D0442353

The Angel Court Affair

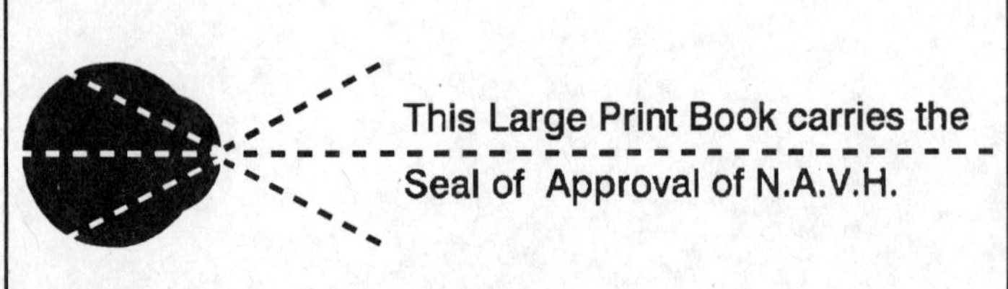
This Large Print Book carries the
Seal of Approval of N.A.V.H.

A CHARLOTTE AND THOMAS PITT NOVEL

The Angel Court Affair

Anne Perry

THORNDIKE PRESS
A part of Gale, Cengage Learning

Farmington Hills, Mich • San Francisco • New York • Waterville, Maine
Meriden, Conn • Mason, Ohio • Chicago

The Angel Court Affair is a work of historical fiction. Apart from the well-known actual people, events, and locales that figure in the narrative, all names, characters, places, and incidents are the products of the author's imagination or are used fictitiously. Any resemblance to current events or locales, or to living persons, is entirely coincidental.

Thorndike Press® Large Print Basic.
The text of this Large Print edition is unabridged.
Other aspects of the book may vary from the original edition.
Set in 16 pt. Plantin.

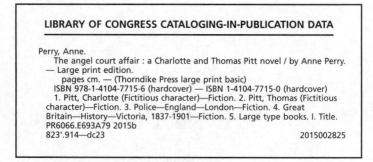

LIBRARY OF CONGRESS CATALOGING-IN-PUBLICATION DATA

Perry, Anne.
The angel court affair : a Charlotte and Thomas Pitt novel / by Anne Perry. — Large print edition.
pages cm. — (Thorndike Press large print basic)
ISBN 978-1-4104-7715-6 (hardcover) — ISBN 1-4104-7715-0 (hardcover)
1. Pitt, Charlotte (Fictitious character)—Fiction. 2. Pitt, Thomas (Fictitious character)—Fiction. 3. Police—England—London—Fiction. 4. Great Britain—History—Victoria, 1837-1901—Fiction. 5. Large type books. I. Title.
PR6066.E693A79 2015b
823'.914—dc23 2015002825

Published in 2015 by arrangement with The Ballantine Publishing Group, a division of Random House, LLC, a Penguin Random House Company

Printed in the United States of America
1 2 3 4 5 6 7 19 18 17 16 15

To Michael Ducker

CHAPTER 1

Pitt stared at the Home Office minister with disbelief. They were standing in a quiet, sunlit room in Whitehall, the traffic outside inaudible.

"A Spanish saint?" he said, struggling to keep his voice more or less level.

"She's not Spanish, she's English," Sir Walter replied patiently. "She merely lives in Spain. Toledo, I'm told. She is here to visit her family."

"And what is this to do with Special Branch, sir?" Pitt asked. Special Branch had been created initially to deal with the Irish Problem, and now in the spring of 1898, its remit had broadened greatly to address anything that was considered to be a threat to the security of the nation.

All Europe was in turmoil as the century drew toward its close. Unrest was escalating and becoming more open. Anarchist bombings occurred in one place or another every few weeks. In France the Dreyfus affair was raging on toward a climax no one could predict. There were even rumors that the government might fall.

Addressing the threat of assassination to a dignitary visiting England was among the duties of Special Branch — but seeing to the needs of a touring nun, or whatever she was, was certainly not. Pitt opened his mouth to point this out, but Sir Walter spoke first.

"There have been letters containing threats against her life," Sir Walter said, his face completely expressionless. "Her opinions have caused some concern and . . . anger. Unfortunately she has been rather too free in expressing them."

"It's a police problem," Pitt said tersely. "I doubt anyone here will care enough to argue with her, let alone cause a nuisance. But if they do, then the local police can take care of it."

Sir Walter sighed, as if this was a tedious argument. "Pitt, this is not a suggestion. You may think that many people are apathetic as to the exact details of religious doctrine, and only deeply committed Christians will argue with her — and even if they do, you trust that they at least know how to behave within the law." He raised white eyebrows. "If so, you are a fool. Some men will argue more passionately about religion than anything else on earth. To many, religion represents order, sanity, the inevitable victory of good over evil. It confirms to them their place in creation." He smiled bleakly. "Somewhere near the top. The appearance of modesty forbids the very top. Something has to be held back for God." His smile faded and his eyes were grim. "But say something to threaten that place near the top, and you threaten everything."

He shook his head. "For God's sake, man, look at how religion has torn us apart throughout history. Start with the Crusades, and the Inquisition in Spain, the persecution of the Cathars and Waldenses in the rest of Europe, the massacres of the Huguenots in France. We've burned both Catholics and Protestants ourselves. You think it couldn't happen again? If Dreyfus were not a Jew, do you think this whole monstrous affair would ever have started, never mind reached this proportion?"

Pitt drew breath to argue, and found the words frozen on his tongue.

It was barely the end of April. Earlier in the month President McKinley had asked the U.S. Congress for a declaration of war against Spain. Cuba had been seeking independence from Spain for many years, and the United States had begun to intervene in the dispute, seeing an opportunity to gain power and position. When the battleship USS *Maine* had been mysteriously blown up in Havana harbor, the powerful U.S. press openly blamed Spain. On 21 April Congress had ordered a naval blockade of all Cuban harbors, demanding that Spain surrender control of Cuba. On 25 April, four days ago, America had declared war. It was the first time they had done such a thing in their brief, idealistic existence. They had focused on internal expansion, had settled the land, built, explored and developed industry. Now suddenly the country was increasing the size of its armies and its navy and looking for possessions overseas, as far away as Hawaii and the Philippines.

This new desire for outward expansion could grow to involve other naval powers, even Britain, if America chose to make it so. If anything went wrong with this Spanish woman's visit, it could easily be misconstrued by Spain. A chilling thought given the state of affairs across Europe. President Carnot of France had been assassinated four years ago. Last year it had been Prime Minister Cánovas del Castillo in Spain, where the violence had reached new abominations.

"She is bringing half a dozen or so of her . . . acolytes," Sir Walter went on, as if he had not noticed Pitt's absence of attention.

"God only knows what sort of people they are, but we don't want any of them killed on our soil. I'm sure you understand the embarrassment that would be to Her Majesty's Government. Especially in light of our history with Spain. We don't want to give them any excuses for war with us as well." He looked at Pitt carefully, as if possibly he had overestimated him and would be obliged to reconsider his opinion.

"Yes, sir," Pitt replied. "Of course I understand. Is it even remotely likely that she would be attacked here?" He asked the question not in a spirit of incredulity, but hoping for some assurance that it was not so.

Sir Walter's expression eased a little, the deep lines about his mouth less severe. "Probably not," he replied with the ghost of a smile. "But apparently this woman's English family do not approve of her at all. She left in the first place over some quarrel of principle, so I hear. Families can be the devil!" There was some sympathy in his voice.

Pitt made a last effort to avoid the task. "I would point out that domestic violence is also police work, sir, not Special Branch's. We have a big case of industrial sabotage at the moment that looks as if it is foreign inspired. It's getting worse and has to be stopped."

Sir Walter's eyes were bright and sharp. "I am well aware of Special Branch's concerns. I will remind you that it is the effect on the nation that determines whose problem it is, Pitt, and you know that as well as I do. If you didn't, believe me, you would not be long in your position."

Pitt cleared his throat, and spoke quietly.

"Do we know the nature of this quarrel within the woman's family, sir?"

Sir Walter gave a slight shrug. If he noticed the change in Pitt's tone, he was sophisticated enough not to show it.

"The usual sort of thing with willful daughters, I believe," he replied, the smile back on his face. "She declined to marry the young man of excellent breeding and fortune, and tedious habits, whom they had selected for her."

Pitt remembered that Sir Walter had three daughters.

"And ran off to Spain and married some Spanish man of unknown character and probably unknown ancestry, at least to Sofia's parents," Sir Walter added. "I imagine it was embarrassing to them."

"How long ago was this?" Pitt asked, keeping his face as expressionless as he could. His own daughter, Jemima, was fast approaching marriageable age. He didn't like to think about it.

"Oh, it has been some time," Sir Walter replied ruefully. "I think it is her religious views that have now compounded the problem. It wouldn't matter so much if she kept them to herself. But she has formed something of a sect. Has her acolytes, as I mentioned."

"Roman Catholic?" Pitt imagined a cult to do with the Virgin Mary, perhaps, causing old persecutions to be remembered.

"Apparently not." Sir Walter lifted one elegant shoulder. "It hardly matters. Just see that no one attacks her while she is in England. The sooner she leaves the better, but alive and well, if you please."

Pitt straightened to attention. "Yes, sir."

"Sofia Delacruz?" Charlotte said with a sudden sharpening of interest. She and Pitt were sitting by a low fire in the parlor, the curtains drawn across the French windows onto the garden. Almost all the light was gone from the cool spring sky and there was a definite chill in the air. Sixteen-year-old Jemima and thirteen-year-old Daniel were both upstairs in their rooms. Jemima would be daydreaming, or writing letters to her friends. Daniel would be deep in the adventures of the latest *Boy's Own Paper.*

Pitt leaned forward and put another log on the fire. It gave less heat than coal, but he liked the smell of the apple wood.

"Have you heard of her?" he asked with surprise.

Charlotte smiled slightly self-consciously. "Yes, a bit."

He remembered Sir Walter's reference to a scandal in the past; he knew how Charlotte loathed gossip, even when it was the lifeblood of investigation. She listened to it, but with guilt, and a thread of fear. She had seen too many of its victims firsthand to take pleasure in it.

"What did you hear?" he said gravely. "She may be in danger. I need to know."

Charlotte did not argue, which in itself was indicative of a different kind of interest. He detected concern in her eyes. She put down the sewing she had been doing.

"You are going to protect her?" she asked

curiously.

"I've assigned Brundage to it," he replied.

"Not Stoker?" She was puzzled.

"Stoker's quite senior now," he pointed out. He did not want to be sharp and set a division between them. This quiet evening alone with her was the best part of his day. Its peace mattered intensely to him. "He has other responsibilities. Brundage is a good man."

"I've heard Sofia's ideas are pretty radical." She was gazing at him steadily.

"For example?"

"I don't know," she admitted, pushing the sewing away entirely and leaning forward a little. "Perhaps I'll go and listen to what she has to say when she arrives. She has to have more fire than our local minister." Charlotte went to church on most Sundays because she took the children. It was a natural part of belonging to the community and of being accepted. It was also the best place for Jemima and Daniel to meet other youths whose families Charlotte knew in a somewhat substantial way.

More often than not, Pitt discovered some pressing duty elsewhere on Sundays.

Pitt nodded agreement, but he was far more conscious of a sharp memory stirring in his mind. His mother had taken him to the parish church on the edge of the estate every Sunday of his childhood. He could still picture the shafts of colored light slanting downward from the stained-glass windows; smell the stone and faint odor of dust. There were shuffles of movement, a creaking of stays, and the dry riffle of pages being turned. Very seldom had he actually listened to the sermons. Some of the stories from the Old Testament were good, but they were isolated, forming no consistent history of God and man. To him the Bible seemed to be more a series of errors and corrections, well-earned disasters and then heroic rescues. A lot of the rest of it was lists of names, or wonderfully poetic prophecies of desolation to come.

Had he believed any of it? And even if he had, did it matter? If he were honest, the stories from his borrowed copies of *Boy's Own* had stirred his heart far more, with their tales of adventure, of heroes any boy would want to copy. He smiled now with quiet pleasure; he felt a sense of identity with his son when he saw Daniel reading. The magazine now had a new name, the stories had different settings, but the spirit was the same.

So what was it that still clung to him so sharply about those old memories of church? The companionship of his mother, the rare sense of peace within her when she was there, as if she were at last safe, loved and completely unafraid? He had thought at the time that her faith was simple and certain. While he was glad for her, because he knew it comforted some of her fears that he could not, he had no desire to be the same way. It was a subject they had never spoken about, out of choice on both of their parts.

He wondered now if perhaps it had not been nearly as easy for her to keep faith as he had supposed, that she had led him to think it was because it took a certain burden from him. It was one area in which he could be a child. She had allowed him that, as she had so many other things of which he had been unaware at the time. She had died without ever telling him she was ill. She had sent him away so he would not notice, not suffer with her.

Charlotte was watching him, waiting. Was she aware of the thoughts inside him?

"You truly want to go and listen to her?" Pitt said, breaking the silence at last.

"Yes," she said immediately. "As I said, I've heard she is outrageous, even blasphemous in her ideas. I'd love to know what they are."

He realized how little he and Charlotte had ever spoken of their beliefs when it came to matters of religion. And yet he knew everything else about her. He knew what hurt her, made her angry, and made her laugh or cry, who she liked and what she thought of them, and what she thought of herself. Often he would read her emotions by her expression. At other times it was in far smaller things: a sudden silence, an unexplained kindness, the letting slip an old grudge someone else could have held on to, and through these small actions he knew she had understood a shadow, or a pain.

"Does it matter to you?" he asked. "If she is blasphemous."

She looked at him with surprise. At first he thought it was because he had asked. Then he realized that she was surprised to not have a ready answer.

"I have no idea," she confessed. "Perhaps that is why I want to go. I'm not sure I even know what blasphemy is. Cursing, or the desecration of a shrine, I understand. But what is an idea that is blasphemous?"

"Darwin's *On the Origin of Species,*" he answered immediately. "The suggestion that we evolved from something lesser rather than descended from something greater. It threatens our entire concept of ourselves." He smiled ruefully.

"Well, if that is what she has come to talk about, she is a little late to cause trouble with it," Charlotte said drily. "We've been fighting about that one already for the last thirty some years! It isn't even interesting anymore."

"So you're not coming, then?" He tried to keep his face straight, as if he were not deliberately teasing her.

"Of course I'm coming!" she said instantly, then realized what he was doing and smiled. "I've never seen a woman blasphemer. Do you suppose there will be a riot?"

He did not satisfy her by answering.

Sofia Delacruz's meeting was to be held in a very large local hall facing a square. Pitt went early in the evening in order to check what precautions had been taken against any protest becoming violent. He also wished to speak to Brundage and hear his opinions of Sofia and, perhaps even more importantly, her followers.

It was a typical April day, sunshine one moment and spatters of rain the next. The new leaves were glistening pale on the branches and there were swathes of yellow daffodils on the grass of the square.

Pitt walked past them, taking a moment of pleasure at the sight, and then up the wide steps and through the double doors to the hall where the meeting was to be held. He noted that there were already several local police around, although there was still an hour before the meeting was due to begin. He asked for Brundage, and was directed to one of the dressing rooms at the back, just beyond the stage. It was bare except for a couple of chairs, a mirror, and a number of hooks on the wall.

Brundage was a large young man, almost Pitt's own height, but more broadly built. His brown hair flopped forward over his brow and he brushed it back automatically as he straightened up from reaching across to a collection of printed papers advertising the event. He had unusual features, blunt and yet in no way coarse.

"Sir," he said politely on recognizing Pitt.

"Evening, Brundage," Pitt acknowledged, glancing around the room, noting the windows and the second door. "Tell me what you've found so far."

Brundage rolled his eyes very slightly. "Wish I could say it was what I expected, sir. The hall is secure enough, and the local police are prepared for a big crowd. Probably more people curious than looking for any trouble, but it only takes a few to make it turn nasty."

"What is here that you did *not* expect?" Pitt asked a little skeptically.

Brundage shrugged. "Someone I can't dismiss as a harmless lunatic I suppose," he answered with a degree of self-deprecation. "I thought her followers would be the usual collection of idealists, dependents and hangers-on. And of course those who want to take her place. I'm not wrong about that. Although they are more intense than I expected."

"A threat to her?" Pitt asked quickly.

"I hope not." He met Pitt's eyes. "But it is not impossible."

"Who are they? Names. Do we know any of them?"

"They're all with her full time. They don't do anything else. They've given their lives to this. The most important, certainly in his own estimation, is Melville Smith," Brundage began. "He is the only one who's English. In his fifties. Ambitious, but denies it. Seems loyal, but I think to the ideas rather than to her. Ramon Aguilar, on the other hand, is about fifteen years younger than Smith, and he's loyal to Sofia over all else. He's Spanish, very soft spoken, gentle."

Brundage smiled. "Sings to himself while he's walking around. The three women who came with her are all harder to read. Cleo Robles is small and pretty, about twenty-five; English mother and Spanish father. I'm guessing there is some tragedy in her background . . ." He left the words unfinished, as he was uncertain what to add.

Pitt formed the instant opinion that Brundage had liked her.

"Elfrida Fonsecca is quiet, watchful," Brundage continued. "Heavier, but in a comfortable sort of way. Womanly, if you know what I mean? And she has a lovely skin, not a mark on it."

Pitt nodded. "Do you know anything about her?"

"She seems devout, withdrawn," Brundage answered with a small shake of his head. "I can't get any history from her. But she bites her nails. Something bothers her."

"Go on," Pitt told him.

"Henrietta Navarro is older. I think she was in some kind of religious order before she joined Sofia. She refuses to speak of it, and I can't press her without causing real anger. I tried, and Sofia herself told me in no uncertain words to leave the subject alone."

Pitt heard a new note in Brundage's voice,

something he had not ever heard before in the year and a half he had known the man. It spoke of a certain awe.

"And Sofia herself?" Pitt asked.

Brundage hesitated.

Pitt waited. Honesty was more important than speed.

"I don't know," Brundage said eventually. "I can tell you about the others. They're not all that different from many I've known." He regarded Pitt earnestly. "But she is. I can't even tell you if I think the threats against her are real. I also can't tell you if she thinks they are, or if she believes some kind of holy angel is going to protect her, so they don't matter."

Pitt stared at him. "Is there anything useful you *can* tell me?" he said with an effort at courtesy. Brundage probably did not want this task any more than he did himself. There were other, genuine and important cases to work on, specifically the industrial sabotage one he had mentioned to Sir Walter, which was growing more serious with time.

Brundage shifted his weight.

"Ramon Aguilar is loyal. If there's going to be an attack from inside it'll be Melville Smith."

They could hear the sound of movement

back and forth along the passage, footsteps, quiet voices.

"Relationships among the followers?" Pitt asked.

Brundage pursed his lips. "Pretty strong dislike between the two men. They think it's concealed, but it isn't. The two older women are distant with each other, but polite. Henrietta Navarro seems to be closer to Smith in attitude. And there's another woman who sweeps and cleans in the yard at Angel Court, where they are staying. But she's new, apparently, only just joined them, and doesn't talk to anyone."

"Then let's see if Sofia Delacruz will speak with me now," Pitt replied. "I suppose she's preparing to give her sermon, or whatever it is."

Brundage looked relieved. He straightened up and went out the door without any further comment.

It was less than five minutes later that the door opened again. Pitt swung around expecting to see Brundage returning with the message that Delacruz was too busy to see him, because she was praying or studying, or whatever she did to prepare herself. Instead he saw a slender woman of more than average height. Dark hair was drawn back from the most remarkable face he could ever recall seeing. His first thought was that she was not beautiful. She was too fierce, her slate-blue eyes too deeply set. Then he realized as she walked toward him that indeed she was beautiful, in a way that was both savage and tender. There was a burning intelligence in her — and something in her expression that might have been amusement.

"I am Sofia Delacruz," she said quietly. "I understand you are Commander Pitt of Special Branch."

Pitt inclined his head. "Yes, ma'am. I hope we can help avoid any unpleasantness occurring for you."

To his surprise she laughed, a rich, spontaneous sound. "I hope that will not be the case. It will mean I am so bland that no one can find anything to object to. Then I need not have come."

Pitt was confused. This was not how he had pictured a woman who was dedicated to religion, regarded by some as a saint. He realized that he had expected a calmness, a purity apart from the world, in fact apart from reality. But Sofia seemed very present, very earthy.

"You came with the intention of disturbing people?" he asked, trying to keep surprise from his voice, and a thread of exasperation. Perhaps she was merely a troublemaker who thrived on attention and shock. He saw nothing holy in that, in fact the opposite. It was contemptible.

She walked across the floor in front of him. She held her head high, proud. The light overhead accentuated the bones of her cheeks and the fine lines about her eyes and mouth. Then she was in the shadows again. She moved with extraordinary grace.

"What do you expect me to say?" she asked him. "Do you think I came here to tell people that there is nothing to do, nothing to worry about? That everyone is perfect, just continue as you are? God loves you and will give you everything you want, so there is no need for you to do anything at all?" She gave a shrug so slight it was barely a movement. "The complacent do not need me to tell them that. The sinless, and those who know in their hearts that this is not the glory possible for them, would both go away empty, and wonder why I had even bothered to come. That is what you expected of me? Why would anyone threaten me, then, Commander? I would be guilty of lying, and of perpetuating boredom, but no one kills for such things, as long as the lies are comfortable enough."

Pitt drew a deep breath. He reminded

himself that whatever it cost him in patience or tact, Sir Walter had made it very clear that any attack on this woman while she was in England would be more than embarrassing; it could be the spark that would ignite an international incident that could escalate into a war.

"So what do you propose to tell them?" he asked as mildly as he could. "What is it that makes someone wish to hurt you?"

"I cannot truly say why someone would want to harm me," she replied smoothly. "But I have had several threats of death that I know of. I believe that there have been others from which Ramon has protected me."

"Only Ramon? Not Melville Smith?" he asked immediately.

The smile was back in her eyes — amusement, not warmth. "No. The ones I did receive were handed to me by Melville. His protection is not of me, but of the faith we share." There was no other expression on her face or in her voice. She was leaving him to draw his own conclusions as to her feelings.

"Do you trust him?" he inquired.

She was startled. It showed in her eyes for an instant, and then was gone. "You are very direct," she responded.

This time the amusement was his. "That troubles you? I'm afraid I have neither time nor inclination to be more tactful. Do you trust Mr. Smith?"

"I trust him to do what he believes to be in the interest of the faith." She looked directly at him as she spoke. "I do not take for granted that that will always be what *I* believe. But before you ask me, no, I do not think Melville will hurt me."

"Does he wish you to stir up controversy?" he pursued.

Now there was appreciation in her face. Her feelings were as swift and as visible as light and shadow on water. "An excellent question, Commander. I am not certain that I have an easy answer for you."

"Do you listen to his advice?"

"Of course. But I do not always take it."

He could imagine their confrontations. Melville Smith would likely be the arrogant type, insistent, perhaps afraid for her, certainly exasperated. She would be fierce, certain of herself, quite plainly listening to him only as a matter of courtesy. She would still do exactly what she wished.

"What are you going to tell people?" he asked, returning to his earlier question. He was increasingly curious to know what this unusual woman believed in, what it was that she cared about so intensely that she had to tell strangers of it, even if it might cost her her life. Was she hysterical, touched by delusions? She would certainly not be the first. History was full of women who saw visions and profoundly believed them to be from God. Joan of Arc was burned alive because she would not deny her "angels."

But this woman in front of him, in a simple, dark blue dress, did not seem in the least emotionally overwrought. In fact she appeared to be cooler than he was.

She smiled, and for an instant he saw uncertainty in her eyes. Then it was gone again. It was not doubt of herself, but perhaps of him.

"I am going to tell them that they are the children of God," she said levelly, watching his face. "As is every human being on earth. That there is no other kind of person."

"Why should that upset them?" he asked, wondering as he said it if it was a stupid question, or if it was exactly what she had intended him to say.

"Because children are required to grow up," she replied unwaveringly. "If we are the children of God, rather than simply creatures of His hands, then we may eventually become as He is. Not in this life, but now is the time to begin, to make the choice that this will be our path. And growing up can hurt. Lessons must be learned, mistakes put right, some errors paid for. Ask any child if he will find it easy to become like his father, especially if his father is a great man."

She smiled slightly, almost in self-mockery. "But what disturbs many people more, what is in fact the 'blasphemy' they cannot abide, is that if we may one day become as God is, then it follows logically that He may, in the infinite past, have once been as we are now. Which is, of course, why He understands us totally; every fear, every error and every need. And possibly even more terrifying to some, He knows that we can do it, that we can become like Him — if we are willing to try hard enough, pay the price in effort and patience, humility and courage, and never give up.

"Most of us want something immeasurably easier than that, far smaller and safer. That is the devil's plan for us — stunted, eternally less than we could have been."

"You are saying that men and God are the same thing?" Pitt asked incredulously.

"Only in the sense that a caterpillar and a butterfly are the same," she replied. "There is no safety, nothing to be bought except by the growth of the heart and the soul. And that is frightening to many. It changes all the rules we thought we knew. There is no hierarchy, except of the ability to love with a whole heart. Obedience is not enough, it is only a beginning. It is a small thing, compared to understanding."

"Are you frightened?" he asked after a long hesitation.

"Yes." Her voice was very quiet. "But the only thing more frightening would be to deny what I know is true. Then I would have nothing left at all."

"We will see that nothing happens to you," he promised. But as he excused himself and turned away he was sure there was nothing to fear. Her ideas might well be offensive, especially if taken seriously, but no more so than any of the activists who wanted economic reform, higher wages, votes for women. Even if what she preached was blasphemy, he did not think that would be enough to disturb anyone to active violence.

The meeting was far better attended than Pitt had foreseen. Word had spread that Sofia Delacruz was controversial, and many people had turned up out of curiosity if nothing else. The large preponderance of them were women.

Pitt checked in with Brundage, and with the regular police, going around the doors, watching the crowd, looking for anyone excitable, furtive or who seemed out of place.

Sergeant Drury was clearly annoyed at being taken from his regular duties for what he considered a frivolous purpose. He was broad-shouldered, a little corpulent, and he stood at the main entrance with a somber look. A gaunt woman in black took in his presence appraisingly, but did not speak.

"She's come to complain, that one," he observed to Pitt, who was standing near him. "But I can't see her being dangerous, can you? What the devil do they think is going to happen, sir? Nobody's going to throw a bomb at this woman! From what I hear, the anarchists would be on her side!"

Pitt's reply was prevented by the presence of a large woman passing by. She glanced at Drury and nodded her approval.

"Ma'am," Drury acknowledged her.

Pitt gave a nod to the sergeant and moved on. He was looking at other entrances, and the increasing crowd, when he spotted Charlotte. It was the familiar angle of her head that drew his attention, and the unique grace with which she turned to the young woman beside her. He smiled with pleasure, until he realized with a jolt that the "young woman" was Jemima. Her long chestnut hair was wound high on her head and she wore one of Charlotte's plainer hats. She was lovely. He had known her all her life, and yet suddenly his daughter seemed almost a stranger. He stared at her a moment longer before he was interrupted by one of his own men coming to repeat a slightly unpleasant exchange. Suddenly he was aware of a cold shiver of warning. The letters to Sofia had not threatened argument, or even ugly or embarrassing scenes — they had threatened death. He must see that it did not happen, not just for Sofia's sake, but for everyone here, including Charlotte and Jemima.

Fifteen minutes later the hall was nearly full. Glancing around it from his position by the stage, Pitt could see less than a dozen empty seats among the five hundred he estimated were in the room. There was a low buzz of conversation. A few heads turned to recognize acquaintances, but the air of expectation prevented the simple pleasure of gossip.

All fell silent as Melville Smith climbed up the steps to the platform and stood facing them. He was of average height, a little pigeon-chested. It was when he spoke that he commanded the attention; his voice was beautiful. He introduced himself and welcomed the audience as if he were the host at some party in his home, and Sofia Delacruz the favored guest.

Finished, he stepped back and Sofia made her entrance. If she was afraid, there was no reflection of it in her bearing. She stood straight, her head high, a slight smile on her remarkable face.

Pitt would have liked to watch her and listen to how she told a crowd of strangers about the extraordinary beliefs she'd shared with him. But it was his duty to look for any threats, even if he felt sure none would arise. It was the regular police's job to keep out any obvious troublemakers, and should unruly behavior begin, to quell it. But tackling any serious attempt on Sofia's life was Pitt's task. He did his best to tune out her words as he faced the audience, watching, trying to judge their reactions.

She spoke as she had warned him she would, gently to begin with: the comforting, familiar ideas of God as a father of all mankind.

In the second row, near the center, a young man yawned conspicuously. It was a discourteous gesture. Pitt glanced at Sofia and saw that she was aware of it. The man had chosen a very visible seat from which to be rude.

Sofia was moving on to the creation of the world, and man's place in it. Her voice was lifting with enthusiasm, the vibrancy in it carrying to the back reaches of the hall.

The young man in the second row was now watching her intently. He was no longer pretending boredom, and his body was rigid, shoulders high.

Sofia continued, moving forward to the front of the platform, as she spoke of the earth and its creatures. The awe she felt toward the beauty she was describing was clear in her face.

"What about Darwin?" a man yelled out, his voice so shrill he sounded close to hysteria.

"Exactly my point," Sofia replied without hesitation. "Things change and evolve all the time. It is possible that we may forever improve, becoming wiser, braver, kinder and more honest, learning into eternity."

"But what about Darwin himself, who says we are little more than monkeys?" Now the man was standing, his fists clenched, his red beard bristling. His face suffused with anger.

Sofia smiled. "Even Darwin," she replied. "There is no one for whom progress is impossible."

Pitt knew she had intended to be funny,

but she had misjudged at least part of her audience. Far to the left someone laughed, but the man with the beard was enraged.

"Don't you dare mock us!" he yelled, his voice even louder. "Blasphemer! No man takes the name of God lightly, still less some . . . some woman! You come here from a godless place and make fun of us, try to make fools imagine they are the equal of God! You —"

The burly figure of Sergeant Drury was getting ready to move forward.

Sofia preempted him. "I mock no one, sir." She said it levelly, but her voice had intense power. "Spain is not a godless country, and as an Englishwoman who has been made welcome there, I am ashamed to hear you speak so of your fellow man, simply because they do not worship God in exactly the same manner you do."

Another man rose to his feet. He was bald-headed and wearing a stiff dark suit. "The insult to Spain is but of ignorance," he said, dismissing it with a wave of his hand. "But to suggest that man is the same as God is indeed blasphemy! I will not stand by and listen to it in silence, or I am guilty of it too." Again he waved his hand. "As are all of us here!"

There was a flush on Sofia's cheeks, but

her voice remained calm, if a little shaky.

"I did not say that man was the same as God now, sir, only that he can follow the same path toward the light, and so become the same. Did Christ not command us to become perfect, even as He was?"

"That's not what He meant!" the man said incredulously.

Another barrel-chested man let out a bellow of laughter. "And how the devil would you know what He meant?" he demanded. He jerked his thumb toward Sofia. "Personally I think she's crazy as a box of frogs, but she makes as much sense as you do, and she looks a lot better."

Now there was laughter all around the hall. Three middle-aged ladies stood up and went out, stiff-backed with outrage.

Somehow Sophia managed to regain control of the discussion and picked up the thread of her narrative about man as a creature capable of becoming all that was noble. She explained the high cost in faith and work: experiences of pain and the conquering of selfishness, ignorance, the instinctive leap to judge others.

There were other brief forays into unpleasantness among the audience, but they were controlled, dissipated with moderate good humor, and finally at a quarter to ten the meeting closed. Pitt was surprised at how tired he was. His head and his back ached, his muscles knotted from the constant expectation of violence. He watched Sofia Delacruz shake people's hands, nod and smile as if she were utterly composed, and then, when the last person had moved toward the door, turn to Ramon and walk slowly in his direction, weariness momentarily acknowledged.

Pitt turned away and his eye was caught by the light glinting off a mane of fair hair as a tall man moved through the crowd. Many people made way for him, smiling, clearly recognizing him. He gave several of them a nod and a smile, then continued on out through the doors, apparently too deep in thought to stop and speak.

Pitt recognized him too. It was Dalton Teague, a gentleman about town, related to many of the great families of power, particularly that of Lord Salisbury, the prime minister. But the deference Pitt had seen here was to Teague the hero of the cricket field, who had outplayed almost every other sportsman of the age. The poise with which he moved was that of the athlete. The attention he commanded could never be bought, it could only be won.

Pitt had no time to wonder what Teague

was doing here. He had to check with all the policemen, and see that Sofia Delacruz left safely. It was another half hour before he was able to speak briefly to Brundage, thank Drury and his men, then with a sigh of relief go outside into the April night.

The streetlamps were already lit, bright, comforting orbs like ornate jewels set in iron, stretching above the footpath. He was walking toward the main road to find a hansom to take him home when a man emerged from the shadow of the nearest building and fell into step beside him.

"Evening, Commander," he said pleasantly. He had a rich voice, well spoken and threaded with a warm humor. "You did well to contain that so unobtrusively."

"Thank you," Pitt said drily. He did not wish to enter into conversation with a stranger, even if it was civil, but there was something in the man's tone that told him this was the beginning of the exchange, not the end.

"My name is Frank Laurence." The man kept pace with Pitt, in spite of being three inches shorter.

Pitt did not reply. Clearly Laurence knew who he was.

"I'm a journalist with *The Times,*" Laurence continued. "I find it very interesting that the commander of Special Branch should be concerned with a visiting saint, as it were. Or do I overstate Sofia Delacruz's holiness?"

Pitt smiled in the darkness, in spite of his irritation. "I have no idea, Mr. Laurence. I don't know how you measure holiness. If that is what your newspaper wishes of you, you will need to acquire your help elsewhere." He increased his pace slightly.

Laurence still kept up with him, without apparent effort.

"I like your sense of humor, Mr. Pitt, but I am afraid my editor will want something more from me than an estimate of holiness." He sounded as if the whole idea amused him. "Something more violent, you know? Scandal, attack, the risk of murder."

Pitt stopped abruptly and faced Laurence. They were close to a streetlamp and he saw the man's face clearly: he had regular features, and his slightly rounded, brown eyes were sharp and intelligent — and at this moment bright with suppressed laughter.

"Well, if you find any violence, Mr. Laurence, I hope you will be kind enough to let me know," Pitt responded. "Beforehand would be good, even if it robs your story of some of its impact."

"Ah!" Laurence said with pleasure. "I think that working with you is going to be less tedious than I had feared. Are you telling me that in your opinion there will be violence? She is a very unusual woman, isn't she? I have always thought that the best saints, the real ones, would be troublesome. There's nothing very holy about telling us all what we want to hear, is there? I think I could probably do that myself."

"I thought that was what you do," Pitt replied waspishly, and then as he saw the laughter in Laurence's eyes he immediately regretted it. He had played into Laurence's hands.

"No, Commander, I tell people quite often what they dread to hear. It is not displeasing them that would be the kiss of death to my career, it is boring them . . . or, of course, being seen as a liar. So. Is she a saint?"

"Why do you want to know?" Pitt found himself engaging with the man, in spite of his determination not to. "Are you hoping for a burning at the stake? I don't think we break people on the wheel anymore."

"We have become very unimaginative," Laurence agreed. "In your opinion, is she merely an exhibitionist, Commander?"

Pitt responded with surprising depth of

emotion to the idea that Sofia Delacruz was an exhibitionist. Even the use of the word offended him, but he knew perfectly well that Laurence was trying to maneuver him into saying so.

"I will not write your article for you, Mr. Laurence. You must write it yourself," he answered.

Laurence smiled. In the lamplight his teeth were white and even.

"Well done, Commander. You are supremely careful to say nothing. I admire that. I look forward to discussing the matter with you again. I am sure we will have many chances." He touched his hat with an airy wave and turned away. "Good night, sir."

CHAPTER 2

Charlotte knew that she must return home with Jemima, and not wait for Thomas after the meeting, but she was longing to ask him what he had thought of it all, especially of Sofia herself. After seventeen years of marriage she believed she knew him well, and herself even better. But most of the remarks the woman had made, and perhaps even more the burning conviction with which she had spoken, awoke in Charlotte many questions. Why had she never examined her own thoughts on such issues?

Was it because she already had all the things that mattered to her: the husband she loved, children, friends, enough money to be comfortable? And she also had the causes she fought for. The world was changing even from month to month. Now political votes for women were far more than a dream, and she was more involved in the fight than she had told Pitt.

She would tell him, of course, but in time. It was exciting. If women had a voice in government, even if it was only the power to withhold their support, it would be the beginning of a new age in reform of a hundred griefs and inequalities.

There were burning reasons to be involved. One of these was an upcoming parliamentary by-election in which cricket hero Dalton Teague was the candidate almost certain to win. Charlotte understood why people admired him, but abhorred the fact that he was against the availability of information regarding birth control. It had been a difficult subject for many years and feelings about it ran very high. The knowledge of such practices was not illegal — it was simply not widespread enough to reach those who desperately needed it: poor women who had child after child until their bodies were exhausted. Ignorance, fear and social pressures were responsible. Religious beliefs had much influence as well.

But it was the women who died because of it, not the men!

It was the recent death of a friend, giving birth to her seventh child, that had brought the subject so forcefully to the front of Charlotte's mind.

Charlotte knew she had so much, sitting

here in the warmth and the dark of the carriage, her daughter beside her. She couldn't help but wonder: Was she too satisfied to need a belief in anything greater, a purpose beyond the immediate future?

What if she lost it all? What strength was there inside her to go on, to stand alone, walk in the darkness? It was a terrible thought, and one that she had had to face several times over the years as Pitt's job, first in the police force and now in Special Branch, took him into dangerous situations. She found herself tense as they drove along, so unyielding she was bumped by every unevenness in the road. Would she, in the face of hardship or loss, find nothing inside her to carry her through?

Jemima also was quiet. She had been very eager to come, and now she offered no comment at all.

"What did you think of her?" Charlotte asked gently, concerned how she would answer if Jemima was confused. The emptiness in her own mind gave her a feeling of guilt for never having found at least some clarity of faith to teach her daughter. Jemima would soon be seventeen, of marriageable age. She would have decisions to make that would affect the rest of her life.

"She's a little frightening," Jemima said

thoughtfully, as though searching her mind for the right words. "Not that she'd hurt you, at least not intentionally. I don't mean that. But . . . she's so certain of what she means that she'll risk everything to say it." As Jemima looked out the window of the moving carriage the streetlights flashed on her face, brilliant one moment, shadowed the next. "She's nothing like the vicar," she went on, frowning as she struggled to explain herself. "He always sounds as if he doesn't mean what he says. I suppose it's the singsong sort of voice he uses, and the fact that he seems to be reciting what he's been told to recite." She turned toward Charlotte. "Do you suppose he would actually love to say what he really thinks; only he doesn't want to upset everyone — or lose his job?"

"I should think it's very likely," Charlotte agreed, picturing the Reverend Mr. Jameson in her mind. He was mild-mannered, a kind man, a guardian of his flock, but not a crusader. He was exactly what they wanted: he offered gentle assurance, unfailing patience and an ability to judge the right amount of hunger within them. But was it what they needed?

"Is Sofia Delacruz right?" Jemima asked bluntly. "Are we all ignoring who we really are, and sitting comfortably in our pews until we turn into statues?"

"She didn't say that!" Charlotte protested, although in truth it was precisely what she herself had been thinking.

"Yes, she did." Jemima was quite certain. "Not in so many words, of course, but that is what it amounted to. We aren't really looking for anything, except to change position now and then, so we don't get a cramp in our . . ." She hesitated to use an anatomical word.

"You may say 'posterior,' my dear." Charlotte was a touch sarcastic because the whole subject was disturbing. "You seem to be happy enough to call the vicar and his flock 'statues.' "

"I'm not happy about it!" Jemima protested, her voice showing the depth of emotion she felt. "But if this woman from Spain can be honest about who we are and what we should be doing, then so can I!"

"We need to be honest," Charlotte agreed gently. "But we also need to be right. And it would be good to be kind as well."

"Is it kind to tell people lies because it's what they are comfortable hearing?" Jemima stared at Charlotte challengingly. "I've never heard you do that! In fact when Grandmama tells me I am too candid to people, she says I am just like you." There was satisfaction in her voice, even a touch of pride. As they passed under another street-lamp Charlotte could see that her daughter was smiling. With the mixture of strength and softness in her features, she did look startlingly like Charlotte had at that age. Charlotte felt a sudden welling up of emotion, and blinked rapidly to hide tears.

"I am not always right," she said, staring straight ahead. "There are ways of letting people know what you think is the truth. Some are destructive. Some are ill-phrased, too soft or too hard. We need time if we are to change, and gentleness."

"I know," Jemima replied. "You catch more flies with honey than with vinegar. You are always telling me, just as Grandmama does." She hunched her shoulders a little and her voice was quiet and very serious. "But when is it the right time to tell people something they don't want to know? If you wait until they want to hear it, it's probably too late. You're always telling me what to do, and even more, what not to do."

"You're my daughter!" Charlotte said quickly. "I love you! I don't want you to be hurt, or make any mistakes that matter, or —"

"I know," Jemima interrupted, reaching

across and touching Charlotte lightly on the arm. "It upsets me sometimes, because it sounds as if you think I'm really silly. But I know why you do it. And . . . and I think I might be frightened, and a bit lonely if you didn't." She smiled ruefully. "And if you ever remind me I said that I'll never speak to you again!"

Charlotte wanted to put her arms around her daughter and hold her tight, but she thought at this moment Jemima was too grown up for that, and perhaps too full of her own emotion to deal with Charlotte's as well. Instead she gently put her other hand over Jemima's, and they rode on in silence.

Charlotte was seeing Jemima and Daniel off to school when the maid, Minnie Maude, brought in the newspaper and handed it to Pitt. Her face was wary because she could read, and she had already seen the headline of the article. Her usually cheerful expression had darkened and she was now watching him unobtrusively, pretending to be busy putting the same things away over and over again, so she could keep him in sight. Uffie, the stray dog she had adopted, was sitting in his basket near the stove, his head swinging around each time she passed. He had begun his life secretly in the cellar, and was permitted to remain in the kitchen only if he stayed in that corner. The rule had lasted less than a month.

Pitt opened the paper and found the piece immediately. He began to read, forgetting his tea and allowing it to go cold. It was well written, which he would have expected from his conversation with Laurence in the street the previous evening. What surprised him was the approach.

Laurence described Sofia vividly. His words brought her presence back to Pitt as if she had only just left the room: the sweep of her hair; the challenge of her eyes, probing, almost intimate; above all, the energy in her.

"Is this woman a saint as her admirers claim?" Laurence wrote. And then he answered his own question. "I have no idea, because I don't know what makes a saint. Am I looking for sublime goodness? Which is what? The absence of all sin? Sin in whose judgment? Or is it mercy, gentleness, self-effacement, humility, generosity with worldly goods, and with time? Meekness?"

Pitt could hear Laurence's mellow voice in his ears as he looked at the printed page. He could hear the amusement in it, the echo of self-mockery. He read on.

Or are saints people who see further than

the rest of us, catch a glimpse of some brighter star? Should they make us feel at ease, comfortable with what we have? Or should they disturb us, make us question, strive for more? As Señora Delacruz demands, reach for the infinite and strive to become like God Himself?

Are saints perfect, or do we permit them to have the same flaws as the rest of us? Why do we want them, or need them? To tell us what to think, and make our decisions for us?

Again Pitt could hear the mockery in Laurence's tone. And yet the questions were seriously meant. People said "saint" easily. It was a catch-all word with different meanings, or none at all.

He turned back to the paper.

Señora Delacruz is going to do none of that. She demands that we "grow up," that we begin now on the infinite journey to become like God, somewhere in the regions of eternity. She even claims that God Himself was once like us! That I find far more troubling. I do not want a God who was even as fallible as any of us. Is that blasphemy?

And I am not at all sure that I want so

much responsibility myself, even in the "forever"! The punishment for failure would be small. A little while in purgatory, and then an endless peace.

Doing what, for heaven's sake? I should die of boredom, if I were not, apparently, already dead!

Am I then irreverent, a blasphemer? Should I be punished for such thoughts? Perhaps I should even be silenced? By force if necessary? I think not. I am a questioner, and I am not at all sure that Saint Sofia Delacruz has the answer. But then neither am I sure that she does not. The only thing I am certain of is that she has disturbed my peace of mind, and that of a great many others. And for that, many will wish to punish her.

Pitt could not argue with a single thing Laurence had written, and yet he expected there would be a torrent of letters from all manner of insulted, angry, frightened and confused correspondents the next day.

"Is it bad?" Charlotte had come into the kitchen while he was reading, and was watching him with a frown of concern.

"As an article? No, it's very good," he said honestly.

"You look worried." The slight furrow

between her brows deepened.

"He's reported what she said accurately, but he's asked a lot of questions. What is a saint? Have we the right to remain ignorant, or the responsibility not to?"

"Did she say that?" Charlotte asked doubtfully.

"Didn't she?" he asked, turning the question back.

Charlotte thought for a few moments. "Yes, I suppose she did, but more subtly than that. I thought the real trouble would be that she said we all had the same chance of becoming divine."

Pitt considered for a moment. "You're right. Most people won't like that."

"Just about everyone thinks they have a better chance than others, either because they're cleverer, or believe the right doctrine, or are just more humble and generally virtuous." She bit her lip and smiled at him with a steady probing gaze. "And I suppose that excludes us pretty well from real virtue, doesn't it? If we loved others we would be seeking to find a way of including as many as possible, not as few!"

"Laurence didn't say that," he replied thoughtfully. "Perhaps he should have."

The letters were there the next day, as Pitt

had expected. Passions were ignited both for and against Sofia Delacruz, with considerably more against than for.

Pitt read them methodically at the breakfast table. Some simply defended their own faith and felt Sofia had made grave errors of understanding. Those were to be foreseen, and were largely harmless.

Others called her outrageous and demanded that she be silenced. A few suggested God would act to destroy her, if man did not. Various biblical punishments were suggested, more colorful than practical.

Pitt was aware of Charlotte watching him read, concern in her face.

"It's only words," he said, smiling at her, trying to defuse the sense of unease he felt. There was an ugliness to the tone of so many of the letters. They expressed not so much a defense of faith as a wish to punish Sofia for the offense of disturbing their certainties and awakening doubts that had been long asleep.

Charlotte started reading over Pitt's shoulder.

"Some of them are pretty vicious," she said.

He folded the newspaper and put it facedown on the table.

"You have to be very ugly inside to write

the sort of things they say," she went on, moving around the table to face him.

"They're angry because she's disturbed them," Pitt pointed out reasonably. "They're frightened."

"I know that." There was an effort at patience in her voice, and it showed through. "But frightened people are dangerous. You taught me that, and I haven't forgotten. Can you stop any of it?"

"No," he said more gently. "She has the right to say whatever she believes. And they have the right to deny it, ridicule it or put forward any alternatives. We can't pick and choose whose opinions we allow to be heard."

"But they could become violent," Charlotte protested.

He stood up, ready to leave. "As I said, my darling, they're only words. The threats are implied, no more." He got no farther than the hall, when the telephone rang, and he went to answer it.

"Brundage." The person on the other end identified himself immediately. He sounded hoarse and a little shaky. "She's not here, sir. We've searched the whole of Angel Court, where they're staying, and it seems she went sometime during the night."

Pitt felt a chill ripple through him, leaving

him cold. "Señora Delacruz? Where on earth would she go?"

"I don't know, sir," Brundage said with a thread of desperation in his voice. Pitt could hear it over the wire.

"Did anyone come, either in the night, or earlier?" Pitt asked. "Any letters, messages?"

"No, sir," Brundage answered a little more sharply. "And nothing seems to be damaged, or missing . . ."

"Except Señora Delacruz," Pitt snapped.

"Not just her, sir." Brundage swallowed hard. "Two other women are gone too. Cleo Robles and Elfrida Fonsecca."

"For God's sake, Brundage, what happened? Nobody could forcibly kidnap three adult women without there being some signs of a struggle!"

"I know that, sir! But there are no signs of a struggle or a fight. Nothing's broken. Nobody heard anything, not even a cry or a thump."

"Or nobody's admitting to hearing anything," Pitt corrected.

"Yes, sir, I thought of that." Suddenly Brundage's anger was gone and he sounded crushed.

It was not his fault, and Pitt knew it. None of them had taken the threats very seriously. They had thought no further than of a little unpleasantness at one of the public appearances: perhaps at worst a loss of temper, a few stones or pieces of rotten fruit thrown. Now, suddenly, she was gone. Voluntary or not, it was disturbing.

"What's your impression, Brundage?" he asked.

There was a moment's silence, and then Brundage answered. "She was persuaded to go, sir. Or else she planned to all along. But I think that's less likely, in the circumstances . . ."

"What circumstances?" Pitt asked.

"She has a meeting tomorrow evening. Melville Smith has canceled it now." Brundage's voice grew harsher. "He seems certain she isn't going to be back for it."

A dark thought entered Pitt's mind. "What did he say about the meeting, as clearly as you can remember?"

"I know exactly what he said," Brundage replied sharply. " 'Due to unforeseen events, which we cannot at the moment explain, Señora Delacruz will not be able to speak at St. Mary's Hall tomorrow evening. We deeply regret the disappointment and inconvenience this will cause, and hope that she will be able to take up her mission again soon.' "

"I'm coming to Angel Court," Pitt said.

There could be any number of reasons why Sofia had gone, willingly or unwillingly: illness, an accident, a quarrel during which someone lost control, possibly something to do with one of the members of her family in London. That last seemed the most likely. But why on earth had she not informed Melville Smith of the reason for leaving, and the date when she would return? It was discourteous, to say the least. Could it be carelessness? A message gone astray?

He was back in the kitchen again and its warmth wrapped around him, the comfortable smell of bread toasting in front of the open grating, a breath of air from the window over the sink.

"What is it?" Charlotte asked quietly.

"Sofia Delacruz has gone from Angel Court, without explanation," he replied.

Charlotte rose to her feet. "What on earth do you mean 'gone'? Has someone kidnapped her? How could that happen with all those people around her, and your men watching?"

"It doesn't seem that she was kidnapped — at least not forcibly," he said bluntly. "She may have had some urgent call from a member of her family."

"Went out alone, leaving no word?" Charlotte said with disbelief.

"We don't know what happened," he replied. "I'm going to Angel Court now. And she wasn't alone. Two of her women went with her."

Charlotte grasped his wrist, holding it with surprising strength. "Is that what you believe, Thomas? That she received a message from her family? It's not, is it? She isn't a foolish woman. If she were in the habit of treating her staff like this, it would become known, and defeat her whole purpose."

"Many so-called saints are tyrants at home," he said gently. He knew Charlotte had liked the woman, as had many others. If this disappearance was intentional then Sofia was letting them down, and he resented it.

"Thomas, she hasn't gone willingly!" Charlotte said with a burst of desperation. "You know that as well as I do! You must find her." She did not add that she feared Sofia had been hurt, perhaps killed, but it was there in her eyes.

Pitt's touched Charlotte's hand gently, loosening her hold, but not letting go of her. "Of course I'll find her," he said gently. "But you have to prepare for the possibility that this is a deliberate piece of melodrama to gain more attention. It's possible none of the threats to her life are real. The fact that two of her women went with her suggests it was planned. And it would be extremely difficult to kidnap a visiting Spanish saint undetected." He leaned forward and kissed her gently.

But Pitt was far less certain of the truth when he paid the cabby and crossed the pavement to the entrance into Angel Court. It was an ancient courtyard, its surrounding buildings three stories high and with mullioned windows. At the entrance to the courtyard stood a stone angel, life-size, its wings gigantic, its arms raised as if in benediction. It was imposing and strangely sinister. There was an old stable half door to the left. The ground was paved with rough cobbles, which were rounded on the surface, green moss thick between them. An old woman moved rhythmically over them with a broom, back and forth.

Melville Smith had clearly been waiting for Pitt. He strode across the open space toward him, tension in every line of his body.

"Thank heaven you've come," he said breathlessly. "This is a disaster. It makes us look like . . . incompetents! It's absurd!" His voice cracked with the effort to control it.

Pitt felt the sting of the word "incompetent." It applied to him far more than Smith.

Smith clasped Pitt's hand, then let go of it. He led the way across the court to the open door of their lodgings, and inside.

Brundage was in the oak-paneled hallway speaking with a dark, gentle-faced man whom Smith introduced briefly as Ramon Aguilar. They were both pale and clearly distressed. Brundage swung round when he saw Pitt.

"Morning, sir," he said grimly.

"Morning," Pitt replied. He might be less civil later, but not now. They needed clear thinking, a logical appreciation of the facts. Whatever was written in the newspapers yesterday, to Frank Laurence, and any other skeptical observer, this would look very much like a stunt to obtain publicity. They had to tread carefully to keep the situation from spinning out of control.

"Was the front door locked and bolted this morning?" he asked Brundage levelly.

"Yes, sir," Brundage replied. "So was the back door into the delivery area. I can't find anything to indicate a jimmied window, but there is an open one on the second floor. It's right near the bathroom downpipe, but I can't see three women dressed in long skirts climbing down the wall in the middle of the night or the small hours of the morning."

Pitt could in fact imagine Sofia Delacruz doing it, if the cause was important enough to her, but he did not say so.

Smith glared at Brundage. "Someone could have climbed up it," he pointed out angrily. "They could have broken in and taken Sofia and —"

"The two other women also?" Pitt raised his eyebrows. "Only with help. And it'd be almost impossible to do silently. I cannot imagine Sofia Delacruz going unwillingly and without a fight. Can you?"

Smith glared at him. "Are you suggesting she went willingly?" he said between his teeth, anger staining his cheeks pink.

"Is it possible?" Pitt responded. "You know her better than most people do. You have supported her for over five years. You have stated publicly, many times, that you believe her philosophy." He smiled very slightly. "You certainly appear to admire her."

"Of course I do," Smith said instantly, then stiffened as if he regretted committing himself so far, and without equivocation. He moved his feet uncomfortably on the wide oak floorboards. "We have our differences though," he went on, aware of now being intensely awkward. "On minor points only."

Pitt purposely allowed the silence to grow heavy. Footsteps echoed across the yard, uneven on the cobbles, and somewhere in the kitchen a saucepan was dropped.

"She was in danger!" Smith finally said angrily. "That's why your people were supposed to guard her! Where were your men when she was taken? Why aren't you asking them these questions? Where were you yourself?"

"Asleep, as I imagine you were," Pitt said softly. "I am not attacking you, Mr. Smith. I am trying to rule out impossibilities, so that we can concentrate on what is possible. A window three stories up is open, but all the doors to the outside were locked and bolted. It seems hard to think of a way in which Señora Delacruz and both the other women were taken by force without a sound being heard. There has been nothing broken, nothing stolen and no indications that anyone was hurt."

Ramon spoke for the first time, his face flushed with anger. "If you are saying that the señora went willingly and has left us, then you are a fool! You know nothing of my people." His accent was very slight but his voice was husky with anger. "You spoke with her, I know that. Do you see that woman stealing out in the night like an eloping maid? Why? What for? Her faith is her life . . ."

"There are different kinds of faith, Mr. Aguilar," Pitt said very gently. The man's distress was clear in his pale face and clenched body. "What about coercion or trickery?" he suggested. "Or a message from her family that someone was ill, perhaps dying, and time was short."

Ramon hesitated. "I suppose it is possible," he said with a flicker of hope. "But why did she not leave a message? And why take both Cleo and Elfrida?"

Smith's mouth was drawn in a tight, thin line. "If she had gone to see her cousin, Barton Hall, then she would certainly have told us," he answered for Ramon. "The situation between them is . . . unpleasant. He has no understanding of her mission. She did say she wished to see him, but I have no idea why. And I am certain that she has not done so yet."

Ramon gave him a withering look. "Her business is private. She certainly would have gone alone, but not in the night, and not without telling anyone."

"An emergency?" Pitt was still looking for an answer that displayed thoughtlessness possibly, but not danger.

"What emergency?" Smith said bitterly. "They were not close. Her family treated her very badly. Without understanding. They are steeped in their own past, their own knowledge, their own importance! Rigid . . ." He stopped and flushed very slightly, aware that both Pitt and Ramon were staring at him. He cleared his throat. "I apologize. I have never met Barton Hall. I know only what she told me, and what I read between the lines of her words."

Ramon was irritated. "I do not believe she spoke ill of him, whatever she thought." He turned to Pitt. There was anger and warning in his eyes.

Ramon's blind defense of Sofia was possibly hampering the investigation, but nevertheless Pitt admired it, which was unreasonable in itself. If any woman looked capable of defending herself, and was willing to do so, it was Sofia Delacruz.

"You wouldn't," Smith said with an edge of contempt. "Your views of her are tinged with affection, even though at the moment only the truth is of any help to us." He turned from Ramon back to Pitt. "Their differences are an old wound to Barton Hall's family pride. To his standing in the world, if you like."

"He has no standing in the world," Ramon snapped back. "He is a banker and a layman in the Church of England. He is important in his community, that's all. When he retires someone else will take his place, and he will sink into obscurity. The señora will be remembered forever. The world will be changed because of her." His dark face with its gentle lines was filled with a passionate enthusiasm that made him momentarily beautiful.

Pitt was momentarily shaken by the man's conviction. Then common sense returned like a cold wind erasing words written in sand. Sofia had gone away, unaccountably. Judging from his face, Smith's feelings were very mixed, but he seemed more angry than concerned. Was that because he knew perfectly well where she was? Or was he unable to contemplate something serious having happened to her?

Ramon's expression was different. He looked fearful of the worst, as if in his vision she was important enough that all the power of evil, human or otherwise, would quite naturally gather against her. It was there in the panic to his voice, the intensity of his speech.

Pitt clung to the details of fact and reason.

"The two women who went with her," he

said, returning to the issue, "Cleo Robles and Elfrida Fonsecca — tell me something of them. I remember seeing them at the meeting. They seemed to be close to her, but why would she take both of them with her?"

Smith and Ramon began speaking at the same time, and then both stopped. It was Smith who began again, asserting his seniority.

"Cleo Robles is very young, twenty-three. She is well meaning, full of enthusiasm, but she has much yet to learn of the way to teach people."

"There are as many ways as there are people to teach," Ramon interrupted. "And often enough it takes more than one person to do it."

"He was asking about Cleo, not about teaching," Smith corrected him. He turned back to Pitt and, with an effort, resumed his formal voice. "She is like a child, eager and friendly. If you imagine she has guile in her, then you know nothing of people."

Pitt was used to being in the center of a disagreement. "She has no guile. Does that mean that she is also gullible?" he asked, looking from one to the other of them.

"Yes," Smith said without hesitation. His

eyes darted at Ramon, then back again to Pitt.

"No," Ramon contradicted him in the same breath. "Not . . . gullible. Perhaps innocent. She has dreams . . ."

"Gullible," Smith repeated, looking away from him. "But she is loyal. Ramon is right: she has dreams of saving the world, and she believes that Sofia can do it." This time his voice did not give away his own feelings, only that he was struggling to hide them.

Pitt wondered what had made a man like Melville Smith join Sofia's group. It had to be alien to him in every way: to his family background, his culture and his upbringing. The reason must have been compelling, but was it a need for what Sofia taught, a hunger he could not deny, even at the cost of giving up all that was familiar? Or was it a flight from something he could no longer bear?

If Sofia did not reappear soon, Pitt would have Brundage look into the man's background.

"And Elfrida Fonsecca?" he asked. "Is she gullible too?"

This time both other men hesitated.

"I don't know," Smith admitted. "She is extremely capable in administrative matters. We could be in trouble without her, which I am sure she is aware of. It would be very unlike her to absent herself from any of her duties. It . . . it mattered to her belief of herself."

"She is much needed," Ramon agreed quietly, a flash of anger in his eyes at Smith's betrayal of the group's vulnerability. "I cannot believe Elfrida would go away from Angel Court willingly. Mr. Pitt, I fear very much that there is cause to be concerned . . . even afraid."

Smith moved a step closer to Ramon. "For once I agree completely. There are certain papers I would like to show you, Mr. Pitt."

Ramon drew in his breath sharply, then looked at Smith and seemed to change his mind about arguing.

Smith turned back to Pitt. "If you would come with me to my office . . ." He began to walk away, his bearing stiff, and very upright.

Pitt nodded to Ramon and Brundage, and then followed Smith down the hall and into a corridor. Ramon's face clearly reflected the trouble within him. He did not seem to be aware of Henrietta Navarro marching toward him, her angular frame stooped a little forward. What she said Pitt couldn't hear, as Smith led him into a room. The office was very pleasant, if a little dark. The mullioned windows looked out onto the courtyard. The direct sun was blocked by the height of the surrounding buildings, leaving only a gentle light. He closed the door and invited Pitt to be seated.

Pitt waited for Smith to open a drawer for the papers he had referred to, but instead the man simply sat down on the opposite side of the desk and folded his hands.

"I am reluctant to tell you so much," he began, "but I fear events have made it necessary. It is after eleven o'clock, and we have had no word from Señora Delacruz, or either of the women who appear to have gone with her. This has never happened before, and is entirely out of her character. She is fully committed to the cause."

Pitt did not interrupt him. He looked at Smith's high-boned, rather pale face and found himself unable to read it. The other man now appeared worried, but not deeply afraid. That could have been so for many reasons. Perhaps he knew that Sofia had disappeared intentionally, to create a stir, and thereby reach a far wider audience.

Worse, it was possible that he welcomed her disappearance because that would leave him as leader of this fast-growing sect, and free to take it in a direction he might prefer.

Smith drew in a deep breath. "Sofia has come to England primarily to meet the family member I mentioned, Barton Hall, who is a cousin in some degree, although he is considerably older than she. She did not hide from me that it is a matter of some urgency, although I have no idea what the matter is. Hall is apparently in good health." He stopped, waiting for Pitt to respond.

"But what about her 'mission'?" Pitt asked curiously. If Smith was right and Sofia's reasons for coming here were less about preaching and more about this meeting with Barton Hall, then it altered the way in which Special Branch would approach her disappearance.

Smith bit his lip. "It was a chance to preach that we could not lose, and I believed it much wiser that we did not make it obvious that meeting Hall was Sofia's real purpose in coming to England."

Pitt looked at Smith. He was sitting uncomfortably, his back straight, his hands clasped in front of him, knuckles white — but there was no wavering in his eyes.

"But you don't know anything of their business?" Pitt asked.

"No," Smith replied. "But I came to believe that my first supposition that it was a family matter was at least partially mistaken, perhaps entirely."

"What changed your mind?" Pitt said.

Smith frowned. "It is hard to be precise, and I feel somewhat foolish about it," he said hesitantly. "If it had been clear to me then I should have prevented this, and you will think me incompetent . . ."

That word again. "Incompetent?" Pitt said ruefully. "If she has gone away in order to whip up greater public interest in her message, then she has duped me, and I assume you also. If something unpleasant has happened to her, then it is my charge to protect her, and therefore my inadequacy that she is now missing. So please tell me what you know."

For a moment Smith looked embarrassed, almost compassionate, then it was gone again. "I have known her for nearly six years," he stated. "If she went willingly then I should have seen it coming. Having seen the threatening letters, I believed those who wrote them to have been no more than cranks, people whose words were violent but who had not the courage to act." He smiled sourly. "At least not so criminally . . ."

"What gave you the thought that she was not here to resolve an old family quarrel?" Pitt reverted to the earlier, still unanswered question.

Smith leaned forward a little. "When she

was in her early twenties, about ten years ago, I think, she was betrothed to be married to someone extremely suitable, in her parents' view."

Pitt knew, at least generally, what was to come — Sir Walter had told him — but he did not interrupt.

"She refused to accept the man," Smith said with a faint shrug of his shoulders. "I have no idea why. She may have known something of him that was repellent to her. She never spoke of it to me. She simply left England and ran off to Spain. Or more accurately, first to France, then later to Spain, ending up in Toledo. There she met and married a Spanish man — Nazario Delacruz."

"Is that unforgivable?" Pitt tried not to sound condescending about it, but it seemed such a trivial thing over which to carry a grudge for a decade. Then he thought of Jemima, and how he would feel if she ran away to a foreign country and married someone neither he nor Charlotte had ever met. "Is she happy?" He asked the one question that would have mattered to him, had it been Jemima in that situation.

"I believe so," Smith replied. "But that is not the issue." He looked away and smiled uncomfortably. "Nazario Delacruz was already married, with two young children. I know little of what actually happened, but it was both tragic and scandalous. That is what her family could not forgive."

Pitt was grieved and confused. Such an action seemed completely out of character for the woman he had met.

Smith was waiting for him to say something.

"Then what is it she feels she can accomplish in coming here now and meeting with Barton?" he asked. It did not make sense.

Smith took a deep breath. "She is not coming with regard to the past," he said quietly. "It is something current. She would not discuss it, even with me." There seemed to be much more that he wished to say and could not find the words, or did not trust himself to control his emotions.

Did he harbor feelings for Sofia that he could not acknowledge? She was beautiful, in her own way, and frightening in the depth of her conviction, her courage, whether well- or ill-judged.

"Do you know Barton Hall?" Pitt changed the direction of the inquiries a little.

"Only from what Sofia has said." Smith made a small, rueful gesture. "He is a leading lay member of the Church of England.

It is of great importance to him socially and, to do the man justice, perhaps spirituality as well." A shadow passed over his face. His voice was softer when he spoke. "There is a sense of continuity to it, the safety of what has been tested and sacrificed over the centuries. Men have died for the right to have the Bible in the vernacular, freedom from the Church of Rome to preach and teach as they believed."

Pitt was struck by his own indifference to irreligious faith in his life so far. To him, faith was merely a comforting presence in the background. Every village had its church tower or spire. Bells rang on a Sunday morning, in city streets or village lanes; people in their best clothes walked along the paths, all in the one direction.

"For Barton Hall, being part of the establishment is necessary to his career," Smith said. "It takes a lot of courage to abandon the familiar and step outside the group as Sofia has. You have to be very certain that the new path is better than the one you are already on."

"Better and truer?" Pitt asked.

Smith smiled slightly. "You can only know that by following it. Stronger and more beautiful, yes. Truer? I don't think even Sofia was without her doubts, at times."

"You said Barton Hall is a layperson," Pitt circled the conversation back to the facts.

"Oh, yes! She told me he is a banker of some considerable distinction. He is an officer of high standing in one of the investment banks. Perhaps even governor. He deals with the investments of the Church of England, which of course are enormous, and also of the Royal Family, whose fortune is not inconsiderable."

Pitt was impressed. It was an almost incalculable weight of responsibility. Presumably Hall shared at least some of it with others. He tried to imagine what Sofia's refusal of marriage had meant to him. Were any of his clients or colleagues aware of her affair in Toledo with a man already married? And a Roman Catholic, at that?

Why had she wished to see him now, so many years after the scandal?

"But you don't know anything about this current matter that brought Señora Delacruz here now so urgently?" he pressed again.

"No," Smith repeated without hesitation. "I have wondered that since she first told me that she must come, and I broached the subject with her. But she refused to discuss it. I knew only that it was of the greatest importance to her. I had the impression that it was something she believed she owed Mr. Hall and it could not wait. She has people in Spain who are desperately troubled and relying on her spiritual guidance. I have racked my mind as to what it could be, and I know no more now than I did the day she first mentioned it in Toledo. I'm sorry."

"Did you know that she was in communication with Mr. Hall?"

"Not before this trip. She never previously mentioned it."

Pitt knew from Smith's face that he had nothing more to say on the subject. "Do you know if the matter might be related to any of the threats she has received?" he said instead.

Smith looked startled. "I had not thought to connect the two. Certainly not any she told me about. But if it was something she kept to herself, then of course it is possible." There was doubt in his voice. "But she was not running away from anyone. If she were it would not be to Barton Hall, or to somewhere as vulnerable as Angel Court. There are places in Spain where she would be far safer, and which would not require such travel."

"So even before she proposed coming here she received threats to her life?"

"Yes," Smith agreed unhappily. "But it

was almost always that God would destroy her for blasphemy, rather than an intent that the writer would."

"You don't think the writers see themselves as instruments of God?"

Smith's lips tightened. "Sometimes. I don't know whether to take such people seriously. Perhaps it is because my conviction is anyone may believe whatever they wish. Intolerance is a greater offense against God than holding a strange or even inconsistent belief. You have the right to worship what you wish — a pile of stones in your garden — as long as you do not injure others. God gave you that, and I have no right whatsoever to mock you, or prevent you doing so. And I know that —" He stopped abruptly, and then looked at Pitt. "I can hear Sofia's voice in my words. But that is the truth, whatever anyone else may believe. Please find her, Mr. Pitt. This whole . . . whole journey has become a fiasco. I must keep up everyone's spirits." He rose to his feet. "There is nothing more I can tell you. I doubt there is anything further Ramon could either, and certainly not Henrietta. Please don't distress them unnecessarily."

"I will do all I can to keep from upsetting them," Pitt promised. "Now may I see these threatening letters, Mr. Smith?"

"Of course." Smith pulled open a drawer in the beautiful old oak desk and removed a pile of letters, still in their envelopes. He passed them over to Pitt, and then rose stiffly to his feet. "I shall leave you to read them."

Pitt opened the first letter and read it. It was written in pen, in a scrawled handwriting that tilted slightly downward at the end of each line.

Sofia Delacruz,
You are a blasphemer against the God who created you.

You are feeding poison to the people who believe in truth and you should be stoned to death, as all liars deserve. You are a servant of the devil and will surely die in hell.

It was signed with a squiggle of lines that was indecipherable. Pitt put it aside as of little meaning.

The second was darker in tone, and written with a strong, firm hand.

Señora Delacruz,
Charity requires that I try to think of you as an ignorant and ambitious woman who has little idea of the damage you do

with your seeds of discontent. Is there not enough violence in the world, enough rising up of the discontented masses, without you giving them the insane idea, the dreams of madmen, that they are destined to become gods one day?

Your ideas go beyond madness into the realms of evil.

You stray over the verge into the realms of sedition, as if your will is to have anarchy. You do not openly advocate bombings, murders and outrages, but they will be the inevitable outcome of your teachings, which give men already primed to murder and destruction the belief that order is unnecessary and should be hurled down, and trodden upon. The order and civilization that has adorned society since the Dark Ages should be overturned! Virtue, modesty and obedience are worthless and courage lies in creating chaos!

Whether you are mad or wicked no longer matters. You preach evil, and must be fought with all weapons at the disposal of decent people. Change your words, take back your teachings or prepare to become the victim of your own sins of pride.

I speak for every man!

Adam

Pitt put down the paper slowly. How deep a threat was intended? The writing was steady, an easy script without flourish, the name presumably symbolic.

The next two were more hasty, written in anger, but the theme was there again: pride, a woman who did not know her place and sowed discontent, disorder, the breakup of hearth and home, which has been the center of civilization, of comfort, art, law, the keeping of peace for countless generations.

The further half dozen or so were less literate and less thought through.

Did they amount to serious threat? Pitt did not know, but he could not afford to ignore the weight of feeling they expressed.

He stuffed the letters into his jacket pockets and stood up to leave.

As he walked across the cobbles of Angel Court, toward the figure of the angel near the entrance, he was still unsure as to whether Sofia Delacruz had left so dramatically in the night in order to whip up even more public interest in herself, and so gain a greater platform for her message. He remembered vividly the passion in her face, the timbre of her voice ringing with certainty. He had no doubt she was a woman who would do what she believed to be right, and take the consequences later. But was that holiness, was it human obsession or was she on the brink of insanity?

The world was full of uncertainty. They were hurtling toward the end of the century. There was social and religious unrest everywhere. There were too many questions that no longer had answers. There was a seed of disorder in belief, not as to which God was true, but in any God at all. It matched the already growing social anarchy in politics throughout Europe. This year had seen an Anti-Anarchist Conference in Rome, and the founding of an international police force. It was long overdue.

And as he turned the corner into the street and walked toward the main road, he noticed the newsboy selling papers. The headline said something about mounting tensions in South Africa.

He shook his head. He must liaise with the Spanish Embassy to make sure his inquiries did not ruffle diplomatic feathers, and tomorrow he would go to see Barton Hall and find out what he knew of Sofia Delacruz and her real purpose in coming to England.

CHAPTER 3

Early the next morning the hansom drew up to the curb in Eaton Square and Pitt stepped down onto the pavement and paid the driver. He walked past the wrought-iron railings and up the steps to the paneled oak door of Barton Hall's home. Apart from the lion-headed door knocker, the house was as elegantly Georgian as all the others facing the square. It was formal and perfectly proportioned. There were no flippant fancies to mar its classic exterior.

Pitt raised the knocker and let it fall. It was only moments before the door was opened by a man of immense dignity, gray-haired before his time. His face had an expression of imperturbable calm.

"Good morning, sir. How may I help you?" He was holding a small silver salver, the sort used to take a gentleman's card.

Pitt dropped his card on it, adding as he did so, "Commander Pitt of Special Branch.

I would like to speak with Mr. Barton Hall. It is a matter of the greatest urgency."

"Yes, sir. If you would like to come in I will see if Mr. Hall is available." The butler stepped back into the wide, marble-flagged hall.

"Perhaps you would like to wait in the morning room, sir?" It was not an inquiry so much as a direction. He indicated the way with a very slight movement of his hand.

Pitt was happy to accept. Morning rooms were often revealing not only of a man's character but also of his means, his interests, and the comfort and discipline of his household.

This one was no exception. As the butler closed the door and his footsteps retreated over the marble, Pitt stared around at the dark curtains, the polished wood floor with its very traditional red and blue Turkey carpet and the one wall entirely lined with books, comprising sets uniformly bound in leather. They were arranged according to size and color, rather than by subject matter or by author. They looked expensive, well cared for, infrequently moved from their places.

He walked over and pulled one out. The shelf was sufficiently well dusted that there was no mark. He smiled and pushed the book back into line. It was a history of Schliemann's excavations in the ruins now believed to be Troy.

He turned and looked more closely at the two paintings on the farther walls. They were rather staid pastoral scenes, undisturbed by any signs of real country life. Everything was artistically proportioned, from the haywain to the slant of the thatched roof.

There was one photograph that caught his eye. It was in a frame on one of the smaller tables. It showed the head and shoulders of a middle-aged woman whose dark hair was pulled back in a fashion of at least ten years ago. At first glance she was ordinary, her features strong but a little heavy for handsomeness. But the longer Pitt looked at her, the more he saw in her not only a frankness, but a humor. She seemed the sort of woman that, when you knew her well, you would miss very much when she was absent. Was she Barton Hall's wife?

His thoughts were broken by the opening of the door as Barton himself came in and closed it silently behind him. He was a tall man with slightly receding hair, which was graying at the sides. He was very formally dressed, bony wrists showing beneath his white shirt cuffs.

"Good morning, Commander Pitt," he said quietly. "How may I be of assistance to you?" Hall's voice was more than pleasing — there was a depth to it, almost a music.

"Good morning, Mr. Hall," Pitt replied, inclining his head. "I believe you are related to Sofia Delacruz?"

Hall winced very slightly. "I am," he admitted. "She is a cousin on my late mother's side of the family." He remained standing. "But please do not hold me accountable for her eccentric views. Believe me, sir, were I able to dissuade her from speaking of them publicly, I would already have done so." He cleared his throat. "I apologize for any embarrassment she may cause. I am acutely aware of it, but helpless to prevent her. All the family's pleading has changed nothing."

Pitt felt a degree of sympathy with him. There were few people who were not embarrassed by their families at some time in their lives, but usually not to this extent. Hall was also clearly touched by anxiety.

"I am not looking for your help in moderating her speaking," Pitt replied.

Hall frowned. He was still standing in the middle of the Turkey rug looking vaguely at a loss. "Then what is it you wish of me?"

"Sofia Delacruz was staying at a residence in Angel Court . . ." he answered. He saw Hall's bleak smile of humor at the name of the place. "She disappeared from there sometime during the night before last," he continued. "Her people are anxious because she left no word, and it has meant they have had to cancel a meeting this evening."

Hall's eyebrows rose in surprise. "And you thought she might have come here? I'm sorry, I have no idea why she should do something so . . . irresponsible." He sighed. "Although I should not be surprised. Her whole life has been a journey of one irresponsibility after another. This is merely the latest."

"Irresponsibilities that were against her own interests?" Pitt asked quickly.

Hall stared at him, a confusion of thoughts racing across his face.

Pitt waited.

Hall swallowed hard. "Perhaps I spoke in haste. I have known very little of her for the last ten years or so." He cleared his throat again. "One always hopes that people may change."

Pitt realized with surprise how angry he was. He had believed that Sofia was sincere, even that she had a vision of a glory in the world that made sense of some of the pain, the waste, and the seeming chaos.

And it seemed now as if she was very probably a charlatan. The taste it left in his mouth was bitter. If Barton Hall had endured a lifetime of this deceit, then Pitt had every sympathy with him now.

Hall was waiting for Pitt to continue. His face was creased with concern and he stood unnaturally still.

"Has she contacted you since she arrived in England?" Pitt asked.

"Oh, yes." Barton Hall spoke wearily. "She sent a perfectly civil letter from Southampton, and then a note when she reached London. She had asked to meet with me the day after they arrived in the city, but I had other arrangements. She agreed that it should be tomorrow."

Pitt wondered at Sofia's keenness to meet with her cousin. Was it simply that she knew it would be unpleasant and thus wished to get it over with as soon as possible, whereas Hall had preferred to delay it, maybe even avoid it altogether?

"She may return before then," he said.

"And if she doesn't?" Hall asked. "I presume you are looking for her? Questioning these . . . people that she has now made her life with?" His shoulders were tight, pulling the fabric of his coat, and there was a thin thread of fear in his voice. "Do you know anything about them?"

"We are making inquiries," Pitt replied. "But all of the group who traveled with her are Spanish, apart from Melville Smith, and we are having to work with the Spanish Embassy —"

"Sofia is English," Hall interrupted. "She was born and bred here, from generations of English! Marrying some damn Spaniard doesn't rob her of that!"

Pitt was surprised by the heat of the anger in Hall's words. His fists were by his sides, but Pitt could see they were clenched so tight his large knuckles shone white.

Hall stared at Pitt for a moment, then apparently realized he had betrayed too much emotion and visibly composed his face into total gravity.

"I apologize, Mr. Pitt. Sofia has always been a deep concern to her family, but that does not mean we are indifferent to what happens to her." He cleared his throat again. "Or that the thought of her coming to some harm is not extremely distressing, especially to me, since I am the last one who was close to her parents. I regret to say both my aunt and uncle are deceased."

"No brothers or sisters?" Pitt allowed himself to be led, at least temporarily.

"She had one brother, who died as a child," Hall said simply. "You understand why I am concerned." It was a statement, not a question.

"Of course," Pitt agreed. "It is perfectly natural. I shall see that you are informed of any progress we make." They were still standing on the middle of the carpet. Pitt did not feel as if he could sit in any of the comfortable armchairs until Hall should invite him to. There was a charge of emotion in the air like the tension before a storm. Any ease would be pretended.

"Thank you," Hall acknowledged.

"Were you in regular correspondence with Señora Delacruz?" Pitt continued.

"Señora Delacruz? For God's sake." Hall's voice was tight, the music that had been in it so agreeably, now completely gone. "No, I wasn't. If our family had not lived in this house for generations I doubt she would have even known where to find me."

"She lives in Toledo?" Pitt asked, trying to judge how much Hall had kept up his information about her.

"So I am told. Is that relevant?" Hall appeared surprised.

"I don't know," Pitt answered. "She seems to have gained enemies long before she came to England, at least according to the threats she has received."

"Hardly surprising," Hall snapped. "She has a gift for it. Her ideas are absurd, which is irrelevant, but they are also deeply offensive to many who revere the teachings of their own Church, whose faith is nearly two thousand years old, and has stood the test of time and hardship!" He started to clear his throat and turned it into a cough. "How can they not be?"

"Christianity has certainly withstood terrible persecution," Pitt agreed, watching Hall's face.

"And from a woman in my own family! Thank God her parents are not alive."

Pitt was taken aback. There was almost a hunted look about Hall that he did not understand.

Hall straightened himself up. "I'm sorry. This must seem absurd to you." His voice was stronger, his composure regained. "Her return to England has come at an unfortunate period for me. I have responsibilities: serious matters to which I cannot afford to give less than my full attention. I'm sorry if I seem heartless, but there are only so many times we can drop all our own affairs to rescue someone who is bent on her own destruction and is willing to take you with her." His voice wavered, strained almost to the point where it could barely escape the tightness of his throat.

"I'm sorry to have disturbed you, Mr. Hall," Pitt apologized, watching him with a degree of pity. "I was hoping she might be here. And since you are her only relative in England, we had to inform you of her disappearance."

Hall sighed. "I understand. I dare say by tomorrow she will have appeared again with some absurd story of hardship, and be too busy talking to the newspapers about it to be aware that she has distressed her poor followers, and wasted your time."

"I hope so." As soon as the words were out of his mouth, Pitt knew that he did not entirely mean them. He hated the thought that the woman he had seen only three days ago, so passionate in her belief, was actually self-serving and manipulative.

Hall pursed his lips. "Do you hope so? I think you speak without realizing the damage she can do, and undoubtedly will, if she returns and continues in her insane crusade." Yet again he coughed and cleared his throat. "Her religious views are socially dangerous, Mr. Pitt. That is what you should be turning your attention toward."

Pitt regarded him steadily, trying to judge whether he was acting or not. Certainly he was laboring under the stress of some extreme emotion. Pitt could see its depth, but there was no way to tell its nature.

"She sees what she wants to, and ignores the rest," Hall went on, the bitterness still in his voice. "There is much in her past she prefers not to recall, as if it never happened. But believe me, Mr. Pitt, she did not leave England with honor, nor did she originally act with any decency in Spain. I don't know how the people of Toledo could forget, but perhaps their values are different from ours." He stopped just short of implying that Spaniards were morally weak.

Pitt hesitated. He did not wish to look too interested, and make Hall realize how far he had trespassed on the privacy he had originally claimed.

"You doubt me!" Hall said with a flare of anger. "And it would be a betrayal for me to tell you more. Sofia may do as she wishes, but I shall not allow her to claim moral superiority by sinking to the level of speaking ill of her — and those dark griefs that are part of our family's history. Sufficient for me to say that she may have many enemies among those she has . . . harmed on her way to her present absurd position."

The thought flashed in Pitt's mind that Hall was deliberately taunting him, but he had no doubt at all that the anger and the pain in Hall's face were perfectly real, whatever their cause. He chose his words very carefully, watching Hall's eyes for his reaction to them.

"Are you saying, as discreetly as you can, that she has injured people in Spain who may have felt sufficiently aggrieved to follow her here to England in order to take revenge?"

Hall swallowed, his throat jerking as if the movement was painful.

"I am," he replied. "And there is always the possibility that at least one of her followers has turbulent and mixed emotions about her. Disillusion is a kind of betrayal, Mr. Pitt." Hall smiled sadly. "You have many places to look for whoever might have wished Sofia harm. Begin with those closest to her, and work from there. You may even need to look at her husband."

"Oh?" Pitt said with interest. "Do you think there is ill feeling between them sufficient to cause some sort of abduction or attack?"

"I don't know, Commander. But to the best of my knowledge she has not been in England for many years. This is very soon after her arrival to have created such enmity."

"Have you been to Spain, Mr. Hall?"

"To Madrid once, a long time ago, never to Toledo. I think I have already told you, sir, I have had no contact with Sofia since she went to Spain a decade or so ago. I wish her well, of course, but I have no real interest in her affairs. I imagine her enemies are in Spain, or at least from Spain, as a matter of common sense, not any specific knowledge."

"And she gave you no idea as to why she wished so urgently to see you?"

"None whatsoever," Hall agreed, holding out his hand toward Pitt. "I am sorry my assistance is so meager and in essence harsh as well." There was a flash of intense bitterness on his face, then the moment after it had vanished. "I regret I cannot spare more time to be hospitable, but I have business that cannot wait longer. Good day to you, sir, I wish you success."

Pitt took a hansom cab to Angel Court, hoping that Sofia might have returned, or at least sent some message with an explanation for her absence. But when he walked in through the gateway of Angel Court, he knew. Henrietta Navarro stood on the cobbles with a bunch of herbs in her hand. She stared at Pitt with a momentary flash of hope, then her eyes filled with tears and she turned away and hurried inside.

Pitt went across the yard and in through the door without looking back.

When Pitt got home, later than he had expected, he was happy not to think of Sofia Delacruz. He was tired of wondering where she was, and if she was there of her own will. However, he had barely finished his dinner in the pleasant warmth around the kitchen table when he realized that Jemima was watching him, waiting. He had been hoping to talk of something comfortable, but he saw the possibility disappearing.

"What do you think has happened to her, Papa?" Jemima asked the moment he caught her eye.

He knew that Charlotte would have told her not to ask him until after dinner. He knew she had been watching every mouthful, barely tasting her own food.

"I don't know," he said honestly. He was careful how he answered his children, trying to protect them from the harsher side of his job, but he never lied. Sometimes that was difficult, but if he did lie, he knew that their trust in him would be broken and someday it would come back to haunt them all.

"People are saying that she went on purpose," Jemima continued. "That she wasn't kidnapped at all, she's just pretending so she can make people scared, and think she's in danger when she's perfectly all right. They're saying it's a trick to make her look more important. That's not true, is it?"

He looked at her. She was so like Charlotte that he could imagine Charlotte as a girl, as if the years had blurred and carried him back to a time before he had known her. Jemima had the same soft curve to her cheeks and mouth, the same steady eyes, yet there was something of himself in her too, the way her hair grew from her brow, like his, and like his mother's. He had only this moment realized it.

"I don't know," he said carefully. "When I met her I thought she believed what she was saying and that it mattered enough never to soil it by trickery. But I've been mistaken in people. We all have."

"Then you're saying she could have been lying all the time!" Jemima challenged, her voice thick with emotion.

Daniel winced. He was three years younger, and very tired of girls altogether, and emotional storms especially. His were yet to come. He was brave, intelligent, very practical. He was interested in the rising possibility of more widespread war in Africa than the present fighting in the Sudan, especially against the Boers in South Africa. The military tactics, the heroism and the sacrifice involved intrigued him. He did not care in the slightest about the philosophy of saints, or their behavior.

Charlotte looked from one to the other of them, anxiety in her eyes, but she did not intervene.

"I don't think she is," Pitt replied. "But Barton Hall, who is her only relative in England, said that she has misled people in the past and that there is a great deal that we don't know about her. He won't tell me exactly what it is, because he feels it would be dishonorable, a betrayal of family secrets."

"That's despicable!" Jemima said hotly. "He will tell you there's something awful, but he won't say what it is, so you can't judge it for yourself. He could be lying. If he won't tell you then he shouldn't mention it at all! That's like being a sneak!"

Daniel looked up, his expression reflecting his agreement. To a boy his age, sneaking was the worst sin imaginable, after cowardice. He stared at Pitt, then at his sister. "You shouldn't listen to him," he said without hesitation. "It all sounds very childish."

A look of both surprise and amusement

lit Charlotte's face. She quashed it immediately. She drew in her breath to speak, then changed her mind.

Charlotte had warned Pitt that Jemima was both excited and afraid of the great changes in her life that were coming in the next couple of years. She had thought of adulthood as freedom, and was just realizing that it had its own kind of restrictions. Marriage meant a gain, but also its own sort of loss, and she was not at all sure she was ready for that yet. Romance could be wonderful or heartbreaking, and sometimes both.

The idea of promising to love and obey anyone else, for the rest of her life, terrified her. Perhaps that was why the courage and the independence of Sofia Delacruz appealed to her so much.

"He was warning me that she might have more enemies than merely those who disagreed with her religious views," Pitt told them. "He was answering my questions."

Jemima blinked rapidly. "Do you believe him?"

"I believe he feels very strongly about it." Pitt wanted to reach out and comfort her, but he wasn't entirely sure how.

"Why?" Jemima asked. "Does he hate her?"

"I think he's afraid of her," he replied.

"That doesn't make sense." Contempt rang in her voice. "She isn't hurting anyone, especially him."

Should he be honest, or was it burdening her with thoughts she would not understand? He desperately wanted to forget Sofia Delacruz and enjoy the evening.

He looked across at Charlotte, and knew that she was not going to say anything. She wanted answers as well, although she would not have asked him, especially not this late when she understood his need to give his mind a rest.

"Papa?" Jemima persisted. "Why would he be afraid of her? Do you think she's dangerous?"

He knew he could hurt her so easily. He must choose exactly the right words.

"He's afraid that people will believe her ideas, and then be horribly disappointed when she doesn't live up to what she has said," he answered.

"She didn't say she was perfect!" Jemima argued. "She just said it wasn't all a big mistake because God didn't know we'd disobey and get cast out of Eden. Which would make Him pretty stupid. She said it was meant to be, and that we can learn from it and get better . . . forever."

Daniel rolled his eyes, but very wisely said nothing.

Pitt was surprised that Jemima had been listening closely enough to be able to put it so succinctly. He was proud of her, and afraid for her in the same moment.

"Don't you believe that?" Jemima demanded.

"I want to believe it," he admitted. "But it's hard to be different from all the people around you. It doesn't come without a price, and I don't want you to be hurt. I look at Sofia Delacruz, and I see the turmoil around her, because she is challenging the order of things and suggesting something new. People like what is familiar. We get upset when people ask us to change. It's hard work. It feels dangerous, and we are afraid we will lose those we love."

She blinked. "Is there a God? I'm trying to think back, but I can't remember you ever saying so." The hope was shining in her eyes, and she would believe what he said.

Charlotte moved her hand slightly, just barely touching him.

"My mother died before you were born," he said quietly. "But she believed. I always knew that. I would like to believe as deeply as she did, but I haven't got there yet. I'm afraid I haven't tried very hard. But I do know certain things are right, and some are wrong, and I don't doubt that. Although there's an awful lot in the middle."

This time it was Daniel who interrupted. "What's always right?"

"Kindness," Pitt answered with certainty. "Keeping your promises. Not giving up just because it gets hard. Owning up to your mistakes, and not blaming other people even if you would get away with it."

Jemima took a deep breath. "You will find her, won't you, Papa? I mean before anyone does something terrible to her?" She wanted him to so intensely he could feel it like a pressure in the air. Dare he promise her he would succeed?

"He can't if she's already dead," Daniel said reasonably. "But she's probably perfectly all right, just lost, or someone knows where she is and is playing a stupid trick, not telling anyone." He pushed his chair back and stood up. "What matters is whether there's going to be a war or not, a big one. Like with the Americans and the Spanish, but with us." He gave a shrug and walked out of the room.

"Yes, we'll find her," Pitt replied to Jemima and Charlotte. "I'll do everything I can for it to be soon enough."

CHAPTER 4

At noon the next day Brundage came into Pitt's office. His blunt face was pale, almost bruised-looking. He was clearly discouraged.

Pitt had been reading reports of a group of anarchists in east London who had suddenly gone quiet, as if they were preparing for some decisive action. He turned the top sheet facedown and pushed the whole pile away. He would return to it later.

"Sit," he directed. He knew Brundage would not do so until he was asked.

Brundage did not obey.

Pitt leaned back in his chair. "No trace at all?"

"No, sir. I've spent all morning questioning Ramon, Henrietta and Smith about all the possible threats they knew of, or even might suspect. I got nothing new, certainly nothing helpful. I did as you said and asked as much as I could about enemies, rivals in

Spain, money, how the Catholic Church treated them. Learned nothing of use." Brundage moved his weight from one foot to the other. "Melville Smith decided to hold a meeting yesterday evening." His face was bleak. "The place was crowded. You couldn't have fit more people in with a shoehorn. He made the most of it."

Pitt could see the unhappiness in Brundage, and he realized with surprise how little he knew of the sergeant beyond the record of his abilities and his service. He had no idea about his personal life, or if he had any faith that could be bruised by Sofia's ideas, or her disappearance. Looking up at him now, he saw something in his face deeper than professional embarrassment, but he was not certain if it was disillusion, or merely his own misery at their failure.

"Sit down and tell me what he said, Brundage," Pitt said quietly. "Do you think Smith is behind her disappearance, or is he just capitalizing on it?"

Brundage sat in the large, comfortable chair opposite Pitt's desk. "I'm not sure if he's trying to hold the group together and keep an audience," he said thoughtfully. "He's being very open about her disappearance. If he knows where she's gone, or why, or if she's safe, he's damn good at hiding it." He smiled a little self-consciously. "But then, I've often thought the best preachers were also the best actors. They get carried away by the story. They're playing a part they may believe in, but they don't have to. They're watching, listening, carrying their audience with them, and they feel it. It's a kind of power, for a little while." He shook his head. "The difference is that their audience is there because they believe they should be, and some of them at least need to hear what is said."

Pitt was impressed. Brundage was far more perceptive than he had expected.

"You look out at them and you can't tell who's desperate inside," Brundage went on. "Who's crippled by fear, or guilt, or loneliness. Do you think he knows? Smith, I mean? He played a hell of a part!"

"As good as Sofia?" Pitt asked curiously. Could this all be a plan they had created together? It was a repulsive thought.

"No," Brundage said without hesitation. "I've been thinking about it, turning over the possibilities as I listened to him. He's not giving exactly the same message. The changes are very small, but they're there." He stopped and looked at Pitt, waiting for his response.

Pitt knew exactly what he was thinking.

The same thought was taking shape in his own mind, the lines of it clearer with each new piece of evidence.

"How is the message different?" Pitt asked.

Brundage frowned slightly, just a faint turning down of the corners of his mouth. "It's safer, easier to accept than hers because the price is less," he replied. "It's more a matter of the parts he left out, like God once being as we are now. That's a big thing to swallow. Doesn't make us more, or God less. What he said is all more manageable to the imagination. Less risk." He leaned forward a little. "I couldn't put my finger on it exactly, but I watched the faces of the people listening. There was much less fear in them. They didn't fidget and sneak glances at one another the way they did when she was speaking. I saw some of them nod. It was as if he promised rather than challenged. He made a lot less out of the price of failure, almost as if success was not expected, and there would be no blame. Like . . . like speaking to children."

"But it worked?" Pitt pressed him.

"Depends on what you count as success," Brundage replied. "He doesn't have the fire she does, nothing like the passion. Yet perhaps that's more comfortable for the majority."

Pitt suddenly felt ashamed; had never figured Brundage to be so thoughtful. He had broken his own rules, judging the man based on his bluff appearance, his slight country accent, his very clear physical fitness, the occasional comment on sports.

"You've given it a lot of consideration," he observed. "You have a faith of your own?"

Brundage blushed. "Not really, sir. I've seen all this sort of thing before. My father's a country vicar . . ."

"You never mentioned it," Pitt said in surprise.

Brundage looked uncomfortable. "It's not the sort of thing you talk about. Ragged about it pretty hard when I was a boy. Thought a lot of my father, but I didn't want to be like him. Couldn't keep up the front, even if I had wanted to. I haven't the patience with people. But I saw a lot of what he did. And the sort of people who come to church. I suppose I should be grateful. Best lesson in human nature, watching a village."

Pitt smiled wryly. "Perhaps I owe your father a word of thanks too. Tell me, do you think if and when Sofia Delacruz comes back, she is going to find her place usurped? Will she have to adopt Smith's alterations, or lose a significant part of her cause?"

Brundage bit his lip. "Maybe. He might have organized this in order to make a kind of coup. He's ambitious. He's played second fiddle to her for a long time. But what happens if she comes back and accuses him of having deliberately had her kidnapped in order to step into her place?"

"Any number of things," Pitt said bitterly. "The whole organization will fracture into pieces, a kind of civil war. It might be ugly, and if neither of them wins quickly then it will drag on until it destroys any credibility in giving a moral leadership, and everyone loses. Or else it simply disintegrates and disappears. Or maybe she'll go on alone."

"Why would he be so stupid as to risk something like that?" Brundage asked.

"People don't always think ahead," Pitt said with a touch of asperity. "If we could see the end of the road, half the time we'd stop before we took the first step. Sometimes if we knew what something would cost, our courage would fail."

"You make it sound both good and bad," Brundage pointed out.

"I meant to," Pitt answered.

"Maybe Sofia will return and never know who arranged her abduction," Brundage said. "And they'll all go back to Spain before she finds out," he added hopefully.

"Or her disappearance has nothing to do with Smith, and he's simply an opportunist," Pitt added. "One thing is certain: if she reappears now, she'll need to have a remarkably good explanation of where she's been."

"Do you think she knew Smith was intending to alter the message, and she did this deliberately in order to smoke him out?" Brundage suggested. "But that would be taking quite a chance."

"I've no idea," Pitt admitted, knowing as he said it that he believed Sofia Delacruz perfectly capable of taking any chance at all, if she believed the prize worth the risk. "I wish to hell she'd chosen somewhere else to do it!"

"Perfect place," Brundage said miserably. "Get us running around in circles, and blame any loose ends on us and our general incompetence."

Pitt felt the sting of that and knew Brundage was reflecting his own failure in not having kept Sofia safe, even if it was from herself. Should he attempt to comfort him? Pitt was his commander, not a fellow officer. Commiseration would make them equals, and that was not what Brundage wished for. It would have been so much more comfortable for Pitt, but also wrong.

"It may well have begun that way," he said. "But if so, it's changed. Something has gone wrong. The publicity was moderately positive in the first day or two. Now it's becoming much less pleasant. She can't have been unaware of the furor she would create. She's frightened people, and they'll hate her for that."

Brundage looked bleak. "Yes, they will. They'll feel she made fools of them. That's a kind of contempt and it hurts."

"I wonder if that's what Smith intended." Pitt remembered Smith's face, the intonation in his voice when he spoke of Sofia. There had been admiration in it, but also something else. Envy? Criticism? Fear that she was mishandling the most important belief in his life? Why did a man like Melville Smith abandon the faith of his family and his youth, and publicly embrace something so different and controversial? For that matter, why did anybody?

"We need to look much more closely at the rest of the disciples, or whatever they call themselves," he added. "What details have you learned so far?"

Brundage recited particulars of birth, family, different places where each of the followers had lived and worked. He added the dates they had joined the group, and the positions they had held, including the little that was known of their relationships with one another. He added any facts that might link into whether they physically could have had anything to do with Sofia's disappearance. He included what he had been able to learn of both Cleo and Elfrida also: more specifically of their devotion to Sofia, and any tales of quarrels or disappointments, however inviolate-seeming.

"It's not enough," Pitt said when Brundage finally fell silent. He thought for a moment, and then when there was still no answer he looked up. "Why do people change religion, Brundage? I want your honest opinion."

Brundage was startled.

"I don't know, sir, but it must be something pretty profound. You don't just change everything at this sort of cost for no reason, no matter how persuasive someone is. But there's no money involved. I did look into that. There's no trace of money changing hands at all. Sofia Delacruz has enough to get by, but not in luxury."

"I understand her, at least I think so . . ." Pitt was thinking aloud. "At best, she really believes what she's saying, whether she has the right way of making other people listen, or not. But what draws them to her? Why the change of faith, the way of life altogether? They are stepping outside the path they'd followed before, and losing friends, even the safety in the ordinary day-to-day life. What are they gaining?"

Brundage frowned. "Does it matter? Are you thinking something made her group so disillusioned with her that they've attacked her?" He bit his lip. "That perhaps they are even covering up a murder?"

Pitt felt a chill run through him, as if he had been touched by ice. "Oh God! I hope not. But it's possible. We need to know why they joined her," he said to Brundage. "Each of them. It's the key to who they are, and why any of them might have helped her or hurt her." He stood up. "There's no trail to follow, no corpse, no sign of her at all. At least one of them at Angel Court knows something."

"Yes, sir," Brundage agreed, standing as well. "I'll also try to find any places in London the others might have connections with. If they are the ones who are keeping her, they can't have taken her very far."

Pitt nodded. "Good."

Angel Court looked desolate rather than peaceful, the sightless angel forbidding. The early May sun was hazy, blurring the shadows. The cobbles were swept but they were still dusty — they always would be — and uneven in places where cracked ones had been replaced.

Pitt walked past the old woman who had been sweeping the last time he was there. Now she was standing with her back to him as she pulled weeds out of the wooden tubs where she was nurturing parsley, chives and purple sage.

He had not reached the door when it opened in front of him and Henrietta Navarro stood expectantly, her dark eyes searching his face.

"What do you want now?" she said bitterly. "I've already told that young man of yours everything I know. You should be out there looking for her!" Her voice quivered slightly.

"He's out there looking," Pitt answered. "But we would do better if we knew more."

"Better?" she said scathingly. "Better than what? Better than nothing?" Then she relented, perhaps realizing she was wasting her own time as well as his. "Come in, then. Come on!" She stepped back and turned to lead him into the hallway where he had spoken with Ramon and Smith previously. She allowed the heavy front door to close itself.

Thinking of what Brundage had said about people's need for faith, he followed her. She led him through the short passage into a small sitting room. The furniture was spare but meticulously clean. There were two hard-backed wooden chairs, a straight-legged table, three upholstered chairs — all well used and different from one another — and a sofa with thick cushions on it. The light slanted in through windows, but there was no view beyond except a smaller yard.

Pitt sat down where she indicated. To him she was the most interesting of the three followers who remained here. It was difficult to tell how old she was, but he guessed her to be in her late fifties at least. She was tall for a woman, square-shouldered and lean, but in her youth she might have had grace, possibly even beauty. Her features were well proportioned and her iron-gray hair was still thick. Now she glared at him out of coal-black eyes.

"Why do you believe anyone would take her?" he asked.

"That's obvious," she said impatiently. "New ideas always stir up passions. If you didn't know that, what are you doing as a policeman?"

He decided to be just as blunt. Clearly she had no respect for authority, especially

English authority, which had so signally failed to protect the woman she had accepted as her spiritual leader. He could not blame her for that.

"What am I doing? I'm looking for an Englishwoman who has adopted Spain for her home, and created a new branch of religion that is causing controversy. Some of her followers think she is a saint, other people that she is deluded and dangerous at a time when the whole world is on the brink of chaos. If she has been taken violently there is no sign of it, no evidence, and no one has made any demand for ransom. If, on the other hand, she went willingly with someone she knows . . ."

Henrietta's face hardened in lines of anger and she drew in her breath to interrupt him.

He ignored her.

". . . and was then tricked, or held against her will," he went on, "I need to know a lot more if I am to find her."

Gradually she relaxed, but her eyes never moved from his. "What do you want from me?" she asked.

He sat back more comfortably in the chair. "Sergeant Brundage listened to Melville Smith speak yesterday evening. He said it was good, but Sofia's message had been considerably blunted, made easier to follow.

Is that true?"

Her reaction was instant, but so masked that had he not been watching intently he wouldn't have seen it. There was contempt, disgust, and a shadow he thought was fear. Fear of what? The discovery of something? Of Smith's involvement in Sofia's disappearance? Or of losing the faith she herself needed? She was a fierce woman, with a past he could not guess at.

"Was Sergeant Brundage wrong?" he demanded of her silence.

"What can I tell you?" she returned, still challenging, evasive.

"You can tell me if Mr. Smith is now saying what he really believes, and perhaps seizing the chance to take over leadership . . . ." He stopped at the blazing anger in her eyes, and then also saw the change as she realized they both knew that it was true, and that saving Sofia, her reputation and perhaps her life, was more important than preserving a false appearance of unity.

She lowered her eyes. "Perhaps," she said quietly. "He is very practical. He would rather have many people beginning their journey toward faith than a few who accept it all."

"And Sofia would rather have the few?" Pitt asked curiously.

She looked up. "You can have everybody, if you make the gate wide enough, and the climb shallow." Her contempt was scalding.

"Do you like Melville Smith?" he asked.

She gave a very slight shrug of her gaunt shoulders. "No. But that is irrelevant. I don't like him because he is a harsh judge, in all the dark, painful things that matter to me. And perhaps I am the same to him. We will smooth the rough places in each other . . . if we survive it!" The amusement was bright in her eyes for an instant.

"But he is ambitious?" Pitt pressed.

"For the faith, or for himself?" she quibbled. An obvious part of her was savoring the exchange. Perhaps it was a relief to quarrel openly with someone and not have to care if she hurt him.

"You've already answered the first," he pointed out.

She smiled suddenly, and he saw an echo of the beautiful woman she had once been. "And the second also," she told him.

"And Sofia?" he asked. "You say Smith is softening the message, robbing it of truth. Was she an even harsher judge than he, then?"

"You didn't listen, did you!" It was an accusation filled with memories of some old wound. She was explaining to him only because she saw no alternative. "The way is hard. Life is hard, if you want anything of real value — knowledge, passion, love. If you hunger for all there is, then you have to learn wisdom. You have to fight all the battles, not just some of them. You can't pick and choose the easy parts." She bit her lip until it must have hurt; her eyes were full of tears.

"But no matter how far you fall, there is a way to get up again. Sofia knew that, and she helped. She never blamed."

"And Melville Smith does blame?" he asked in little above a whisper.

"Oh, yes."

He changed the subject. "And Ramon? Is he ambitious?"

"Ramon is a good man!" she said between her teeth, her anger back in full force. "If you suspect him of harming her, or of altering a word of her teachings, then you are a fool!" She closed her eyes momentarily. Seeing the pain in her, the white skin stretched across the knuckles of her hands, Pitt could imagine the scenes that might be playing across her imagination.

"Tell me," he asked.

She opened her eyes and looked at him, weighing her decision.

"Ramon grieves for the dead in his family

who sinned, at least according to the Church, in his own land," she said finally, her voice filled with pity. "Perhaps it was no more than the sin of doubt — and who can help that, if they are honest? We all stumble, in our different ways."

He did not speak his answer because he knew she could see it on his face.

"He cannot bear that they should be shut out because they fell now and then, because they doubted and feared, and wanted above all to be loved." Her voice dropped even lower. "Do not hurt Ramon. It would not only be wicked, it would be pointless."

"What do you know of Barton Hall?" Pitt changed the subject. "Why was it so important to Sofia that she see him? Would she have gone away voluntarily before speaking with him?"

The watchfulness was back in Henrietta's face, and indecision.

He waited.

"I don't know," she said eventually. "I don't know what she wanted with him, only that it was desperately important to her. She feared something too terrible to share with any of the rest of us. She said it was for all our sakes."

Pitt spoke to Ramon next, and he could tell

at once that the man was frightened. He hid it well, but Pitt had seen fear too often not to know it with a familiarity. Old ghosts were back again from times he had thought forgotten.

In that moment Pitt was certain Ramon had not hurt Sofia. But had he feared she would be attacked, even assassinated, and taken her against her will in order to save her life?

How many times had he rescued Charlotte from an impossible situation because she was on a crusade for some cause, and had taken a risk from which she could not escape?

"Do you know why Señora Delacruz wished so much to speak with Mr. Hall?" Pitt asked. "He does not seem to me to be likely to change his opinions about her cause, or his judgment, and I don't believe Señora Delacruz is naïve enough to think that he would."

"It was nothing to do with reconciliation," Ramon agreed quietly. "It was something she wished to help him with, or at least try. She did not tell me what it was. She trusted me, but she did not wish me to know it, for my own protection."

"She was afraid of it?" Pitt asked.

"Yes. I think she was," Ramon admitted.

Pitt searched his face and saw no guile in it at all. Pitt suddenly wondered if Sofia could have gone of her own accord, just to escape the weight of living up to everyone else's unbearable need. He could understand that, he thought with a shiver that for a moment took his breath away.

"Thank you," he said to Ramon. "You have given me an awareness of thoughts that had not occurred to me. Would she have gone away willingly before seeing Mr. Hall, do you think?"

When Ramon spoke his voice was hoarse. "No, señor. In my opinion, she would not."

Pitt was late home, after going through the threatening letters yet again. He still found himself disturbed by the anger in them, the hatred generated by those who professed to worship a God of universal mercy and love for all mankind.

"It's fear," Charlotte said quietly. They were sitting in their usual chairs in the parlor, a brisk fire burning in the hearth, and the curtains drawn against the sudden, hard spring rain and the wind that drove it against the glass. Daniel was upstairs in his room, his head buried, as usual, in the *Boy's Own Paper.* Jemima was having supper with her aunt, Emily Radley, and her cousins.

She would very probably stay the night, which pleased Pitt more than it should have. He could delay any further questions at least for a day. He imagined Charlotte had arranged it so.

A momentary shadow crossed her face. "I don't want Sofia to be hurt, but I realize I would almost rather that than proof that she is actually a fraud." Charlotte shook her head. "What she said was frightening and different, but it was beautiful. I would like it to be true . . . I think."

Pitt thought of Ramon and his fierce defense of mercy. The man needed the tenderness, the hope that Sofia gave him. In fact, it seemed that he could not bear to live without it. In defending her he was clinging to the most precious thing he knew, spiritual survival.

And Henrietta needed something also, a mercy perhaps for herself, and everyone else she had known who was like her. To destroy that hope would take away her courage to live.

What did Melville Smith need, other than to be valued, respected, perhaps to be leader rather than one of the many followers of a woman? Did that offend his own sense of manhood, of that order of things that some of the angriest letters had expressed?

Charlotte was waiting for him to speak again. Ever since they had first met, at the time of the murders in Cater Street, they had found it easy to talk to each other, to explain possibilities, to disagree without rancor.

"How much do you believe what Sofia teaches?" he asked. "Really?" He wanted to know, not to understand the case, but because it intruded into his own life, his thoughts and above all the memories that suddenly would not stay silent in his mind. Mostly they were of his mother. There were so many things he had not said to her. He had not thought of the words until it was too late.

In spite of all his efforts to block it out, the day he returned and heard the news of her death came back to him now, sitting quietly beside his own fire. He could remember the light from the windows slanting across the hallway of the big manor house, and Sir Arthur Desmond's voice gentle and full of grief. He could smell the floor polish, and the scent of flowers in the big vases on the side table.

Did he want there to be an eternity where it could all be put right, pain forgotten, guilt healed, where there was laughter and friendship rather than some amorphous existence in spirit? Sofia's idea of eternal learning and creating seemed so much better, filled with purpose, even joy.

Charlotte had considered for several minutes before she replied, and when she did, her words were measured.

"It makes more sense than what I can remember from when I was growing up," she said. "That was comfortable, if rather boring. Of course, the music was marvelous and the light through the stained-glass windows of the church was beautiful, calming. I think a lot of the comfort came from the sense of timelessness inside. People had worshipped God there for a thousand years, maybe longer."

A log settled in the fire and sent up a shower of sparks. Outside the wind gusted, and then was quiet again.

"I suppose if you accept something long enough," she went on. "And everybody around you does, you come to believe that it must be true." She looked at him with a brief smile. "If we change, we lose all that. We're sort of . . . adrift . . ."

She stopped for a moment but he did not speak, wanting her to continue.

"I don't understand it," she admitted, looking at him earnestly. "I remember being taught about Thomas Cromwell, in the religious struggles during the Reformation, signing away his freedom to be Protestant, and then later being burned alive for his change of mind. He thrust the hand that had held the pen into the flames himself, to pay for that denial." She winced. "I've burned myself on the flat iron once or twice. How it hurts! I admire a faith so powerful, but I'm also frightened of it. If you would burn your own living flesh, and bear the pain without screaming, what else would you do?"

Pitt drew in breath to argue that Cromwell had been one man, and nothing like others. Then before he could speak, he realized that he had no idea how many other people might care as much. They may not even know it themselves, until the certainties beneath them shifted violently, like the ground in an earthquake, opening up fissures in the earth's crust and bringing mountains down. To imagine wars over religion could happen only in the past was naïve to the point of irresponsibility.

The Reformation, with all its dreams, its slaughter and martyrdoms, was born in the minds of individual people, visionaries convinced they were acting for the greater good. Was Sofia one of those? The idea that one could know someone of that passionate vision and belief was strange.

Charlotte interrupted his thoughts.

"Do you think Sofia is still alive?" There was urgency in her face.

"I have no idea," he admitted. "I think her own people may have hidden her in order to keep her safe. But if she doesn't reappear soon, with an excellent explanation, then she will have destroyed her reputation."

"Could that be the purpose?" Charlotte asked quietly. "To let someone more moderate take over? Like Melville Smith? He's turning the message much more into being not a break from tradition but merely an addition to it."

"That's what Frank Laurence is suggesting in the paper, anyway."

"Is he supporting Smith?" There was a look of distaste on her face.

"I doubt it," he said seriously. "He's probably just commenting in a way most likely to stir up controversy."

"He's right." She did not hesitate. But, Smith hasn't the passion for it, the blazing light that stops you in your tracks and makes you suddenly see a new way. It's steep, but you can climb it if you want to enough."

"Do you?"

She laughed suddenly, breaking the tension. "I shouldn't think so." Then she was desperately serious again. "But I'm happy. I have all I love and want. All I need is to keep it . . . but that's a big thing, perhaps the biggest."

The next day was the fourth since Sofia Delacruz had disappeared, and there was new speculation in the newspapers that she was either dead or had intentionally run off to escape the responsibility of the position she had chosen, leader of a cult in which she had lost faith. Perhaps she had even eloped with some lover no one knew about.

Neither Pitt nor Brundage commented on the articles, but both were aware that there could be truth in them. Instead they studied new threatening letters that had arrived at Angel Court. Some were warnings to Sofia not to bring her foreign heresies across the Channel into a Christian and Protestant country. One even referred to Queen Mary's marriage to the Catholic King of Spain, and then to the Spanish Armada and the attempt to conquer England in the time of Queen Elizabeth.

The current war between Spain and America was brought unpleasantly back to Pitt's mind at that. He reached for another letter.

"She's not preaching Roman Catholicism," Brundage said in disgust. "I should think the Catholics dislike her even more than we do."

"Did you see this one?" Pitt passed across the letter he had just read, watching Brundage's face as he read it.

He went through it twice, then turned it over and looked at it carefully. "It's different," he said at last. "There's something wrong with it, but I don't know what. It seems the same as some of the others, but not quite."

"Read it again," Pitt requested. He did not want to say anything further, in case he influenced Brundage's response to the contents.

Brundage obeyed, and then looked up again, frowning. "All the phrases are right, falling exactly in line with others, but that's it . . . . they're all picked from other letters."

"Right," Pitt agreed. "Which means it was written by someone who had access to all the others."

"One of her followers at Angel Court." Brundage spoke the obvious conclusion.

Pitt studied the letter again. "But why? To frighten her further? To convince her to hide?" He had a sudden thought. "See if there's some old family place, under a different name. Maybe she repeated there. What was her name before she married Delacruz? I can't believe we didn't check that earlier."

Brundage stood up. "I'll have it within half an hour, sir."

It was barely a few minutes more than that when he returned and handed an address to Pitt.

"This is a family home, sir. It was actually in Sofia's mother's name. The only place I could find. Do you want to go alone, sir? I don't think we should warn anyone."

"I wasn't going to," Pitt replied. He put away the reports he was reading and stood up. He walked over toward the door and took his coat from the stand. "The two of us should be sufficient."

Brundage followed eagerly, matching his pace to Pitt's, down the hall and out into the windy street. Neither of them even noticed the first spots of rain. They took a hansom to the address Brundage had provided, and sat silently for the short distance. It was mid-morning and the traffic was light.

Pitt's mind raced. Were they about to find Sofia? And if so, would they discover her there of her own will, or kept prisoner, unable to communicate?

They pulled up at the curbside and alighted at number 17 Inkerman Road. Pitt paid the driver but told him to wait. It was a quiet residential area and some distance from any main thoroughfare. He followed Brundage across the pavement and up the short footpath to the front door. There were a few pink and blue lupines blooming in the garden, and pink tulips under the front window. The garden looked cheerful, and also well tended. There were no weeds at all and the earth was damp and rich.

Brundage glanced at Pitt, then lifted the polished brass knocker and let it fall.

There was no answer, and even after waiting, no sound of movement from inside. None of the lace curtains across the windows twitched.

Brundage tried again.

Still no answer.

Pitt did not insult Brundage by asking if this was the right house. Instead he gestured for them to walk around the end of the short block and go to the back. If they needed to break in, rear windows were less observed. Pitt had already made the decision not to ask the neighbors. According to Brundage's check with the local police, the house was supposedly unoccupied.

They opened the gate into the back garden. Brundage walked rapidly up the narrow path past the woodshed, across the paved yard to the rear doorstep and the scullery. He peered in the window, then stepped back, missed his footing and stiffened. When he turned toward Pitt, his face was ashen.

Pitt pushed forward past him and stared in through the glass, his heart beating so hard in his chest he struggled for breath. Then he saw what Brundage had seen. There was a woman lying on the bare wooden floor, skirts crumpled around her, flies crawling across her face and a massive dark stain covering the lower part of her body.

Pitt felt the sweat break out on his skin and a wave of nausea swept over him. It took all his strength not to stagger back as Brundage had, and he succeeded only because he had been forewarned. Slowly he swiveled round, keeping his balance.

"We have to go in. I expect the door lock will hold. However, the window over there looks comfortably large enough to climb in through, with a bit of effort."

"Yes, sir." Brundage straightened up, pulling his shoulders back. His face was almost gray. He walked over toward the shed with an effort not to stumble. He kicked the door open and came out a moment later with a long-handled garden spade. Within moments he had broken the pantry window and cleared away all the glass from the frame so they could climb in without the loose shards stabbing them.

Even before Pitt opened the pantry door into the kitchen the smell caught in his throat, making him gag. The buzzing of flies was louder. He took a deep breath and pulled the door open.

The body on the floor was that of a young woman. A glance at her face was enough to know she had been dead for at least twenty-four hours, and the heavy odor suggested at least that long. Her eyes were wide and glazed, her whole body slack. It was not Sofia Delacruz.

Even in his horror and pity, Pitt was drenched with relief. He did not know her. Then he looked farther down and realized that the dark mass around the lower part of her body was not an apron crumpled up, but her own intestines, where her belly had been torn open. Then almost with relief he saw the knife buried deep in her chest, and knew that the mutilation could have been done after death, sparing her at least that pain.

"Please God . . ." he murmured, keeping

himself from gagging with difficulty.

"It is Cleo Robles," Brundage said hoarsely. "She was only twenty-three." His voice choked with anger and grief. "She thought she was going to save the world, or at least a good part of it. She believed in everything . . . in God." He stopped abruptly and swallowed hard, and then he barged out of the room into the rest of the house.

Pitt followed him, knowing he had to. Elfrida and Sofia were probably lying just like this, somewhere close by. He needed to be angry too. Grief was no use now; revulsion and fear were even worse, more disabling. Pity could come later. Now they must do their jobs.

Elfrida Fonsecca was in the hall, at the bottom of the stairs, curled over against the bloody mess that had been her internal organs. She too had been stabbed in the heart. She was older than Cleo, perhaps in her forties. There were a few gray threads in the hair unraveled around her face, and her skin was touched with lines at the eyes and mouth.

"Who the hell would do this?" Brundage asked blankly, his voice trembling. He had been in the army before joining Special Branch; he was acquainted with violence, but not this obscenity against women. "This can't be religious . . . can it?"

"I don't know," Pitt admitted. He was trembling himself, his hands slipping on the banister, his legs weak. He pushed past Brundage and went on up to the top landing. It was empty, but a potted plant in a stand had been knocked over and there was soil scattered over the carpet.

His hands stuck on the doorknob, his throat tight, while he opened the first bedroom door. The room had been lived in recently. There were hairbrushes on the dressing table and a nightgown laid out neatly on the bed, the sheets smooth, blankets tucked in.

He walked around slowly, then kneeled down and looked under the bed. There was nothing there but a few pieces of fluff, as if no one had swept for a day or two.

He stood up again, awkwardly, and looked in the wardrobe and the drawers of the chest. There were a few undergarments, clearly a woman's. Whoever it belonged to had brought at least sufficient to stay for several days. She had not been snatched without warning.

The other bedroom had two beds in it; both had been occupied, but left neat. Pitt and Brundage searched from attic to cellar, but there was no sign of Sofia Delacruz.

Chapter 5

Pitt sent Brundage to find the nearest telephone and inform the local police. He had considered for a few moments the possibility of not telling them, but eventually they would have to know. Special Branch did not deal with crimes other than those that endangered the state. Police cooperation was critical.

He also told Brundage to send for more of their own men, most specifically Stoker, usually Pitt's right-hand man. He had not been involved in this so far because it had seemed such a trivial case at first.

These murders were going to make headlines though. There was no way to avoid it. And the more he attempted to try, the worse it would look. The neighbors would already be wondering what was going on. Any minute now someone would come to look. The first journalists would not be far behind. He shuddered at the thought of what

Frank Laurence would write.

When Brundage was gone Pitt steeled himself to go back and study the bodies. The local police surgeon would be among the first to arrive. Pitt knew he had maybe thirty or forty minutes to learn what he could while the scene was undisturbed.

He would look at Elfrida first. Reluctantly he went back to the hallway and the foot of the stairs. Gazing at the wreck of Elfrida's body he felt a momentary wave of fury at the flies and lashed out at them, sending them buzzing crazily.

Within seconds they were back and he felt ridiculous.

When he had learned all he could by studying her, he would find the linen cupboard and put a sheet over her. It was a decency for his own sake. It made no difference to anything else now, certainly not to her.

Had Elfrida been coming down the stairs, perhaps hearing Cleo cry out? Or had she been going up, trying to run away or warn Sofia, even defend her?

Pitt wondered how the murderer had got into the house. The front door was unmarked and no windows at either the back or front appeared to have been jimmied. Had one of the women let him in? At which door, back or front?

He stood staring at the body, picturing it in his mind. She was lying slightly sideways, her head a couple of steps higher than her feet. The knife was in her chest, and yet she seemed to be going upward. She must have turned to face the killer. Had she been going down then he would have been behind her. She would have fallen forward much farther.

If it was someone she knew, had she run only after he had killed Cleo? If she had been afraid immediately then she would surely have gone out the door and into the street, screaming for help.

Or maybe Sofia had done that. But surely someone would've reported it. And then, where was she? Escaped? Still alive and taken somewhere else? Or dead, but the body in some other place?

He went upstairs and found the linen cupboard. He took two sheets and spread one out over Elfrida's body, then returned to the kitchen and forced himself to look at Cleo.

Again he had to swallow his rage at the flies and study the way the body lay, the clothes, her position relative to the table, the stove, the door. He must learn everything he could.

One leg was twisted half under her. She must have turned. He worked out which way she had been looking when she fell. It was toward the back door. But had that been to run out of it, or could her attacker have come in that way?

He studied the few articles on the floor: a wooden spoon, a cloth, a china bowl broken into two pieces. There was spilled egg yolk on the boards, dried hard now. She had been starting to make something. Whatever else she had been going to use was still in the pantry. It must have been a calm hour of the day when they were busy doing simple chores and then violent and terrible death had come on them, with perhaps only seconds' warning.

It was another twenty minutes before the local police arrived accompanied by the surgeon, and the formal process of investigation began. Pitt had found only a few further signs of struggle, slight but there. There was a dent in the wooden table in the hallway. There was a small tear in the net curtain by the window beside the front door. He saw three other small tears neatly mended, suggesting that this one was recent. It could mean anything or nothing.

Inspector Latham was a tall, spare man. He introduced himself to Pitt, glanced around the kitchen and noted the body covered with the bedsheet. He cleared his throat as if to say something, then changed his mind. He nodded to the police surgeon, a Dr. Spurling, who nodded to Pitt, then bent down, removed the sheet carefully, and began his examination.

"Thank you, sir," Latham said to Pitt. "Very nasty indeed." He had a long, sad face and it expressed his emotions perfectly. "We'll take it over from here. But before you leave, you'd better tell me what you know. Who are these women?"

Briefly Pitt told him about Sofia Delacruz and her mission in England.

Latham shook his head. "Oh dear." His voice was grave. "Well, if we find anything we'll let you know. We'll question the neighbors. There are half a dozen of them hanging around. We'll keep you informed. Any trace of Señora Delacruz and we'll report it." He nodded. It was a dismissal, and Pitt was happy to leave.

Pitt arrived home late and tired. Charlotte had already heard of the murders at Inkerman Road. They were in the late editions. He did not tell her the details, or how he felt about discovering the bodies of the two women, but she knew him well enough not to need words. The news had spread like a flood tide through London. By morning all the newspapers carried the story in various degrees of horror, from the stately loathing of the most respectable to the lurid gore of the pamphlets in the East End. Common to them all was the speculation about religious vengeance and the shame that such a crime should happen to foreigners visiting London. The police were excoriated everywhere. Pitt felt a rising anger in their defense, and an embarrassment that Special Branch, which had been given the specific task of protecting Sofia Delacruz, and forewarned of the threat, should have so signally failed.

At first glance Laurence's article in *The Times* was less cruel than it might have been. Pitt looked at it with trepidation, and when he came to the end he felt a breath of relief. Then he looked across the breakfast table at Charlotte and saw her expression.

"You've read it?" he said quietly.

She nodded, her face bleak with sympathy. He looked at her for a moment or two, then scanned the article again. It avoided all the direct and obvious criticism, but it was sharper, and also funnier, than the others, and filled with additional information about Sofia Delacruz and the substance of her philosophy. It explained quite clearly why it could be so disturbing to the Establishment. It raised questions the other accounts did not. It caught the attention, made one laugh and shiver at the same time.

It ended by reminding the readers of the radical changes of the last half century. Science had given people new worlds, but it had also shaken the foundations of the old.

> The advances of science make it difficult for many of us now to believe in the Bible as the literal truth. If it is figurative, then who is to interpret it for us? Science is impartial. It offers no comfort, no moral authority and certainly no help or mercy. The strong survive. But the strong are not necessarily the funny, the brave, the wise or the gentle. And they are not necessarily the ones we love. Why did Sofia Delacruz's message frighten people and make them so angry? Is this what we have become, killers of those we do not understand?

Frank Laurence's article would be read, and remembered, by the people with influence, and the power to call Pitt's position into question. None of it could he disclaim.

Charlotte said nothing for a moment; when she did speak it was very quietly. "Is

Laurence right, Thomas? Whether she means to or not, is Sofia Delacruz eating away at the foundations of the Church, and therefore also at the Throne? The Queen is the Protector of the Faith, and so at least nominally the head of the Church. Do you suppose Sofia has even thought of that?" She bit her lip. "Or is it exactly what she is meaning to do?"

"That would be one reason for silencing her," Pitt admitted unhappily. It was a possibility he did not want to think about, and yet he must.

"Should we let anyone silence her?" Charlotte asked. "What if she's right? What if she won't be silenced, except by violence?"

"Thank God that's not my decision," Pitt said with intense gratitude.

"And if it were?" she persisted.

"I don't know what I believe." He found the words hard to say. "I wish it could be as simple for me as it was for my mother. She believed. It was there in her face, in her eyes. It's all I can remember about her really clearly. Sometimes I see her, for an instant, in Jemima, although really Jemima looks like you. It's just in the turn of her head, an expression sometimes. Or maybe I just want to see it that way." He smiled at her very slightly, and felt her hand close round his and her fingers tighten.

In the office, Brundage was waiting for Pitt, and almost as soon as he had finished his report on the few facts they had gained from Latham's men, Stoker came in also. His bleak, bony face was grim. He acknowledged Brundage, and then spoke directly to Pitt.

"The police surgeon, Spurling, has nothing useful to add, sir. From the postmortem, seems the two women were both caught pretty much by surprise. The one in the kitchen, immediately. Never had time to defend herself. The older woman on the stairs seemed to be trying to run away. Neither of them were able to fight hard; no wounds where you'd expect them if they had. That suggested that maybe they knew whoever did it, didn't immediately attack him, poor creatures. At least the bastard didn't cut them up alive." His expression registered a marked degree of anger. Pitt realized suddenly that the younger woman, Cleo, had had lovely hair, auburn in color, just like Kitty Ryder, whom they had spent so long searching for only a few months ago, and who had held Stoker's imagination so tightly.

"We've got to find this swine," Stoker said

with a wave of fury. "I don't care if this killer thinks he's on some religious crusade, or what he believes about anything. This is plain, brutal murder."

"We'll get 'im on the end of a rope, sir," Brundage said suddenly. "I don't know if it's a help or not, but this case has got a hell of a public outcry."

Pitt winced. "I know. I suppose now we have to closely examine every lunatic who threatened her. Sort out the dangerous ones from the crackpots."

"I'll do that, sir," Brundage said quickly. "I'd like to scare them witless. Let them think I believe they ripped those poor women's bellies out. They won't open their mouths again in a hurry."

Stoker gave a rare smile at the thought.

"While you're about it, don't forget that some of them might actually be respectable," Pitt said bitterly. "Religious lunacy doesn't know any bounds. If you doubt it, take a look at some of the things we did in the Reformation. We burned a fair few people for their beliefs."

"We?" Stoker's eyes opened wide.

"Yes, 'we,' " Pitt answered decisively.

There was a knock on the door and a young man looked in, his face pale, eyes wide.

"What is it, Carter?" Pitt asked.

"Mr. Teague is here, sir," Carter replied breathlessly. "Dalton Teague. He'd like to speak to you, sir."

Even Stoker looked impressed, in spite of himself.

Pitt understood. Dalton Teague was a national hero. He excelled at many sports, but at cricket he was supreme. He played not only with such skill and leadership that he seldom lost, but he had a grace that was a joy to watch. He typified the courage, honor and sportsmanship that was the essence of the game. Pitt remembered seeing him at Sofia's lecture; he was equally surprised the man was here now. Had he come to exert some influence in the search for Sofia? He *was* standing for Parliament. But as a Conservative candidate he must loathe everything Sofia Delacruz stood for.

"What on earth does Teague want?" Pitt said with exasperation. He was not in the frame of mind, or the position of strength, to receive a national figure at the moment. He searched for an excuse, and found none. He glanced at Stoker, then at Brundage.

"You had better ask him to come in," he conceded to Carter.

Almost immediately after Carter went out, the magnificent figure of Teague filled the doorway. With his pale-colored clothes and fair hair he seemed to carry the light with him.

Pitt rose to his feet and stared at him levelly. "Good morning, Mr. Teague. What may we do for you?" he said courteously, offering his hand.

Teague shook it with a powerful grip, then sat down gracefully in the nearest chair. He did not acknowledge either Brundage or Stoker, not like he had not seen them, but as if they were servants, to whom one naturally did not speak.

"Good of you to see me," he said casually. His features were excellent, his skin burnished golden by the sun.

"I imagine you have no time to spare for calling on anyone without a specific purpose," Pitt replied, keeping up his own pleasant expression with something of an effort.

"Precisely," Teague agreed. "So I shall come to the point. Like everyone else, I am aware of the murders of the women from Angel Court, and the disappearance of Sofia Delacruz. I am not an admirer of her teachings. Frankly I think them preposterous. But I am an Englishman, and I do not wish her to come to harm while in my country. I shall be happy to do all I can to help find her, and if it should be necessary, help to rescue her from whomever is responsible for this." He smiled very slightly, holding up one hand as if to prevent Pitt from interrupting him.

"I have considerable means at my disposal," he went on. "You may not be aware of the extent of my interests, but I can call upon scores of men all over the Home Counties to do whatever is necessary to search for Señora Delacruz. You cannot be unlimited in the number of men you can deploy, since your responsibility is far wider than this one miserable incident." He smiled bleakly. "God knows, the world seems to be on the brink of a precipice, and losing its balance. Even America, which I've always thought of as the sanest and most idealistic of countries, is setting out on wars of aggression.

"But of course you must know that. They have already declared war on Spain so they can take Cuba. Then Dewey's Asiatic Squadron steamed into Manila in the Philippines and destroyed the entire Spanish fleet there, and most of the shore batteries. Who knows how many people they killed."

He clenched his teeth. "Europe is in chaos. Only God and the devil know how this damn Dreyfus affair is going to end. By the look of it, either the government will fall, or the army will. Dreyfus is rotting his life away in prison on Devil's Island, innocent or guilty."

Pitt drew in breath to speak, but Teague carried on.

"I'm sorry, I have gone off on a tangent. As I said, I am to offer whatever assistance I can in order to find Señora Delacruz."

This time his smile was wider. "Also I am not without influence in various . . . other circles. For instance, when it comes to certain branches of the press who could be of more use, and of less nuisance, than they currently are. Permit me to help, Mr. Pitt. We have common cause."

It was the last thing Pitt had expected. His immediate instinct was to refuse. Special Branch worked alone. It was out of necessity, and under sufferance, that they cooperated with the police. And yet even as the words rose on his tongue, he saw the advantages of Teague's offer. The situation was desperate, and Pitt did not have sufficient men to comb the countryside for one woman who could be anywhere. She had been gone for several days now, which was long enough for her to have returned to Spain, or anywhere else.

What a full-blown manhunt might result

in, were she found, was another question. She might be perceived as a dangerous woman, in league with anarchists and involved in acts of criminal violence. She might well be running because she was very understandably terrified for her life. On their record so far she had every justification for believing that Special Branch either could not, or would not, protect her.

Dalton Teague was waiting, a slight shadow of impatience on his face, his arms tense on the sides of the chair. He was not a man Pitt could afford to insult; Pitt had already earned himself more than sufficient enemies. In the past he had saved the Queen's life, but before that, he unfortunately made a mortal enemy of the Prince of Wales, who in the near future must succeed his old and increasingly frail mother.

"Thank you, Mr. Teague," Pitt said. "That is remarkably generous of you. Any information you are able to collect will be of use, and of course your influence will be enormous."

Teague relaxed a little, his arms again lying loosely on the chair.

"Good. I thought you would welcome help. Before I can deploy all my people, naturally I would need to know which of the facts I have read are actually true, which are false and which are as yet unknown."

Pitt tried to choose his words with great care. A mistake now could be irredeemable. "It is too early to say on most issues, Mr. Teague, but as soon as there is something you can act on, I will be happy to tell you. So far the evidence is minimal. I can say that both women were killed at least twenty-four hours before their bodies were found. And, incidentally, the worst wounds were inflicted after death."

Teague leaned forward. "Really?" He took a deep breath and let it out slowly. "A small mercy." His voice was quiet and curiously unemotional. Was that lack of feeling, or so much feeling that he dared not allow it out of control? "Is that information confidential, Mr. Pitt?"

"I would prefer you not to reveal it for the time being," Pitt replied. He met Teague's eyes, and knew that the man understood it was a test. Pitt wished profoundly that he could afford to refuse Teague's help, but he needed all the influence and the additional manpower he could obtain. There were no secrets of state involved in this case. But it was a cold, bitter thought, which he could not dismiss, that maybe the disappearance of Sofia Delacruz was the first step toward being dragged into war with Spain. Teague was right. The consequences could be far reaching. He knew more than Teague did, knew that America needed a canal linking the Atlantic and the Pacific, and naturally the land around it to protect such a monumental investment: land that was currently Spanish in culture, language and spirit.

Britain could not afford to be part of that dispute.

He felt his mind racing and the sweat breaking hot and then cold on his skin. He must force himself to keep control. He smiled back at Teague, feeling as if it must look ghastly on his lips.

"I appreciate your assistance, sir. I'm sure your influence will be greatly helpful in keeping the press from causing panic with thoughtless speculation."

"I will do all I can," Teague agreed. "The best remedy would be to put a fast end to the whole story. Find Sofia Delacruz, alive or dead, and arrest whoever was responsible for her abduction. Unless, of course, it is possible she has gone voluntarily. But I suppose you have already thought of that."

"Yes," Pitt agreed. "It might be useful for you to know that we rely a great deal on the public's observation in cases of missing people. No one literally disappears if they are alive. Cabdrivers, sailing parties, people behind counters in shops, waiters, chambermaids, folks out walking their dogs. Someone must've seen her."

"Yes, I understand." Teague rose to his feet. "Just as I thought, it is a job for an army of people. My employees and my colleagues are at your disposal, Commander. I shall keep you apprised of anything I hear, sir. Good day." This time he glanced at both Brundage and Stoker as he walked elegantly out the door, leaving Brundage to close it behind him.

It was Stoker who spoke first.

"Can we afford to do that, sir?"

Brundage was still standing, his eyes wide. "He's even . . . bigger in person, isn't he!"

"We can't afford not to," Pitt replied to Stoker. "He's right. We don't know enough about this situation. There's still a possibility she escaped, and is off on her own. We haven't enough men to track her down if she's alive and free to move as she wishes."

Brundage looked at him coldly. "Do you believe that, sir?"

"No, I don't," Pitt answered sharply. "But I have to acknowledge that it's a possibility."

Stoker's eyebrows rose. "We also can't rule out the possibility that she murdered the other two women, can we? In which case she's a criminal lunatic, and we should find her and hang her for it."

Pitt controlled his emotions with effort. "I don't believe that to be true, Stoker. But you are right. If she committed such a terrible crime we'll find a way to have her face the consequences. We are Special Branch. We do all we can to defend our country from any attack that could threaten the safety of the government, wherever it comes from. We do not choose the result we want, we pursue the truth, and when we find it, we deal with it the best way we can. We cooperate with the police, and hope to hell that they will cooperate with us."

"Dalton Teague isn't the police," Stoker pointed out.

"Right at the moment, he is help we could probably use, and an enemy we can't afford."

That evening, Pitt decided to see Vespasia and ask for her advice regarding Teague, though he felt very much less confident than he had when talking to Stoker and Brundage. And now that Vespasia was married to Pitt's previous commander in Special Branch, Victor Narraway, he would almost inevitably see Narraway also.

Narraway had previously lived in apartments in the center of London, but had been more than happy to move all his belongings into one of the wings of Vespasia's large and very gracious house, which was in a more residential area. Pitt had already noticed a few differences here and there. Narraway had set up his own study, but the beautiful drawings of trees from his — now Pitt's — office at Lisson Grove, were in Vespasia's sitting room, which faced the garden. They fitted in remarkably well, as did the other chair beside the fire, opposite hers. Its darker-toned seat was less feminine, but it sat comfortably with the shades of the room, giving the entire space a new kind of weight.

Pitt was welcomed in not by Vespasia's maid, but by Narraway's manservant, now elevated to butler. Pitt imagined, with a smile, the rearrangements that must have gone on belowstairs among two households of servants required to blend with each other and keep their ambitions and disappointments from showing. The coming to terms in the kitchen, the new order of precedence, he did not even wish to think about.

It was Vespasia who met him as he was shown into the sitting room.

"Good evening, Thomas," she said with

evident pleasure. "You must be tired and harassed. Would you like tea, or whisky? I have a whisky that Victor assures me is excellent." She smiled gently, a very faint color in her cheeks as she said Narraway's name. In her prime she had been considered the loveliest woman in Europe. Now time had left its marks on her face, but they were of laughter and experience, knowledge of pain and how to endure it with grace, never bitterness. Pitt found the beauty in her deepened with each passing year.

"Tea would be excellent, thank you," he accepted. "Also it would give me time to collect my thoughts and ask you the questions I need to." He sat down near her, but not in the chair opposite her. He hoped Narraway was in, or would arrive shortly and join them.

Vespasia reached for the bell beside her and rang it. When the maid answered she asked for tea.

When the maid had gone again, closing the door silently behind her, Vespasia looked at Pitt expectantly.

Though she undoubtedly knew of the situation from the papers, he briefly gave her the details about Sofia Delacruz's disappearance, and the discovery of the mutilated bodies of the two women who had been her followers, and apparently gone with her, whether willingly or not.

She listened without interrupting him, her face grave until at last he fell silent, waiting for her to reply.

"So you are inclined to believe that she was taken against her will, but you do not know the reasons for it," she concluded.

He shook his head.

"I am uncertain about so many things. I don't know whether she's a woman of deep and original convictions, or a charlatan. I don't know whether she was kidnapped, or went willingly with intent to exploit the notoriety that must follow, or even without giving it any thought. I don't know if she is laughing at us, or terrified, hunted, possibly caught and tortured. For that matter I don't know if she is alive at all." He looked at her steadily. "What made you think that I was inclined to believe she was taken against her will?"

"Your choice of words, my dear," she said gently. "To me it is clear that you believe that she is honest, if deluded, and you are afraid that she is either in very serious danger, or already dead."

He had never prevaricated with Vespasia. Certainly he was not going to begin now.

She had read him far too well, as she often did.

"I'm afraid the implications are much deeper than the individual tragedy of these murders," he continued. "This is a very public failure of Special Branch to protect people. Many of the press believe we should not exist at all, and they will excuse us nothing."

She had more respect for him than to argue. She smiled at him now, but her silver-gray eyes were candid.

"I have read Mr. Laurence's articles," she told him. "I don't know whether I like the man or not. I have never met him, and I might find it interesting to do so. On the other hand, so often one is disillusioned. I would be very disappointed to find his wit existed only on paper, and that he was actually the most fearful bore in person."

"He isn't," Pitt admitted. "But he has no mercy."

"Of course not," she agreed. "He is a journalist. However entertaining he is, you surely have more sense than to trust him?" A shadow of anxiety crossed her eyes. "Use him if you have to, my dear, but never allow him the upper hand, or you may lose it."

He was saved from having to respond by Victor Narraway's entrance into the room.

One of the servants must have told him of Pitt's arrival. There were three cups on the tea tray the maid brought in almost on his heels.

Narraway was of average height, lean rather than slender. Pitt had had occasion several times to learn that he was actually far stronger than he looked. Long ago, at the time of the Indian Mutiny forty years before, Narraway had been in the army and served with some distinction. Since then he had advanced through various parts of the secret services, ending in the position Pitt had now occupied for such a short time.

"Wondered if we'd see you over this affair," Narraway said, coming into the room with a glance at Vespasia, then taking his place in his chair, on the other side of the fireplace.

Pitt watched their interaction with interest. He had known Vespasia far longer than Narraway had, and had watched their friendship, at first so guarded, grow into something immeasurably deep. Pitt had a loyalty to Narraway and a growing regard for him, respect mixed with understanding. But his love for Vespasia — and "love" was not too strong a word — was a stronger and more emotional thing. If Narraway hurt her, even unintentionally, Pitt would not be able to forgive him for it. She was older than Narraway by some few years. She was proud, wise, brave and so very vulnerable. No one who fractured her present happiness would escape Pitt's fury.

"Thank you," Pitt accepted his tea, and one of the tiny chocolate sponge cakes. He must remember not to eat it in one mouthful.

"Do you think Barton Hall had anything to do with this mess?" Narraway asked, sitting back comfortably and crossing his legs. He was naturally elegant in a way Pitt never would be. Birth and education gave him a confidence no later learned skills could ape.

"It is possible," Pitt replied.

Narraway looked pensive. "Do you know the man's importance, Pitt? I don't mean socially, I mean in banking circles?"

"He's head of one of the smaller banks that cater to major figures," Pitt replied, wondering what Narraway was thinking. "Including the Church of England, and some members of the Royal Family. Sofia is an embarrassment to him, that much I gathered when I met with him. But I really can't see him kidnapping her, or her followers, whatever he thinks of her theology. I did wonder if he would try to have her arrested, or even deported. Not that that matters now. This is far beyond embarrassment. The murders on Inkerman Road were two of the most awful I've seen."

Narraway glanced at Vespasia, then back at Pitt.

"You're thinking emotionally. Consider the financial implications."

"Of what?" Pitt tried to keep his voice calm, but he wasn't sure what Narraway was saying. Was there some piece he had missed? "If Barton was involved in these murders, I have no doubt the bank would disown him, publicly and vehemently, within hours."

"I don't doubt it either," Narraway agreed. "But scandal of any sort is bad for banking, almost all of which is built upon confidence. Money is largely a fiction, a piece of paper that represents real assets, or the trust that assets exist. Take away this trust and it is worth nothing. A run on one bank is like a contagious disease. People panic and follow with runs on other banks. No doubt you played dominoes as a child?"

"One or two fall and they all go," Pitt answered. "But if personal scandal about a banker could do that then there wouldn't be a bank in Europe still standing."

Narraway smiled bleakly. "Not personal scandal, for heaven's sake! Or there wouldn't be a throne standing either," he said drily. "Power would be changing hands every season. Every form of stability would go, and investment would go with it. I'm talking about loss of confidence as a motive for actions that otherwise seem out of proportion. Don't lose sight of Barton Hall as a man with extraordinary interests to guard."

Pitt looked at Narraway closely, trying to read behind the cool dark eyes. "Perhaps I should investigate your new interests since you were elevated to the House of Lords."

Narraway's smile reflected his amusement at what seemed to him an absurdity, and the still painful memory of having been betrayed by his own men, which had resulted in his being dismissed from a job he loved, and at which he was extraordinarily gifted. Pitt was still awkwardly aware that he far from filled Narraway's shoes. No one had been condescending enough to lie and tell him that he had. The kindest thing that had been said had come from Narraway himself. It was that Pitt had qualities to bring to Special Branch that Narraway lacked, qualities such as mercy and self-doubt, which meant he would not allow the power of it to go to his head. He might have attained power, but he would never exercise it too much. Doubt would always creep in and question.

"By all means do," Narraway said mildly. "I am not on the board of his bank, but I have acquaintances who are."

"Do you know Barton Hall personally?" Pitt pursued it. "Can you tell me anything about him that might be useful?"

"I know his background," Narraway said, pursing his lips. "He comes from a wealthy county family. Studied at Cambridge and did very well. Economics, of course, and the humanities. I don't know what specifically, but he graduated with a good first. Mixed with all the right people and was surprisingly popular for a man who played few sports and has very little social charm."

Vespasia was watching Narraway. It flickered through Pitt's mind to wonder how well they were coming to know each other in the radically new situation of sharing not only a home but a bed. He recalled vividly with both affection and amusement his early days with Charlotte. But they had been so much younger, and therefore perhaps less vulnerable. Vespasia had been long widowed from a moderately comfortable marriage. The greatest love of her life had been an Italian revolutionary named Mario Corena. He had been killed several years ago, here in London.

That she loved Narraway, Pitt did not doubt. They had both helped Pitt in some of his past cases, struggling against crime and confusion. Some cases had been small: an individual injustice, a single death or an innocence shattered. Others had been large; the cost of failure would have been terrible.

They had worked side by side, sitting around the kitchen table planning, questioning, counting the risks and the price of failure, and always finding a way to push ahead. Trust, and the shared passion in victory and defeat, had become love. Pitt hoped, perhaps with a degree of naïvety, that these would turn out to be the happiest years of Vespasia's life.

Narraway, on the other hand, had never been married. Without question he had had affairs, some more honorable than others, but he had allowed Pitt to form the opinion that none of them had tested the depth of his ability to love wholly and passionately. If he had married Vespasia without loving her more than he could control, more than he could ever walk away from, then Pitt would not forgive him. And he would pity him. The inability to love was an affliction, not a sin. He realized that as he watched Narraway looking at Vespasia now, and thought of his own feelings for Charlotte.

"What about Dalton Teague?" he said at last.

Narraway turned his attention back to the moment. "Interesting. Why do you ask?"

"He offered his help today," Pitt replied, waiting for the response.

"I assume you accepted it?" Narraway asked curiously.

"You didn't accept it!" Vespasia said at the same moment.

Pitt saw Narraway's head lift and a sudden expression of doubt cross his face. Then he controlled it and it was gone, as if it had been no more than an illusion of the light.

But Pitt understood. It was fear. Narraway had come only lately into Vespasia's life. He had no idea whom she had known in the rich years of her past, who had loved her, or how deeply, and perhaps how unwisely. He felt vulnerable, because it was a part of her life in which he had no place, and the exclusion hurt.

"I'm afraid I could think of no good reason to refuse him," Pitt said ruefully. "He has many admirers all over the country, and financial investments employing people who would do anything he asked of them. I have very few men I can spare from what they are already doing, and he knows that."

"I'm sure he does," Vespasia agreed with a

twisted little smile.

Vespasia clearly had much to say about Dalton Teague. Pitt decided he would ask her more about her opinion later, when they were alone.

Narraway nodded slowly. "I imagine you have considered that the purpose of this atrocity could be primarily to attract attention and engage a large part of your forces? Yes, of course you have. That was not intended as a question." He looked across at Vespasia and saw the flicker of amusement and acknowledgment in her eyes.

"Yes, I have," Pitt agreed. "This solves that problem. Teague is also a man I cannot at the moment afford to have as an enemy. God knows, I have enough of those."

"No," Narraway agreed. "You can't. But be careful, Pitt. Be very careful."

Chapter 6

Pitt stood in front of Sir Walter again. He was not surprised to have been asked to report, although he had nothing useful to say, and it was a waste of time that he could have used to more effect. Sir Walter probably knew that, but he had to appear to be in control.

"Yes, sir," Pitt said respectfully, standing before Sir Walter's desk. Sir Walter himself stood by the window, the sunlight making a halo of what was left of his silver hair.

"Ugly business," Sir Walter muttered, as much to himself as to Pitt. "Very ugly indeed. I'm sure you're doing what you can . . ." His blue eyes narrowed and were surprisingly bright. "You damn well better be, anyway."

Pitt felt even more uncomfortable than he had foreseen. "It's a police matter, sir. Regular murders don't concern Special Branch, even if they are brutal. I can't take it out of police jurisdiction. But finding Sofia Delacruz is certainly a priority."

"Damn it, man!" Sir Walter said savagely. "The two women were Spanish citizens. What do I tell the Spanish ambassador?" He waved his hand impatiently and paced a couple of yards as if his pent-up energy needed release. Then he stared at Pitt again. "That's beside the point. What really matters is that I'm beginning to wonder if this mess with Ms. Delacruz is the beginning of something, not the end. Have you consulted with Narraway? If not, you should."

He swiveled round and knifed his hand through the air again before Pitt could respond. "He's not a petty man, Pitt. He'd give you advice, if you've the humility to ask it, and the wisdom to accept it."

Pitt felt a cold prickle of anxiety. Special Branch had been specifically asked to look after Sofia Delacruz, which meant it was Pitt's responsibility. He had taken it too lightly. He had let her down, and therefore also Narraway, who had recommended him for the position. And of course, all the men who served under him. And Charlotte, who believed in him always. He wondered whether to apologize again, or if that would make him seem even weaker. Heaven knew, the evidence was bad enough.

Sir Walter was staring at him, waiting.

"Yes, sir," Pitt replied. "I saw him only yesterday evening."

"Hmm. Say anything useful?"

Pitt knew it was unwise to say he had not. "Only that there may be far more behind this than at first appeared. Possibly someone is using her —"

"Yes, of course someone is using her, damn it!" Sir Walter cut across him. "But who? Spanish anarchists, probably. God knows, they have enough cause to be desperate." He pulled his mouth into a thin, bleak line. "What do you know about them, Pitt? Worst of it was a bit before your time . . ."

Pitt could not hide his amazement.

"Not your time alive, man!" Sir Walter exploded. "Your time in the job! Superintendent of Bow Street, what the devil would you care about Spanish disasters and their repercussions? Nothing to do with your homegrown murders. No reflection on you. Can't bear people who can't keep their minds on their own jobs! What do you know about Zarzuela?"

Pitt didn't know if it was a place or a person.

"Nothing, sir."

"January of '92," Sir Walter began. "Andalusia. Dirt poor. Peasants worked all the hours of daylight for the price of a loaf of bread." He resumed his pacing back and forth in front of the window, turning at exactly the same spot on the carpet each time. "Four hundred of them, armed with scythes, pitchforks, whatever came to hand. Marched on the village of Jerez de la Frontera."

Sir Walter cleared his throat and continued, his voice quieter. "They meant to rescue five of their friends who had been imprisoned for life because they were involved in a labor dispute ten years earlier."

Pitt thought of the labor disputes he had known in London, the terrible poverty of the people involved, the injustice, finally the desperation. Many such disputes had become violent, but usually in a minor way. There had been no reprisals of the sort Sir Walter was suggesting. He waited for the end of the story, the part that echoed today, into 1898 and the murders in Inkerman Road, where two women had been eviscerated, and a third remained missing.

"It was not done by the military." Sir Walter stood still while he spoke, but his voice shook a little and his eyes were shadowed and intense. "Four of the leaders were garroted. They do it by tying the person to a post, then from behind, putting a scarf around their throat and twisting it until they are strangled to death. Zarzuela was one of them. He died calling out to the crowd to avenge them."

Pitt waited.

"Heard of General Martínez de Campos?" Sir Walter asked.

"Yes," Pitt said quickly. "Wasn't he behind the restoration of the Spanish monarchy in '74?"

"Yes, among other things. He also put down a Cuban insurrection pretty brutally. Damn fool. By late '93 he was Minister for War in Spain. He was recruiting the troops in Barcelona when an anarchist named Paulino Pallas threw a bomb, killed one soldier and five bystanders and, unfortunately, the general's horse, poor beast. But not the general."

"Pity." The word was out of Pitt's mouth before he considered the wisdom of it.

"Quite," Sir Walter agreed. "Pallas was tried and found guilty, of course. Not even allowed to say good-bye to his wife or mother — God knows why. He was shot by a firing squad, shot in the back. He too promised 'Vengeance will be terrible!' "

Bits and pieces of foreign news began to come forward into Pitt's memory.

"November '83," he said aloud. "The

bomb at the opening night of the opera season in Barcelona. Lots of people killed . . ."

"William Tell," Sir Walter agreed. "Not one of my favorites. Prefer Verdi, myself. Teatro Lyceo. Chucked the damn bombs off the balcony into the crowd. Fifteen killed instantly. Rest panicked. Hysterics. Fought one another like animals to get out. Blood all over the place. Twenty-two dead altogether. Another fifty wounded."

Pitt could imagine the reprisals for that, but he let Sir Walter tell him.

"Police raided every damn place they could think of," Sir Walter continued. "Thousands were arrested and thrown into the dungeons of Montjuïc. That's the huge fortress seven hundred feet above the sea. So full they had to shackle the rest in warships in the harbor below. Tortured them." The skin across his face seemed to be pulled tight and his voice shook. "Burned them with irons. Forced them to keep walking for fifty hours at a time. Even dug out some of the more inventive tortures from the Inquisition. God forgive them. Their people won't."

Pitt was cold. He tried to force the pictures out of his mind, but they would not leave. If Sofia Delacruz knew of these things — and surely she must if here in London Sir Walter did — then she might well make it part of her mission to crusade against the police and the government of Spain. Was that what lay at the heart of her disappearance?

Sir Walter was staring at him, watching the emotions in his face, waiting for his response.

"I'll send a couple of men to Spain to see what they can learn of the political situation. And I'll ask Melville Smith if Sofia Delacruz had any connection to the unrest." Pitt found the words slowly. "He may lie. But I might learn from his silences, whatever he doesn't tell me."

"Good point," Sir Walter agreed. "Don't tell all your men about this yet, Pitt. Tell one or two, perhaps, but not the rest. We don't want anyone jumping to conclusions or making incorrect assumptions in such a delicate situation."

Pitt said nothing. He felt numb.

"Get on with it, man!" Sir Walter said suddenly.

Pitt found his voice, hoarse and tight in his throat. "Yes, sir."

"Good. If you need anything, say so."

"Yes, sir. I will."

Angel Court was quiet and dusty in the

sunlight and there was no one in sight inside the arched entrance except the old woman who seemed to spend all her time sweeping the cobbles, scrubbing the few steps into the kitchen and scullery or tending the ancient pots holding her herb garden.

She looked up as Pitt passed her.

"Good morning," he said with a slight nod.

Her eyes were watchful, her face brown, the skin worn with exposure to sun and wind. She cannot ever have been beautiful, but there was humor and strength in her features. Yet this time, looking more closely, Pitt saw also a consuming fear.

She had been snipping off small pieces of rosemary and sage, and the pungent smell of the herbs was in the air. Now she turned away from him, without answering, and went back to the plants. He noticed her drab skirts were a little short for her, exposing bony ankles. Her shoulders were bent, hunched protectively over her flat chest.

Pitt wondered if she was a believer, someone rescued from one kind of misfortune or other, one of Sofia's projects. He was curious. She might have observed much of the people here, seeming almost invisible herself, but she clearly did not want to talk to him. He would mention it to Stoker.

He knocked on the door and it was answered by Henrietta. As soon as she recognized him the demand was in her eyes. She read the lack of news without waiting for his words.

She pulled the door open silently.

"Thank you." He stepped inside. "Is Mr. Smith in?"

"Yes," she said shortly.

Pitt changed his tactics. "I see he has been busy keeping up the schedule of speaking that Señora Delacruz had planned." He watched her expression, the moment of anger, taken over by helplessness, then something he thought was a deep disgust. He wondered again what story lay behind her joining Sofia's group. What had she not found in the Church in which she grew up? Was Melville Smith aware of how she despised him?

She was regarding him now with frustration and disappointment. How much of it was religious, how much personal affection for Sofia? He could not imagine living in what amounted to a religious order with its closeness, the discipline, the passion and the lack of privacy, the watchfulness for error.

"Will she be grateful to him when she comes back?" he asked suddenly.

Henrietta's eyes widened, then she smiled bitterly. "She will be furious," she said with a hollow smile. "You want me to say it?" she challenged him. "Yes, Melville Smith is taking the chance while she is gone to twist all that she taught so that it faces another way. It is all gentler, without the edge that cuts through hypocrisy. It has a sweet smell, like something that is beginning to rot! Is that what you want me to say?" She stood with her body all at sharp angles, as if she would be rigid to the touch, bones and muscles locked.

"Did he create the chance, or only seize the opportunity?" Pitt asked.

Some of the anger seemed to drain away from her. "I don't know. I think he hasn't the courage or the imagination to have made it happen. He is just using it . . . and I hate him for that! You see, don't you? It's in your face. I have allowed him to make me into what I do not want to be! Perhaps it is myself I hate. Sofia would say he holds up a mirror to me and I see the worst in myself. The mirror she held showed me the best." Her eyes filled with tears.

For a moment Pitt had no answer. A memory came to him of Sofia Delacruz standing in the hall talking, her face alight with the passion of her faith. For that brief time in her presence he had believed what she was saying. Now in the emptiness afterward, with the confusion of stories about her and the mutilated bodies of Cleo and Elfrida, all her fire of purpose had disappeared.

Then he recalled himself to the reason he was here, and Henrietta watching him.

"Was Smith against coming to London?"

She looked startled. "Yes. But she said she had to come. There was no choice." Henrietta closed her eyes. "I could not dissuade her, it was pointless because she had decided. Preaching had nothing to do with it. But there is no point in asking me over and over again. I don't know anything beyond the fact that she was scared. I'd never seen her so scared."

She blinked, indecision in her eyes. For seconds she fought it, then overcame the temptation. "I've known Melville Smith for five years," she said quietly. "He would not . . . not kill anyone, not ever anything so . . . violent. His feelings are always . . . as if he had swallowed them."

Pitt thought he understood what she was saying. "And Ramon is the same way?"

This time her reaction was instant. "No. He would never hurt someone else. He was always for helping. Sometimes I think he is too soft."

"Too soft how?" he asked.

"Innocent," she replied with a smile. "Saw what he thought should be there, whether it was or not. Like his own family." Then seeing Pitt's surprise she instantly regretted it. "I shouldn't have said that. That's what we should be . . . family. Not that you've got to like family. Sometimes they're the worst . . ."

He considered pressing the thought, but he saw in her eyes that she was angry with herself for giving away a confidence. He did not want her to transfer that blame to him. He needed her trust now.

"I know," he agreed. "Do you think Sofia is soft as well?"

She let her breath out with relief. She was too frightened to smile, but the ease in her face was back. "No. She took risks with people, but she did it with her eyes open," she answered.

"What kind of risks?" He asked it mildly, as if it were of no great importance.

"Protecting them, giving them second chances. Helping to make bad things right again. She helped many people burdened by guilt for their past mistakes. There was a constant stream of penitents of all kinds to her door."

"Anyone in particular you remember, just

before you all came to London?" He thought of all those labeled as anarchists, merely because they wanted a living wage, that were driven to violence because no one would listen to them. Hunger changed people. He had seen it often enough in the backstreets of London too. It could create a kind of madness. Who could watch their children starve, and stay reasonable?

Henrietta stared at him. Why should she trust him? He was the law. At least he was supposed to be. He should have no sympathy with madness, whatever the cause.

"There was one poor man in terrible fear — for his life or his soul, I don't know which," she said after a moment. "But Sofia had to leave him to come here. I told you before, she was hell-bent on seeing Barton Hall," Henrietta reminded him. "But she wouldn't tell any of us why. Melville was furious, but it made no difference. They quarreled about it. She won." She said that last with considerable satisfaction, even though she knew nothing of the issue at stake.

"So Cleo and Elfrida didn't know?" he asked.

"No." She blinked rapidly but it did not stop the tears, or the sudden pallor of her face.

He thanked her and then went to look for Melville Smith. He found him in the room that had been Sofia's study. He was sitting at the desk, clearly deep in thought, a pen in his hand and a sheet of paper half covered with neat handwriting. He looked up blankly as Pitt came in.

Pitt closed the door behind him with a sharp click of the latch.

Smith's face creased with annoyance. It was a long, silent moment before he decided not to express it in words.

"Have you news, Mr. Pitt?" he said with a sudden eagerness, which was better prepared than Pitt had expected; it forced him into immediate apology.

"No, I am sorry. The police seemed to have learned very little, except that the murderer was not any of the people already known to them for violence, and there was nothing taken of significance." He sat down in the chair opposite the desk.

"We *have* nothing of significance," Smith said tartly. "Except our lives! Those were certainly taken."

Pitt felt the sting of the rebuke, but he did not acknowledge it. "Why did the three women go to Inkerman Road, Mr. Smith? Surely whatever the threat, they would have been far safer to have remained here at

Angel Court with the rest of you?"

Smith looked at him steadily. "Of course they would! Who knows why Sofia did half the things she did?" He smiled bleakly, merely a twitch at the corner of his lips.

Pitt refused to be put off, or to allow his irritation at Smith's disloyalty to distract his attention from his purpose. He smiled back.

"You are too modest, Mr. Smith. I think you know Señora Delacruz very well indeed. I don't believe you could have worked so closely with her for five years or that she would have trusted you were she not certain of your loyalty and your grasp of the fundamentals of her faith."

Smith sat rigid, a faint color slowly staining his cheeks. "I do what I can," he said awkwardly. "But . . . but I find her behavior difficult to understand sometimes . . ." He left the words hanging, unable or uncertain how to finish.

"She confided in you?" Pitt asked, implying that he knew the answer already. "Or Ramon?"

"No," Smith answered quickly. "Ramon is . . . very loyal, a good man, but his admiration of her is intense, greater than his judgment. I regret saying this, but this is a time for honesty. His need to believe her doctrine, for his own intensely personal reasons, did not leave him room for doubt, or . . . or acknowledgment of the reality of her strengths and . . . weaknesses. She knew that, and she would not have burdened him either with her own fallibility, or with the very real fear that something might happen to her."

"But you knew." Pitt made it a statement, investing his voice with a touch of respect.

"I'm afraid so," Smith agreed.

Pitt nodded gravely. "It must have been very distressing for you."

"Yes . . . I wish . . ." Smith floundered for words, studying Pitt's expression, seemingly trying to ascertain how much he knew, or guessed.

"I'm sure you did all you could," Pitt said gently. "Even in the short time I knew her I could see that she was a difficult woman to persuade . . . even in her own interests."

"Very . . ." Smith agreed quickly. "I . . ." Again he stopped.

"They were brutal killings." Pitt kept his voice level, his eyes on Melville Smith's face. He saw the fear, naked for an instant before the mask was replaced. It was a consuming terror, but was it imagination or knowledge? There was guilt in it. Yet anyone would feel to blame, simply because they had not prevented the whole disaster. The mutilated bodies of the two women were lying in the police morgue, and Smith was sitting here in his office, alive and well, preparing speeches so he could take over Sofia's position as leader of a brave and passionate group of people.

He looked at Smith, now ashen pale, sweat beading on his brow.

"Sofia did not come here to preach, Mr. Smith," Pitt elaborated. "She came to see Barton Hall about something so secret she could not tell any of the others, and so urgent that it could not wait. Henrietta says that she gave help, sanctuary perhaps, to many people in trouble. But before you all came here, was there someone in a different kind of trouble? Far bigger than some sin of faith or domestic betrayal? You may hate those whose preaching you abhor, but you do not follow them into another country and hunt them down in the quiet streets, break into their houses and tear their entrails out on to the floor! Whatever happened here is dark, and I must find out where Señora Delacruz is before it happens to her — if it hasn't happened already."

Smith gasped and for a moment Pitt thought the man was going to vomit.

"I have no idea who killed them!" Smith protested, his voice strangled in his throat.

"I told you before, Sofia wanted to see Barton Hall, and nothing I said could dissuade her. But she would not tell me. I swear I did all I could to learn so I could help, but you cannot argue with her!"

"I believe you," Pitt agreed. "So when she wouldn't listen, did you consider taking matters into your own hands?" He watched Smith as the color flooded back into his face; his eyes evaded Pitt's gaze, then came back again.

"I did," Smith said very quietly, his face scarlet. "And perhaps what happened was my fault. I don't know who did it, or why! Dear God, all I meant was to keep her safe!"

"It was you who sent her to the house on Inkerman Road," Pitt concluded. "And you kept it from us all this time! Who else knew?"

"No one." Smith said fiercely. "Unless she told them! I don't know if she was ever afraid. She thinks she's invincible, God help her. She's . . ."

"A fanatic?" Pitt suggested.

"Yes! She . . . she doesn't look at reality. It makes her a great preacher, but an impossible woman to work with. She doesn't listen to anything she doesn't want to hear."

The man was obviously deeply afraid, and Pitt needed to find out exactly what he feared, and why. "What did you tell her? Did you add your own letters to the pile you had already received?" he asked.

"Yes. But the danger to her life was undoubtedly real," Smith answered so quickly that Pitt was certain it was in some way less than the truth. It was a prepared answer. "That is what I told her."

"How did you know of the house in Inkerman Road?" Pitt asked innocently.

Smith flushed. "I was told of it by a . . . a friend."

"For what purpose?" Pitt persisted.

"As extra accommodation, if we required it," Smith said, looking so unwaveringly at Pitt that the commander knew it was a lie.

"So if Señora Delacruz was not here at Angel Court, then this friend might assume she would be at Inkerman Road." It was a conclusion, not a question.

Color drained from Smith's cheeks, leaving him gray. "He is above reproach," he said firmly. "A good and decent man. He must be as appalled as we are." His normally beautiful voice was hoarse. "If I thought it was possible, let alone likely that he'd had any hand in this whatsoever, I would have told you immediately."

"So it was Barton Hall." Pitt concluded bitterly. "If Sofia didn't know of the house herself, only Barton Hall would've known of it — It's in her mother's name. A man who profoundly disagrees with her teachings, but I imagine would find your amendments less . . . extreme, dismissing as they do the whole notion of anarchy against the order of God."

Smith sat paralyzed, as if staring at a snake. He struggled for the right words of denial, indignation, anything at all, and failed.

"I don't care about your religious ambitions, Mr. Smith," Pitt said very quietly. "I do care very much about what you have done to realize them. Whatever you believe, if it professes to be any form of Christianity, it does not justify the terror and the pain of those women . . ."

"I didn't have anything to do with their deaths!" Smith cried out desperately, lurching forward in his chair. "All I wanted was . . ." he stopped, sweat running down his face, ". . . to keep her safe and silent for a while. She has no idea what trouble she is causing, completely unnecessarily. Teach slowly! Not . . . everything at once. People will reject it because the change is too big! She has no patience, no . . . no understanding of people's fears —"

"That doesn't matter now." Pitt cut across

him. "If Barton Hall knew where she was, then either he is responsible, or he has told someone else who is. Do you know who?"

"No . . ."

Pitt stood up. "It would be very much in your interest, Mr. Smith, to be honest with me. It is more than your own credibility that is at stake. If you want to emerge from this a free man, never mind one with any honor left, then you will do everything you can to see that Sofia Delacruz returns to Angel Court alive and well. Unless, of course, if she is already dead, and you had a part in it. Then you might be better to get in my way by any means you can."

Smith's horror was so palpable it was unnecessary for him to make any protest at all.

Pitt walked out quietly and closed the door behind him.

Pitt was sitting in his office with Stoker across the desk from him. It was littered with reports from the local police and from the few men Pitt could spare for the case, plus a few messages from Dalton Teague.

"You going to face him, sir?" Stoker asked when Pitt told him of his visit to Angel Court, and Smith's admission of his arrangement with Barton Hall to use the house in Inkerman Road. "There's got to be something pretty black that we still don't know about. Hall's a pompous sort of man, a bit cardboard, but he wouldn't rip a couple of women apart simply because they disagree with him religiously. And it wasn't even Sofia . . ." He bit his lip and winced. "At least we don't know that she's dead too. Even if murder wasn't morally unthinkable to him, the sheer risk of it is terrifying." He pulled his face into an expression of bleak acceptance. He had been in Special Branch far longer than Pitt, although he was several years younger.

"Then who was it? And what the devil did she want to see Hall about?" Pitt said it as much to himself as to Stoker.

This time Stoker had no ready answer. He turned to the papers on the desk.

"The police have come up with nothing," he said unhappily. "They spoke to all the other households in the area, cab drivers, delivery boys, tradesmen. Nobody saw anything unusual. No strangers reported. Those that even noticed the women said they were quiet and polite." He shook his head.

Pitt did not bother to reply.

"You going to see Hall?" Stoker asked.

Pitt was not yet ready with his answer.

"Has Dalton Teague come up with anything useful?" he said instead.

Stoker's bony face was unreadable. Emotions flashed over it and were gone too rapidly to register. "No, sir," he said, then picked up the police reports and went to the door.

"Stoker!" Pitt said abruptly.

Stoker froze, and then turned around to face the desk. "Yes, sir?"

"Have Teague's men done anything at all?" Pitt demanded.

"Oh, yes, sir. They're everywhere already, like fleas on a hairy dog."

"Your choice of comparison is highly suggestive," Pitt said drily. "They are getting in your way?"

Stoker smiled, showing his teeth. "No, sir. Wouldn't allow that. Just ask a lot of questions about Special Branch. I respect people wanting to know who we are and what we do. Too often they don't understand and don't want to. They think us a nuisance, worse than the police, because we're not investigating crimes they can see. But I haven't got time to be answering such questions, and frankly I don't think they should know everything about the way we work, even if they're trying to be helpful."

"What sort of questions are they asking?"

Pitt said curiously, a small nail of anxiety digging at him.

"Detailed ones," Stoker replied, watching Pitt's face. "All supposed to be good manners, I suppose. Make us feel as if they care about what we do." He hated to be patronized, and it showed in every angle of his body. He could take orders, or even criticism; he could not abide condescension.

"They are likely just awkward," Pitt judged. "Wanting to be helpful but not knowing how."

Stoker gave him a sour look and went out of the door.

Pitt had a brief, late lunch of bread, cheese and pickle away from his office, and he was walking toward the main thoroughfare to catch a hansom to speak with Barton Hall when he became aware of someone falling into step beside him. It was Frank Laurence, looking well dressed and politely interested. His shirt was immaculate, his suit remarkably well tailored. He was actually far tidier than Pitt. For a start, he had nothing in his pockets to drag them out of shape, nor was he overdue a haircut, as Pitt seemed to be most of the time.

"I have nothing additional to say," Pitt told him without preamble.

"Of course not," Laurence agreed. "You don't know anything, and if you did, you would not tell me."

Pitt was stung, as he knew Laurence meant him to be, but he would not rise to take the bait. He smiled. "You are quite right, I would not."

"Are you finding Mr. Teague helpful?" Laurence was undaunted. "I know he has vast resources. His family owns half of Lincolnshire."

"How is that helpful?" Pitt asked curiously.

"Oh, it isn't," Laurence said with a laugh. "But you have to be enormously wealthy to own half of anything. It gives one an air of assurance, as you will have noticed. He is used to people considering it a privilege to oblige him. He is definitely a good man to have on your side."

"Is that a warning that he is a bad one to have against you?" Pitt asked, keeping his voice level and affable, as if they were discussing the weather.

Laurence laughed again. "My dear commander, if you need me to tell you that then you are not the man for the job you have."

Pitt did not answer.

"Did Mr. Teague tell you that he has known Barton Hall most of his life?" Laurence managed to look both innocent and amused. "Or did he omit that piece of information?"

Pitt froze, and he knew instantly that Laurence was waiting for just such a reaction from him — he was angry with himself for giving it to him.

"You did not know," Laurence observed. "Since schooldays, to be exact. Neither of them mentioned it I see. My dear fellow, it is written on your face."

"Your investigations found this?" Pitt asked him.

"Oh, no, not at all. I happen to have been at the same school myself, a few years behind them, of course, but things don't change a great deal. Same rules, you know? Same kind of people who break them. We all have our heroes."

"And Teague was one of yours?" Pitt asked. For some reason, the thought seemed incongruous with what he knew of Laurence. He didn't seem the type to put Teague on a pedestal.

For an instant there was a curious kind of anger in Laurence's face, all the humor vanished.

"Oh, hardly," he replied. "I was several years behind him. As I said, I didn't know him at all. But no one ever forgot the way he played on the cricket field." He gave a slight shrug. "I hated cricket. Not a team player!" He smiled. "Rather good at chess and fencing though."

Pitt could imagine him at both very easily. The thrust and parry, move and countermove would appeal to him, a honing of natural skills. Were he anything other than a journalist Pitt would have liked him immensely.

"Good luck with Mr. Hall," Laurence added. "He is also more interesting than you may yet appreciate." He turned and walked away, leaving Pitt to ponder what he had just learned.

Chapter 7

Before Pitt went to see Barton Hall at his bank, he returned to Lisson Grove to check if there was any news from Latham and the investigation at Inkerman Road, or from the men he had sent to Spain. Not that he expected them to find much. But the more he thought of it, the more concerned he was that the origin of Sofia's troubles and disappearance lay in Spain. Perhaps it was time he sent one of his senior men to see the Spanish ambassador and ask a few pertinent questions — tactfully, of course.

Five minutes later James Urquhart stood in front of him, smiling slightly. He was a good-looking man in a gentle way, and very well spoken.

"I think it's time we paid a friendly visit to the Spanish Embassy," Pitt began. "Don't make a big issue of it, just assure them as a courtesy that we are doing everything we can to find Señora Delacruz, and to bring to justice whoever killed the other two women. You could ask the ambassador if he has any advice to offer us." He looked at Urquhart closely to see if he understood both the delicacy and the urgency of the situation. He had been a diplomat before joining Special Branch. There were times when both his knowledge and skill were remarkably useful.

"Yes, sir," Urquhart nodded. "I doubt they will be of much help, poor devils, but you never know. What is it exactly that we need?"

Pitt had given it some consideration. "What they know of Señora Delacruz, or suspect but would not wish officially to say," he replied. "Hints, suspicions, confidences, things they would rather not have attributed to them."

"Right," Urquhart agreed. "Understood, sir." He excused himself and left.

A moment later Stoker came in looking unhappy. "Sorry, sir, there's nothing from Latham." He half sat on the edge of Pitt's desk. Pitt stood by the window. "There were three strangers who were seen entering the house, but they turned out to be a plumber and two delivery men, all accounted for, all left well before the time we think the women were killed." Stoker went on. He frowned. "Are you convinced it's political now?"

"Yes." Pitt was surprised how easily he answered. He had not realized he was so certain. "Not that it would be beneath a politician to use a religious maniac to carry out his aims."

"Spanish?" Stoker asked.

"The politics, or the maniac?" Pitt inquired.

Stoker smiled for the first time. "Both."

Pitt smiled briefly in response. "Henrietta Navarro told me how Sofia took in all kinds of penitents and fugitives: the Church's outcasts, or society's. Why not political anarchists running from the law after an atrocity, whether they were guilty or not? Some of the poor devils were driven to their wits' end, and beyond."

"Why not?" Stoker agreed. "But what's Hall got to do with it?"

"I don't know," Pitt admitted. "I am going to see him now. He has a lot of explaining to do about the house on Inkerman Road."

"I'll come with you," Stoker straightened up immediately.

"No need." Pitt shook his head.

"If it's anarchists, sir, and they murdered these two women, and took Sofia, and Mr. Hall is on their side . . ."

"We have no facts to suggest any of that is

true," Pitt pointed out, stopping at the door and blocking Stoker's path. "Hall is supremely established, right at the heart of the Church, Crown and money. How much more rooted in order can you be? If Sofia has any sympathy with rebels, anarchists or just the hungry, he wouldn't share them. They're natural enemies."

"Bloody hunted and prey!" Stoker said, then blushed at his own outspokenness.

It was the first time Pitt had laughed in a while. It was not so much amusement as surprise. "Indeed," he said with feeling. "Unfortunately we can't do much about it." He walked as far as the coat stand and took his jacket off the hook.

Before Pitt could put it on there was a knock on the door, and when he opened it Brundage was standing there with Dalton Teague a yard or two behind him. Brundage looked embarrassed. Before he could announce the obvious, Teague stepped forward.

"Afternoon, Commander." He held out his hand.

Pitt had no alternative but to accept it. "Good afternoon, Mr. Teague." It seemed almost redundant to ask if he had anything to report. The gleam of satisfaction in his eyes belied the gravity of his expression. Pitt put his coat on the hook again, stepped backward into his office and invited Teague in.

"Thank you." Teague sat down in the large, leather-seated captain's chair, leaving Pitt to sit in the other, opposite him. He crossed his long legs and leaned back. "I've tried to quell it, but the newspapers are getting a little hysterical about this entire matter, which doesn't help. Not that helping is what they have in mind, of course." He had a bitter little smile on his face. " 'Give aid and comfort to the enemy' at times."

"Very ugly," Pitt agreed. He wondered what Teague had come for.

"I suppose you've read some of the articles Frank Laurence has written? He seems to be taking this whole business very seriously as a political threat, although he doesn't make it very clear of what kind. War with Spain, I suppose? But then, he is better at suggestions than facts. Always was."

"You've known him a long time?" Pitt kept his tone casual, but he was suddenly interested in what Teague had to say. Laurence had made it clear that he disliked Teague, but he had also said it was by repute. That they had been at the same school and university, but not in the same years, and so hadn't known each other well.

Teague gave a slight shrug. "Since school days, Commander. He hasn't changed so much. He was an eager little bastard then. Always inquisitive, looking, listening, adding up. Memory like an elephant."

"You know him well?"

Teague's eyes widened.

"Good God, no! He was very junior. But he ran errands for older boys, you know? Traditional. We all do it. Fetching and carrying, that sort of thing. He did it for me for a while."

Pitt could imagine it easily. He had never been to such a school, but he knew some who had. The hierarchy was rigid, with traditions going back not decades but centuries.

Pitt was aware of Teague watching him. He kept his face expressionless, although Teague would notice that too. It was unnatural. He must find some response to make.

"Do you think he has any concern in this, other than to make a good story?" he asked. "And of course get credit for it."

Teague smiled. "Commander, I don't think Frank Laurence has any object in life other than to get a good story, and credit for it, let the chips fall where they may."

"Have you something to report, Mr.

Teague?" Pitt asked quietly.

"Ah," Teague leaned back in his chair. "Time to report to the team captain?" He was smiling, but his eyes were expressionless, guarded. Pitt had no idea whether the remark was a joke, or a jibe.

"You are not a man who wastes his time," Pitt pointed out.

Teague's body relaxed a little.

"The house on Inkerman Road where the murders took place belongs to the Hall family. You must already be aware of that? Yes, of course you are. Which is not so surprising. It has come to my notice, through certain connections I have, that Sofia Delacruz has been known to extend both sympathy and a degree of assistance to fugitives from the law in Spain."

"And how does this pertain to the murders?" Pitt said softly.

"Sofia's sympathies are with the persecuted, for whatever cause, justified or not," Teague replied, watching Pitt's face closely. "Some who fought for the rights of the poor in Spain are admirable. Others are not. Some anarchists simply want to destroy. They might welcome any violence, even that of this new, miserable war. They worship chaos and hate anyone who possesses what they do not. The authorities make little distinction."

It was what Pitt himself had been thinking, but he was still acutely interested in what Teague had to say, and why. Another thought came to him that was increasingly disturbing as he listened to Teague's reasoning: How much of what he was saying had he learned from listening to and watching Pitt's own men in Special Branch? Was he now leading or learning? Why? How much else was there he had observed, and was not speaking about?

As Pitt listened to Teague he tried to work out whether this entire business could be a form of revenge against Sofia by the Spanish government. The question also remained as to whether Teague was here to give him information, or to gain it: even whether he had some personal interest that he was using Pitt, and Special Branch, to pursue.

Teague was related to half the aristocracy of England, even indirectly to the prime minister himself. That might mean everything or nothing. Traitors could come in the highest places. He must direct Stoker to speak discreetly to the men about exactly what they said in front of Teague, or any of his employees.

Or was it already too late?

Was it even possible Teague's purpose was

to test the discretion of Special Branch? The organization had enemies in government as well as friends. Pitt's dismissal would please the Prince of Wales greatly. There were many other men he would consider far more suited for the position, not only more skilled, but who would understand the unspoken rules of how gentlemen treated one another, what secrets were kept, who owed what and to whom. Narraway had known. Pitt was learning, but slowly. And he had made mistakes.

"I have some contacts in Spain," Teague was saying. "But there's no point in calling in favors to learn something you already know." His eyes searched Pitt's face. "For example, you must be aware of the political climate in Spain at the moment . . ."

"Of course," Pitt agreed blandly.

"Is it possible Señora Delacruz might be protecting one of the fugitives after the murders in Barcelona? Or some other episode like it?"

Pitt was aware of the tension in Teague. He was awkwardly still, as if his muscles were locked tight to stop some involuntary movement that might betray him. But why? Surely it was impossible for a man like Dalton Teague to have sympathy with the Spanish authorities?

Pitt's thoughts raced before he answered.

"It is possible," he said slowly.

"But you don't know?" Teague urged. "Smith has said nothing to you about her protecting anyone?" Again his eyes searched Pitt's face. Then he suddenly became aware of his posture and broke the tension with a small laugh. "If she had some mistaken pity for the wrong man it would become embarrassing for us . . . even more embarrassing than it already is."

Pitt was acutely aware of how embarrassing it was now. He knew Teague had mentioned it for that reason, but he kept his expression carefully neutral.

"Or perhaps she betrayed them," Teague went on. "Or they thought she did. Is that possible, from what you know?"

"I don't have enough information to answer that," Pitt replied evenly.

"Perhaps when you do, you will tell me?" Teague smiled.

"You've given me a lot to think about." Pitt replied, not answering Teague's question.

As Teague rose to his feet, Pitt did also. This time he was the first to offer his hand.

It was now too late to see Barton Hall, so Pitt went home. He was still deep in thought, and unprepared to face Jemima's questions, though he knew he could not avoid them.

They were sitting in the parlor after dinner. Unusually, all four of them were present. Homework had been completed and no one had any other commitments.

"Do you know anything more about Señora Delacruz, Papa?" Jemima asked anxiously.

"Not yet, but we are looking for her and following every clue we can find," he answered, aware that it sounded empty.

"She could be dead," Daniel pointed out.

Pitt was about to tell him to be quiet; the words were on his tongue, when he realized there was no point in denying that possibility. "Of course she could," he agreed. "But the most likely thing is that she is being held prisoner somewhere, and when everyone is really upset and desperate, whoever is holding her will ask for a ransom."

"Who'd pay?" Daniel asked.

"The people at Angel Court, of course," Jemima said sharply.

"Have they got any money?" Daniel asked with surprise. "And do they want her back anyway? The newspapers say that they might not."

"Not wanting someone is not the same as

letting them be killed if you don't pay," Charlotte said quickly. "You'd do that even for someone you really disliked. And they didn't dislike her."

Jemima looked at Pitt. "Is she right in what she is preaching, Papa? Is it possible for anyone to become like God?"

"Oh, really!" Daniel said with exasperation. "Nobody's perfect! She's just letting people hear what they want to hear! That it doesn't matter how bad you are, there's always a way back? Try hard enough and you can become like God? There isn't any inequality in 'forever,' we're all exactly the same?"

"She didn't say that!" Jemima said angrily, her voice raised. "And anyway, it isn't what people want to hear! They like to think that they're special. If anyone can get to heaven, what's the point? They only want it if they can shut someone out. Don't you listen at all?"

"She's just a woman, Jemima," Daniel said patiently. "She's not a saint. She doesn't know any more than the rest of us."

"Yes she does," Jemima retorted. She swung around to Pitt. "Doesn't she, Papa? She is different. She has courage, and passion. She's seen something that other people haven't . . . hasn't she?"

Pitt was at a loss as to how to answer his daughter. She was so trusting, and eager to believe in Sofia. What if he told Jemima that Sofia was honest, and then it turned out she was helping political terrorists?

"I am truly not sure what she's seen." He picked his words slowly. "But you should judge what she says for its own intrinsic value. Flawed and imperfect people can still speak the truth."

Daniel frowned. "Are you saying it's the truth, Papa? Or that you know she's imperfect?"

"We're all imperfect." This time Charlotte stepped in. "Even you, my darling. We love you anyway."

Daniel ignored his mother and kept on staring at Pitt, waiting for him to answer.

"Your mother might have said it with a smile," Pitt told his son, "but I think she meant it very seriously. Everyone has imperfections. It's part of being human. I don't know what has happened to Sofia Delacruz, but I am doing everything I can to find out and if possible to rescue her and punish whoever is responsible for killing the two women on Inkerman Road. All of this may have to do with religion, or politics, or money, or some private hatred. I don't know, and I'm not going to judge until I do.

That is the end of the subject for tonight."

Jemima drew in her breath and started to say something else, then evidently changed her mind and gave Pitt a quick hug before saying good night and leaving the room.

"She's going to be sick as anything if that Sofia turns out to be a fake," Daniel said unhappily. "She shouldn't build people up like that. It's really bad."

"She might be upset depending on what we discover about Sofia," Pitt agreed. "But it is also important to have faith in people."

Daniel stood up slowly. "I'm not sure I like religion much. It's either boring or it's dangerous." He walked slowly toward the door, touching his mother lightly on the arm as he passed her.

"Life is a bit like that," she said quietly.

"Boring or dangerous?" Pitt asked with surprise.

"Safe or risky," she replied. "Risks can hurt, but at least when you take them, you know you tried. And that can be wonderful." She smiled at him, and he felt the warmth flood into the room. He smiled back without arguing.

A little while later, Charlotte stood up and quietly left the room. Jemima's distress troubled her. There was something deeper in it than concern for the safety of a woman she had seen once, on a stage.

She went up the stairs and knocked on Jemima's bedroom door. Hearing a muffled answer, she took it for permission to go in.

Jemima was sitting on the bed, had clearly been lost in thought until Charlotte's interruption. She looked up questioningly.

Charlotte closed the door behind her and sat at the foot of the bed.

"What is this really about?" she said directly. "Why do you care so much about Sofia Delacruz?"

"Is she trying to create a stir, or does she really believe what she says?" Jemima asked.

"I think she means it. Why?"

Jemima did not answer for a moment. "Nobody knows whether it's true," she finally said, looking up and meeting Charlotte's eyes. "Nobody can know. If you know, for sure, then it wouldn't be faith at all."

"That's right," Charlotte agreed. She told herself to be patient, to let Jemima tell her what was worrying her when she was ready. "And why does that matter?"

"They hate her because she's clever, and she speaks out. Some of what she says makes more sense than what they're saying." Jemima's face was pinched with anxiety.

Charlotte wanted to comfort her, but no platitudes were going to do that. "Yes," she agreed again.

Jemima took a deep breath and let it out in a sigh.

"Do you remember the party at Lady Cromby's?"

"I remember you going to it, yes."

"Her son was there. He was really very nice. No, that's a stupid word!" There were tears in Jemima's eyes now and she blinked them away angrily. "He was funny and clever, and . . . very handsome. He liked me. I could see it in his face. Everyone could. We started to talk really sensibly. He asked me what I thought about certain matters, and I told him. I shouldn't have. Because it wasn't what he thought, even though what I said was right. Some of the others could see it. Earlier he had asked me if I would go to the theater with him . . . properly chaperoned, of course. At the end of the evening he said, 'I'd better not go to the theater after all, because I wouldn't like the play.' " She stopped, her throat too tight to speak.

"I'm sorry, darling," Charlotte said gently.

Jemima fished for a handkerchief and

found one.

"I've had that happen before, and it didn't hurt as much. But I really like him. Annabelle told me afterward that if I had any sense I would agree with boys, because that's what they like, no matter how wrong they are. It isn't right and wrong! It's just being able to think what you want to, and talk about it. But what if I do that and nobody ever loves me? Am I going to have to pretend all the time, or be alone for always?"

She fished again for her handkerchief. "To care about what happened at this one party is just stupid, I know that. But do I always have to tiptoe around things and say I don't know, even if I do?"

Suddenly Charlotte saw it all very clearly. What could she possibly say that would help Jemima? She saw herself in her daughter so vivdly. She remembered being Jemima's age. Her friends had got married one by one, and she had not. She had been handsome enough, just as Jemima was, but also like Jemima, she had been far too opinionated.

Was there another Thomas Pitt around to love and marry Jemima? And how much hurt lay between now and finding him?

She chose her words with care. "You don't

have to say you agree. Sometimes silence is wiser."

"I asked him to explain why he felt that way," Jemima said reasonably.

"Oh, darling!" Charlotte sighed. "He can't possibly explain if he doesn't understand himself. And if you think about it, you'll realize that."

"Is that why someone killed Señora Delacruz? Because she asked too many questions, instead of being silent?"

"We don't know that she's dead, and if she is we don't know who killed her, or why."

"But will anyone love me if I say what I believe, and it's not what they believe?" Jemima persisted.

"You may not find love easily, but if you do, it will be real, and it will last. Even so, it's a very good idea to keep your own counsel at times. Believe me, I have learned that the hard way myself, at times. Not just with men, with anybody. Being right is not the same thing as wise."

Charlotte leaned forward and hugged her, relaxing at last as Jemima hugged her back.

There was another large article by Frank Laurence in *The Times* the next morning. He did not belabor the fact that neither the police nor, as far as anyone knew, Special Branch had made any progress in discovering who had murdered the unfortunate women on Inkerman Road, or what had happened to Sofia Delacruz. He did not even speculate as to whether she was alive or dead.

Pitt read on, and was startled to see what it was that Laurence was really addressing. It was written with such searing honesty that he could hear Laurence's voice as if he were beside him at the table. He could even see in his mind's eye Laurence's face with its high intelligence and quick, bright humor.

"If she is dead it is a tragedy, and unquestionably one of the ugliest crimes in this city," Laurence wrote.

> But if she is alive and well, able to contact us if she chose, then it is a sin of a deeper nature. There are many ways of cheating people, of robbing them of money, land, opportunity, of office or even glory they have earned. Often it is by deluding us so that our own greed is our undoing. The prospect of getting something more than we have deserved is a lure for many of us. I've tasted it! I've been tempted. In small ways I've taken the bait. Who hasn't?

It can be as small a thing as making a wager when you have the odds far better than the other person.

But if Sofia Delacruz has deceived us then she has taken our dreams, our trust in prayer, and the most sacred words on the lips of a believer. A man in terror for his life cries out to God for help. How many soldiers' last words on earth are a prayer? How many of us weighed down by guilt plead in prayer for forgiveness? A woman nursing a sick baby begs God to help her, save her child's life, ease her pain at any cost. How many of us are children, overwhelmed by life, confused and stumbling, turning to God for a light anywhere along the path?

And we look to heroes. We search for those who have found a faith in the God we only seek somewhere in the darkness around us. We see honor in them, and courage to do what we long to. We see mercy and wisdom, and above all faith. If they can find a way, then so can we. Is there anything more blessed, more healing than hope?

How deep is the sin of those who ask for the trust of the innocent, then destroy it? And we are all children at heart when we are frightened, alone and in need.

Of course there is a place for questioning one doctrine or another. There is a place for doubt and for argument. But it is not on the lips of those who promise hope. If you take the role of hero and accept the trust of the vulnerable, then you have made a covenant with them. We do not expect perfection, but we expect honor.

Has Sofia Delacruz blasphemed the God she claims to believe in by betraying that promise? We don't know yet. We are working on it, striving day and night, doing all we can, because it matters. If she has not, then there is something beautiful we can treasure. If she has, then we need to find a way to heal, to find another light to follow. Perhaps one of us needs to become that light. It doesn't always have to be someone else.

To Pitt it would almost have been better if Laurence had done as so many of the more lurid newspapers had, and simply focused on the horror of the murders. Even anger against a woman being outspoken, inappropriate, opinionated and self-seeking would be only what was expected. Those who agreed would be satisfied, and those who did not would ignore it.

Laurence appealed to the thoughtful, the

fair, those who were looking for hope and trust in these desperately uncertain times.

He folded the newspaper and rose from the table. "Not very helpful" was the only comment he made to Charlotte as he left.

When Pitt arrived at Lisson Grove Stoker told him he had made an appointment for him to visit Barton Hall, but it was not for an hour and a half yet.

Pitt thanked him. "Any news from Spain?" he asked, without expecting any more than a perfunctory answer. Stoker would have told him already if there were.

"Nothing that helps, sir. But I looked into Laurence a bit more." Stoker was standing halfway between Pitt's desk and the door, as if he could not make up his mind whether to stay and share his information, or leave without speaking further.

Pitt felt a sudden misgiving. "What did you find?"

"Odd, sir," Stoker replied. "He told you he knew Teague at school only by repute."

"Yes," Pitt agreed. "But Teague said he knew him a bit better than that. One of them obviously lied."

"Laurence lied, sir." Stoker stood stiffly in the middle of the floor. "He was really bright, ahead of his years. Smart-arsed little beggar, so they said, but easily up to it academically. Lot better student than Teague. Though of course rubbish on the sports field."

"I wonder why Laurence lied," Pitt said thoughtfully.

Stoker frowned. "Could Laurence be a suspect in this?" he asked dubiously.

"I can't see how," Pitt said. "But he doesn't like Teague. Maybe he doesn't want us to know why, but if he wants me to damage Teague for him, he's wasting his time," Pitt said irritably. "I don't particularly like Teague, but I've got nothing against him either, and I'm not picking Laurence's chestnuts out of the fire for him. Anything more on Barton Hall?"

"Yes, sir. On your desk." Stoker went out and Pitt sat down and began to study the papers Stoker had left.

Pitt alighted from the hansom and paid the driver, then walked across the pavement to the entrance of the bank. It was magnificent, a flight of marble steps up to colonnades of pillars and a door fit to have graced a Renaissance palace. He went into a hushed anteroom and was met by a footman who inquired politely how he might be of assistance. Pitt told him that he had an appointment to see Mr. Barton Hall. The footman accompanied him up another flight of stairs and along a silent passageway to a large door.

The knock was answered immediately. Barton Hall stood up from behind his magnificent desk and inclined his head very slightly. He looked perfectly in place in this austere, expensively furnished office with its leather-bound volumes on the shelves, its Chippendale chairs and Adam fireplace.

"Good morning," Hall said almost expressionlessly. He was formally dressed, his hair combed back off his brow, revealing where it was thinning a little. He looked tired, although it was only half past nine in the morning.

"Good morning, sir," Pitt replied.

"I can only suppose you have some news of Sofia that you feel you must tell me in person. That is courteous of you, but unnecessary."

Pitt felt a momentary pity for the man. He was very clearly in some distress, but the cause of it could have been any of a number of things, including guilt, or fear.

"I have no news, Mr. Hall," Pitt told him. "Of course the regular police are doing all they can to discover who is responsible for the appalling deaths of the two women. And

Special Branch are making our own investigation. But my reason for speaking with you again is to learn more about Sofia."

"I really have no idea what else I can tell you," Hall said sharply, waving his hand for Pitt to sit down, and doing so himself behind the desk that formed a considerable barrier between them.

"Please let us start with her contacting you to say that she was coming from Spain to see you, especially," Pitt replied. "You must have asked her why."

Hall hesitated just long enough to betray that he was weighing his answer before giving it.

"Most financial questions are confidential, Mr. Pitt . . ." he began.

"So she was consulting you financially?"

"No, of course not!" Hall snapped. "But the matter had to do with money. She said it was a very considerable amount involved, but refused to clarify it. I pressed her, but she insisted that we speak face-to-face. I could not persuade her otherwise. And as you know, I never did see her."

"What is 'considerable'?" Pitt asked.

"I . . . am . . . I am very loath to tell you so much, Mr. Pitt. It is not Special Branch's business, but the amount of money she mentioned ran into millions. I don't know if she was speaking the truth, or hopelessly exaggerating," Hall retorted. "And as I have already told you, since she vanished before we could meet, I know no more than that."

"And yet you offered Melville Smith the use of the family house on Inkerman Road for Señora Delacruz and two of her women to hide in. From what, Mr. Hall?"

Hall was very pale. "From whatever religious zealots she had outraged by her crazy preaching!" Hall snapped at him. "What else?"

"You offered her the use of your house on Inkerman Road, and she accepted it, but you told no one else? Did you think it was her own people she had to fear? Why? What happened that day to give you such an idea?"

"I told you, I did not ever see her, I saw Melville Smith. He was concerned and I told him they could use the house." Hall was lost, struggling for an answer. He clenched and unclenched his hands. "I wish to God now that I hadn't."

Pitt started to speak, but Hall cut him off. "I'm sorry," he said. "This whole terrible business has distressed me profoundly. Those . . . poor . . . stupid women! Nobody deserves to be killed in that way, no matter how foolish they are." He stared at Pitt. "I should not be angry with Sofia," he said with an effort.

"That's very compassionate of you," Pitt said; the silence seemed to demand it.

Hall shrugged. "It is easy to allow anger at horrible outcomes to blind you to the fact that those committing the offenses may have had little idea of what they were provoking." He sat still, his eyes almost closed. "The world is changing very rapidly, Mr. Pitt. In fact one might say it is careering toward the edge of the cliff."

Pitt again felt pity for the man, but he wanted to find out what Hall was imagining, and the only way to do that was to allow him to continue.

Hall leaned a little forward across the desk. "Perhaps because she was in Spain, hiding from reality in her religious fantasy, Sofia didn't truly realize what dangerous times these are," he said with his eyes wide, brows raised. "And I have no idea what this Spanish man is like that she married except, of course, that he was abominably irresponsible, and had no control over himself when it came to Sofia. God knows what his political beliefs are." He waited for Pitt to challenge him.

Pitt merely nodded, as if he understood.

Hall was staring at him, his face very

grave. "You must be even more aware than I am of the gathering momentum of rebellion in Europe," he said grimly. "In Russia it is appalling. The Tsar has all kinds of plans about peace conferences, but he hasn't the faintest idea what he is doing. His leaders nod and smile and agree with it all, and then go on doing exactly what they were doing before — preparing to build up their armies till they outnumber all the rest of us put together."

Pitt felt cold at the thought, but he believed Hall was wildly overstating the case. Special Branch was far more concerned about the buildup of armaments in Germany, which was very much closer and openly more belligerent. The vast machinery of manufacture there was creating ironclad monsters that would crush the old-fashioned cavalry that had once been so effective.

"Money," Hall went on gravely. "Attack and defense both depend upon money. Ours most especially rests with our navy. America has begun to see that, which of course is why they are building warships like mad. They intend to dominate the entire Pacific from San Francisco to Manila, and all the Caribbean, hence the Spanish-American war for Cuba."

Pitt did not argue. He knew perfectly well that the idea of liberating Cuba from Spain was irrelevant. All the intelligence he had heard said that Cuba had no wish to be liberated and pass from one imperial power to what they saw as simply another.

"It looks as if the Americans have learned a few of our tricks," he observed.

"Yes, I suppose so," Hall conceded reluctantly. "But more to the point is the chaos in Europe. That is on our doorstep. If this Dreyfus case goes against the French army, and the government falls, then we are on the edge of a precipice. We must re-arm, get up-to-date. We still carry delusions that we can fight Trafalgar and Waterloo again. Some people think modern machines of war are so overwhelmingly destructive that they will never be used. Would God it were true, but it's a complete fallacy."

Pitt knew that Hall might have deduced all sorts of things from international banking circles, but he was not privy to information of the British government or the secret services.

"Do you believe all of this is related to Sofia, or her disappearance?" he said carefully.

Hall sighed and relaxed some of the stiffness in his shoulders.

"Not intentionally, perhaps," he said with a shrug. "I don't think she is wicked, just selfish and a little unbalanced where certain beliefs are concerned, and self-serving, of course. Perhaps her husband has thoroughly used her? He might be an anarchist, or have some sympathy with them." He raised his eyebrows even higher.

For a moment Pitt was thrown into complete confusion, then a sudden thought bolted across his mind like a shaft of light. He had a dreadful premonition as to what Hall was talking about. How stupid of him not to have seen it before! He had been looking at a tiny picture, just as Narraway had said. He was being a policeman instead of being the head of Special Branch.

He observed Hall again, his serious, rather academic face, his big hands, the severity of his collar and black tie, the tension of his body in this old-fashioned and magnificent room that spoke of tradition, order and safety.

Pitt found himself growing colder inside, as if it were January, not May. His mind flew to H. G. Wells's recent novel about a Martian invasion of earth and a terrible and total defeat. Of course it was complete fiction, but it mirrored in ways another book, *The Battle of Dorking,* which had shown a successful German invasion in England.

It had been written by Sir George Chesney, with the intention of drawing people's minds to the fact that Britain was still living in the age of her victories over Napoleon nearly a century ago, as if nothing had changed. But the book had made no difference to the apathy and self-satisfaction of those in power.

It was time to change the subject. Hall had very successfully drawn it away from Sofia and into the realm of anarchy and international finance. Sofia's disappearance had not yet escalated so far.

"We have gotten off topic. It is time you told me everything you know about Sofia," he said calmly. "It is too late for discretion and family secrets."

"I suppose it is unavoidable now," Hall agreed with a sigh, at last leaning back in his chair. "It is not a pleasant story and I dislike telling it."

Pitt waited again.

"In her own way she was a beautiful woman," Hall began. "But fierce, not to every man's taste. Most men prefer someone a little more . . . accommodating, more comfortable. Nevertheless, she received several offers of marriage as she reached about twenty. Her father found one extremely suitable."

"But Sofia refused him?" Pitt asked, already knowing the answer.

"Yes," Hall agreed. "And she gave no reason. Instead she traveled as companion to an elderly woman of great distinction, first to Paris, then to Madrid, and finally Toledo, where I understand the woman eventually died.

"In Toledo she met a young Spanish man, some few years older than herself," Hall continued. "He was married, with two children. Despite that, he courted Sofia and the result was even more disastrous than was foreseeable." His mouth tightened and curved in a downward line. "His wife moved out of the home, taking her young children with her. This did not curb her husband's behavior, or Sofia's. They continued with their affair. A short while later, abandoned and in total despair, the wife killed herself and both her children. Burned all of them to death." He stopped abruptly, his skin pale, and pulled tight across the bones of his face.

For moments there was no sound in the room.

"Are you quite sure of this?" Pitt said at last, amazed at how revolted he was, and his intense desire to prove it wrong. He thought again of Laurence's article in *The Times* that morning. Any disillusion was painful, but that of faith eroded the foundations of everything else, all that hope and trust were built on. He felt a brush of it now himself and knew with a jolt of surprise that he had cared what Sofia had said. The ideas were beautiful and while he did not consciously accept them, he wanted the chance that they were true.

Of course he understood falling in love. He had fallen in love with Charlotte when it looked impossible that she would wish to marry him and give up her own comfort and social position to share the home and comparatively negligible income of a policeman.

But it had not altered his moral judgments or made him imagine doing something so appalling as apparently Sofia had, and the man who was now her husband.

Would he even have considered it, were Charlotte married to someone she did not love? Please heaven, no! But was he certain? Can you ever be certain of such a thing, beyond any doubt at all? It was so easy to judge when you had not been tested.

Hall was watching him, judging his response.

"I'm sorry," Hall said quietly. "I can see

that you had no idea. Imagine how those people who believe her doctrine will feel should they discover the truth. I don't think I exaggerate if I say that her deception is a betrayal. I would have protected people from it, had I the power. I tried everything I could think of to persuade her not to come to England, but she insisted."

Pitt struggled to choose his words carefully. Whatever she had done, the murder of the two unfortunate women who had followed her was a monstrous crime. If she had suffered a similar fate herself, it might well develop into an international incident with tragic and dangerous consequences. He could imagine what Laurence would write if her mutilated body were found.

"What do you think Laurence will make of it if she is never found?" he said aloud.

"What?" Hall was startled.

"Frank Laurence," Pitt said. "He wrote a very powerful article about disillusionment and responsibility in *The Times* this morning. You knew him, I believe."

Hall looked confused.

"You were at the same school," Pitt reminded him.

"Was I?"

"You and Dalton Teague."

For an instant Hall's face was frozen, then

he regained his composure with a faint look of confusion. "Oh, yes, Teague, of course. I don't remember Laurence. Unless he was that smart-mouthed little beggar who ran errands for Teague, practically hanging on his every word. Mind, I suppose there were several like that. Practically thought Teague was God. You don't need to part the Red Sea if you can hit a cricket ball out of the field." He straightened his shoulders. "Sorry. School days weren't my best. Bit of a swot."

"You never played cricket yourself?" Pitt kept his tone light.

"Tolerable fielder, that's about all." Hall dismissed the subject. "Is there anything else I can help you with? I have an appointment with the Dean of St. Paul's in half an hour." He reached for a pile of papers close to his hand, as if to resume studying them.

"Just one more thing," Pitt said. "Apparently Sofia helped a great many people one way or another, especially those who had committed offenses they deeply regretted."

"Possibly. Sounds like something she would do," Hall said lightly, but his hand over the papers clenched till the big knuckles shone white. "I told you, we had no communication about that."

"Apparently she felt there was a way back from any sin, if you were prepared to make such amends as you could," Pitt continued. "She gave penitents who believed the same sanctuary and pardon."

Hall swallowed. "Really." His voice was flat, as if he were scarcely breathing.

"It was part of her ministry," Pitt went on relentlessly. "There was one man in great trouble, terrified for his life, just before she left to come to England. Apparently she felt that seeing you was for some reason even more important than this man's redemption. She didn't mention him, did she?"

"No, I'm afraid not. Now, Commander, I have a great deal of urgent business to attend to. If you please . . ." Hall turned away and picked up the telephone attached to the wall near him and Pitt heard his voice, tight in his throat, ask for a number.

He opened the door and stepped through it, hesitated for several moments, then turned back in time to see Hall's face turn ashen pale and the phone almost slip from his fingers.

Chapter 8

Pitt sat at the breakfast table, his tea ignored and the toast going cold in his hand. The letter had come by the first postal delivery of the day. Charlotte had brought it from the hall minutes ago. There was one sheet written in a scrawling hand, addressed to him personally. The lines went down at the end, and there were no commas.

> Commander Thomas Pitt
>
> I have the self-styled prophetess Sofia Delacruz in my keeping for the time being safe and no more than slightly injured. Well not a lot more. Of course that could change for the better or the worse. This depends on your skill.
>
> You must be aware by now of the nature of her marriage to Nazario Delacruz and the resulting terrible death of his first wife Luisa and of their two little children. If by any chance you are

so naïve you do not know of this it is easily verifiable.

Your choice is simple. Find Nazario Delacruz in Toledo, and have him write in detail exactly how Sofia seduced him into betraying his family and abandoning them for her. Publish the account in the personal column of the London *Times.* I appreciate that he will be reluctant to do this. It will make her a laughingstock and those who previously loved her will end up hating and despising her. Her preposterous religion will crumble into dust.

But on the other hand it will save her life because if she does not then she will die most unpleasantly. The deaths of Cleo and Elfrida were comparatively quick. Hers will not be so.

The decision of course will be her husband's not yours. You must convey this choice to him. Naturally that will take some time. I will allow you exactly two weeks from the date you receive this letter. If by then I do not see Nazario's confession of guilt in *The Times* and believe me I will not be fooled by a fake edition then Sofia will receive the martyrdom she professes to crave.

I don't think that is what you wish. You

are something of a squeamish man and you have a wife and children yourself!

See what you can persuade Nazario to do. We shall discover where his loyalties really lie!

There was no signature.

Pitt was aware of Charlotte watching his face, her brow wrinkled in concern as he tried to figure out what to say to her. He felt cold, numb. His first dreadful thought was what he would do were he in Nazario Delacruz's place. He could hardly fail to know Sofia's nature and the depth of her belief. To write the letter that was asked of him could destroy everything she had built and betray every person who had believed in her.

And yet he could not doubt that the man who held her would murder her, violently and terribly, if he did not. It explained why he had killed the other poor women in such a way. Not because they had done anything to incur his fury, they were simply a demonstration of his seriousness.

"Thomas!" Charlotte said urgently, fear in her voice now.

He needed her opinion, her understanding of Sofia. There were no women in Special Branch. He handed her the letter.

She read it through again, slowly, to be certain she had really seen it as it was. When she looked up her face was white.

"Do you know anything about him?" she asked huskily.

"Of course I don't," he replied, confused. "We've no idea who it is. Except it is a complete muddle. The handwriting is awful, in places almost indecipherable, and yet the spelling is correct. And he uses some unusual words as if with ease: 'martyrdoms she professes to crave.' And there are no commas."

"Not who wrote this!" Desperation made her tone sharp. "Sofia's husband! This . . . Nazario. What will he do? Does he love her, or is he some religious fanatic who would accept her death as the greatest boost to her faith?"

"You think he could be behind all of this?" The thought was appalling.

"Couldn't he be?" she insisted. "And if the story of him leaving his wife for Sofia is true, what about the first wife's family? They could easily want revenge."

"Why would they wait all this time?" he asked, as much to himself as to Charlotte. "Wouldn't they have taken revenge back when it happened? A lot of people would have understood that. Why do it in London?" He drew in a deep breath. "What a mess. And none of this explains why Cleo and Elfrida were murdered. None of it was their fault."

Charlotte raised her eyebrows. "You're expecting bereaved and distressed people taking revenge to be reasonable?" Then she saw his face and came forward, standing very close to him and touching him gently on the cheek. "I am sorry. You're right, it is a mess."

For several moments he said nothing, trying to picture Sofia's face accurately from the brief times he had spent with her, recall if she had said anything about her husband. He could recall nothing. She had spoken only about her belief. But that was all that he had asked her about.

What if this was, as they had feared, some plot to involve England in the Spanish-American war, which was getting uglier by the day? Was that why Sofia had been kidnapped in London, not Toledo? Then the obscene murder of the two other women could have been to make certain it was news in the headlines everywhere.

"The kidnapping is all over the news here," he said quietly. "*Anyone* could have written this letter. She could be already dead." He felt Charlotte's body tighten, her hand freeze. He pulled away and looked up at her.

"But what if she is not? This could be her only chance!"

"But do we take this choice — either destroy all her work, deny her faith, disillusion heaven knows how many people, or let her be tortured to death — to her husband without knowing if the person who wrote this letter truly has her? Or if she is alive?"

Charlotte was very pale. Instead of letting her hands fall, she clung on to him more tightly. "No. You're right. You need to know this is genuine before you ask Nazario Delacruz to make the decision. But how are you going to do that?"

"The writer of this must expect that I will ask for proof she is alive."

"But he hasn't given you any way of answering him to say so," she pointed out.

"If he truly wants me to do anything, he'll write again."

She swallowed. "You mean we just . . . wait?"

"Not quite. I think I'll go and find Frank Laurence. I'll get him to write a specific article. See if we can shake something loose."

"You like him, in spite of yourself, don't you?"

"Definitely in spite of myself," he agreed ruefully. "And I'd like to know why he lied about knowing Teague at school. It seems a silly thing to do."

"Maybe that's all it was."

He shook his head. "People don't lie for no reason."

"Be careful, Thomas."

She had not said it, but he knew what she was thinking. He was still new at the task of leading Special Branch. He was still struggling to think like a politician and see a wider view than the solution of one crime, regardless of where it led.

"I'll be careful," he promised.

"You want me to write a piece about ransom?" Laurence said with interest. He picked up his tankard of ale and stared at Pitt over the rim. They were sitting in a noisy, crowded public house where their conversation could not be overheard by anyone. A burst of laughter and loud cheers made it necessary to lean forward across the table to hear each other.

"Only a fool pays ransom without proof that the victim is alive," Pitt replied. "If we waited, he might get in touch with us, but I would rather take that decision from him. And I don't know how she is, or if she will last if I wait and play a slow game."

"Last?" Laurence said quickly, leaning forward over the table. "You mean she's injured? Or they are torturing her? Pitt, I hate to say this, but do you think they can afford to hand her over alive, even if you do pay?"

Pitt could feel his body go cold. He could see the pity in Laurence's eyes and he believed it was real.

"No," he admitted. "I don't. And it isn't money they want."

"What do they want?"

"I'll tell you when you need to know, if that ever happens."

"The street runs both ways, Pitt," Laurence said carefully. "I want something in return."

Pitt stiffened, possible threats running through his mind.

"I'll do it," Laurence said quietly. "But when you see her, I want to be with you. I give you my word I'll do nothing except look at her."

"Then write it up in *The Times* for everyone to read," Pitt said bitterly. "No."

"You want my help . . ." Laurence began.

"I can go somewhere else." Pitt started to get up.

"No . . . No! I'll write it," Laurence

conceded. "Interesting subject, ransom. And you really won't tell me what it is they are asking for?"

"Not yet. But I'll owe you."

"Oh, yes," Laurence agreed. "Indeed you will!"

The answer was swift in coming. A letter written in the same hand as before was delivered to Pitt's office at Lisson Grove.

Well done Commander

Wise of you to accept my offer. Of course you wish to see that she is still alive. At least for the time being. Come to the old chandler's shop near the Horseferry Stairs this evening at seven o'clock. I doubt you would be foolish enough to do anything stupid like attempt to seize her or anyone with her. If you do you will not pay for it but she will.

Do I need to detail that for you? The human body can take a great deal of pain without finding the release of death.

Do as I tell you and you will see that Sofia is still alive.

Pitt stared at the piece of paper for long, silent moments, then he went to the door and called for Brundage.

Pitt and Brundage walked quickly and almost silently along the narrow road. There was nothing but warehouses between them and the river, and on the inland side of them, a few shops, and lodging houses.

"Left here," Brundage said quietly, and led the way through an alley into the street at the other end. It was even more deserted, and only one of the dozen or so streetlamps was unbroken. The chandler's shop was right opposite it.

"He chose well," Pitt said with disgust as he picked his way across the broken cobbles of the street. The door had been forced open some time ago and the rusted lock hung on the frame. He pushed it open and Brundage went in behind him, half lifting the door to get it almost closed again.

The glass in the windows was still whole, and sufficiently clean to let in the light from the lamp immediately outside.

Pitt looked around. The shop was deserted. There were a few broken candles on the floor and the remnants of the boxes they had come in, some nails and old screws, rat droppings.

"Watch where you step," he warned. "Don't want a nail through your boot."

"No, sir," Brundage agreed. "Good place, though. Come at us out of darkness, and go back into it. But we'll see him clear for a moment or two, just enough to see her . . . and if she's alive."

"It's all we need," Pitt replied, then settled into silence to wait.

"Can't we do something?" Brundage said restlessly as the minutes passed by. Seven o'clock, five past, ten past. "He isn't coming!" he said between his teeth, anger making his voice hard-edged. "He's set us up as fools!"

"Maybe," Pitt agreed. "More likely he's just exercising his power. He is enjoying watching us wait, and fume. Be patient."

"I'd enjoy watching him swing by the neck!" Brundage snarled.

"I'm working on it. Actually if it's done right, they don't swing. They just drop."

"Pity," Brundage replied.

He froze, and then turned to face the window as they both heard the sound of hoofs on the road outside. Brundage took a step forward toward the door and Pitt grasped him by the arm as hard as he could.

"We can't do anything about it now. She'll pay for it, not us," Pitt hissed at him.

Brundage stopped.

Outside under the lamp a hansom

stopped. Pitt strained his eyes to see who was in it. There looked to be two people: a woman close to them, a man sitting on the far side beyond her, his figure no more than a shadow.

The woman turned toward them. She moved awkwardly, as if her body was stiff. Her right arm, closer to them, was heavily bandaged, her fingers curled over as though useless to her. Her thick hair was wild and matted. She turned toward them, staring straight at the window as if she could see through its panes and recognize them staring back at her. One of her eyes was puffed, the cheek below swollen and dark with bruises. There was blood on the other side of her face, and bloodstains on the collar of her clothes. But she was still recognizable as Sofia Delacruz.

"God in heaven!" Brundage let out his breath.

Pitt said nothing. He let his hand fall from Brundage's arm. He knew neither of them would move.

The driver of the cab flicked his whip and it started forward again, leaving Brundage standing stiffly, and Pitt feeling as if he had been turned to ice.

It was well after nine when he got home.

He told Charlotte nothing of what had happened, except that he had seen Sofia and knew that she was alive. He was glad Jemima and Daniel were in bed. He was not certain he could have hidden his horror from them, or the feeling of being overwhelmed.

He was sitting on the sofa in his own home, the French windows onto the garden closed and locked for the night. Although the room was warm, and he could smell the perfume of the flowers on the side table, tonight he did not feel its comfort.

"I'll have to send someone to Spain to tell him," he said to Charlotte, trying to think who could carry such a message.

Charlotte bit her lip. "Whoever has her must have a great deal of power. They seem to know a lot about Sofia's life in Spain, and also here. They very cleverly engineered her capture, even though she was expecting trouble, and her own people were supposed to be looking after her." She tactfully forbore from saying that Special Branch had been watching Sofia as well, but Pitt was bitterly aware of it, and knew that she was too.

Pitt looked up at her. There was something in her not totally unlike Sofia Delacruz. The root of it might be a different faith, but Charlotte was hot-headed, passionate in causes that touched her heart, burningly angry at injustice far beyond the stage where she weighed her own safety. If that was taken from her, if she was made to betray her beliefs to protect herself, what of her would be left?

Would he prefer to see her dead rather than eaten away and destroyed? It was a meaningless question because he would always seek another way; cling on to the hope of finding it, even until it was too late. Then blame himself. Nazario Delacruz was probably just the same — unless of course he was behind everything.

If he was, maybe Sofia would rather die than be forced to know it! Except her captor had sworn it would be a slow, desperate and terrible way to go, and Pitt believed him.

"Why don't you go speak to Nazario Delacruz yourself?" Charlotte asked.

"I can't leave London right now," he replied. "She's here, and so is whoever took her. I need to send someone who understands the situation and everything involved in it, and who speaks fluent Spanish."

"Have you any men like that?"

"I've already sent the best ones out there. But I don't know if any of them have the tact or experience to handle something as delicate as meeting with Nazario. They've been tracing the threats to her that we know about, from the letters. So far they're all noise and no substance. I shall see if I can find a diplomat whom I can trust with the confidentiality of it," he said. "Narraway may know of someone."

"A good idea," she agreed, relaxing a little at last.

On Vespasia's doorstep Pitt felt intrusive, and oddly resentful that he could no longer call on Vespasia anytime he chose, and expect to be welcome. He had not appreciated before just how much he had taken that for granted.

But tonight he needed Narraway's advice, and it would not wait. He was prepared to inconvenience anybody.

The maid who answered the door held her surprise at seeing him so late. She was too well trained to have done otherwise, regardless of what she thought.

Fortunately Vespasia and Narraway were still up, and Pitt was shown to the quiet sitting room. The moment the maid withdrew, Narraway spoke with concern.

"What is it? Have you found Sofia Delacruz?"

"Yes, and no," Pitt replied. "I have a kind

of ransom letter." He pulled it out of his pocket and passed it over to Narraway. His voice shook a little. "And I know she is alive, as of a couple of hours ago. I saw her. But she has been beaten, and perhaps has a broken arm." His voice wavered.

Narraway took the letter and read it silently, then without asking Pitt, handed it to Vespasia.

"Oh dear," Vespasia said softly, putting the letter down on the table beside the small crystal bud vase with its single peach-colored rose. "You have to respond, Thomas. It is very clever, and I believe he means it. In fact quite possibly he has deliberately asked for something he knows cannot be given."

"He means it," Narraway agreed. "But I am not sure why. Have you any idea yet who it is, Pitt?"

"No. It might be someone in her church. I know Melville Smith has taken over a good deal of the leadership. He may have told himself it was to moderate her doctrine and make it more accessible to a greater number of people . . ."

Narraway smiled very slightly, but there was no joy in it.

"But do you think he planned this?" Vespasia said. The shadow of deep emotion was in her eyes.

"No," Pitt said without hesitation. "He is merely an opportunist, as Henrietta said. I believe Barton Hall is more involved than he has let on, though. He gave me the impression he was hiding something great. He does not look well."

"Why?" Vespasia said practically. "How would kidnapping her serve him? Because she is an embarrassment to the family? That is absurd. Of course he would rather she had remained in Toledo and not brought her crusade to England. But not to the point of committing the gruesome double murder of her largely innocent followers. If he is involved, perhaps it is because someone else is exerting an irresistible pressure on him, Thomas."

"I know he is terrified, but I don't know exactly of what," Pitt answered slowly, considering Vespasia's words. "I saw his face when he spoke on the telephone, just as I was leaving his office. I had told him about Sofia's habit of helping fugitives, penitents in trouble."

Vespasia's eyebrows rose. "Really?"

Pitt thought back to Hall's expression. "I think he suddenly realized something rather than intending malice from the beginning. I had the impression of a man unexpectedly and severely out of his depth. You could be right that someone has made use of him. . . ."

"Hall is very traditional, even for a banker. Has always done the appropriate things, since the day he was born," Narraway said. "It seems unlikely anyone could blackmail him."

"He is appropriate as far as you know," Vespasia said with a smile. "Perhaps he is rather better at concealing his adventures than we suppose?"

"I have never been as sensitive to the whispers of society as you are," Narraway answered, smiling back. "What do you hear of Mr. Hall?"

"Very little," she admitted. "He is a widower of impeccable reputation, which is probably well deserved. His passions seem to be entirely of the mind. He is well educated, a natural scholar who has found his field and remained within it. I think he is virtuous, in Society's sense. He has neither the imagination nor the appetite to step out of it."

Narraway winced. "What a complete damnation in one sentence."

Pitt agreed with him, but even the most tedious of people could surprise at times, if the spur were sharp enough. He could not forget the terror in Hall's eyes. "He is very afraid," he reiterated.

"Interesting," Narraway murmured. "I wonder what would frighten Barton Hall."

"Before I find that out, I must find someone to take this message to Nazario Delacruz in Toledo," Pitt replied. "Or wherever he is. Please God he is not the man behind all of this."

Vespasia winced. She did not need to speak the thoughts that filled her mind; they were visible in her face: the knowledge of love, the belief in it. If Nazario was involved in Sofia's kidnapping, it was the ultimate, terrible betrayal.

Narraway glanced at her, then at Pitt. "I'll go myself," he said firmly. "I haven't used my Spanish in a while, but it's pretty good. And I could pay for a Spaniard to assist me. I have before. But Pitt, none of this makes sense with the information we have so far. There has to be at least one major factor we have no idea of yet. Do you know anything about Nazario Delacruz?"

"Not enough," Pitt admitted. "That is one of the things you will need to find out. Is the story true that Hall told of Delacruz abandoning his wife and children for Sofia? Is his family involved in this? Or his dead wife's? They may well hate Sofia, but this seems an extraordinary degree of vengeance, and oddly timed. The wife did not die recently. And the two other women, Cleo and Elfrida, were in no way involved in Sofia's personal affairs, so why kill them, and so abominably?"

"I will find out all I can," Narraway promised.

"We will," Vespasia corrected him.

He looked at her, indecision naked in his face. It was not what to say so much as how to say it. "I will need to travel rapidly, and not necessarily in the most comfortable way possible," he began. "And anyone who would murder two women simply as an example of his intent is extremely dangerous. I think . . ."

"That you can do it better on your own?" Her silver eyebrows rose in surprise, and a degree of amusement, but there was no yielding in her face.

It was clear to Pitt that this was one of the testings between them, now that the bond was so much closer than before. Vespasia was not used to anyone guiding her or telling her what she may do, still less what she may not. There was more than pride or practicality involved now; there were deep and complex emotions. She clearly had every intention of going to Spain with him, yet she needed to find a way to do it that did not openly defy him.

And he needed to yield without appearing to do so.

"Are you afraid that I will hinder you?" she said gently. "Or that your concern for my safety will be a distraction?"

"You are always a distraction," he said with a smile that held a certain pleasure, even a pride in it.

Pitt, watching and keeping silent, was suddenly very aware how deeply Narraway was in love with Vespasia, committed for the first time in his long and varied life. It was new to him, dangerous in that it could wound him in a way he had never known before, and full of pitfalls for precisely that reason.

Suddenly Vespasia's pride vanished. "It is far too important for us to disagree over," she said quickly. "This poor woman's life is at stake in the most urgent and terrible way. Neither your feelings nor mine are important by comparison. If I can help, then you must allow me to come. My Spanish is more fluent than yours, and I have friends in Madrid and Toledo. On the other hand, if you need to move more swiftly than I can, or my presence will be a hostage to fortune for you, then I will remain in London. Not that London seems to be so very much safer, certainly not for poor Sofia."

Narraway drew in a deep breath, and then let it out in a sigh.

"I will make arrangements immediately. Prepare to travel as lightly as possible, one case of moderate size. And dress for convenience rather than fashion. We shall be on trains for some time. I'm afraid it will be impossible to take a maid." He looked at her very levelly; to be certain she was aware that there was no room for argument.

"I am perfectly able to dress myself, Victor," she said, smiling at him. "And I have traveled before on journeys that were far more interesting than they were comfortable." She turned to Pitt. "We shall accomplish all that is in our power to do."

Pitt rose to his feet, as she did. "Thank you," he accepted.

CHAPTER 9

Narraway and Vespasia set out on the train to Dover the following evening. They had less than two weeks in which to travel to Toledo and speak with Nazario Delacruz, tell him what had happened and persuade him to return to London with them in order to face the appalling dilemma of the ransom demand.

"He should not be hard to find," she said as they made themselves comfortable in the carriage seats. "Toledo is not a very large city, and Sofia will be known by repute, if not personally, by any local church."

"It's not finding him that concerns me," he replied. "It's how to do it in the least cruel way . . ."

She looked at him with a level, candid gaze. "There is no gentle way to tell him the truth, my dear. And you must not lie to him. That would be really unforgivable."

He felt a twinge of guilt. "I am not thinking of sparing his pain," he answered quietly, although there was no one else in the carriage. "I need his mind clear, not clouded by emotion. It is necessary that he listen and think as clearly as possible."

She smiled ruefully. "Of course. How do you propose to do that?"

"I don't know," he admitted. "But before I approach him at all I would like to find out how much of Barton Hall's version of his first marriage and its end is true."

"Even if Sofia is extremely to blame, and Nazario's first wife took her own life in despair of being abandoned, does that alter what we must say or do now?" she asked.

"No, of course it doesn't. But it may cast a totally different light on what sort of a man he is. I need to know what to expect of him, whether I can trust him, rely on him, or not."

Vespasia looked away from him for a moment. "I know," she agreed. "You have to consider the possibility that he is involved in the plan himself. He may have grown tired of her, as he apparently did of his first wife, and be willing to permit someone to murder her, and thus set him free."

"Vespasia!"

She turned to look at him.

The sunlight on her face showed the

beauty of it, the strength of the bones beneath the flesh, the high cheeks and arched brow. But it also picked out the fine lines with which candlelight was so much gentler.

"You think that is brutal?" she asked. "Of course it is. But Sofia is a professional woman, beautiful in her own way, certainly articulate. He may have been fascinated with her to begin with, and then accustomed to her, and finally tired of her endless drive, her opinions, her very hunger for life. Perhaps he has found someone younger, more easily impressed with him, more pliable to his will. It can happen."

"If in the first place it was only infatuation," Narraway said with conviction. "Not if it was love."

"That is one of the things we must find out, if we can," she agreed. "She might grow tedious after a year or two. People consumed in a crusade can be. I have known a few."

Beyond the carriage windows the rich fields and pastures of Kent streamed by, dotted with woodlands here and there. It was not far to Dover and the sea.

"I must see what I can learn about her," Vespasia went on. "The woman, not the saint. I have been thinking who I might know that would still be in Spain. Another woman's assessment could be useful."

"How do you know anyone in Spain, especially Toledo?" Narraway asked. "In fact how do you speak Spanish at all?" He was puzzled. She had never spoken of Spain before. He realized that in spite of their friendship and the many things they had spoken of there were decades of her life about which he knew very little.

"It's not very interesting," she said. "When I was newly widowed I went to Spain because I wanted to escape the London Season's endless sameness, people's commiserations and encouragement, their transparent plans to arrange my life for me." She looked away and Narraway saw pain in her face. He wanted to touch her, but it seemed intrusive.

"I felt as if I had escaped," she said very quietly. "And I was ashamed because I should have felt as if my life had ended, not as if it had just begun. I felt a very strong desire to begin it somewhere else, where I was not known. I suppose I see something of myself in Sofia, just a little. I gather she too was escaping when she went to Spain."

"Perhaps there is a likeness," he said with a smile, and a sudden upward surge of happiness that she had not felt such a loss of her husband that it could cloud her happiness now — his happiness for the future.

She raised her eyebrows slightly. "Indeed . . . then I shall look up old acquaintances and see what I can learn informally about Sofia, and her friends or enemies, what was thought of her by those who did not regard her as a saint. By the way, do we know when she had this religious conversion?"

"No."

"Then I shall try to find that out as well."

"And I shall see what I can learn of Nazario, and of his first marriage, and if he has any other romances in view."

"I hope not," Vespasia murmured. "I would very much like to believe differently. We have only Barton Hall's word for any of that part of her life."

She was right, and as the train rattled on its way Narraway brought to mind all he knew of Barton Hall. He was a banker, one of the invisible people who held the reins of financial power so steadily one forgot they were there.

They authorized huge loans and advised on the investment of fortunes. They probably had an unspoken knowledge of what most of the great families were worth, and exactly who owned which vast tracts of arable land or small blocks in the heart of

London on which palaces were built or the residences of foreign princes. Such knowledge was a power in itself.

Before leaving London Narraway had reminded himself very briefly of exactly who Hall's bank dealt with. It was mostly those silent giants of respectability, the Church and the Crown. The Prince of Wales had borrowed money for years, and frequently not repaid it. But that was done largely privately, from friends rich enough and unwary enough to lend it. The Church of England's property and income ran into the millions, but were untouchable by scandal, largely because they were extremely discreet. It invested in things that those of sensitive conscience might find distasteful. There was an aspect of profiteering. Beyond doubt the Church were sham landlords, but to what degree he did not know. "Residential property" covered a multitude of things. They also invested in coal, heavy industry and arable land. Was there a degree of speculation, perhaps less respectable?

So why was Hall so afraid, to the point where his fear had disturbed Pitt?

The answer must lie in another area of his life. He had been a widower for some years, and appeared to be perfectly content to remain so. His pursuits were academic, and in keeping with his position and reputation. Was there a darker and far more secret side to him?

Narraway doubted it. But then he had not foreseen any of this appalling shambles with Sofia Delacruz. He had feared no more than the Englishman's traditional embarrassment at public and inappropriate emotions. Religion was observed quietly, and largely in private. If one questioned at all, it was in writing that nobody else read. And of course it was not done by women!

Hall had been a gifted academic, gaining firsts at Cambridge in economics and history, very appropriate to a man whose ultimate aspiration was to become governor of the Bank of England. Narraway could not imagine Hall falling madly in love, enough to sacrifice all he had and plunge into the unknown.

But then he could not have imagined it of himself either!

He glanced at Vespasia beside him, and wondered for a hectic moment what wild, unforeseen things he might have done, had she asked him to! Probably anything. But the key to that lay in the fact that it would not have been wrong. She would never have asked that of herself, still less of anyone else. Which was the other great difficulty that weighed on his mind. If this whole trip to Toledo turned out to involve issues of crime, vengeance or matters that genuinely concerned Special Branch, it might require him to take moral risks, decisions that were gray, hard to justify.

The ugliness of that was part of his responsibility in the past, and now was the heaviest weight Pitt carried. In fact it was the reason Narraway felt Pitt was so good for the role. His sensitivity to moral judgments would mean they were never easy for him. He would never justify, or shift the blame to others. He would make mistakes, and learn to live with them. The man who could take them in his stride was not safe with such power.

Nor was Narraway safe now. There were many things he had done that he preferred Vespasia did not know about. Some were hard decisions, but right ones. Others he thought he knew about at the time, but now was much less certain. He would never ask her about past acts of hers, past secrets, certainly not past lovers. In fact he was quite certain that he preferred not to know. He was a bit startled to find himself jealous.

But the present issue was whether he would have to take decisions and actions that would make Vespasia see him in a different light. She might understand, at least intellectually, but would they disturb her in a man with whom she was intimate, a man whose name she had taken, and therefore was allied with not only privately but publicly?

There had to be secrets between them, matters from the past that remained confidential and always would.

He knew already that Hall had been to Eton and Cambridge, an impeccable pedigree! Dalton Teague had done the same. Was that why Teague was now involving himself in looking for Sofia? An old school loyalty carried on through university? They would also have been there at the same time, but unlikely friends. Hall was brilliant, a natural scholar, without charm or athletic ability. Teague had been the exact opposite, handsome, charismatic, one of the best cricketers who had ever played for England. Everyone had expected him to fail his exams — and he had surprised them by passing well.

But friendships could happen between the most unlikely people — just like marriages. Some of them even prospered.

Again he looked sideways at Vespasia and she turned suddenly and met his gaze, smiling at him, and he was ridiculously pleased.

He nearly put out his hand and touched her, then realized how sentimental that would be, as if they were twenty! He felt the heat burn up his face, smiled awkwardly and turned to look out of the window at the wide expanse of countryside speeding past them.

They made a late afternoon crossing of the Channel to Le Havre, from where they were going to catch the train south to San Sebastián, on the northern coast of Spain, then south again to Madrid, and from there finally to Toledo.

It was one of those lazy, early summer days when from the deck of the ferry the whole world was blue. The sky arched over them almost unblemished and the light seemed to brim over and dazzle the breaking water that foamed away at the stern. Gulls followed in their wake echoing its pattern with their wings, swooping, climbing then drifting as if life were all one exquisite pattern of the tide.

The breeze moderated the warmth of the sun, although not its ability to burn, but it was barely strong enough to unravel Vespasia's hair as they stood together in the stern watching the white cliffs of Dover recede in the distance. It was hard to remember that their mission was urgent and terrible.

"Victor, what do you make of Dalton Teague's concern in looking for Sofia?" she asked. "I can't believe that he agrees with any of her teachings. They go against every privilege of birth or wealth. She regards gifts of any sort as an obligation of service, not a birthright."

"The aristocracy originally regarded it so, and the best of them still do," he pointed out. "Teague is related to several of the old families. The Salisburys, and the Dukes of Devonshire at the very least."

"I know," she agreed, still staring at the white wake curling over behind them.

Of course she knew. She was related to most of them herself. She was born to her title; she had not married into it. Now that he knew her so much better, and she was real to him in the intimacy of flesh, laughter, physical joy and pain, and he had touched the delicate, private moods of her heart, Society's world was revealed to be a mirage. Inextricably wound in with incidents he would prefer to forget.

When he had been younger in Special Branch, long before he was its head, he had worked in some of the more complicated areas of personal loyalties and intrigues in the earlier years of the Irish troubles. Narraway had been just into his forties,

Teague at the height of his sporting career. Narraway had seen Teague's charm, and his weaknesses, and he had used both to his advantage to create a dangerous trap, and to spring it. It had accomplished its purpose, but they had both been hurt, as had others who were no more than bystanders, shallow and careless perhaps, but not wicked. The whole fascinating and ultimately tragic episode with Violet Mulhare still lingered in his memory with embarrassment. Perhaps that was the reason he disliked Teague, who had been able to walk away from it without embarrassment? There was something to be said for a man who could at least feel guilt for the pain he caused.

He would rather not have had Vespasia know anything about it, but he could not evade it without lying to her, and perhaps it mattered to the present case. Probably not, but it was the implicit lie to Vespasia that mattered.

"I think you are right about Teague, and the last thing he would do is agree with Sofia's beliefs," he said slowly. "At first glance I would say he is seeking the limelight as usual. He is posing as the hero, using his money and power to help someone very visibly in trouble. The fact that he does not subscribe to her creed only heightens the nobility of what he is doing."

Vespasia gave him a wry look, a bleak amusement behind her smile. "You really don't like him, do you? Not that it surprises me."

He had a sudden, terrible thought that Teague might once have been an admirer of hers, even a lover. His dislike of Teague crystallized into a blaze of hatred.

Then he saw himself as ridiculous, and regained at least some control. He had had affairs. What normal man of his age had not? In some of them he had cared passionately at the time. Only later did he look back and see the flaws, the self-deception, the veneer of romance hiding a more pedestrian, physical reality, and maybe also a loneliness temporarily dispelled, only to close in more tightly afterward.

"I didn't expect you to like him, my dear," she said gently, watching the white gulls dip and swerve above the water. "He is essentially an opportunist, I think, a man empty of any convictions, except those that serve the moment."

"Do you suppose that Pitt sees that in him?" he asked.

"Thomas is not as naïve as you fear," she answered. "Gentlemen don't impress the servant class nearly as much as they like to think they do."

"The servant class?" he said incredulously. He had never thought of Pitt in that way.

She smiled patiently. "His mother was a laundress in one of the great houses in the Home Counties. Sir Arthur Desmond, I believe. A very good man, but human, nevertheless, with his flaws and eccentricities. Thomas was a policeman many years. He has seen the frailties of the rich and powerful more than most of their fellows imagine. It's not the wealth or the breeding of Teague that bothers me; it is his grace and courage on the cricket field. Out there in the white flannels, and the sun in your eyes, you become a demi-god to millions. That tends to make people imagine you are innocent to the limitations of the rest of us."

Narraway considered that for minutes, looking into the distance where the chalk cliffs were beginning to fade into the skyline. She was right. That was where Teague differed from other men of position and wealth.

"Why do you dislike him?" she interrupted his thoughts.

"I don't know. Completely unfounded suspicion," he admitted, then realized she would know he was evading the issue. "Actually, I ran across him in a case, a long time ago. Twenty years, at least. He was on the fringes of it."

She remained with her face half turned away, still looking at the gulls. "I know that many things must remain secret, Victor. I am not asking for confidences, only to know if Thomas is in a danger that he is not aware of. It is the present that matters, not the past. Is your reason for doubting Dalton Teague anything that may affect Thomas now?"

There was no sound but the swirl of the water and the whisper of it against the sides of the ferry, and now and then a cry of birds.

"It was an old case," he said at last. "I didn't behave very well. I was in love with Violet Mulhare. At least I thought so at the time. I used Teague, and then I caught them both. Teague betrayed her so that he escaped and she was caught, as was the man I was after. Teague told me afterward that he knew all the time."

Vespasia said nothing.

"I know," he admitted. "I used both of them."

"Did you believe Teague?" she asked.

"No. I think he lied. He changed sides at the last moment, when he knew I would turn them both in. But I couldn't prove it."

"Of course," she said wryly. "Teague is far

too careful for that."

Did Vespasia care if he had loved Violet or not? He looked at her and had no idea. It mattered to him in a way he could not explain. It shouldn't, not now. That past happened to different people, more impulsive and so much shallower than now.

Slowly Vespasia turned to face him, searching his eyes. He felt uncomfortably stripped of pretense. He was not accustomed to being so vulnerable.

"I think your judgment of Teague is probably correct," she said gently. "I knew him very little, but I chose not to. I felt I was being very unfair about it, but what you have said makes me feel less guilty of prejudice. Possibly it was a better instinct than I thought." She took a last look at the pale gleam of cliffs in the distance, almost vanished as the sun lowered. The long summer dusk was beginning to fade. They would disembark in Le Havre in the early morning and catch the first train south.

Vespasia wanted to stay up here on the deck until there was no light to see any longer, perhaps until the first stars pricked the sky. It was not that she did not wish to relax, or to be alone with him in the small cabin. That would be a pleasure. She had been married before, and borne children, but that seemed like another life. Long, long ago, when she was very young, she had fought at the barricade in Rome, in the Revolutions of '48. She had loved Mario Corena, and thought that she would never love like that again.

Her first marriage had been one of affection, but never passion. The long years afterward had held romances of differing kinds. She had not expected to care beyond her ability to savor, and lose without unhealable wounds.

At first she had seen Victor Narraway as an ally in the desperate battles that Pitt had faced. Gradually she had come to think of him as a friend. Perhaps that was the difference that mattered. He was not a lover whose fire had tamed itself into a kind of friendship; it had been a companionship in a common cause, which had deepened into one that had changed everything in his life. He had accepted it and swallowed whatever trepidation he had felt. And she knew that he had felt fear, even though it had been deep, and very private, the sort one hides inside oneself.

She thought back to her own life, the loves great and small, the good times and the pain. She and Mario Corena had had no time together except in the hectic battles of youth. She could not be sure how much she had idealized it in her mind.

Victor Narraway was real, witty and resolute, cynical in worldly matters, startlingly vulnerable at heart. And for all his experience in the Indian Army, the government and the secret services, Special Branch with its secrets and betrayals, he had little day-to-day understanding of women. Part of him expected her to be so much more fragile than she was, idealistic, unaware of the grubbier realities of life. It was part of the myth that women were gentler than men, purer and more delicate. She would have to disenchant him of that very carefully. Some dreams are hard to let go of.

There was a moment's silence, then she continued, reverting back to her original question. "Why do you think Teague is so interested in this case, Victor?"

"I don't know," he replied. "But I'm certain he has a reason. There's something he wants."

"Revenge?" she suggested quietly.

"No. No, it's far too long ago." But even as he said it he knew that time would make no difference. Teague might have been waiting for the perfect opportunity. He would not damage Narraway; he would deliberately injure the man who had taken Narraway's place, his friend and protégé, which would wound him far more painfully and add guilt to the depth of it. There was an elegance to it that was exactly Teague's nature.

"Is it?" Vespasia asked.

"Yes." He tried to sound far more certain than he was. He would fight this case to the end. He must not let Sofia be destroyed or the murder of the two women go unsolved, but above all, he must not let Teague revenge himself on Pitt.

Vespasia moved a little closer to him and linked her arm through his.

They landed in Le Havre and went straight to the train. It was a long journey to Madrid, where they spent the night before going on the following day, arriving at Toledo a little before sunset. It was a magnificent walled city dating from the great days not only of Spain's growing worldwide power, but of its medieval splendor. Tolerance had reigned supreme, Christian, Muslim and Jew had lived and worked side by side, sharing the wonders of art and knowledge freely and all profiting from its glory. Of course that was before 1492, and the expulsion of both Moors and Jews, and the rise of the Inquisition, when to be different became a sin and all questioning was forbidden.

They went straight to the hotel they had booked in advance of their arrival. They had discussed all the plans they had made and all the possible variations they could think of beforehand. Now they sat back in the carriage in silence and enjoyed the ride through the ancient streets. Many of the buildings were as they had been centuries ago.

It brought back memories to Vespasia and the years slipped away until she felt the same sense of exhilaration she had when she had first come here, seeking excitement, novelty and adventure. She had found at least some. It had been a good time.

Now she was happier than she could ever remember, even in the heady days of youth. The fact that she and her husband had come in an attempt to avoid a tragedy did not sour the underlying sense of peace.

The hotel was excellent, and after an early dinner they returned to their room.

"I have a message from one of Pitt's men," Narraway said quietly. "He followed up on a lot of the threatening letters, but didn't find anything except angry people who have nothing else about which to feel articulate or important. The main thing is that he did actually find all of the ones who put their names to their words. There are more of them in England. Once they put their rage on paper that seemed to be enough for them."

Narraway sighed. He stood with his back to the light, but not directly in front of the great window with its view over the ancient city.

"I don't think this has anything to do with Sofia's rather eccentric religious views," he said quietly. "Deeply as they will offend some people, their weapon of choice would not be to attack Cleo and Elfrida."

Vespasia frowned. "Was that not so vile in order to make us believe that Sofia really will be killed in the same way if her husband does not ruin her cause by denouncing her? That sounds religious to me, even if it is a creed of the devil." She took a breath. "That's melodramatic, isn't it? I'm sorry. But I think both you and Thomas have underestimated the power of the belief people have as to who they are in the universe. People have died for it before, tens of thousands of them."

"I know that," Narraway said gently, moving a step closer to her. "But there's something more behind this. Pitt said that Barton Hall is deeply afraid, and it's not of losing a religious battle. There is something real and measurable that's frightening him. And he daren't tell Pitt what it is, which means that it's illegal, or it's a scandal that would ruin him, or someone he cares about."

"His reputation," she agreed. "Or it's to do with a vast amount of money. And since he invests for the Church, and some of the Royal Family, either way he would indeed be ruined."

Vespasia had not told Narraway, nor anyone else for that matter, but she had read a little of the writings of certain self-proclaimed revolutionaries. They burned with anger and pity at the injustice of all social orders, the power that robbed people of dignity and hope, and too often even of life. They believed that without government, men would revert to a natural goodness, and it would be the dawn of a new age. Only one passionate, violent act was needed to initiate it and give everyone else the courage. None of them explained why the violent wars of the past had not caused such new birth.

She understood their rage and pain, but she thought them totally deluded in their philosophy, perhaps driven mad by the injustice they saw, and in most cases also experienced.

Sofia Delacruz was not angry, she was full of hope. At least that was how she had seemed. Was Vespasia so easily misled? Did the key perhaps lie in the nature of Nazario, the man she had married, and presumably loved?

But if what Barton Hall had told Pitt was true, then they were joined by an act of selfishness that had ended in tragedy for others. A woman and two children were dead as a result of adultery and abandonment. Could any happiness, let alone a bond of trust, be founded on acts so utterly callous?

Was repentance enough to expunge such horror? Sofia herself had said that repentance was incomplete if you kept the fruits of your sins. There was a natural justice that demanded you repay in some fashion. Words mattered, but if the acts negated them then the words were an added offense, a hypocrisy.

She hoped intensely that she could find some other answer to Sofia's actions, something that fitted with her words. Except, of course, that sometimes it is the bitterness of knowing what you have done that teaches change, and the understanding and need for your own forgiveness that makes you forgive others.

She must be prepared for whatever she learned.

■ ■ ■ ■

Narraway prepared to leave early, telling Vespasia only that he had no idea how long he would be gone, but that there was no cause for anxiety if he did not come back by dark.

He stood near the door from their room into the passageway to the stairs down into the main hall. It was a very comfortable hotel. He had decided they would be more conspicuous in a smaller hotel than here in what would have been a natural choice were they simply tourists. Neither had any wish to be taken for people on honeymoon, which was perhaps what they were.

Vespasia in particular felt self-conscious and rather absurd to be so happy in a condition that usually belonged to people a third her age. And yet she felt few young couples would have treasured their time together so deeply, or been so acutely aware of how precious happiness is, how easily wasted, or scarred with small acts of thoughtlessness and self-importance.

She stood now looking at him. She would like to have touched him, perhaps kissed him, but would he find it inappropriate, misplaced when he was about to go out in search of answers to horrific murders.

And yet a moment not taken might be regretted for a long time, and never completely undone. Then was her decision complete in her mind.

She walked over to him, head high as always, and touched his cheek gently. She was almost his height. "Good luck," she whispered, and kissed his cheek.

He put both arms around her for an instant, then let her go and turned to leave, but she saw the smile on his face, and the emotion that for a moment almost overwhelmed him.

When he was gone Vespasia's first action was to obtain copies of the local newspapers for the last few days, and study the Society pages. She was searching for any names with which she was familiar, and a reasonable guess as to where she might contrive to meet these people in a manner that would appear to be chance. It needed to be as soon as possible. The letter the kidnapper had sent to Pitt did not allow for much time to find Nazario Delacruz and persuade him of the issues, then accompany him back to England. More importantly than that, and weighing far more heavily, how much longer could Sofia endure such misery and pain? Her abductors might even kill her without intending to.

As Vespasia considered the matter, the obstacles to success seemed immense. And yet haste might jeopardize their slim chances of making the right decisions, choosing the right words, judging Nazario correctly. She could not start imagining the heartbreak of the decision he'd have to make; the pain of it would distract her from the only useful thing she could do.

Having studied the newspapers carefully, she knew exactly what she needed.

Accordingly, the late afternoon found her tired, suffering a little from the weariness of traveling and the considerably greater warmth of southern inland Spain, as compared with London. She dressed in one of the few more fashionable gowns she had brought with her, a warmer color than she usually wore, and very flattering.

At half past five she alighted from her hired carriage at the entrance to classical gardens where an early evening soirée was being held.

She entered with her head high, and such an air of both elegance and command that no one questioned her right to be there.

It took her half an hour of polite and completely meaningless chatter, compliments and name-dropping before she came face-to-face with the woman she had come to meet.

Dorothea Warrington was not beautiful, but she had money and a certain flair. She possessed a sharp wit and remarkable hair and she made the best of both. She stood still by the fountain in the center of the garden and stared with growing incredulity as Vespasia approached her.

"Good evening, Dorothea," Vespasia smiled. "I had no idea you were still in Spain, but it suits you admirably. I have never seen you look so very well. You make the rest of us seem positively insignificant."

Dorothea, who had left London Society under something of a shadow, and who Vespasia recalled as hating her dark, almost swarthy looks, suddenly seemed to feel much better about herself. She looked Vespasia up and down, noting her fair skin and the high carriage of her head.

"How generous of you," she replied with a tentative smile. "You are right, of course. I am enjoying it here very much." Vespasia knew she was lying. But in Toledo no one knew of her past misjudgments. "Surely at this time of the year you are here for the climate?" Her sharp eyes tried to assess Vespasia's fortunes and what kind of disaster could have driven her from the heart of the

London Season to a relatively small place like Toledo. The gleam of interest in them could be taken for concern, but it had the brilliant sheen of curiosity.

Vespasia had foreseen exactly that and was prepared.

"I have a goddaughter who has fallen in love, most unsuitably, as it turns out," she replied with a slight, graceful gesture of her shoulders as if to shrug it off.

"Oh dear," Dorothea said quickly, moving a step closer. "How unfortunate."

"Indeed." Vespasia restrained herself from moving back. "Her mother is naturally beside herself that the matter should be ended without . . . scandal. She has already made her feelings known, with the worst possible results."

"Oh dear," Dorothea murmured again, moistening her lower lip. "Young people can be so headstrong. But when we think we are in love . . ." She let the conclusion hang in the air, waiting for Vespasia to furnish more details.

"Exactly," Vespasia nearly choked on the words. She had forgotten how shallow Dorothea could be. Since her own disgrace, she seemed to relish that of others. "I see you understand. I thought I might prevail. She will at least listen to me, if I can speak to her alone. She knows that I will have her interests at heart." She wondered how much more to embellish the lie. Watching Dorothea's face, she decided to put another confidential touch to the story. "I have been in love a few times myself, and afterward wished I had listened to advice."

Dorothea's black eyebrows rose. "Haven't we all," she said softly. "Not always with fortunate results." That was possibly a bleak reference to her own exile in Spain. "Can I be of any assistance? I know a number of people."

"Perhaps," Vespasia agreed. "It may be somewhat . . . urgent."

Dorothea was elated, her eyes gleaming.

"Have you heard of a woman called Sofia Delacruz?"

Dorothea gasped. "But of course! She is very well known. For heaven's sake, you don't mean that your goddaughter has become caught up in that absurd cult? Is she in love with one of them? Then you must do all you can."

"You know something of her?" Vespasia asked innocently, her brows arched above her wonderful silver-gray eyes.

"Personally? Of course not. But I have heard. She is quite beyond eccentric. I am embarrassed to say that she is originally

English, though. But of course she married a Spaniard, so she is no longer really one of us."

Vespasia repressed a shudder of distaste for Dorothea's snobbishness.

"What is she like? Do you think it would be worth appealing to her?" she asked.

Dorothea spread her hands. "Not in the slightest. She listens to no one. She is a religious fanatic. She'll tell you all kinds of preposterous things about who she thinks you are. At least that's what I've heard. I've never met her." She waved her thin hands dramatically. "I can't stand all the earnest abstract passion. Such poor taste, don't you think? Nothing worse than a crushing bore. What on earth can you do with them?"

"Pass them on as rapidly as possible," Vespasia said instantly. "Unfortunately we cannot all agree as to who they are. Is this woman really such a bore?"

"I have no idea," Dorothea admitted. "I suppose if you truly are serious, you could go and ask the people in her organization."

"Will they not be more than a little biased?"

"You could always try the opposition," Dorothea suggested. From the flatness in her voice it was clear she was losing interest.

"Opposition?" Vespasia asked.

Dorothea gave an elaborate shrug of her shoulders. It was a gesture that fell short of elegant. "Well, my dear, she is hardly universally admired, is she? Her past is rather worse than questionable . . . don't you think? Or do you not know about it?"

Vespasia presumed she was speaking of Nazario's first wife, the tragic Luisa, but just in case she was not, she affected ignorance. Even if she were right, another more colorful and less charitable version of the story might be useful, tasteless as it would be.

"I see you don't!" Dorothea said with relish. "Very beautiful in a weird, melodramatic sort of way, if you like that kind of thing. Apparently Nazario Delacruz did . . . like it, I mean. Doesn't look like an Englishwoman in the least! All black eyes and Spanish pride. Walks as if she is on wheels."

"The . . . wife?" Vespasia had very nearly slipped and named her.

"No, of course not! Sofia! Luisa was a gentle creature, a little spoiled, perhaps. And boring, for all I know. But so are half the women in London . . . at least half."

Vespasia was beginning to feel as if she were paying dearly for these scraps of information, if they were even that.

"Indeed," she said shamelessly. "Unfortunately the interesting ones tend to leave. One cannot help wondering if that is cause and effect."

Dorothea turned that remark over in her mind suspiciously, then decided it was a rather delicious compliment.

"From a good family, of course," she continued. "I was always surprised Luisa's people didn't take some kind of revenge, on both Nazario and Sofia. Perhaps it will happen yet. I think I would want justice! Wouldn't you?" It was a direct question.

Vespasia decided to pursue it. "Yes, I think I might, if I had the courage," she agreed. "But I also could be content to bide my time, until I could do it really well, and not be caught at it."

"Don't you think the courts, or whoever it is, would understand?" Dorothea asked. "Or the police, at least?"

"I don't know. Maybe it would depend upon what private grievances they had, I suppose. Even so, I think I would prefer not to have to explain myself, or my family's tragedies, in order to avoid being punished for the vengeance . . . whatever it was."

Dorothea gave a little shiver of delight. "I'm so glad you came to Toledo. Life is going to be so much more interesting now that you are here."

"What is the name of this family?" Vespasia inquired.

Dorothea's eyes widened. "For heaven's sake, you are not going to call on them, are you? That would be . . . daring!" She meant brazen and inappropriate, and she would be delighted if Vespasia did such an indiscreet thing.

"Not at all," Vespasia denied. "But you did remark upon how surprising it is that they have not taken any vengeance on Nazario or Sofia. I wonder if there is a reason for that." She saw Dorothea's look of intense and sudden interest. "It does seem . . . unusual, don't you think?"

"Now that you mention it, yes! Yes, I do. I wonder why that should be. It's been years. I couldn't wait so long. I shall make some discreet inquiries and let you know."

"Their name?" Vespasia prompted her.

"Oh, I shall let you know," Dorothea replied airily. "Didn't I say?"

Vespasia refused to take the bait. Perhaps she had deserved this. She would despise herself as much as she despised Dorothea were the stakes any less high. Now she forced herself to smile. "I should be interested to know more about Sofia herself. But I don't imagine you could help with that."

"I . . ." Dorothea colored faintly. "I have a slight acquaintance with a nun in one of the convents on the outskirts of the old city. She might be able to help. If you wish, I can have my carriage take you there."

"Thank you, Dorothea," Vespasia accepted. She lied without hesitation. "You were always generous."

Dorothea looked startled, suspecting sarcasm, but she did not argue.

The following morning at a little after eight o'clock, Dorothea's carriage pulled up outside the high walls of the convent. The building was probably a hundred years old, beautiful in its simplicity.

Vespasia alighted and walked to the entrance, where she gave the gatekeeper her name, and requested to see Sister Maria Madalena. She also gave Sofia's name, and said that the need was very urgent.

Five minutes later she was conducted through a huge barred oak door into the silence of stone colonnades, motes of dust whirling in the slanted morning sunlight. The floors were worn uneven from centuries' passage of feet, the center of each step on the flight of stairs hollowed out.

She was shown to a quiet room filled with patterned sunlight coming in through the wrought-iron grille on the window. She sat in one of the two chairs in meditation until the door opened and Sister Maria Madalena came in.

She was a small woman with a gentle face and a very slight limp. She looked to be about Vespasia's own age. There was in her eyes a great peace, not untouched by humor.

"Lady Vespasia Narraway." She smiled, bowing very slightly, in a curiously graceful gesture. "I believe you are inquiring about Sofia Delacruz. I can tell you only what I know."

"Thank you, that is all I ask." Vespasia accepted. "Do you know her well?"

"Oh, yes," Sister Maria Madalena answered with certainty. "She came to visit us. She liked it here, the apartness from the world, you know? We often sat and talked together. We agreed about all the little things, the daily things." She smiled. "Just not on who we are, where we came from or where we are going to, or even why. Just the step by step of it." She smiled, and it illuminated her face. "It is the step by step that counts, don't you think?"

Vespasia made a sudden decision to be honest with this quiet nun who judged so wisely. "I am afraid something extremely unpleasant has happened to Señora

Delacruz, and I hope that by learning more about her, we may forestall it becoming a complete tragedy. I cannot tell you much more, except what is publicly known in London. She has been kidnapped, and two of her followers violently and very terribly killed."

Sister Maria Madalena's face showed pain, but not horror, and no incredulity at all. Vespasia wondered for an instant if she had not understood, even though Vespasia's Spanish was good.

"Oh dear," Sister Maria said quietly. "There is such terrible tragedy in the world, and such wickedness. But blazing a path isn't easy, wherever it leads." The ghost of a smile touched her lips. "Perhaps it would be wiser of me not to admit that, but an error of doctrine is a small thing compared to the love of one person for others. She does not lack courage, which will possibly be her undoing."

"Was she much resented for her beliefs?" Vespasia asked.

Sister Maria smiled. "Here, in Toledo? You do not know our history. And why should you, when you have so much of your own? But in the past we were famed for our tolerance, before the days of fear and the judgment that only one way was right. That was before the driving out of most of those whose ideas were different from our own, and the persecution of the few who remained. Then art and science flourished. Differences were no threat; they were the path to greater learning. Fear is a terrible thing, Lady Vespasia, a disease that leaps like fire from one mind to another, and burns away so much of the best in us. We stop listening and strike out too easily, before we think.

"Your question? In Toledo, the old quarters, no, we found her ideas strange and interesting. She made me reevaluate some of my own faith's teachings. I saw certain things in a different light, and at least one of them seemed the more precious for it. She made me realize that we love certainty, and often imagine we see it where in fact we do not."

"Your face says that you are not afraid," Vespasia said quietly.

"I am not. I am certain of the things that matter. Kindness and honor are always good. Do not build God in your own image, with your doubts and fears, your need to judge and condemn, your need for safety, and to be right whatever the cost to others, and ultimately to yourself. Let your soul be still, and know that God is never capricious, never cruel and never wrong. It is our understanding that stumbles. Even the cleverest of us are yet children, and the wisest of us know that."

"Was Sofia one of the wisest?" Vespasia asked.

"Good heavens, no! One of the bravest, certainly. And one of the gentlest, in her own way. She was forever seeking to help the truly penitent to find their way back to the light. That is a godly thing to do."

"You are not surprised that she should have been abducted?"

Sister Maria considered for a moment before replying, then she measured her words carefully. "Sofia worked with a great many people. I heard that she turned no one away, although a good many went of their own accord. Some of her teachings were hard, others were very gentle. She never denied food and shelter if she had it to give." She bit her lip and hesitated, then reached some inner decision. "One man came to her, shortly after there was a very brutal murder committed. A man had been found with his throat cut, and his body mutilated. I do not know what the fugitive man said to Sofia. She did not tell me and of course I did not ask. But he sought shelter with her. He was very afraid, mortally so. She was deeply disturbed by it, and confided in me that she was afraid for his life, and for his soul."

"She told you this?" Vespasia said with surprise.

"She would not have, had she not needed my help. She said he had confessed a deep sin to her, but that it was not violent, although the harm it would do was terrible. She asked me to find him shelter where he could not be reached by outside forces seeking to kill him. She gave me her word that he had not confessed to this murder, but admitted that his fear was in connection with it."

"And you believed her?" Vespasia asked, sudden new ideas whirling in her mind. Was this fugitive the key to Sofia's kidnapping? Did "outside forces" mean Sofia's abduction was political after all?

"I did. I still do. I never found Sofia in a lie of any sort, even to herself. She is the most blisteringly honest person I know, and I choose my words with care and intent. Of course I do not know if the man deceived her."

"But you sheltered him?" Vespasia said, trying to keep her voice level. "Is he still with you?"

"No. I did. It was just for a few days, and

then Sofia found her own way to protect him. I did not ask what it was, nor did she offer to tell me. I think she obtained money to look after him elsewhere, but that is only my guess."

"Thank you," Vespasia acknowledged her help. "It seems very possible that her rescue of this man may have been the cause of her present trouble. Is there nothing more that you can tell me about him? For example, how long before her departure to England did this happen?"

"Less than a month," Maria Madalena replied, her expression suddenly grave. "That is why I felt compelled to break her confidence and tell you. Please . . . do what you can to help her. Her beliefs are blasphemous to my Church, or they seem so, but she is a good woman, and to me that is all that matters. She is a child of God as much as anyone."

"I will," Vespasia promised. She rose to her feet and grasped Maria Madalena's hand for a moment. "I will," she repeated.

CHAPTER 10

Pitt stood in Inspector Latham's small, untidy office. The desk was littered with piles of reports, and two enamel mugs half full of tea. On the ashtray rested a pipe. The wooden bowl of it was stained dark with use, but it gave off a warm, rather pleasant odor.

"I've already told you . . . sir," Latham said tartly, his patience wearing thin. "Police surgeon says they died early in the evening before we found them. As near as he can be sure, within minutes of each other. It was fine and warm that day. Windows open, flies around. Unpleasant, but it helps fix the time. Probably no later than dusk. Twilight's long this time o' the year. Clear night, an' all. Light enough you wouldn't be afraid of answering the door, dark enough neighbors was inside an' probably having their dinners. If anyone did see, they'd think it was likely someone come to dinner. Two hansoms were noticed, but the witnesses can't say if it was the same one twice."

"How far apart?" Pitt asked.

"For heaven's sake, sir, people don't look at their clocks unless they're expecting someone who's late. Could've been a few minutes, or an hour. The neighbors are just beginning to get themselves together again. If you go clomping up and down asking any more questions, like those damn fellows of Mr. Teague's, you'll just upset decent people, and get a whole lot of stupid stories from those who don't know their backsides from their elbows, but want everyone to listen to them anyway. I don't know what you called him in for! We can do our job, if it can be done at all. There are some people you never catch. We had half of England trying to catch the Ripper, but we never did."

He took a deep breath and controlled his anger with an effort. "Why don't you just go and chase them dynamiters, or whatever it is you do, and leave us to sort this one? If we get even a whisper there's anybody political here, we'll call you. And can you get Teague out of the way, please? I'm all for heroes, but in their own place, not ours."

"I didn't invite him in, Inspector," Pitt said wearily. "And Sofia Delacruz *is* a political figure, and she's still missing."

"Thought she was some kind of preacher?" Latham shook his head. "Don't have no truck with it, myself. Go to church on Sundays and mind my own business. Who'd want to argue with the parson? What for?"

"Some people would argue with God," Pitt said with a sigh. "I suppose there's no more material evidence?"

"Nothing you haven't heard. Sharp knife used. Aren't many in the kitchen, but no way to know if it was one of them that was used, and the killer took it away, or if he brought his own."

"Do you know for certain that it was one man?" Pitt asked.

"Looks like it," Latham answered. He picked up his pipe from the ashtray but did not relight it, just held it comfortably in his hand, as if he liked the feel of the smooth wood.

Pitt frowned. "How? Would you go alone to kill two women and kidnap a third who would certainly fight you? In fact probably attack you to try to save the other two? I would take someone with me. Sofia Delacruz would be sure to attack right back. She wouldn't run to save herself. And she'd scream for certain."

"I've thought about it, sir," Latham answered. "First off, if I were going to do something as horrible as this, I wouldn't be letting anyone else know I did it, or he'd have me for the rest of my life. Unless I killed him too, that is. But I'd be afraid he'd think of that and get me first."

Pitt nodded.

"I'd go alone," Latham went on, his voice quiet, his confidence growing as Pitt did not challenge him. "I'd watch from outside. Dusk already. There'd be lights on in the house, so I'd have an idea where the different women were."

Pitt thought of the garden and places near bushes, on the edge of the property where a man could linger, perhaps with a dog, or to smoke a pipe without raising suspicion.

"Makes sense," he said quietly. "Find any evidence?"

"Some," Latham answered. "Soil's a bit dry, but there are clear enough parts to show that someone stood for a while near the bushes up the side path next door." Latham sucked on the stem of his pipe for a moment. "No way to know if it was him, but could have been."

Latham put the pipe aside. "I would have watched there before, seen their habits, then that evening I would have waited until one of them was upstairs and the one in the kitchen was alone. I'd have dealt with her quickly, got the second one while the third one was upstairs, not able to come down without passing me and escaping."

"Got to be very quick," Pitt said thoughtfully. "It looked like he killed the one in the kitchen first, then when the other one ran away, he chased after her up the stairs. Why she didn't go out into the street, I've no idea."

"The front door was locked," Latham answered. "Top bolt and side one. She was a small woman. Couldn't have reached up and undone it before he'd have grabbed her. And he was between her and the back door." As Latham spoke, Pitt could picture it in his mind and it turned his stomach with pity. "And Sofia still upstairs too. Poor soul," Latham added bitterly. "Cleo or Elfrida must have let him in at the back. He wouldn't have bolted the door himself, an' neither of them could 'ave reached it. Taller woman could have, I suppose."

"Only if they were expecting him to stay all night," Pitt answered. "Which would mean one of their own."

"Perhaps," Latham thought aloud. "Thought he was there to protect them — poor devils. Couldn't 'ave been the little

Spanish chap, then. He wouldn't have reached the top bolt either."

"Melville Smith could have," Pitt said. "But his time is accounted for all evening. Might anyone have come back? Bolted the door later?"

"Why, for God's sake, would anyone come back?" Latham said reasonably. "I used to think we'd got a common-or-garden lunatic. Nothing to do with who she was. But the ransom makes it different. Now I don't know what to think, except that it was the kind of violence you don't use on a stranger, unless you're barking mad. Makes more sense it was someone who knew her, and hated her, as well as wanting something so bad he'd do anything to get it. We checked everyone who came with her, and we didn't see anything that . . . personal.

"As far as opportunity — they all vouch for one another, and why wouldn't they? If one of them did it, they're likely all in it, or got reason to cover for whoever it is. If you ask me, they're all a bit touched."

Pitt did not argue. He thanked Latham and took his leave.

Outside it was a brisk and windy day. People on foot were walking quickly, one or two women clutching at hats with brims that lifted and threatened to blow away.

Pitt was deep in thought, grateful for Latham's cooperation. The police did not always work easily with Special Branch. They felt a clash of jurisdiction and as if they were left with the worst to do while others took the credit.

He had reached the curb of the main thoroughfare when he became aware of Frank Laurence beside him.

"A little desperate, are we?" Laurence said cheerfully. "Kidnapper hasn't asked for a ransom yet? That doesn't look good. Don't suppose they accidentally killed her, do you? She looked like the sort of woman who would put up a good fight."

Pitt stopped abruptly and swung around to face him, aching to wipe the smirk off his face.

"This is not a game!" he said furiously. "She is a human being with people she loves, dreams and beliefs just like the rest of us. She's not some figure of your imagination you can manipulate to sell more of your damn newspapers!"

Laurence's eyes widened, but he was not in the least taken off balance. Pitt realized in that instance that Laurence had said what he had precisely to provoke Pitt into losing his temper. Angry men make mistakes, say more than they mean to.

"You really are afraid she's dead!" Laurence said softly. "Ransom too high, is it?"

"That is none of your business," Pitt snapped, starting to walk rapidly across the street.

Laurence kept pace. "If it's come down to money, perhaps the noble Mr. Teague will come up with it. That would really make him a hero, wouldn't it? I can see the headlines now: Dalton Teague pays a king's ransom to save the life of a Spanish saint whose every word he disagrees with! Perhaps he kidnapped her in the first place, so he could rescue her in public? Pay his fortune back to himself. Do you suppose there is some insurance that would cover it?"

"Why don't you write it and find out?" Pitt suggested tartly. "Except that of course Teague would ruin you."

"Indeed," Laurence said with a twisted smile. "That is exactly what he would do. And I wouldn't be the first man he ruined. You should think of that, Mr. Pitt. Take a good look at Dalton Teague's career, and what has happened to those who stood up against him."

"Did you?" Pitt asked. "Did you stand up to him, and suffer for it? Is that what this is really about?"

"It's about Sofia Delacruz, and whoever murdered Cleo and Elfrida," Laurence answered. "Isn't it?" He gave a slight shrug. "Or is it about terrorism, and the war between Spain and America, and whether it eventually escalates into a world war? If it does, which side do you think we will be on?"

"Have you got anything helpful to say?" Pitt asked.

"Yes, as a matter of fact I have," Laurence retorted. "You might look into the relationship between Teague and Barton Hall."

"You said that before," Pitt agreed. "They were at the same school, at the same time. As were you, which you rather neatly evaded when we spoke about it before, yet you talk about Teague at every opportunity."

Laurence raised an eyebrow. "Have you ever been on a school sports team, Pitt? Or a college team? Do you know the kind of loyalty that creates? Do you know how sports teams are worshipped by others, especially those who almost always win? What it is to be part of the 'in' circle?" His face darkened. "Or what it is like to be the swot, the one who doesn't hit the ball, doesn't score the runs?" There was a bitter edge to his voice. "And yet you can pass the exams . . . can't you? You can do the maths, write the essays, even understand and remember the lessons of history. Wasn't it the Duke of Wellington who said that the Battle of Waterloo was won on the playing fields of Eton?"

He looked quizzically at Pitt. "Well he was right; a lot of things are won and lost on school playing fields, Commander. You might remember that." And with a little mock salute he turned and walked away, leaving Pitt standing on the pavement, trying to see order in the confusion. He could not pin it down, but there was something there, something to do with Teague and Spain, and Laurence intended Pitt to find it.

Dalton Teague was brought to Pitt's mind again within the hour. He returned to Lisson Grove to find Stoker fuming with anger. His bony face was white and he was so stiff he refused to sit down.

"His damn men are everywhere!" he said as soon as Pitt was through the door. "Now he's got Russell eating out of his hand. It's Teague this, and Teague that! Doesn't listen to me anymore! And what's the result? Gone careering off up to Nottingham on a false trail. Turns out the woman's a damn gypsy. No more Sofia Delacruz than I am."

It was not the first time Special Branch had followed a lead that turned out to be useless. Rather a lot of them had come through Teague on this case, but their own leads had been no better.

"Papers got it?" Pitt asked, walking past Stoker and sitting down at his desk. He saw the pile of reports on it and realized how much was being set aside because of Sofia's disappearance. He hardly even recalled the details of the sabotage in the London factories. Dalton Teague's meddling, his pronouncements to the press, were all keeping it at the forefront of people's minds, so imaginations were running wild.

Was Teague being manipulated by someone far cleverer than he? That possibility had crossed Pitt's mind lately. Did they look at this handsome man with his grace and his connections, and play on his hunger for adulation? Could it all be a sleight of hand, and Pitt was taking the bait?

Or was Laurence trying to lead him into finding some fact about Teague that held a real meaning?

Current unrest was mild in Britain, compared with the rest of Europe. Even in the United States they were having troubles of protest and unease, a new class of urban poor uniting and demanding privileges previously unthought of. There had been very considerable violence. Was it building up here too, but Pitt was too busy being a policeman, too focused on one problem as he used to be in his Bow Street days, and so was blind to the greater picture, the very thing Narraway had cautioned him against?

"Russell's a good man," he said aloud. "Tell him not to be such a damn fool. Take a look at those reports," he waved toward the papers on his desk. "I'm going to find Teague and tell him to lower the profile."

"He won't do that," Stoker said flatly. "He's like a hardmouthed horse with the bit between his teeth. I don't know what you think you'll achieve."

"I don't expect to change his mind," Pitt replied with a tight smile. "I want to learn a bit more about him, see if I can work out what he knows, and what he's really trying to do."

Stoker's eyes widened. "D'you think he has anything to do with her disappearance, sir? That would mean he knows who killed the two women. But I can't see him as an anarchist or anything like that. He's a dyed-in-the-wool aristocrat. Generations of privilege behind him. Probably got ancestors back to the Norman Conquest!" He said it with an air of disgust.

"We all do, Stoker, it's just that his were on horseback and yours and mine were on foot, and on the wrong side," Pitt observed. "And no, I don't think for a moment that he's intentionally with anarchists. Teague is with Teague, and a man like that can be used."

"Yes, sir!" Stoker was already sitting at Pitt's desk and beginning to go through the piles of paper by the time Pitt reached the door.

"And Stoker," Pitt said, pausing at the threshold.

"Yes, sir?"

"Find out if Teague has any connections in Spain, will you? Any at all."

"You think he does?" Stoker said with surprise.

"I don't know. Just something Frank Laurence said."

Pitt reached Teague in the quiet lounge in one of the gentlemen's clubs. Teague leaned back in the armchair, stretching out his long legs, ankles crossed, staring up at Pitt, a crystal sherry glass in his hand.

"Dear fellow, good to see you," he said with a casual smile. "Do sit down. Can I have the steward bring you a glass of sherry? I can recommend the Amontillado."

Pitt knew perfectly well that the phrasing of the invitation was intended to leave him uncertain if he was being offered the sherry, or expected to pay for it himself. He was not a member of the club, although Narraway had convinced him of the necessity of belonging to a couple of others. It had nothing to do with the cachet of social acceptance, but rather a matter of who was confiding in whom, who was in and who out. Sometimes it was as subtle as a tone of voice, the lifting of an eyebrow, the omission of some seemingly trivial topic, two people avoiding leaving at the same time so it might be assumed they were not close.

"No, thank you," Pitt replied. "A little early for me."

Teague smiled, but his eyes were cold. "Very right of you," he agreed. "No doubt you have a great many other issues to take care of." He uncrossed his legs and recrossed them the opposite way. "I admit, I am beginning to appreciate rather more just how enormous Special Branch's task is. How on earth do you keep track of it all? It is sort of . . . amorphous! Thousands of people across Europe are restless, looking for a way to lash out at authority. You can't possibly watch all of them. How do you know which one is reveling in the sound of his own voice, and which will actually throw a bomb one day?" He looked interested, his head a little to one side, the late sunlight through the window creating a halo around his magnificent hair.

"Most of them are not my problem," Pitt said with a smile, sitting down opposite him, almost as much at ease, at least on the surface. "It is largely their own leaders they want to blow up rather than ours."

"That's your answer?" Teague said incredulously. "It's not your problem?"

Pitt realized his flippancy was going to be turned against him, very rapidly, if he were not more careful. "We watch and observe," he replied levelly, holding Teague's eye. "We warn other governments if we learn anything they should know. As they warn us."

"How do you know they are telling the truth?" Teague pressed.

"We don't. We file it away, and make our own judgments."

Teague's eyebrows rose. "You must have a memory like an elephant, keeping all those thousands of lists so you can put them together and see some sense. That's what one of your fellows told me. You can make any picture you want out of most of them. Takes a very clever man to make the right one." He looked as if he were half asleep, even a little drunk, but Pitt noticed that his hand around the stem of his glass was rock steady and under the drooping lids his eyes were needle-sharp.

"One gets used to certain patterns," Pitt answered. "Quite often it's the one piece that doesn't fit that makes you see the picture's real shape."

"How interesting," Teague murmured. He put up his hand to catch the steward's attention and the man was at his side in moments.

"Yes, Mr. Teague, sir? May I bring you something?"

"Thank you, Hythe. Commander Pitt is still engaged in business. May we have a pot of tea?" He turned to Pitt. "Do you prefer Chinese, or Indian?"

"Indian, thank you," Pitt accepted. He would definitely enjoy a cup of tea, or several, but whether he did or not, to refuse would be clumsy.

"Yes, sir. I'll bring it immediately." Hythe bowed and left.

"I prefer Indian myself," Teague agreed. "Back to this likeness of a jigsaw that you mentioned. It is a most vivid analogy. The piece that doesn't fit, eventually, because you are trying to make the wrong picture out of it. If I understand you rightly — and

I have observed your men gathering all kinds of pieces that seem trivial, unrelated — they never ignore any of them. The intelligent ones don't anyway. Stoker is a good man, quiet, steady, observant, loyal, and I should think the right man to have beside you in a fight. Does it ever come to that?"

"Very seldom." Pitt leaned back, reclining as casually as Teague was. He would never be as elegant, but he knew how to look at ease.

"All the same, there must be times when it counts. Although speed and strength will never surpass intelligence." Teague was looking at Pitt very steadily. His eyes were as much green as blue. "These pieces you collect. For example?" He ticked them off on his long fingers. "Sofia Delacruz is a beautiful woman, lit from within by an extraordinary passion. She is married to a Spaniard who lives in Toledo. She has started this eccentric and absurd new religion, which she seems to believe, and is prepared to cling on to at whatever cost. She left England, and her family, in rebellion against a marriage she did not want. She fell in love with a man who was already married. His wife killed herself, and their children. Sofia has come to England to preach this extraordinary creed. She is upsetting the Establishment. Her only relative is Barton Hall. She says she wishes to meet him, but doesn't say why. She makes no moderation in her radical preaching. She disappears, possibly with the connivance of her own people. There are threats against her life, at least some of which have to be taken seriously. Am I correct so far?"

"Yes." Pitt could not argue. "What picture are you making of the pieces?" He was curious to know.

"I'm certain we don't have them all," Teague replied, his eyes not moving from Pitt's. "Why did she really come? She doesn't care about Hall, and he certainly doesn't care about her. In fact she is a considerable embarrassment to him. They have a far better chance of reconciliation if they leave as wide a distance between themselves as possible. Surely she knows that?"

"Then one necessary piece is the reason she really came," Pitt concluded. He knew that Teague was watching him just as closely, judging every conflict, every shadow, every word said or unsaid.

"Of course you know that," Teague smiled very slightly. "Let us consider what shape that piece is. I think it fits right in the middle, don't you?"

"Yes," Pitt agreed. "I would be surprised if it didn't." He allowed Teague to lead. He wanted to know where he was going.

"Have you ever noticed how a room changes if you move the light?" Teague continued. "Shadows fall in different places. Different directions change the look of everything."

Pitt was startled by his perception, and a little uncomfortable. It was an image he had not thought of. His mind started to play with it.

Teague smiled quite openly now. "You have had the light on Sofia. What if you move it to Barton Hall? What do you see then?" He was watching Pitt intently, as a cat watches a mouse hole in the wall.

Pitt considered for a moment. It was not a question of what he saw in Hall, but of what he wanted Teague to think he did, and perhaps even more, of what Teague wanted him to see! This was an opportunity to shine the light on Teague. Without appearing to, he could ask all manner of questions, and what he would not say to Teague was how much you could learn not only from what a person answered, but how they answered, what they volunteered even though you had not asked, the silence they had filled in unnecessarily. Above all, it was what they did not say. This was an opening he might never have again.

"I see a man who is related to a very troublesome woman," he answered. "But who is closely involved in spite of himself because he is the only family she has in England. He disapproves intensely of her beliefs, and finds her open preaching of them in his own country most embarrassing."

Teague smiled tolerantly. "But that is not new, Mr. Pitt. She has apparently been doing this for years."

"Not in England." Pitt saw a sudden opening. He pursued it. "This is the first time she has come here and commanded large audiences, right under his nose."

Teague smiled. "So you think he was so hysterical about it that he had her kidnapped?" His voice was gently reproving, as if a favorite pupil had disappointed him. "With what result? She is now known by millions rather than a few hundred. She is no longer the troublemaker disturbing people's quiet, habitual certainties. She has become the victim of brutal suppression, by murder, of a person's right to believe as they choose, and speak their faith."

He leaned forward with a sudden urgency, so his physical presence was intense. "Barton Hall is not a fool, Pitt. He is a highly intelligent man. His brain works swiftly and easily. He may be a little hide-bound in his imagination, but he has some vision, and a fine grasp of detail, judgment and, at times, courage. He is responsible for investing part of the great fortunes of the Church and of the Crown! Do you think he would do something so foreseeably idiotic?"

Pitt had to keep the excitement out of his voice. "You sound as if you know him quite well, Mr. Teague."

"I do! For God's sake, man, I went to school with him. I probably knew him better than his own family did. He was a swot, but a damn good one. He sailed through exams the rest of us labored for." He pursed his lips very slightly, as if he were dismissing something in modesty. "Not I, but . . . most people. We studied together sometimes, helping, challenging . . . you understand it?" He knew perfectly well that Pitt had not been to any university, let alone Cambridge. He did not know that Pitt had actually been privately tutored at the manor in which Pitt's mother had worked, before his father's conviction and transportation to Australia.

Pitt smiled. He spoke with calculation. "Yes, I do. I was tutored with Sir Arthur Desmond's son. Privately, of course, but the principle is the same. A little friendly rivalry, perhaps a little not quite so friendly. It was both a help and a spur."

Teague's eyes widened. For a moment he was caught wrong-footed, a rare experience for him.

"We came to know each other very well, and perhaps in ways no one else could have," Pitt continued. "I should have taken more notice of your opinion of Hall." He smiled, waiting.

Teague was still on the wrong foot and for a moment not sure how to reply. He made the decision quickly. He was used to it. When a cricket ball is flying through the air at you, you have less than a second to decide exactly how you will strike it.

"My fault," Teague said ruefully. "I should have informed you. I admit, I had not until very recently appreciated how responsible Hall might be in this whole business. I was entirely bent on trying to find out where Sofia Delacruz is. Or was."

"You have evidence to suggest she's not alive?" Pitt asked.

Teague drew in his breath. "Oh, no, not at all. Surely if anyone wished her dead, they would simply have killed her there on Inkerman Road, with the other women? Why keep her alive, if not for some purpose? If a ransom is asked, you will not give it unless you know she is alive . . . will you?"

"No," Pitt agreed. "Of course not."

"But no ransom has been asked?"

Pitt had no hesitation in answering. "Not a penny . . . so far. Perhaps they are playing a cat and mouse game with us, until we are so desperate we make a mistake?"

Teague stared at him. "Maybe. But the time will come, and I think soon, when they will have to make a move. Can we afford to delay? What if they become desperate and lose their nerve?"

"Then they will kill her, and escape," Pitt answered. "I'm curious — knowing Hall as you do, what do you see when you turn the light on him?"

Teague answered straightaway. "I see a man who has plunged into something far deeper than he realized, and has found himself drowning." His voice was perfectly level, and yet there was emotion in it, curious and impossible to identify. Part of it was pain, but there was no way to tell if it was old or new. "He is terrified and has no idea where to turn." He looked straight into Pitt's eyes without flinching.

"I agree with you," Pitt hesitated only a moment. To have disagreed would have tipped his hand. Teague knew he was not that much of a fool. If he earned Teague's contempt intellectually as well as possibly socially, he would have put himself at a great disadvantage. As it was, Teague was playing with him, enjoying the game. Pitt needed to play it too, in order to learn, to read and interpret the omissions, to play it at Teague's pace, his way, let him reveal what he did not mean to. He kept his own face bland. "But that does not mean his fear is to do with Sofia's disappearance, or any guilt he has in it beyond lending Melville Smith the house on Inkerman Road."

He saw the flash of understanding in Teague's eyes, just a very slight widening, but for the first time the man hesitated before replying. Then he recrossed his legs again. It was a casual, very elegant gesture, consciously so.

"I agree," Teague said. "It might be quite unrelated. I am sure you are already familiar with his professional responsibilities. His anxieties may be in that direction and Sofia no more than a distraction. It would explain why he did not find time to see her, or insist on making the opportunity, immediately after she arrived in England. To a banker, religion is part of the bedrock of society, but not a matter for any kind of question, still less any change. Bankers hate change.

Money and trust are the realities. He does not wish to appear callous regarding her disappearance, but it is not the cause of his fear. Have you the power to investigate that?" For an instant there was a shadow across his eyes.

Pitt saw it. "Not easily, but if there is some cause, I can inquire." He watched Teague minutely, his face, his long hands lying in his lap, even the tension in his body so gracefully sprawled in the chair. "Do you think I should?"

Teague took a shallow breath, and let it out slowly. "I think you would be unwise not to, Mr. Pitt."

By late afternoon Pitt had learned little of Barton Hall that was not already in the public knowledge, and he was again sent for by Sir Walter.

"What the devil does Hall's banking have to do with Sofia Delacruz's disappearance?" Sir Walter demanded when Pitt stood in his office, the late sun golden on the carpet bringing out the colors. "Do you have any idea what you are asking?"

"Yes, sir," Pitt replied gravely. Sir Walter was clearly tired and no doubt beginning to taste failure in the case. Pitt played his strongest card. "I know that Hall's bank holds a considerable amount of money for both the Crown and the Church of England, therefore its reputation must be above reproach."

"Exactly," Sir Walter agreed. "Questioning them would be tantamount to a suggestion that there could be something . . . amiss. Banks around the world survive on the world's confidence in them. It's all one vast house of cards. A bad enough disaster in one of them can spread until they are all tainted. Then panic sets in . . ."

"I want to prevent such a suggestion from ever happening." Pitt kept his voice level, free from the anxiety he felt. "Before it is even whispered about."

"Before what is whispered about, Pitt? Stop dancing around like a damn ballerina and tell me what you mean."

"The suggestion that I look into a few matters, very discreetly, was made by Mr. Dalton Teague, sir. In view of his standing, and his long acquaintance with Mr. Hall, I dare not ignore it."

"I see." Sir Walter thought for a moment, weighing the two sides of the matter before conceding. "Then I suppose you had better do it. I'll get you the appropriate permission. Best not to let Hall know himself. Keep this very quiet indeed, Pitt. Even a whisper could bring ruin to a great many important families. Only takes a word to start a run on a bank. You had better not tread heavily with those big feet of yours!" He smiled bleakly, the shadows of exhaustion like bruises on his face.

"No, sir," Pitt said quietly. "You won't even find my prints."

Before going to the bank with the necessary documents of permissions, Pitt went back to his own office. He read again through Sofia's letters and papers that had been taken from Angel Court. With notes from them he then went to the bank, where Sir Walter had smoothed his path to absolute discretion and he read the records of Hall's investments, working far into the night. His eyes were weary in the gaslight, and the bank guard was pacing impatiently outside the locked private office when he finally found what he believed was at least the beginning of the answer.

Hall had invested a great deal of money in land in Canada, an amount that to Pitt seemed like a king's ransom. Most of it belonged to the Church of England, and at first it seemed no different than the many other purchases of land the Church already possessed, and from which it drew a huge income. Only with several handwritten notes, hard to read, did Pitt realize that Hall was now trying desperately to raise a similar amount from other sources.

Was it possible that it was this that had brought Sofia to London, and to see Hall? Was it speculation from which she expected to profit? Or was it a disaster she hoped to prevent?

He did not wish to think that it was a terrible error for which she intended to manipulate him into some act he would not otherwise contemplate, but of course it was possible. Had she meant to warn him, help him, blackmail him, or ruin him? And how had she learned about it in the first place?

Whatever the answers were might now cost her her life.

He made notes, incomprehensible to anyone else, then he returned all the files and documents to exactly the places he had found them and told the guard he was ready to leave.

The man looked at him with suspicion and resentment.

"Thank you," Pitt said graciously. He was perfectly happy to lie; he could see the necessity for it. "I believe what I am looking for is not here, but I appreciate your time so that I could assure myself of it. Good night."

"Good night, sir," the man replied, somewhat mollified. "Glad you didn't find it here, sir, if you'll not mistake my meaning. We take care of some very important people. Wouldn't do for them to be uncomfortable. Might lose their business."

"Quite," Pitt agreed. And he felt the weight of that knowledge heavy on his mind as he went out into the warm night oppressed by possibilities that had not even crossed his mind before. Perhaps Narraway was right, and it was to do with money after all. If the anarchists wanted to bring down governments, then a scandal that ruined a bank, and the ensuing collapse that would spread around the world like fire across the plains, consuming everything, would be far more effective than any individual assassinations, no matter who was killed.

Chapter 11

Vespasia finished talking with Narraway about what she had heard from Sister Maria Madalena. He had listened without interrupting her, his face grave. When he finally spoke it was with more emotion than she had expected.

"There's something very major that we don't know," he said softly. "The more I hear about Sofia, the more I am obliged to take her faith seriously. Not that I believe it is true, but I have to accept that she does. The dilemma about what to do gets worse with every new fact." He took a deep breath, his eyes unmoving from Vespasia's face. "I think she will die before she denies it."

They were sitting in the hotel on a balcony overlooking a small square, the evening light gold and long-shadowed across the cobbled street. It was completely without wind; the leaves hung motionless. A lean, handsome young man swaggered up the middle of the street as if he owned it. He went into the engraver's shop opposite. Toledo steel was famous around the world.

"She knows something that they will torture her to death in order to learn," Narraway went on quietly. "And it has its roots here in Spain. Someone confessed something to her."

"Will it help if we know what?" Vespasia asked.

"Possibly. But we need to know who too," he answered. "The details might matter."

"Maybe the man Sister Maria told me of, who confessed to Sofia, lied about the violence," she suggested. "Perhaps he did kill the man they found eviscerated, or at least knew who had done it."

Narraway frowned. "I think she would have made him repent of it, and tell the police, at least to stop anyone else from being blamed."

"Are you certain it is not anything to do with revenge by the family of his first wife? It's a fearful grief to lose your child by suicide, and your grandchildren by murder. I suppose it's impossible Nazario caused it directly somehow? Do you think that would be what this is about? Whether it is true or not, they believe he killed them all?"

"There's a great deal still to learn," he agreed.

Vespasia looked at him in the fading light. The gold in it made his skin look even darker, his eyes black. He easily could have been Spanish himself. Only because she knew him did she see the anxiety in his face.

"What is it?" she said quietly. "What are you thinking?"

He smiled bleakly. "I have no reason to believe Nazario himself is guilty, but we mustn't forget that possibility."

"Do we know if his wife's family blames Sofia?" She was afraid of the answer, but she had to ask. Why would it hurt her if they did? Did she really admire the woman she was coming to know so much that it would darken a hope, or a dream, if she was to blame? Did Sofia forgive so passionately because she understood the need to be forgiven? If so, had Vespasia never walked that path herself that she was so quick to judge, or to be disappointed?

She was aware of Narraway watching her, perhaps more closely than she wished. How vulnerable it made her to care so much about what he thought; how much of her he read!

"No," he said with slight surprise. "I wasn't able to get a sense of who was truly at fault in the matter. I would like to know more, but there isn't time. I think I must go and see Nazario himself tomorrow."

But it proved far more difficult than he had expected. Inquiries at the old abbey where Sofia and Nazario lived elicited the fact, told reluctantly, that Nazario had spent the last several weeks in a monastery many miles outside the city, where he had been helping the people of the nearest village. It was apparently something he did regularly. No one knew when he was due back to Toledo. There was nothing for Narraway to do but hire a guide, and a horse, and travel to the monastery.

He returned to the hotel and told Vespasia of it, somewhat to her alarm. He saw, wryly and with a degree of self-consciousness, that she was afraid for him.

"My dear," he said gently. "I began my career in the Indian Army. I am perfectly comfortable riding a horse. I have even fought battles with a saber in one hand and reins in the other. I shall manage to ride at a decent pace along a rather good road, I promise you." He leaned forward and touched her cheek, closing his eyes and feeling the softness of her skin. In part he did not wish to embarrass her further by seeing the hot color as she blushed, but he was also aware of how much they did not yet know each other.

She searched for words, and found none, so she touched him gently, and bit her lip as she watched him leave.

It was several hours' ride through the deepening evening light from Toledo to the monastery, but Narraway enjoyed it. It was a long time since he had ridden a horse at all, let alone a strong animal such as he had now, both eager and biddable, picking its way along what was clearly a familiar path. To begin with he sat in the saddle comfortably, but he knew that by the end of the journey his body would be aching. He must not let his pride make him ridiculous by denying it. It would be an easy mistake, and the thought of it brought heat to his face.

He relaxed and gave the horse its head. He stared around him with interest. Some of the landscape he could see brought back memories of India, even though it resembled it very little. It was a quality in the light, the width of the view and the shadows on the horizon, the warmth of the air on his face, but perhaps most of all the sway in the saddle, the constant adjustment of his weight, the smells of earth and dust and crushed herbs.

And he admitted this was also the chance to put off a little longer the need to face Nazario Delacruz and tell him of the ransom demand. He was further pleased to delay the time when he must come to some judgment of the man. It was instinctive after so many years to make assessments of people, but he disliked it more and more as he moved away from command of Special Branch. There was a freedom in not having to be right. Now mistakes, however serious, would be no more than an embarrassment. The responsibility was all Pitt's.

Except that if you had the power, you also had the obligation. It was not society that told you that, it was your own inner consciousness. So there was nowhere to escape.

Some of the time the pathway was steep and it was natural to ride behind rather than beside his guide, but on the occasions when he could, he struck up a conversation with him.

"Señor Delacruz comes to this monastery often?" he asked.

"Yes," the guide agreed.

"How often? Every month?"

The guide shrugged and smiled. "Maybe."

"Why?"

"Is good place." The guide crossed himself absentmindedly. "Good men. Care for poor, for sick."

Was this where Sofia had hidden the fugitive she was protecting? Perhaps Nazario was looking after him now?

"And penitents?" he asked aloud. He had no idea how to say "fugitives seeking asylum" in Spanish. And if he did, he might be taken for an agent of the Spanish government, or an informer in general.

The guide shrugged and turned his face forward, evasive again. The conversation was finished.

They arrived after dark, when the summer sky was burning with stars. They were so dense here, far from any city lamps, that the arch above them was like a milky smear across to the darker rims of the horizon.

The monastery stood alone on high ground, its squared outlines like battlements. The path toward it was steep and the horse slowed. Narraway dismounted to walk his animal, and found he was indeed horribly stiff. He was glad of the darkness to hide it. Not that his guide would have been rude enough to have remarked on it.

The guide knocked on the huge iron ring mounted on the oak door and when it swung wide he explained in Spanish as much as he knew of Narraway. There was no mistaking the warning in his voice as he told the gatekeeper why Narraway had come. Narraway understood enough of it to know that their earlier conversation about the penitent was repeated.

The monk rang an iron bell hanging from the rough stone of the entrance. Within a couple of moments another monk appeared and took the horses.

Narraway and the guide were led in, everything said once in Spanish and again in English. They were offered food and shelter, but before accepting, Narraway explained to the abbot that his business was with Nazario Delacruz, and concerned a profound danger to his family. He must be informed immediately, and privately.

The abbot made no demur, and within ten minutes Narraway sat across a wooden table, polished by centuries of use, and faced Nazario.

"What can I do for you, señor?" Nazario asked courteously. He was a man of approximately Narraway's height, perhaps an inch taller, but he was also lean and wiry, and dark.

Narraway hated what he had to do, but there was no possible escape. To be evasive only added to the inevitable pain. He must stop visualizing himself in the same dilemma. And remember that this man had apparently left his wife and children for Sofia, the grief of which had brought about their deaths. Narraway wondered if this had been deliberate cruelty, or simply self-indulgence, weakness, Nazario's yielding everything to his own needs.

And of course nothing ruled out the possibility that he himself was in some way, directly or indirectly, responsible for Sofia's abduction.

Narraway must tell him what he had to in such a way that if there was anything at all to be learned from Nazario's reactions, he would do so.

"My name is Narraway," he introduced himself. "I used to be head of British Special Branch, to do with —"

"I know who they are," Nazario interrupted him. "What do you want in Toledo? If we have revolutionaries here, I don't know of them. And before you ask any further, I don't wish to know." He spoke in fluent and easy English, even though Narraway had spoken to him in Spanish.

"Actually, so far as I know, this has nothing to do with revolution," Narraway replied. "But it is interesting that that is the first thing that comes to your mind."

Nazario frowned. "You are British Special Branch. What else could it have to do with?

What do you mean, so far as you know?"

Narraway drew in his breath to explain that he was retired, and then changed his mind.

"I'm deeply sorry, Señor Delacruz," he said, his mouth unexpectedly dry, "but your wife has been kidnapped. We don't know by whom. We have done everything —" He stopped, seeing the stunned incomprehension on Nazario's face, and then almost immediately the beginning of a terrible comprehension. "Do you have any idea who would do this?"

Nazario shook his head as if words were impossible for him.

"But you understand?" Narraway insisted.

"Of course I understand," Nazario said sharply. "I speak English!"

"I know you do," Narraway said gently. "I meant that you are not amazed, not incredulous."

"No . . . no, there have been threats against her, many times. None of them has resulted in anything beyond unpleasantness before though. This is different, isn't it?" His voice wavered a little. His eyes searched Narraway's. "I see by your face that there is more. What is it? Please do not play games of words with me. You are speaking of my wife. Is it to do with anarchists or not?"

"We don't know what it is to do with," Narraway said frankly. "But two of the women who were with her were killed." He watched Nazario's face intently.

"Who?" Nazario asked.

"Cleo and Elfrida," Narraway replied.

Nazario's face was pinched with grief and he maintained his composure with difficulty. "But you think Sofia is still alive?" There was a desperate hope in his eyes, and yet also an even sharper fear than before. He knew something far beyond what he was revealing.

"I am almost sure of it," Narraway answered. "I know nothing for certain, or I would tell you." With a vividness he would rather not have felt, he imagined this man's terror. His love for Vespasia, his total commitment to her, had altered his ability to play the game of interrogation in the old way. Perhaps it would also give him a compensating new insight? He needed it, however painful it would be.

"What do you know?" Nazario pressed. He was clearly clinging on to his dignity with difficulty, trying not to break down in front of a stranger, and a foreigner. Narraway knew it did not help that he was English, of all things. They were a famously unemotional race.

"They have asked for a ransom," Narraway told him. "They know that before we paid anything at all we needed proof that she is alive. As of seven days ago she was."

Nazario leaned forward.

"Ransom? How much? I have very little, enough to live on, no more. But there are many people I can ask." There was a lift in his voice as if he dared to hope. "How much, Señor Narraway?"

Narraway felt sick at what he would have to say to this man sitting across the table from him.

"It is not money," he replied. "Señor Delacruz, I need your help, your honesty and clear sight in this. The situation is, I believe, extremely complicated. You know some of the people involved but possibly not all of them. I am not willingly playing with your feelings in telling you this a piece at a time, I am trying to learn from you all that I can. I think knowledge is the only effective weapon that we have."

"Knowledge?" Nazario said hoarsely. "Knowledge of what? What do you need?"

"I will tell you what has happened as far as we understand it, and I expect you to explain it for me, if you can."

Narraway told the facts simply, without

complicating the narrative with other names.

"We were warned that there might be threats against your wife. We took what we thought were reasonable precautions. However, she disappeared, along with the two women who were very brutally murdered, in a house on Inkerman Road, only two miles from Angel Court, where they had been staying."

Nazario remained motionless.

"We had thought at first that it might be a deliberate tactic to gain some attention . . ." He saw Nazario's face darken with anger, and that he controlled himself with difficulty.

"Melville Smith has admitted to helping them, and finding the place in Inkerman Road," Narraway went on. "Not for publicity, although he did cash in on that, but he said to protect Sofia, and we believe that was true, even if his motives were mixed."

"He wants a simpler teaching," Nazario said, his voice tight with strain. "Gain more followers by making it softer, easier . . . and untrue. He has for years, and she would never agree with him. Even so, I did not think he would kill."

"Neither do we," Narraway agreed. "The house belongs to Barton Hall, whom I believe was the real reason your wife went to England . . ." He waited, watching Nazario.

"Yes," Nazario conceded, lowering his eyes. "Hall is a cousin of hers." He looked up again, his eyes desperate. "She would not tell me why she was going, only that it was absolutely necessary. I begged her not to, or to allow me to go with her, but she insisted I had business here, which I do, and that this was something she must do alone. She said my being with her would attract more attention, and therefore more danger." The muscles of his jaw tightened and a tiny nerve ticked in his temple. "I should not have allowed her to persuade me!" His anger was directed at himself and again he looked away, as if Narraway had voiced the same thoughts of blame, and he could not face him.

It was the moment to press, and Narraway did not allow himself to hesitate. "Why, Señor Delacruz? What was the additional threat? This is not the moment to protect anyone! Whoever it was, they murdered Cleo and Elfrida to show us that they are in earnest. They cut them open with knives, and tore out their entrails, just to ensure we knew that they are not only capable of anything, but willing to do it."

Nazario was white, as if he had been drained of blood. Narraway was afraid that he had gone too far. A witness horrified into paralysis was no use.

"Señor Delacruz . . ." he said more gently. "They have kept Sofia alive because they very badly want to give her back, in exchange for certain actions on your part. They will win nothing from you if she is not alive and well. You have some fearful decisions to make. You need as cool a head as —"

"What decisions?" Nazario demanded, glaring at Narraway. "What can you mean? I will do whatever they want. Are you suggesting that I would refuse? What kind of a man are you?"

Narraway almost smiled; it was no more than a tightening of the lips. "One who is also married to a woman of courage and conviction, who would not have me do something I know to be wrong, even in order to save her. And certainly would not thank me for making a decision she would consider a coward's way out, whatever I thought."

"I don't understand." Nazario's voice cracked and he was close to losing control. "For the love of God, stop talking in riddles and tell me what you want! Who is it? Do you know who it is? Is it something to do with your government? Do they want somebody else in her place?"

"No." Narraway realized he was drawing it out more than he had to. "The government has no hand in it at all, and nothing to lose or gain, except whatever morality they believe in," he replied. "What the kidnapper wants is for you to come to England and say that Sofia is a fraud, a woman who deliberately seduced you from your first wife, and your children, and was the immediate cause of their suicide by fire. That you both covered up those facts to avoid the disgrace of it. Of course, it would ruin all that she has fought for and preached for these years, but the reward would be her life."

For terrible, aching seconds there was absolute silence.

"And if I don't?" Nazario said at last.

"Then she will be killed, in the same manner that Cleo and Elfrida were." Narraway felt sick as he said it, and he thought Nazario looked like he was going to faint. "I'm sorry," he found his own voice almost strangled in his throat.

"It is not true," Nazario said slowly, choosing his words as if English had suddenly become a strange language to him and he had to think to frame his sentences. "Luisa and I had parted before Sofia came to Toledo. Of course we were not divorced. Our faith at the time was Roman Catholic, and such a thing was forbidden. We could not obtain an annulment because there were no grounds." He stopped, the memory clearly painful.

Narraway did not interrupt or try to hasten him. It was not out of practicality so he could observe him, but for the compelling need for a decency toward a suffering he could not help.

"Luisa went to live in a small house her family owned, and she took our children with her," Nazario continued. "I did not stop her, for the sake of the children, as well as the fact that I could see no way in which we could be reconciled. I think now that Luisa was ill in her mind. I did not realize it at the time. Perhaps I did not want to.

"I lost myself in whatever good work I could find, mostly connected to this monastery here, but based in Toledo."

"And Sofia?" Narraway asked.

"That was when she came to Toledo. She was a companion to an elderly woman of some means. As the woman became ill, I was of assistance to her."

"You are a doctor?" Narraway asked.

"I qualified in medicine," Nazario said, nodding. "Then my father died, leaving me sufficient means for the rest of my life, without practicing. I did it for mercy's sake, not for payment. I came to know Sofia during that time. It was a friendship in the service of the woman whose companion she was, and for whom she had the deepest regard. More, I think, than for her own mother."

His face became bleak. "But Luisa mistook the relationship for something else. As if I would fornicate with a woman I had come to love, in the house of her dying patron and friend!" His voice was raw with pain. "So little did Luisa think of me! She tried to persuade me to abandon them, even as the poor woman lay in agony. I would not do it."

Narraway maintained his silence.

Nazario drew in a deep breath and let it out slowly. "Luisa's belief in my infidelity became more and more hysterical. She threatened to kill herself, and our children. To my everlasting grief, I did not believe her. I should have. She did exactly that. Killed the children quickly, I have to believe, mercifully, then set fire to the home and cut her own wrists."

Seconds ticked by.

"The police doctor told me this, but he allowed the coroner to say that it had been an accident. Luisa's family is powerful. They are old and respected, with considerable wealth, but more than that, there are many priests, even a cardinal in her recent ancestry. It would have been an appalling shame for them. Suicide is an unforgivable sin, not to mention killing her own children." The tears now ran down his face, in spite of his attempts to blink them away.

"They allowed it to be recorded as a terrible accident, and she was buried in a Christian grave. Of course, when I married Sofia there were those who said Luisa died of grief. Perhaps she did, but it was not for that reason. I committed no sin and Sofia even less so. But I let it be, for the sake of my children. And I suppose for Luisa also."

He smiled with a bitter self-blame. "And of course you could say that Luisa's family would not have allowed me to do anything else! But Sofia felt for her, even though they had never met. Sofia loved me, and she knew how another woman could have also. But that's Sofia. Now tell me, Mr. Narraway, how do I let her die?"

Narraway could not answer, and even to try would be insulting.

"Or how do I tell the world that she is a

whore who lured me from my wife and children? She was a woman who nursed her dying patroness, whom she loved as a mother, and only came into my arms, or my bed, after I had married her, and Luisa was dead, by her own hand. How can I do either of those things? Tell me!"

"I can't tell you," Narraway said honestly. "I don't know what I would do myself."

"Don't you?" Nazario asked. "Wouldn't you say that there must be a third way, and I will give my life to find it?"

"Yes," Narraway said in a whisper, seeing Vespasia's face in his mind. "I would."

There was a knock on the door and Nazario stood up to open it. The abbot came in, glanced at Nazario, then at Narraway. He read the distress and the exhaustion in their faces.

"Brothers, I think it is time you allowed yourselves time to rest, perhaps meditate a little, and certainly sleep. With peace will come new strength." He turned to Narraway. "We have prepared a room for you." He gestured toward the door and Narraway was happy to stand also, and follow him.

In the morning, long after sunrise, which was very early at this time of year, Narraway arose and inquired his way to the refectory. He was welcomed and shown to the table where Nazario was dining. He looked weary, his eyes hollow and heavily shadowed.

He looked up as Narraway pulled out the heavy wooden chair and sat down. After the table had been set with bread and finely sliced ham, olives and herb butter, Nazario broke the silence.

"I have been thinking about this most of the night." Nazario looked up from his plate. "Sofia did not tell me so, but there were other events that I believe may have caused her to feel impelled to speak to Barton Hall. She did not discuss it with me because she knew I would rather she did not take the risk herself, and God knows, I wish I had been wrong!" He stopped abruptly and took a long drink from the pewter mug of rough wine beside him.

"I had better tell you the whole story, so you may judge which parts of it, if any, may have connection with what has happened. You mentioned that the house where Cleo and Elfrida were killed was owned by Barton Hall. I had not thought it relevant before, and it may not be."

"Tell me anyhow," Narraway insisted. Perhaps at last this was going to be about the fugitive she had protected.

Nazario thought in silence for a few moments before he began.

"Several weeks ago, not two weeks before Sofia went to London, a man came to her in great distress. It is not an unusual happening. She is widely known for her mercy. This man said that he and a friend of his, whom he named only as Alonso, had perpetrated a hoax of almost unimaginable size. It had succeeded beyond their dreams, and now threatened their lives. Alonso had been murdered, very violently. Knifed to death and left almost torn apart, out in the country, but near the road where he was bound to be discovered."

Nazario glanced up at Narraway, then back at his plate again.

"There is no point in killing someone as a warning if the corpse is not found," he went on almost under his breath. "Juan Castillo, the other man in the hoax, understood the message and he was terrified for his own life. He knew he would be next. Above all, he was afraid of dying without having made a confession and receiving some absolution he could believe in. He came to Sofia and told her all that he had done. I have no idea the nature of this hoax or what it was because of course she did not tell me."

"What happened to Castillo?" Narraway asked.

"I don't know," Nazario replied. "But she

hid him — so far as I know, successfully. At least she believed he was still alive when she went to England."

"You don't know where?" Narraway knew the answer, but he had to ask.

"I have no idea," Nazario replied. "She would tell no one. And the police have never found any clue at all as to who killed Alonso, or why, and whether Castillo had any part in it. But from the description of how Cleo and Elfrida were murdered, I fear there is some connection."

"You have no clue at all as to the nature of the hoax?" Narraway had to press the matter as far as he could. Sofia's life might depend on it; and maybe more than that.

Nazario hesitated.

This time Narraway did not wait. "Even if she did not tell you, you must be able to piece some of it together," he said urgently. "We need every shred we can get. We're fighting in the dark."

"Money," Nazario replied. "A vast amount of it, a king's ransom."

"How? You say a hoax. That implies a trick rather than a robbery. Why did she want to see Barton Hall? Is he connected to it?"

"I would guess so," Nazario answered. "Or perhaps he could have done something to help? I know of no other reason she would go to see him now. Their quarrel was years ago, and is a difference of belief that cannot be mended. Neither of them will change, and she would not wish him to pretend. What *he* would wish I don't know. I've never met him."

"But she said that she must go to him alone?"

"She told me there could be no discussion about it, and certainly no argument. I saw from the look on her face that she dreaded it, yet she had no honorable choice but to go."

"Was she afraid?" Narraway asked.

Nazario smiled bitterly. "If you knew her, you would not ask that. I think so, but certainly not of murder. Something has happened she did not foresee, not even in imagination. But I have no idea what."

"Could she have known who killed Alonso, and therefore who would be trying to kill Castillo?" Narraway suggested.

"And that person killed Cleo and Elfrida?" Nazario's eyes narrowed. "Then why take Sofia rather than kill her too? It doesn't make any sense. Sofia had no part in the hoax, whatever it was about, and neither did Cleo or Elfrida."

"Then Sofia is hiding something, possibly concerning the whereabouts of Castillo,"

Narraway concluded. "And therefore the key to the hoax."

"Where does Hall fit in? Whose side is he on in this?"

"Probably his own," Narraway said bleakly. "You said the hoax has to do with money? He is a banker, with fortunes in his charge. It seems unlikely they are not connected."

"Are you certain Sofia did not speak with him?" Nazario asked.

"Yes, at least according to Hall," Narraway sighed. "It's possible he lied, of course. And I wish I knew what happened to Castillo."

"So do I," Nazario agreed. "He comes to Sofia to help him save his soul. She gave him all the passion, honor and pity she could, and I loved her for it. But I will not let it cost her life."

"Then come to England with me and we will face the dilemma."

Nazario was ashen-faced. "I can't let them kill her . . . but neither can I say she was a whore, and responsible for Luisa's death. That would destroy everything she is, all she believes and has worked to teach."

"I know," Narraway agreed. "We must try to create a third way. But we need to have all the facts to do that. We have a few days yet. I dare say they will know when we have returned to London. Take time to study all the possibilities, and fast and pray, or whatever you do."

Nazario sank his head into his hands and did not reply. Narraway saw the man's shoulders heave in sobs he could no longer control, and stood up silently. He could at least give him privacy.

They rode back through the night, hoping to arrive in Toledo by dawn.

Narraway was pleased to have the same horse, even though he had told the guide that he would leave earlier and go in the daylight.

The vast sky stretched above them, glittering with stars, and the wind was cool in their faces, blowing from the east. One huge shoulder of hillside gave way to another. The slow moon, three-quarters full, rose to the southeast and made their shadows black as Indian ink on the road, pooling and shifting and gathering again as the angles shifted against the light.

They did not speak. Narraway was glad. Nazario rode in front of him, and conversation would have been difficult, and there was nothing to say. Perhaps Nazario was lost in memories. Narraway would have been. He would have lived again every moment of happiness, even the smallest things: sunlight on his face as Vespasia turned to smile at him, the touch of a hand at a moment of beauty when to speak would have interrupted it, like a stone breaking a pool of still water.

Sunsets changed from second to second and finally died. But there would always be another. Next spring would be as beautiful as this one, yet one could hardly tear one's eyes from blossom trees, or the sheets of bluebells strewn across the ground like fallen skies, so thick there was nowhere to tread without crushing a flower.

How could anyone love, and bear to let it go? Was there always a last day, a last time, a last touch?

With a sudden, almost unbearable pain he wanted Sofia's idea of eternity to be true. Anything less was unendurable. Now that he loved, the thought of being alone again was one that he fought against as a drowning man fights for air.

Maybe Sofia was a fantasist, but her vision was a dream of such loveliness he longed for it to be true. The strength of it should survive. He knew why she would die before she would be made to deny it. But how long did they have before her captor realized that?

As they came over the last hill with the sun blazing above the horizon in the east, Narraway was so tired his whole body ached, yet the view of the city in the distance still caught his breath with its ancient splendor, its memory of a kinder age.

They rode the last distance without speaking, by mutual agreement. The streets were stirring with the first business of the day when they parted outside Nazario's home and Narraway went on to the hotel. He gave the horse to the groom and went inside and up to his bedroom.

Vespasia was asleep on the bed, still in her clothes, as if she had been reluctant to give herself over to exhaustion. He stood in the doorway looking at her. Her hair was loose, but more as if it had come undone than that she had deliberately unfastened it. Her face was peaceful, the lines of anxiety smoothed out of it by sleep. She looked both younger and incredibly vulnerable.

He was tired and dirty after the long ride, and the emotionally harrowing experience of watching Nazario's pain. He was also unshaven, and acutely aware of it. He wanted to lie down beside Vespasia and sink into oblivion himself, even if it was only for a couple of hours, but he would disturb her, and he knew he must smell of leather and horse sweat.

He watched her silently a moment longer, then went into the bathroom, took off his clothes, washed and shaved, then went back and lay on the bed.

It seemed only minutes before he woke again, his head aching and his body so stiff he winced to move at all. Vespasia was standing over him, fully dressed, her hair casually curled and pinned, and a cup of steaming tea in her hands. He saw both anxiety and a thread of amusement in her silver-gray eyes.

She did not speak, and he realized she had woken him by touch.

"I'm sorry," she said gently. "But I had to wake you." She put the tea down on the small table beside the bed. "Drink it, and tell me what happened. What is Nazario like? He must feel bruised to the soul by this. What must we do next to help?"

"I have to get up . . ." He moved, trying to mask the pain.

"No, you don't." She pushed him back softly, but with her weight behind her arm. "You will drink your tea, and tell me what you learned. No one does their best work when they are exhausted, not even you, my dear. If we had the time, I never would've woken you."

He stared at her, and drew in breath to argue. Then he realized not only was she right, but she was quite aware he knew it also.

He sipped the tea. It was hot, but exactly the right temperature to drink. He was glad she forbore from making any comments about his soreness, or his riding in the Indian Army, or cavalry charges. It had been a long time ago.

He told her what Nazario had said, adding only a little of his own impressions of the man. He wished her judgment to be untainted by his feelings.

She waited until she was certain he had finished.

"Well?" he prompted.

"You believe him, don't you." It was not a question.

"Yes. But nevertheless I intend to confirm it, as much as I can. And we can only do it here in Toledo. It will cost us a couple of days, but that will make no difference. Whoever has Sofia will not act until we have replied. I believe whoever it is will kill her only when they are certain they have failed in their demands."

She looked at him with horror, but she did not argue. That in itself was chilling.

Vespasia was always ready to fight if she thought there was any hope at all of winning.

"Sleep a few more hours," she said finally. "I have made some contacts, and it should be possible for me to learn more of this English-woman whom Sofia cared for. She will have had servants, and servants see a great deal."

"Vespasia, be careful! Whoever it is —"

"Of course I will be careful, Victor," she said briskly. "I shall ask the hotel to bring you something to eat in a few hours. If I am not back by dinnertime you may send the dogs to look for me."

"Vespasia!" he called out as she reached the doorway.

She turned to look at him. He was struck again by what an extraordinarily beautiful woman she was. For an instant he caught his breath.

"You are not following me," she said with a smile. "You are wearing your nightshirt. You will look absurd. I shall see you this evening." She gave him a sweet smile, and left the room.

"Damn," he said quietly, but he was so tired that sleep overtook him before he could think about it anymore.

CHAPTER 12

Pitt went home from the bank with his mind in turmoil. He had lost track of time while he was looking through the papers and records, which had drowned him in information and only at last had he seen some order and connection in the large amounts of money.

At first it had looked to him as if the monumental investments in land had already given returns far exceeding what even the most optimistic could have hoped for. Then after reading the papers several times, he had realized that the money coming in was from different sources altogether, and what seemed to be a connection was not in fact so.

But what remained a mystery was whatever it was that Barton Hall had feared so much that he had been driven into the panic of suddenly raising such vast sums and had then gone to so much trouble to conceal something that was perfectly legal.

And of course the ultimate thought that Pitt tried to put away was always there at the end. Was there treason involved? Was this money actually invested in foreign armaments? Germany's heavy industry was overtaking Britain's and openly boasted about. Was that why Hall had concealed it?

The hansom pulled up at the curb. Pitt paid the driver and thanked him absent-mindedly before going across the pavement and in at the door.

He found Charlotte sitting up waiting for him, as if he were often this late, and it caused her no anxiety, let alone inconvenience. She put down her sewing and stood up, giving him a quick kiss, then disappeared into the kitchen.

He took his boots off and sat down by the embers of the fire. Even this far into May it could be cool in the evenings.

Less than ten minutes later Charlotte came back with a tray of hot tea, cold beef sandwiches and a large slice of fruitcake. She put it down on the table beside him and poured tea for both of them. The sandwiches and the cake were for him. He had not realized until now that he was hungry.

He thanked her and sat back to enjoy the

few moments before he needed to think again. The French doors to the garden were closed because it was dark and the air was cool, but the smell of flowers and cut grass still lingered. It would have been a good time to forget everything and let himself sink into the peace and the silence, let it unravel the knots inside him. If he did, he knew that as soon as he had finished eating he would fall asleep.

He realized that Charlotte was watching him. He smiled and eased himself back a little farther. He wished he could tell her what he had discovered. It seemed like a bright island, a long time ago, when he had been merely a policeman and crimes had been at times appalling, but individual, involving only a handful of people. Now his job was about impersonal injury and sharing it with her would have been no help or pleasure.

This case was different, however. The murders of the two women and the torture of Sofia were fearful; but the future of whole countries could be affected, if what he began to dread was true. America and Spain might be only the beginning.

The thought that he had not understood this huge international responsibility when he took the position was the sort of self-indulgence he would have despised in another man. But it was hard to put the burden of it aside, especially when he was tired, and confused by too much knowledge in some areas, and too little in others.

He had enjoyed asking Charlotte's opinion of people, especially either of women, or of her own social class with which he was not familiar. Of course she had interfered in his cases, sometimes at considerable risk to herself, but she had actually proved very astute, and more than one case he could not have solved without her.

Since he had joined Special Branch everything was different. There was too much that was based in secrecy. It made the job far lonelier. He missed the balance of another judgment and very often a subtler view than his own.

It was Charlotte who broke the silence.

"Is she still alive, do you think?" she asked, her voice quiet. He had not told her about seeing Sofia, beaten, swollen-faced in the hansom.

"She was alive just before Narraway and Vespasia went to Spain," he answered. "I don't know about now. I . . . I don't know how long she can last. But they'll kill her as soon as she tells them whatever it is they want to know. I think it's about someone she is protecting, I don't know who or why."

Charlotte sat very still, her face pale even in the glow of the gas lamps on the wall.

Had he told her too much?

"I'm sorry," he held out his hand, palm open. "You didn't need to know that."

She put her hand on his, gripping him, glaring at him through her tears. "Were you ever going to tell me? How can I protect Jemima, or explain anything to her, if I don't know?" she demanded. "She's terrified, Thomas. She thinks all women who speak their beliefs or fight for what they want won't ever be loved. They'll be respected, feared, hated, admired, but no man will ever want to marry them."

It was absurd, painful and desperately easy to understand. History was marked with heroines who were essentially alone. What girl of sixteen wants to be excluded for any reason?

"That's how she sees Sofia: brave and betrayed by a husband who grew tired of her courage and battles," Charlotte went on. "Is she nearly right?"

"I don't know," he said. "I just don't know."

She must have seen his exhaustion, because she said nothing more but leaned into him and put her head on his shoulder. He closed his arms around her and held her more and more tightly.

The next day Pitt was again waylaid on the street by Frank Laurence.

"Good morning, Commander," Laurence said soberly, falling in step with Pitt as they passed a boy selling newspapers. A current scandal had replaced Sofia's disappearance on the front pages.

"I have nothing to tell you, Mr. Laurence," Pitt replied.

"Actually, much against my better instincts," Laurence replied, "I care what happens to Sofia Delacruz. You know the remarkable thing is that I don't think she expects this God of hers to rescue her. I'm not even sure that she expects you to. Which makes it the more remarkable that she had the courage to do whatever it is she is doing. By the way, you haven't worked out what that is yet, have you?"

Pitt knew that if he lashed out at Laurence in words it would betray no more than his own desperation. So with an effort he controlled himself.

"I believe you," he said calmly. "What is it you intend to do to put her, and yourself, back on the front pages?"

Laurence winced. "Not I, Commander.

Mr. Teague. He will do something to keep it in the public eye. You can't need me to tell you that, surely?"

Pitt stopped again. "You really hate Teague, don't you? Enough to lie about how well you know him, quite unnecessarily. Until you lied, I didn't care at all. Now I wonder why."

Laurence looked uncomfortable. For a moment he did not meet Pitt's eyes, and then when he did he was hesitant, as if deciding whether to lie again, or finally tell the truth.

Pitt let out his breath and turned as if to walk away.

"You're right," Laurence agreed. "There are things I know that I cannot prove, and I was reluctant to mention them. My slight evasion was to avoid the subject altogether."

Pitt turned back to him. "If it's irrelevant to the case, I really don't care. It is a lie without a purpose, which suggests to me that you are a man with no respect for the truth. You invent in order to make some story in your mind more interesting . . ."

Laurence blushed. It startled Pitt, who had imagined him incapable of such a thing. For once he was certain that whatever Laurence felt, it was a real emotion, and painful. For all his manipulations, on some level integrity was important to him.

"I can't prove anything against Teague," Laurence said quietly. "But I know what I know. If I could do so, I'd have ruined him years ago." For a moment the emotion was naked in his face, both fury and a dire and extraordinary pain.

Pitt believed him, but was puzzled as to what would have happened in school days that would still bite so deeply inside a man like Laurence, with his worldly wisdom, his intelligence and dry wit.

"Cheating," Laurence replied, as if reading his mind, and this time his eyes were absolutely direct and without pretense. "Cheating in games is despicable, a thread woven into the grain of a man's character, but cheating in the examinations that determine your future career is profoundly more serious. It is a lie to the future, to all the men and women who will trust your ability to practice your skill in their lives. And it is an injury to those who have examined your knowledge and ability and staked their own honor on their word that you have such qualities. You go to a doctor, see his degrees, and believe such an institution of learning has said he is fit to prescribe medicine for you, or even take a knife and cut open your body! Or, with an architect, that the house he designs will stand. If you need a lawyer to defend your life or your liberty, that this man is skilled in the law, and can do so." He gave a sharp little gesture with his hands.

Pitt had not thought of it in those terms, but it struck him that Laurence was right. It was a trust one took for granted.

"You know he cheated?" he said.

"Of course I do."

"How? If you saw it, why did you not report it then?" Pitt pressed. "Were you afraid you wouldn't be believed? Or of retribution?" He said it in a calm tone, because he knew the words would sting. And yet it truly confused him. Laurence was still deeply angered by the incident, and he had been outspoken enough in his articles to demonstrate that he was not a coward, in any sense.

"No, Commander," Laurence said so softly Pitt moved a step closer to be certain of hearing him. "I was not afraid. Although perhaps I should have been. I wondered at the time at the odd friendships, the loyalties and favors I couldn't understand. The main one of which was why a boy like Hall, studious, physically awkward, what is known unkindly as a swot, should be allowed into First Eleven. He was barely adequate, and yet he remained, while more skilled boys were passed over."

Pitt wanted to interrupt with the answer, but he had learned from past errors that patience was key in allowing someone to confess something they might normally not have said.

Laurence smiled with a harsh turn to his lips, full of regret. "It was a master who saw it and made the mistake of speaking out. At least he told me he had, and I believed him. I still do."

"I found no scandal attached to Hall's name," Pitt replied. "And we did look."

"There was none," Laurence said bitterly. "The master concerned told me he had been listened to with courtesy, and disbelief. But before he could present his proof there was a fire. His papers were destroyed and he succumbed to the smoke. Died of it. No one was suspicious. He was judged to have let a cigar butt fall into his wastebasket, not appreciating that it was still lit." His voice was thick with emotion, as if even after all these years he could still have wept, if he would permit himself.

Pitt felt first a wave of sympathy for Laurence. For that instant he liked the man without reservation. The master's death was a grief he would have felt himself. And then it was an anger he would also have felt, scalding hot inside him, a rage for justice, and he admitted, for revenge on the arrogance that could destroy with impunity, and move on as if nothing had happened.

"Hall?" he said.

Laurence heard the fury in Pitt's voice, saw the pity in his eyes, and for an instant he knew he was not alone. Then it vanished and the hard humor returned. "Of course," he answered.

"For Teague?" Pitt asked.

Laurence's smile widened. "I am wise enough not to tell you that," he replied. "You will have to look for yourself. If you can't put it together, then I have done Special Branch a favor. Because you are not fit to lead it."

"I imagine he cheated for several people," Pitt replied, watching Laurence's smile. "Which opens up some appalling ideas."

"Oh, yes, indeed," Laurence nodded. "The power is appalling, at least potentially. It's odd how the uselessness one sees in school can dog all one's adult life, not only in your own memory, but even more dangerously in the memories of others."

"But you have one person in mind," Pitt pointed out. "You would not have come here, to catch me in the street, now, to make a general observation, no matter how enormous."

"Of course not," Laurence agreed. "That is where your much-praised detective skills will come in handy. I've heard you're brilliant. Can't remember who said it, but I'm sure someone must have."

"Not recently," Pitt let a touch of his own bitterness into his voice.

They matched paces for a dozen yards or so before Laurence spoke again.

"Can you imagine the hatred between the two of them, the cheat and the man who owes him?" he said with a curious mixture of relish and disgust. "The loathing for their own dependence: 'I was a poorer boy than you, I hadn't your grace or skill, above all your popularity, so I bought acceptance from you, at the price of becoming a cheat! I prostituted my academic intelligence to buy your friendship!' " He gave a little shudder of bitter pity and revulsion. " 'You didn't make me into this, but you gave me the chance to make myself this way, and I took it.' "

They walked a few more steps before he went on.

"And from the other man's view. 'I had the skill and grace. I could make almost anyone like me, but I couldn't pass the damn examinations. I hadn't the brains. I was obliged to let you see my failure and buy your intelligence to cheat for me and get my degree. I had to walk up there in cap and gown, with you watching me, knowing I hadn't earned it — you had chosen it for me! All my life I shall look at you, and wonder who you told, who laughed at me because of it!' "

His voice was thick with his own emotions. "Can you think of it, Pitt? Can you smell the stench of that hatred, like acid burning in the gut?"

Laurence was waiting for a reply.

"Yes, I can imagine it," Pitt answered him. "With a lot of different possible outcomes, all of them ugly. You said he cheated on exams for several boys. Do you think they would know of one another? Or might they all believe they were the only one?"

"Hadn't thought of that one," Laurence admitted with surprise. "I think they might have suspected. You develop a sense of how much a boy has his brains sharpened and applied, and who really are either stupid — or clever enough but lazy. But it's only a guess. There are surprises, I mean honest ones. Why?" He glanced sideways at Pitt curiously. "You think they would protect one another? I doubt it. Far more likely they'll lie through their teeth about it, and steer well clear of anyone they think might know. If it was me, I'd take very great care not to show it — at least until I could protect myself, and strike back lethally. Rule of hunting, you don't wound the prey and leave it to come after you. You either kill it, or leave it alone."

"Doesn't sound like you, Laurence," Pitt said with a wry smile. "I thought you were the fearless crusader for truth!"

"Sarcasm ill becomes you, Commander." Laurence's tone was light again, if a little forced. "You know perfectly well that this is real, and I have no more wish to be burned alive in my armchair than you have! I have no desire for you to avenge my murder, I want to be alive to taste my . . . 'revenge' is such an ugly word, don't you think? Whatever — I want to survive this, and I would like to see Sofia Delacruz come out of this alive too, even if she is touched with a little madness. The world needs a few of its better lunatics, even if only to relieve the tedium of the eminently sane. Even if forever doing the predictable is actually sanity. I have philosophical doubts about that, at times."

"Kill it, or leave it alone," Pitt said thoughtfully. "Of course if you can find anybody fool enough to fire your bullets for you, then you will be in no danger."

Laurence laughed. "You are a cynic, Commander, and not as innocent as I presumed. Yes, indeed, I would like you to fire my bullets for me, and I would have preferred you not to have realized it. But only because I think your aim is much better than mine."

"Really," Pitt said with skepticism. "Then you'll have to be a little more honest about where I am to point the gun."

"You won't shoot until you know," Laurence said with absolute conviction. "That's my advantage. I trust you." He smiled suddenly, a gesture of great charm, then he turned and walked away at surprising speed.

Pitt went on toward Lisson Grove, so lost in thought that several times he only just stopped himself going in the wrong direction.

How sincere was Laurence? Surely by now Pitt had more sense than to believe any journalist, particularly one as openly manipulative as Frank Laurence.

Yet there was something honest in him that Pitt did believe, in spite of all the experiences, and the warnings inside him. All that Laurence said made sense. Of course he was far too intelligent to do less than that. All the same, Pitt would have

Brundage check on the public facts. Had there been a master who had died in a fire in his lodgings, while Hall was a senior and Laurence a new boy? Had this master, if he existed, both taught Laurence and been in a position to know if Hall had helped anyone in their exams in a way that amounted to cheating?

Instinctively he believed Laurence, but he would be a fool not to check.

If the boy who had cheated had both possessed and kept any proof then the possibilities for blackmail were enormous. Except, of course, that in ruining the boy for whom he cheated, he would also be ruining himself. That would be a very powerful incentive indeed for the boy he cheated for to make very sure indeed either that his benefactor had a rich and successful life, or a very short one! The master who knew had refused to be bought — he had probably not imagined the possibility of murder. Maybe that was the warning that the cheater needed, and it had proved horribly effective.

Like the murders of Cleo and Elfrida. The similarity leaped to his mind with a sickening immediacy. He all but gagged at remembrance of the house on Inkerman Road.

Barton Hall might be the next Governor

of the Bank of England! Was that the prize he was playing for? But then Pitt wondered how Sofia had learned anything of it.

He could think of no way in which that would make sense. Hall was as English as tea and scones, if rather less agreeable.

He reached the offices in Lisson Grove and went in, to find Brundage waiting for him, looking awkward. Pitt's heart sank.

"What is it, Brundage?" he asked apprehensively.

"Mr. Teague is here to see you, sir," Brundage replied. "He said he wants to give you his report personally."

Pitt swore. He was in no mood for Dalton Teague today.

"He won't see anyone else." Brundage cut off Pitt's answer. His usually pleasant face was strained, the shadows around his eyes deeper. "I think he wants to see what you have to say, sir. He's here more to ask than to tell . . . I think . . . sir." Now Brundage looked worried, as if he thought he might have overstepped the mark.

Pitt smiled reluctantly. "I'm sure of it. But before I see him, I've got a job here for you." Briefly he told Brundage the essence of what Laurence had said.

"Is that true, sir?" Brundage said in amazement. "It could mean . . ." He stopped, overwhelmed by the ugly possibilities that opened up before him.

"That's what I intend you should find out," Pitt answered. "And, Brundage!"

"Yes, sir?" Brundage stood up straight.

"For heaven's sake, be discreet."

Brundage smiled widely, and went out with barely a lifted head in acknowledgment.

Teague was in the room outside Pitt's office. The door to the office was locked, as he always left it that way when he was out. As soon as Pitt came in Teague rose to his feet. He did it in a graceful movement as if he gave it no thought, but for the first time since Pitt had met him, he looked tired. He would never be ungroomed, or untidy, his valet would see to that. But there were shadows in his face as if he was strained, and his usually thick hair looked a trifle flat, as though the vitality had been leached out of it. He held out his hand to Pitt.

"This must be hellish for you," he said with a degree of sympathy Pitt would have preferred not to hear.

"It's unpleasant," Pitt conceded, taking Teague's hand briefly, then unlocking his office door and inviting Teague in.

The moment they were seated Teague began.

"I never believed that Sofia Delacruz had disappeared of her own will," he said earnestly. "But of course that avenue had to be explained. We would have appeared absurd if it had been a simple, rather grubby affair." Teague's clear sea-blue eyes never wavered from Pitt's. "I've wondered occasionally if some supposed saints have grown tired of their own images and longed to escape them and behave just like anyone else. Are saints allowed to laugh? Or to make mistakes like the rest of us, do you suppose? Or is it a relentless regime of being right, fair, just and sober?"

"Good God, I hope not!" Pitt said impetuously, then instantly regretted it when he saw Teague smile. "Is that sanctity?" he asked. "Nothing I've seen in nature is so . . . self-righteous, or essentially absurd!"

Teague sighed and sat back in his chair. "I don't know the woman. But if she had wanted to escape that, I wouldn't blame her. However, all that I've been able to gather — and it's a great deal — indicates that she did not go willingly, either before her pathetic followers were killed or after. In fact from what my men have reported, I don't believe she left the area of London within a mile or two of Inkerman Road."

Suddenly it was no longer a matter of

polite conversation, to be got over with as soon as possible. Pitt found himself tense, listening not only to Teague's words but to the tone of his voice, and watching his face, the strong hands in his lap, even tension in his shoulders.

"Why do you believe this?" Pitt asked as levelly as he could.

"Diligence," Teague answered, his voice almost expressionless. "I have a large number of men I can call on, Commander. Not just servants of one sort or another, but old colleagues, other sportsmen in social disciplines, not just casual. Men I knew in school, county players when I was in my twenties. I played for Surrey for a while, all around the Home Counties. Teammates, opponents, grounds men, lovers of the game, all kinds of people are willing to help. Damn it, she was a good woman as far as she knew how, and a guest in our country. A word here and there, friend of a friend, you know? Different from being questioned by police. There is no sign of her anywhere. She couldn't have walked. I don't doubt she put up a fight! Do you?" He looked at Pitt closely, watching his eyes, his posture, just as Pitt was watching him.

"No, I don't," Pitt admitted. "You think she was hurt, even then?"

Teague's eyelids flickered. "Even then? You think she has been hurt since? You have heard something? Found something?"

Pitt wondered for a moment whether to lie or not. Should he tell this man the truth?

Teague was waiting, watching.

"I wish I could say I had," Pitt answered. "But as you said, it is very likely she put up a fight. In fact I have to face the possibility that she is dead."

Teague's jaw tightened and he ran his tongue over his lips. "Have you given up already?" There was a very faint note of contempt in his voice or perhaps he would call it disappointment, as if Pitt had let him down.

"Possibility," Pitt said the word slowly. "Not probability. I think she was taken alive for a reason."

Teague's eyebrows rose. "Indeed? A deduction or a guess?"

Pitt gave a half smile. "A deduction, and a hope. As you said, she is a remarkable woman."

"From what do you deduce it?" Teague demanded.

Pitt made a decision, his muscles aching from the tension of fear that he was being rash. "From the fact that we have not found her body, and yet the other two women were killed immediately and brutally," he answered. "I think whoever took her did so for a reason."

Teague thought for a moment, and then spoke slowly. "What . . . reason . . . Commander? Money?" He was still watching Pitt intently.

Pitt had no intention of telling Teague of the demand.

"I don't think so," he replied. "None has been asked for. If that were what was wanted, why wait so long?"

Teague considered for a moment. "To heighten the tension?" he suggested. "Her followers are bound to be distressed, and increasingly so with time."

"They were distressed by the deaths of the other two women," Pitt pointed out. "I think if they had been asked for money they would have given it immediately."

"You may be right." Teague nodded very slightly. "Then what could the kidnapper want? A denial of her faith, do you think? Or to force her to change her message?"

Pitt kept his face totally impassive.

"Do you think she would do that?" He turned the question back to Teague.

Teague thought for several moments, and then a thin smile touched his lips. "Even if she would, why kill the other two women?

That makes little sense. Surely it would have been more effective to take the other two and tell her that if she doesn't publicly repudiate her beliefs, they would pay with their lives?"

Pitt nodded. "That would make far more sense," he agreed. "We are assuming that whoever took her did so with a plan. I hope that's true, but I'm not certain of it."

Teague turned it over in his mind.

Pitt waited, watching him, studying him.

"I have learned a little about her," Teague went on. "From past sermons, if you can call them that, and listening to what her colleagues say of her. I imagine you have had reported to you the rather different message that Melville Smith is now giving, as if on her behalf?"

"Yes."

"Very . . . watered down. I dare say he means well, but in his own way he is betraying her."

"I doubt that is how he sees it," Pitt replied. "But what were you going to say about it?"

Again Teague's eyes were fixed on Pitt's as if he could read his mind in the depth of his gaze.

"That she forgives indiscriminately, and that God would be more careful," Teague replied to the question. "Which makes me wonder if perhaps she has formed some alliances that he considers criminal or maybe even politically dangerous."

"The same thought has occurred to me," Pitt said honestly.

"Then they may be behind the kidnapping," Teague said. "Although I can't see why they would take her, if she has given them comfort, or pardon."

"Neither can I. But there has been some difference of approach among different groups," Pitt told him.

"I see." Teague did not say whether he had been aware of that or not. "Smith seemed to be certain she had come to England to speak with Barton Hall. Does Smith know what her purpose was?"

"He says not," Pitt replied. "Do you have any idea?"

As if he had seen a flicker of accusation in Pitt's eyes, Teague responded with a guarded question. "I know we've spoken of him before, but how well do you know Frank Laurence?"

"Not very well. Why?" Pitt asked.

"He's a bit irresponsible," Teague replied. "I raise his name because I think he knows, or suspects, that Hall has something to do with Señora Delacruz's abduction," Teague went on. "Hall is profoundly ambitious, you know? Or perhaps you don't know. He would dearly like to become Governor of the Bank of England one day. A man like Frank Laurence wouldn't be above guiding the news in a way to help him, if it was to his own profit. Or equally, destroying him, if that was."

Pitt drew breath to disagree, then changed his mind, and let it out in silence.

"A dangerous little man." Teague was still watching Pitt. "Plenty of ambition, but he hasn't the power or the nerve to be behind this."

"Laurence?" Pitt asked, trying to sound as if he thought it was a real possibility. He didn't want to openly insult Teague.

"Yes," Teague said with a slight shrug. "Paid by someone, I imagine."

"Who?" Pitt asked.

"I don't know." Teague stood up slowly, again holding his hand out. "I won't give up trying to find out, but I admit to feeling disheartened."

Pitt took his hand, briefly, felt the firmness of his grip, then let go. "Thank you, Mr. Teague."

As Teague left the room Pitt sat back in his chair and thought over what Teague had said. He had been trying to find out how much Pitt knew, how determined he still was to rescue Sofia, if he was beginning to feel defeated. He was always probing. And it was he, not Pitt, who had raised the subject of Laurence, almost as if they had agreed on him as a suspect.

And Teague seemed as willing to discredit Laurence as Laurence was to discredit him. Was that coincidental? Or could it matter?

The evening of the next day Pitt received a hand-delivered note to say that Narraway and Vespasia were home, and would Pitt accompany the messenger back to Vespasia's house to meet with them.

Pitt kept the man waiting no more than ten minutes.

He rode in silence in the carriage, his mind racing over the possibilities of what they might have to say. As soon as he arrived he thanked the driver and went straight to the front door. It was opened by the maid before he had time to knock.

Narraway was standing by the fireplace, his face pale with exhaustion. Vespasia sat in her usual chair, and on the sofa was a slender, dark-eyed Spanish man whose haunted expression proclaimed his identity as Nazario Delacruz.

There was a pot of tea on the table and a

plate of freshly cut sandwiches. Narraway introduced Pitt and then stood back.

Very quietly, with many halts, Nazario recounted how Sofia had taken in penitents, including Juan Castillo, the one who was so terrified after the murder of the man left eviscerated in the road, in a manner hideously like that in which Cleo and Elfrida had also been killed.

"She took him in and agreed to protect him," Narraway added quietly. "She hid him, on condition of his repentance for the crime he had committed, and that he should do all he could to redeem the effect of it."

"What was the crime?" Pitt asked, looking at Nazario.

"I do not know," Nazario answered. "Those things she never told me. But I do know that he was very frightened that he would be murdered next. He came to Sofia because he did not want to die without making a confession. He feared hell. She was determined that he should make amends for the crime, but she never mentioned what it was."

"It was straight after that when Señora Delacruz said that she had to come to London and meet with Barton Hall," Narraway said.

"It all circles back to Barton Hall," Pitt

said quietly.

"Yes," Narraway agreed.

Pitt turned to Nazario, but before he could speak, Nazario answered the question.

"I will go straight to Angel Court, and think, weigh it in my mind, and pray. Tomorrow I will answer you as to what choice I will make."

Pitt bowed his acknowledgment and no one else argued.

CHAPTER 13

Pitt was still tired from the late evening and the rapid pace of events when he arrived at Lisson Grove next morning. He felt bleary-eyed and a trifle stiff as he sat at his desk.

Stoker came in with a mug of tea for him.

"For heaven's sake, sit down," Pitt told him, accepting the mug of tea gratefully. He took the first sip before he started to tell Stoker about Nazario Delacruz, briefly and without sparing the horror of the situation. Nor did he have to warn Stoker that Nazario might be erratic, mistrustful of them and possibly even seek his own answer.

"Poor devil," Stoker said when Pitt had told him all that he needed to know.

"Indeed," Pitt said quietly. "I should have taken the whole threat issue a great deal more seriously from the beginning."

Stoker did not argue. "I did look into Barton Hall's Canadian investments, as you asked." He shook his head. "I can't find any trace of his using the money himself. He lives in the house he was born in. Belongs to a few gentlemen's clubs, some for years. Pretty frugal with his general expenses. Good tailor, but you'd expect that in his position. You don't bank with someone who looks like he can't afford a decent coat. Doesn't own a carriage, doesn't give expensive gifts to people. In fact, as far as I can see, he doesn't have any lady friends. His wife died, and he hasn't courted anyone since.

"And I checked gambling in just about every form it exists, and any payments that could be past debts, or even blackmail. There wasn't anything." Stoker looked earnest and frustrated. "I really don't know what he's done with the money, sir. But it's nothing I've seen before. I asked Darlington, he's an expert in financial matters, and he couldn't suggest anything else."

"Thank you," Pitt said bleakly. "The investment in Canadian land seems to be paying well, so why is it secret, and what is he so desperate about, and needing more money for?

"Yes, sir. He's the reason she says she came to England at all. But why? Could she be blackmailing him over this cheating business so long ago? Even if she is, I still can't see him murdering these women like that. He looks so . . . like a banker! With the imagination of a dish of custard!"

Pitt smiled in spite of himself. He agreed that on the surface, everything seemed predictable about Barton Hall. "An excellent way to look, if you wish to be invisible for what you are."

"I suppose so. Something I did turn up, sir. He travels quite a lot. Mostly Europe, Paris especially, and of course he could go anywhere else from there."

"Interesting," Pitt agreed. It was, but he found himself unable to keep his mind on anything other than Nazario Delacruz, and the moments in the streetlights when he and Brundage had stood in the chandler's shop and saw that hansom go by, with Sofia's bruised face staring at him out of the window.

"Put somebody on finding out where else Barton traveled, especially if it was Spain. But we can't afford to wait for him to get back to us. Sofia may not have more than a day or two, if she's even still alive now. Nazario has to make up his mind in the next few hours."

"They gave us longer than that, sir."

"That doesn't matter. They might torture her to death before then, even if they don't mean to!" Pitt said with a sharp note of desperation in his voice.

"Yes, sir," Stoker agreed grimly, his face pale. "But I'll put someone on it anyway."

Pitt went to Angel Court early in the afternoon. There was no more time for delay. With Sofia missing and none of them knowing for certain if she was alive, let alone how much she may have been tortured, they were all deeply distressed. And they were still mourning the fearful deaths of Cleo and Elfrida. Neither shock nor grief is so quickly recovered from, let alone the constant struggle to keep faith in such disaster.

Pitt had warned Nazario the previous evening that Smith had continued to preach, but that he had considerably moderated the power of Sofia's message. Nazario had not appeared surprised.

No two people saw issues or leadership in exactly the same way. Pitt was not leading Special Branch exactly as Narraway had. And even if he could have done the same, judgment for judgment, would he have? No, the loyalty was always to the job, not to the predecessor, regardless of admiration for them, or friendship.

Melville Smith should have done what he thought the faith required, not copy Sofia, if he believed her judgments were flawed.

Pitt turned in at the entrance to the court, passing the stone angel with its huge wings. He crossed the cobbles toward the door and saw the old woman watering the tubs of herbs. She glanced at him curiously, then as soon as she recognized him, turned away again. She looked even more haggard than before, her skin dark, eyes hollow. Her hands on the watering can were embedded with dirt.

Pitt felt a moment's compassion for her. Perhaps she mourned over Sofia's loss as deeply as anyone else, but she seemed excluded from the fellowship of the others remaining. Pitt was not sure if she spoke much English. He thought of saying something to her now, but if she did not understand him it would only embarrass her. And she had her back to him, bending over the tubs, pinching off leaves here and there and holding them in her other hand, the watering can beside her on the stones.

The door opened just as Pitt raised his hand to knock. Henrietta stared at him and wordlessly beckoned him in.

She led him back inside after closing the door firmly. Her face was gaunt, as if she had slept little. Her thick hair was pulled back severely, showing the bones of her cheek and jaw. Her eyes were hollow, as if with illness, but it was still possible to see that she had been beautiful once, perhaps not so long ago. She walked ahead of him from one room to another, leading him to the same place where he had spoken to Melville Smith before. Her feet were silent on the ancient boards, and she did not turn back to see if he was following her. She walked stiffly, as if her joints hurt, but he could not say whether her pain were entirely physical, or if most of it lay in the burden of grief in her mind.

Melville Smith and Ramon were waiting for Pitt, with Nazario Delacruz standing between them. They all looked ill at ease. Nazario was tense and pale, the marks of exhaustion plain on his face and in the way his shoulders were hunched forward, without energy, yet without comfort.

He nodded to Pitt, as an acknowledgment rather than a greeting.

Ramon Aguilar was clearly afraid, but Pitt believed it was for Sofia, not for himself. He glanced at Pitt, gave the ghost of a smile and then turned back to Nazario, waiting for him to lead.

Melville Smith avoided Pitt's eyes. He looked strained, even guilty, but that could have been no more than the bitter awareness that Sofia had gone missing while he considered himself in charge. Pitt felt sorry for him. It was a delusion. No one, probably not even Nazario, had been in charge of Sofia.

Nazario cleared his throat.

"I will speak this evening." He made it a statement, and instantly Pitt saw both Smith and Ramon Aguilar stiffen. The disagreement was unmistakable, but neither said anything. Clearly they had already made their views plain.

Smith looked at Pitt, waiting for his reaction.

"I think, Señor Delacruz, that we should discuss this privately," Pitt said. "You may repeat to anyone whatever you wish, or ask counsel as you think right. But there are certain facts I would like to make sure you are aware of." He turned to Smith. "May we use your office?"

Smith hesitated, surely not because there was any decision for him to make, but because he was reluctant to let go of the shred of control he still had.

Nazario answered for him.

"Of course. Come." He turned and led the way without looking to see if Pitt was following him.

Once in the office he closed the door and

took one of the two chairs away from the desk, leaving the other for Pitt.

"What is it you wish to say, Commander?" he asked.

"Have you discussed your reason for wanting to speak this evening with them yet?" Pitt needed to know that before he went any further.

Nazario's black eyebrows rose. "No. I do not want them to hear from anyone what the kidnapper is saying of Sofia. It is untrue, as I told Señor Narraway. Melville Smith might not care, but Ramon would be deeply distressed to hear such things and know that anyone else might hear them and imagine them true." His face filled with gentleness. "He is a simple man, tender. He had a sister he loved, and she fell from grace for a very human passion, which the Catholic Church does not forgive in women. He still grieves over it and this would hurt him unnecessarily, and perhaps make his judgment less balanced than he would afterward wish. I will not allow anyone else to carry the blame for what I do."

"Admirable," Pitt said as gently as he could. "But is it wise?"

"Wise?" Nazario's voice cracked a little. "What is wise, Mr. Pitt? What would you do in my place? Have you reached a wise decision?"

"You have a right to blame me for not having prevented this in the first place," Pitt said miserably. "However, you and I arguing now is an indulgence we can't afford. I want us to do the right thing. I don't care whose idea it is, or how we reach it, only that afterward we are still sure it was the best we could."

Nazario leaned back a little in the chair, as if his body had lost the strength to be angry anymore.

"You want to know what I have decided. Time is short. I understand that. So I will preach this evening. Not Mr. Smith's new, softer philosophy, but the beautiful, burning truth Sofia speaks. I know why I do it, so there is no use in trying to persuade me not to. I know Sofia, Mr. Pitt. That is what she would do, what she would live or die to defend."

Pitt looked at him steadily, remembering the bruised face he had seen in the cab, for a moment in the lamplight.

"Are you sure? I have not lied to you that they will kill her brutally and without hesitation."

Nazario shuddered and seemed to shrink further into himself, as if he had become a smaller man.

"I know that. Whatever happens, I shall not accuse you of misleading me. Now let us make certain I do not mislead you. I imagine you love your wife? Yes, I see by the look on your face that you find the question less than real, as if there were no more than one answer possible."

"There is only one answer," Pitt agreed. He did not say that he also loved his children. He thought of Jemima and Daniel, a rush of memories from all ages in their lives. And he remembered that this man's children were lost to him forever. He could not imagine it, the ceaseless pain that he would not see them grow up. They would never be young men, young women, have lives and loves of their own, perhaps children of their own. Thousands of people dealt with such loss, but each one was an individual loss, irreplaceable by any other.

As if Nazario could see the thoughts naked in Pitt's face, he smiled very slightly. "I love my wife too, Mr. Pitt. But I love her for who she is, not just for what she gives to me. For myself, I wish her home safely, and what the world thinks of her is little to me." He leaned forward with a sudden urgency. "But what she thinks of herself is of infinite importance. Do I value my desires at the expense of destroying what she is? Is that love? Yes, love of my own momentary comfort, not of her."

Pitt stared at him, trying to decide if he agreed with Nazario's reasoning.

"Do you believe in God, Mr. Pitt?" Nazario asked suddenly, throwing Pitt off balance.

"Not one that is going to step in and save your wife," Pitt answered. He said the next words with pain, but Nazario had to hear and believe the truth. "They have already tortured her! I have seen her, briefly, but it was perfectly clear. She was horribly bruised about the face. What I could not see might have been worse. The way she sat was as if her arm and her back both gave her more than discomfort. God is not going to help her!" He heard the anger and fear in his own voice. He knew he was seeing not only Sofia's face swollen and blackened with bruises, but his mother's pale face, strained with the losing fight against illness, which as a child he had not understood. Had she imagined the God she believed in, that she worshipped every Sunday, was going to save her?

"Only a child believes in that God, Mr. Pitt," Nazario said quietly. "A child who does not understand that the path is long and hard, filled with shadows that are sometimes very dark, just as the light is marvelous. It carves of us a deep vessel, if we will allow it to. It can hold all the joy there is, in the end. Sofia knows that. I know she has her moments of doubt, even of despair. Those of us who think will all have them. It is then that faith counts, the belief in the good, even if it seems denied to you at that moment."

"So you are going to let them kill her?" Pitt found the words hard to say. He was angry with Nazario for his complacency, his acceptance. Would he still be so sure of himself if he had seen the corpses of Cleo and Elfrida? Should Pitt describe them for him? The blood and the flies, the obscene indignity of it, never mind the pain!

"No, I am not," Nazario cut across his thoughts. "I am trying to make you understand. And the God who would save her was your invention, not mine. Is that the God you think has hurt you so much?"

Pitt was startled. "I didn't say that!"

"It is in your face," Nazario told him. "The God you were told about has disappointed you somewhere in your life. And I think you have taken up the role of mending things, putting them right yourself, because you desire them to be so."

Pitt wanted to argue, but there was a touch of truth in Nazario's words. He smiled instead. "You think I imagine I can do God's work?" he said incredulously.

"A little of it," Nazario agreed. "Perhaps one act at a time, as the chance comes to you. You don't like the thought of it, but it is so."

Again Nazario was right; ever since his mother's death he had been denying the faith she believed in. It had let her die. He had tried to rebuild it in small certainties, one act at a time, values he was sure of. But that was not faith because there was no trust in it, no belief in a power beyond his own.

"I do what I think is right, in my job," he said. "So do most men."

"You didn't answer me whether you believe in God or not," Nazario pointed out. "Of any sort."

"I don't know," Pitt said impatiently. "But what I believe is not the point."

"Well, I do know what I believe," Nazario snapped. "I am trying desperately to cling to it, in spite of my whole soul crying out to save her because I want to . . . now . . . more than anything else. I would let them take me, if they would, but that would do them no good. I don't know what it is she won't tell them."

"And if you did?" Pitt asked quickly. "Would you?"

Nazario sat back a little. "I'm glad I don't have to choose," he said softly. "She is protecting someone, but also protecting the value she believes not just for this life, but for eternity. Do you believe in eternity, Mr. Pitt? Is there a forever that matters? Is goodness a reality, or a convenience, a fiction to make life bearable, trying to give meaning where there is none?"

Pitt did not answer. He thought again of his mother, of all the people he had known and loved. He understood now that she had been ill for a long time, and had hidden it from him to protect him from the fear of losing her. She had created for him a safety, a time of happiness unshadowed by fear, because she put his well-being before her own. It has not been lack of trust in him, but a greater trust in her faith in the God she believed in, and in love. Now that he had his own children, he understood that.

He had never accepted that the people he loved were temporary, here and then dissolved into nothingness. But was that faith, or simply his own need? He had refused to think about it, because he had no answer. Loss hurt too much to risk examining it, looking for an eternal healing, and finding nothing there. That was why when Jemima asked him, he would not tell her what he believed. He had let her down by not knowing, not going on seeking, even in the dark. And Daniel too, when he should ask. The answer was becoming clearer. His mother had not denied him the chance to help her, she had turned to the God she believed in, and protected her child in the best way she knew. He had failed to see it.

"Is it easier for you not to look?" Nazario pursued, almost as if he had understood Pitt's thoughts. "It isn't for me. I have to look until I see something, even if I have to change it a little day by day. There is meaning. I will not accept that every brave and beautiful thing, every moment of tenderness, every act of love vanishes and is lost. Whatever I find, or don't find, I will go on looking. If I deny what Sofia believed, then I deny her whole life."

For a moment Pitt felt exactly the same need, and the same courage to seek. Then he remembered what they must do. "So you will let her die," he concluded gently, but even while he said the words, he knew that was not what he meant, nor did Nazario.

"I have told you what I will do," Nazario replied. "I will preach her doctrine this evening."

Suddenly Pitt was cold inside. He could see it as vividly as if it were already happening.

"There will be violent responses," he said quickly. "Take your head out of the clouds of your philosophy and look at what is real. It will stir up violent emotions, both in those who are afraid of her, and those who cling to what she said and desperately want her rescued. There may be rioting, hysteria. Think what you're doing!"

"I am thinking," Nazario said, his voice quiet again, his body hunched up in the chair. "They have had her for many days now, Mr. Pitt. If they have not killed her by now, they soon will. I believe they want to know where she has hidden Juan Castillo, the last man who came to her for redemption. She will not tell them. She herself will die first. I think she has proven that, to them if not to you. If she tells them, they will kill her anyway. She must know that too."

"You know who it is!" Pitt said in amazement and momentary anger. "Why in God's name are you protecting him? Who is he? Is this political after all? Is the religion no more than an excuse?"

"No, I don't know who it is!" Nazario started up from his chair. "But I believe I know why. And in a sense it is religious, but only because everything in this world is of God! Faith is not something you mouth words for on Sundays, and forget for the rest of the week. The way you live is what you really believe, no matter what you say. Sofia believes there is no darkness from which you cannot come back, if you want to enough. She has believed that, and lived it for years. Castillo came to her for help. He confessed something to her, and of course she did not tell me what it was, except that the man who was his partner in some conspiracy had been murdered. His entrails were torn out of him and his body left on the side of the road as a warning." Nazario's face was gray under the olive of his skin. "I know what they could do, Mr. Pitt. Don't treat me as if I were a dreamer whose visions have blotted out the reality of pain."

He stared at Pitt earnestly. "Faith is supposed to give you hope, not dazzle your vision that you don't see the darkness, or the need to work, to face the truth in all its sorrow and its joy. If you don't see that then you didn't listen to Sofia. I am going to preach this evening, Pitt. You cannot prevent me. I have committed no crime, and you know that. I shall keep all your laws, but I shall try to save my wife, if she is still alive, and I shall do it my own way."

Pitt looked at his dark, unwavering eyes, and knew that argument was a waste of time he could put to a better use. There was no more he could do about the way Nazario Delacruz chose to face his dilemma. Pitt honestly did not know what he would do in the man's place. He could only thank the grace of God that he was not.

"Well?" Charlotte asked him when he got home that afternoon. He was tired, his feet ached, and he would have liked nothing better than to spend the evening with his family, listening to their talk of anything at all — except politics, religion or Sofia Delacruz. But it was not possible. He had already spent a couple of hours with Stoker and Brundage arranging for a degree of police protection at the hall where Nazario was to speak.

His mind kept going over and over all the possibilities. He told this to Charlotte as he hung his hat on the hall stand and followed her as she led the way.

The kitchen was warm and full of nice smells. The dog, Uffie, sat in his basket by the stove and his tail thumped gently on the floor as he recognized Pitt. He didn't move toward him, because he had learned that he was not supposed to be in the kitchen at all, and the delusion that no one noticed him was by far the safest way to stay there.

Pitt sat down in the chair nearest to him and leaned over to stroke his ears. The tail thumped louder.

"Hello, Uffie," Pitt said to him softly. "You are a lucky dog. I hope you appreciate it. Everyone tells you their troubles, and nobody expects you to reply."

Charlotte understood the remark, and ignored it. "What is Nazario going to do?" she asked.

Minnie Maude came in from the pantry with a large apple pie in her hands. She looked from Pitt to Uffie, then at Charlotte. When no one spoke she put the pie on the bench and went out again. Uffie stayed where he was, with Pitt's hand on his head.

"Preach this evening," Pitt replied. "I couldn't persuade him not to."

Charlotte sat very still, her face pale.

"Oh, Thomas, do you think he means to let her be martyred . . . for the cause?"

Pitt had known that thought was at the back of his own mind, but he had refused to consider it. Now he had no choice.

"I don't think so," he replied. "The man Castillo he mentions is no one we know, nor does anyone in Spain that we can reach.

But of course that doesn't have to be his real name. And it all has to do with her reason for seeing Barton Hall and, I assume, the large amount of money tied up in Canadian land that seems to be unexplained."

"Money, religion, politics," she said with a bleak humor in her eyes. "Not very precise, is it?"

He was too tired to concentrate. He had to force himself to think logically. "Somebody wants to know from her where she has hidden Castillo. He has to be at the heart of it. It all started when she took him in, and then hid him somewhere. He has committed some act that he believes is a crime, and Sofia wants him to make amends for it, redeem himself. Then she says she has to come to England in order to speak with Barton Hall."

"Did she ever speak with Hall beyond telling him she wanted to meet?" Charlotte asked. "Even if she didn't see him, there's always the telephone. I'm sure he would have one."

"I don't know. He says she didn't, but she might have."

"Couldn't he be the one who is torturing her to find Castillo?"

"But why? Hall's an English banker, with

ambitions to be Governor of the Bank of England. Why would he have anything to do with a Spanish criminal, possibly terrorist or revolutionary? Then there's Laurence — he says Hall and Teague have been friends, of a sort, since they were about eleven or twelve years old. Laurence dislikes them both, but what he says about them is definitely true, as far as it goes."

"Was he at school with them?"

"Same school, but a few years younger. He says Hall cheated to help people pass their exams. He wouldn't tell me who or how. He hates Hall for it, and because the one man who knew, a teacher, died in a fire, and Laurence believes he was murdered."

She looked at him steadily, sorrow in her eyes. "And was he?" she said softly.

Before Pitt could answer, he heard a slight sound at the door. At first he thought it was Minnie Maude come back, then turned and saw Jemima. She looked puzzled and unhappy. It was probably the emotion she'd overheard that troubled her more than any facts she guessed at.

"Is she dead, Papa?" she asked immediately.

"I don't know," he replied honestly. "Whoever has her asked a ransom so terrible I don't know whether her husband will pay it or not."

"Does he have enough money to pay it?" she asked.

"It's not money they want. The man holding her wants her husband to deny all her teachings by saying she was an awful and deceitful woman, responsible for the deaths of his first wife and his children." He heard Charlotte draw in her breath, and saw the look of pain in Jemima's face. But if Nazario did deny her, then everyone would know that he had, including Jemima. Telling her now might prepare her for it.

Jemima took a deep breath. "Is that what you don't know? If he will, or not?"

"He has a plan. He won't tell me what it is, probably because he is afraid I'll stop him. But he says he won't betray her by lying and saying she was ever greedy or selfish."

She thought for a moment. "Would you do that, Papa? Deny everything you believe is true, to save Mama's life?"

How hideously simply she put it! Like that, it sounded easy. Courage or cowardice? Life or honor?

"I hope not," he answered. "But I'm not sure if I wouldn't do it to save yours or your mother's. Or Daniel's, of course. I love you very much."

She smiled and suddenly her eyes filled with tears. "I know, Papa. Maybe it doesn't count if it's somebody you don't like, or maybe don't even know. If she dies, will she be a martyr? That's what a martyr is, isn't it? Someone who will die rather than say they don't believe in God?"

"I think you can be a martyr to any cause," he replied. "It doesn't have to be God."

"But God is the ultimate, isn't He? Because we don't really know if He's real, do we?"

"I don't know," he confessed. "But I'm beginning to think that perhaps my mother did . . ."

"Can you know something if it isn't true?" she asked.

Out of the corner of his eye Pitt saw Charlotte bite her lip.

"You can think you do." He drew in a deep breath. "But I am seriously considering that she might really have known, in her own way."

"Are there different ways of knowing things?"

"Definitely. Some things are very complicated. You come to them only slowly, a step at a time, and because you want to badly enough to keep trying."

"Like mathematics," she said with a tiny glint of humor. "Or how to play the violin? That's terribly difficult. You have to make all your own notes and know if they're right or not."

"You have it exactly," he agreed. "It's difficult, there are mistakes, but the music will be wonderful in the end."

"I want wonderful music before the end," she said gravely.

"I shouldn't have said 'end,' " he corrected himself. "If there is a God like the one my mother believed in, then there isn't any end."

Pitt went to the hall early to help Stoker and Brundage prepare for Nazario's speech. Not only were attacks to be forestalled, but the possibility of panic and the injury that would occur as a result was to be dealt with.

"Do you really think he's going to start a riot, sir?" Brundage said with disbelief. "Is that his way of getting back at us for letting all this happen in the first place?" He looked thoroughly miserable. Pitt could see in his face that he still felt bitterly responsible for Sofia's kidnapping.

"She came here knowing the risks, and when she got really worried her own people suggested she hide in the house on Inkerman Road," Pitt said patiently. "She went with them willingly! She didn't climb down the drainpipe, and nobody broke in. It was probably very quiet. We were supposed to protect her from attack, not hold her prisoner in Angel Court! If they hadn't lied to us, she might still be all right."

"I wonder why Hall didn't tell us about the house on Inkerman Road," Brundage added. "Didn't he trust us either? Or did he have some other reason, do you think? I know he says he didn't see her, but what's that worth? For that matter, what's that land in Canada worth? You asked me to look into that, but I can't find anything about it. There's land farther east, and west with mineral deposits, even gold, but not there!"

Pitt froze suddenly. "Gold, but not there!" Was that it? Hall had been duped into investing a fortune in land reputed to have gold in it, or some other massively valuable mineral — perhaps diamonds? Gold had been found in California in '49 and both gold and diamonds beyond calculation in the Kimberley mines in South Africa.

That could be what Sofia had known. That it was a hoax, formed and carried out by Juan Castillo, and the man who had been murdered on the road near Toledo.

No wonder Castillo was hiding! Hall would crucify him if he got hold of him. And he would tear Sofia apart slowly to make her tell him where he was, to insure the man was silenced.

Hall was not stealing money; he was trying to disguise the loss until he could find a way to hide it completely. No wonder he was panicking and close to despair. People lost money all the time. Any investment was a risk, but for a banker of Hall's repute to be hoaxed by a couple of Spaniards, and out of a fortune belonging to the Church and the Crown!

Was that what Sofia was coming to tell him? It must have been. A warning and perhaps a way out.

Except it could not have been, or he would not now be torturing her — for what? Not to help him; if she could do that she would. Surely that was why she had come to England.

Hall might want vengeance on Castillo, and if he had murdered the other man, Alonso, then he would have to pay for that in some way. Sofia did not let people walk away from their mistakes.

Is that what Hall wanted? To find the original hoax money, get it back, and walk away? Then of course he would have to silence Sofia, and the only certain way to do that was to kill her.

But not before she had told him where Castillo was.

Brundage was still staring at him, waiting.

"Thank you, Brundage," Pitt said fervently. "I think perhaps you've just solved it! That part, at least."

"Yes, sir," Brundage replied, his expression indicating that he had only the faintest idea what Pitt meant.

The evening began with a surprisingly large crowd assembled before Nazario ever appeared. Pitt had advised Charlotte not to come, and certainly not to bring Jemima. He had no idea what to expect, but it was possible it could be dramatic, even tragic. Jemima would have to know, but calmly, only in words, not be present to see the hysteria, above all, not to see Nazario's grief — if that was how it turned out. Though he didn't think it was likely, Pitt was aware that Sofia's abductor could still turn out to be Nazario himself. Maybe Sofia had outgrown his first passion for her, or even the message of her faith, and now become an embarrassment. If Pitt would find that painful, the destruction of something he had scarcely believed in, and yet had thought to have a beauty he could not forget, how much more bitter a disillusion would it be for Jemima?

Charlotte had given him a very tiny smile, and declined to obey. She had dared him to make an issue of it, and he knew it would make him look absurd to insist. Charlotte would understand his reasons, but Jemima would not.

"She will think you don't believe her able to face truth, Thomas," she had said so quietly he had barely caught her words. "She will feel shut out of something that matters very much to her."

"I know it does!" he had argued. "That's why I don't want her to have to see it, if it becomes ugly."

"If it becomes ugly she will have to accept it," Charlotte had answered. "She is nearly seventeen, Thomas. She is not a baby you can protect from reality. If you do, you won't ease the pain when the first real disappointment comes, you will just make her the more confused by it, and above all you will send her the message that you don't think she can face the truth. She won't forgive you for that."

He knew Charlotte was right, and he could see the fear in her too, when he stopped to recognize it.

"Look after her," he had replied, knowing

that it was a completely unnecessary plea.

Now he stood in the large hall where Nazario was to speak, and watched as more and more people came in, jostling one another to try to find the seats they wanted. Some of them were excited, some somber, some already spoiling for a fight. Many came in groups of four or five, a whole family together. They kept glaring toward the empty stage, frightened the preaching might start before they were seated and they would miss something.

Pitt noted where the police were, and where his own men stood, far more discreetly, and obviously without uniforms. They were quite a few, but perhaps not enough when compared with the ever-growing numbers of the crowd.

He saw some apprehensive-looking clerical men, all recognizable from their collars and robes, all of them in their senior years. He recognized Vespasia easily, not just because the light was on her face and her pale hair, but by the way she stood. One could never mistake her. Narraway was there at her side, pushed up against her by others pressing forward for seats.

Then he saw Charlotte a step behind and Jemima beside her, just as tall now and in some ways so like her. His chest tightened and he forced himself to breathe in deeply, and look away.

That was when he saw Teague, half a head taller than those around him. He saw him turn and acknowledge a portly man a few feet away, inclining his head as a gesture of recognition. The man was a senior cabinet minister, like so many others probably a relative of Teague's. Pitt wondered why the man was here, and who else in the government might have come.

Why? To hear Nazario Delacruz? Or to observe whether the police and Special Branch were adequate to the situation, if the whole thing got out of control? Was Pitt being judged?

"Gathering of the vultures," a voice said beside him, and he turned to find Frank Laurence at his elbow.

"They're a little early," Pitt answered tartly. "There's no corpse yet."

"If you are lucky, they will betray themselves," Laurence continued. "But I dare say you know that! Did you arrange this little exhibition, or merely allow it?"

"How would you suggest I stop it?" Pitt could hear the edge of tension in his voice.

"Point taken," Laurence replied. "Have you seen Barton Hall yet? He is bound to be here."

"Is he? Why?" Pitt turned to face him.

Laurence was smiling. "To see what Nazario will do, how much you know, and above all perhaps, what Dalton Teague will do. In his place, wouldn't you?"

"I don't know. What is his place?" Pitt looked straight back at Laurence with equal challenge.

"Oh, a very interesting question," Laurence said. "Surely you have not ruled him out as a suspect?"

"Is that why you're here?" Pitt raised his eyebrows. "Are you hoping that somehow you can manipulate me into putting Teague into the dock? It is Teague you really hate, isn't it?"

"Why should I hate Teague? It was Hall who cheated!" The darkness, the bitter anger was there in Laurence's eyes again.

"I think more precisely what you said was that he enabled someone else to cheat," Pitt corrected him. "Hall's own marks were honestly won. Wasn't that what you said? He cheated for someone else, because he craved acceptance. A very human weakness. Haven't we all, at one time or another?" He looked at Laurence candidly, without any softening at all. "Haven't you?"

Laurence colored very faintly. It made him seem different, vulnerable.

"Yes, of course. But I didn't cheat for it."

"I am sure you have never cheated academically," Pitt agreed. "I would find it hard to believe you needed to. But you'd be lying if you said you have never used your sharper wits to trick someone into telling you far more than they wished or intended to. And then you have gone off and published it."

"A bold wager, Mr. Pitt!"

"Not at all. You've done it to me." Pitt smiled back at him with exactly the same bland good humor that Laurence had used earlier in their acquaintance.

"Touché," Laurence said softly. "To answer your question. I could see Teague in hell, with pleasure. From a great height . . . I hope!"

Pitt smiled more widely. "Naturally. But if you put him there, you may find that the distance is so very much smaller."

"Do you still suspect Barton Hall?" Laurence asked.

"I have no intention of discussing it with you," Pitt replied.

"I think you do suspect him," Laurence contradicted him. "You found something that interested you greatly when you went to his bank, and came out several hours later."

Pitt felt cold inside. He could not prevent

Laurence following him, but he had not realized he was in the street near the bank.

"Did you not expect me to investigate every possibility?" he said, keeping his voice light. "I found nothing missing." He was not about to tell Laurence what he had found regarding the land in Canada.

Laurence masked his disappointment almost completely. There was only the very slightest shadow across his face.

They were prevented from further conversation by a sudden hush in the crowd and then a cheer as Nazario appeared on the stage. He looked quite small in the lamplight, although he was of average height. He was dressed in dark clothes and with his black hair his features seemed all the more gaunt. His eyes were so shadowed in their sockets they looked enormous, and his high cheekbones caught the light.

He bowed very slightly, with just an inclination of the head, then he began to speak. His English was excellent and his accent so slight it was no impediment to understanding.

He introduced himself by name, then as Sofia's husband.

There was silence in the hall, barely even a shifting of position, only the whisper of fabric and a letting out of breath.

"I have come to speak in my wife's place," he went on. "I know that my friend and colleague Melville Smith has been doing this in my wife's absence . . ."

Pitt looked around to see Smith, and it was a moment before he recognized him. He was pale and stiff; his face seemed so expressionless it could have been a clay mask.

". . . keeping the flame alive," Nazario said. He did not attempt to smile. "It was a brave act, and I thank him for it. He knew, as I know, that Sofia was abducted, and even as we gather here together to speak with one another about faith and honor, and the long journey toward understanding that binds us together, she is somewhere alone with her torturer, who may very well in the end murder her."

There was a gasp of indrawn breath right round the room. Someone let out a cry, and immediately stifled it.

Pitt saw Hall then. He looked terrible. He seemed oblivious of the large woman to his left and the small white-haired man at his right. Laurence was a yard away from Pitt, staring in horror at the stage.

"I am prepared to say all that she would have said to you," Nazario went on, his voice carrying right to the back of the room.

"Melville Smith speaks gently, in part because he is a gentle man, but whatever he truly believes, he moderated it in the desperate hope of saving her life."

Pitt stared at Nazario but he could see no dissembling in his face. That was a lie. Surely he must know it.

"Sofia believes that we are all children of God," Nazario said now loudly, and more clearly. "From Christ to Satan, we are cut from the same cloth, every one of us. And we have the choice to be in eternity anything we wish. Man or woman. Genius or idiot, and all between. Physical beauty means nothing. God sees the heart. Wealth is only a test of what we would do with it. It is a loan from God, as are our talents, a way to prove whether we will use them well or ill. The judgment is awaiting us."

No one fidgeted, but they were waiting for him to say what had happened to Sofia, and what he was going to do about it. They would not wait silently much longer.

"How have we behaved toward the poor, the lonely, the slow of word or wit?" Nazario demanded. "Have we patronized or condescended to the meek? Have we taken advantage? When you bullied your wife, when you condescended to your servant, when you insulted your employee, did you see Christ in their place? Would you have done the same to Him? Of course you wouldn't. Neither would I! Do I always trust people as I would were I to remember that God sees what I do? Of course not! But I should!"

Now there was rustling in the audience. Someone shouted out Sofia's name and asked where she was. Another took it up, then others.

"You want drama?" Nazario asked loudly. "You want me to tell you what has happened to Sofia? I don't know! I know only that she has been abducted, by force, and her two companions butchered, their entrails torn out the way a beast of prey kills what it is about to eat."

The audience was appalled. A dozen or so men stood up and cursed Nazario for his crudity in such speech. A thin woman accused Nazario of having killed Sofia himself.

"You came here to be told how wonderful you are?" Nazario cried out loudly, struggling to be heard. "You are wonderful, and terrible — like all mankind. You are whatever you choose to be! Whatever you want enough to pay what it costs. I think they are torturing Sofia to make her tell them what she has done with a man to whom she offered sanctuary, because he was afraid for his life."

Gradually the crowd fell silent again, the noise ebbing slowly.

"He had committed a crime, not a violent one, but one of which he was ashamed," Nazario went on. "I don't know what it was, because Sofia never betrays a confidence, not even to save her own life. She helped him to repent and make right what he had done wrong. The man who abducted her is torturing her to tell him where this man is. She will not. She will die first."

Now there was horror in the audience, but this time no one interrupted him. Some women were weeping quietly.

"I can save her, so I am told," Nazario struggled to continue, his voice was cracking. "If I tell a lie about her, and say that she is a whore, a loose woman who seduced me, and was the cause of my first wife's suicide. She was not, and I will not say she was. Should I? To save her life? Should I deny the truth, even to save her? So that he will let her go? Broken, bleeding, tortured to betray the man she tried to save so that her abductor can do to him — God knows what?" He spread his arms wide, beseechingly. "Is there any man or woman here who believes this creature would let her go? She knows him. She has seen and spoken with him. She might even know who he is. Do you imagine for one instant that he can let her go? Even if she forgave him, or I did, the law cannot! He has torn apart two women and left their bleeding bodies on the floor to be found."

Pitt could just see Brundage at the far side of the hall turning to signal to one of the police on duty. More police appeared at the doors, but Pitt did not wait for them. He started forward, pushing through the crowd himself, forcing his way forward.

Nazario was still talking, his voice barely audible above the struggling, the moans and accusations from the audience at him and at one another.

"Where is she?" a white-haired man shouted above the others. "What have you done with her?"

Someone else shouted back at him, words inaudible.

A tall man hurled his heavy, black walking cane at Nazario. It caught Nazario on the shoulder and clattered to the floor. Nazario took a step back.

Melville Smith appeared from the wings and moved into the center of the stage, trying to protect Nazario, who evaded him and came farther forward.

"Is this what Englishmen do?" he demanded. "Is this how you 'Christians' behave?"

There was a sudden hush. It caught everyone by surprise.

Pitt looked around and saw Teague, his fair head visible above the mass. For an instant he too looked taken aback. Then he turned and spoke to those close around him, his arms held up in a gesture of calm.

Not far from him Barton Hall stared directly at Teague, ashen-faced, hatred in every line of his features. Teague did not appear to have seen him, although he was not more than ten feet away.

Nazario was still speaking, but half his words were drowned out.

"Let's go find her!" someone shouted. "Search for her!"

Half a dozen allies took up the cry and pushed toward the exits.

"Stop it!" Nazario shouted, and then the noise obliterated his next words. He spread his arms beseechingly. "Please! You can't help like this . . ."

"You want her to die!" someone else yelled furiously. "You're behind this!"

Nazario's answer was lost.

More people changed their minds about leaving and started to swarm up toward the stage again.

Police were beginning to come in from all the doorways, slowly clearing the hall. Even from where Pitt stood now, almost at the steps up to the stage, he could see scuffles here and there, the occasional hat knocked off, or deliberately thrown. One man was trying to clear a way by lashing out with his walking stick.

More people were surging up to the steps on the far side. Someone had already reached them and was starting to climb up.

At the back of the hall a woman began to scream, a high, thin wail rising in pitch.

There were two men on the steps up to the stage at the far side. One of them reached the level and lunged toward Nazario, shouting abuse.

Nazario turned to defend himself a moment too late. He was struck on the side of the head and collapsed to the floor. The man who had attacked him raised his arm high. Pitt saw the gleam of light on a blade. He started up the steps two at a time, but before he could reach the man an old woman flew forward out of the wings and launched herself at him, hands around his throat. They both crashed to the floor as Nazario began to haul himself up onto his hands and knees, dizzy, unable to get his balance.

The woman lashed out at the man with the knife, hitting him so hard he let the knife fall, grabbing the woman by the hair, which came off in his hand. He tore at her clothes, and they too came apart.

Pitt reached them and put his hand on the woman's shoulder and felt the iron-hard muscles beneath the cloth. This close, he recognized her. It was the old woman who swept the yard at Angel Court, except that it was now quite obviously a man.

Castillo! Of course. Hidden where everybody looked at him, and nobody saw.

Pitt threw all his weight and strength into dragging him off the man who had attacked Nazario. As he finally pulled him up, he saw the attacker lay motionless on the boards of the stage, his neck at a crooked, broken angle.

Castillo suddenly went limp in his arms, no longer resisting.

Nazario clambered to his feet, still dazed.

The knife lay gleaming on the floor, the stage lights angled upward, making it almost invisible.

Teague was on the stage now too. He was staring not at Pitt or Nazario, or the dead man on the floor, but at Castillo, who was wigless, still clad in the remnants of the dress.

Castillo stared back at him for a frozen second, then wrenched himself free from Pitt and fled the stage, disappearing into the wings as if somehow they would have closed behind him.

Teague made as if to pursue him, and then gazed for a moment at Pitt, and with a half smile waved one of the police forward to do it instead. Brundage went to the outside to catch Castillo should he reach the back door.

Teague stood facing Pitt, then turned to Nazario, his face utterly wiped clear of expression.

"What the devil are you doing, Pitt? This is a complete fiasco." He glared at the dead man on the floor. "Who the hell is he?" Finally he turned to Nazario. "Do you know him?"

Nazario smiled bitterly, and did not answer. He was still shaking.

There was silence in the audience. They were stunned, embarrassed, some even ashamed.

Teague turned toward them, holding up his hands for attention. Instantly even the faintest stir of movement stopped. They faced him expectantly.

"Ladies and gentlemen," he said gravely. "This terrible tragedy must come to an end.

I have done everything I can, with all the time, money and influence I can offer. I had intended to tell Commander Pitt of Special Branch first, as a courtesy, but these circumstances tonight have changed all that. I must tell you all, and send you home in some peace and assurance."

He glanced at Pitt, but his expression was unreadable. He looked back at the audience.

"I am certain that I know where Sofia Delacruz is being held prisoner."

He was obliged to stop by the cries and cheers. Several people waved their arms.

Teague gently urged silence again. He turned to Pitt and offered his hand.

Pitt could not refuse. He would appear surly and ridiculous. He took it, trying to force a look of happy surprise to his face. He felt like a gargoyle.

"We must rescue her," Teague said loudly and clearly. "My men are ready and willing. What do you say, Commander?"

There was only one possible answer Pitt could give.

"We will make plans immediately. Thank you."

Teague smiled broadly and turned to face the crowd.

Brundage appeared at Pitt's elbow, breathless.

"Castillo escaped, sir," he said. "Poor devil could be anywhere."

Teague turned to Pitt and his face was still inscrutable. But Pitt felt a sudden chill, as if his blood had turned to ice.

Chapter 14

Pitt took a deep breath. Now he had no choice at all. It did not matter whether it was Hall, Teague or circumstances that had outwitted him, he must move tonight; as soon as they could gather the men together and make some sort of plan. Whoever held Sofia would hear of this within an hour or two, if they didn't know already.

"Don't worry about Castillo," he said to Brundage. "Get Stoker and as many other men as you can find in the next quarter of an hour." He turned to Teague. "We must plan this carefully. Any mistake could be fatal."

He did not bother to ask how Teague had found Sofia. He wouldn't get a straight answer, he was sure. But he didn't doubt that the man was telling the truth about locating her — he wouldn't risk his reputation by announcing it to the crowd if he hadn't. Pitt didn't trust the man, but for now he would follow his lead — it might be their best, and only, chance to save Sofia.

"Of course," Teague agreed immediately. "There's got to be somewhere quiet in this place where we can meet. I have half a dozen men I can have here in thirty minutes, once I find a telephone." He looked at the crowd still milling around, excited, frightened, angry, unintentionally blocking the ways out.

"One along the street, sir," Brundage said, pointing to his left. "Couple of hundred yards."

Teague thanked him. "I'll be back," he said to Pitt, then went quickly down the stage steps and started to pick his way toward the doors.

Pitt turned back to Brundage. "What happened to Castillo? Is Nazario all right? He took a pretty hard blow. Does anyone know who that lunatic was? I suppose he is dead?"

"Yes, sir." Brundage looked a little pale. "Don't know whether it was just an unlucky blow, or if he meant it. Either way, no one is sure where Castillo went. From what the local police say, Nazario's assailant was known to them. A bit off his head. Took religious fancies and thought he was an avenging angel, or something of the sort. He's been in trouble for abusing people before, even attacked one or two, but nothing like this."

"And Nazario?"

"He'll be damn sore for a while, but at the moment all he can think about is finding Sofia."

"Good. Be back in twenty-five minutes at the outside, with whoever you have."

Brundage hesitated. "Are we going to rely on Teague's men, sir?"

"I was thinking rather more of keeping an eye on them," Pitt said grimly. "We can't afford to have them go ahead without us."

Brundage looked relieved. "No, sir. I wouldn't trust that lot half as far as I could throw them. They might make a pig's breakfast of the whole thing, or if they do get her out alive, next day's newspapers'll be full of how they did Special Branch's job for them!"

"There's also the matter of catching whoever has her," Pitt added.

"Alive?" Brundage asked.

"I don't know that I care," Pitt replied frankly.

"As long as it's not Teague who kills the bastard. Papers would make a big thing of that too," Brundage said. " 'Special Branch arrests hero of the hour.' That would make us look even worse."

Pitt understood exactly how Brundage felt.

"You think it's Hall, sir?" Brundage asked.

"It seems most likely. If he bought this enormous portion of Canadian land after being led to believe there was gold or diamonds there, and then discovered it was a hoax, he'd be desperate enough to do anything. The fact that it was in any way connected to Sofia Delacruz, who had already caused his family considerable embarrassment, would only add to his fury."

"Right, sir. I'll get everyone I can." He started to move away.

"Brundage!"

"Yes, sir?"

"Also get guns for as many as you can. This could turn very nasty."

"Yes, sir. May take a little longer."

"Make it a very little!"

"Yes, sir."

Pitt went to find Nazario. He wanted to see for himself if he was all right, but even if he was not, he had a great many questions to ask him, starting with how much of this fiasco with Castillo he had foreseen, and intended. If he had lied about anything at all, now was the time to admit it.

The first two side rooms were empty. Nazario Delacruz was sitting in a very old armchair in the third. One of Pitt's men was with him.

"Thank you, Hollingsworth," Pitt said with a nod to the man. "Wait for me outside. We've got to get started as soon as I've had a talk with Señor Delacruz. Let me know, regardless, when Mr. Teague gets back. Regardless, understand?"

"Yes, sir." Hollingsworth stood to attention for an instant, then turned on his heel and went out, closing the door behind him.

Pitt studied Nazario. He was clearly very shaken and in some pain, but his eyes were clear and there was a gravity and an understanding in them that reassured Pitt he was fully conscious and alert.

"We're going as soon as Teague gets back from collecting his men," Pitt said, pulling up one of the hard-backed chairs and sitting down. The room was sparsely furnished, just a plain table large enough for half a dozen people to sit around, presumably for meetings of some sort, and sufficient chairs.

"And your men?" Nazario asked, straightening with a wince as the pain caught him from his injured neck and shoulder.

"Brundage will have them here by then."

Nazario nodded, just a brief movement of his head without involving his neck. "I'm coming with you." It was a statement.

"If you can keep up." Pitt smiled very slightly. "But before we get to that, it's time you tell me the truth about all you know of this. We could make a fatal error through ignorance. And on the assumption that you did not set this up with the intention of martyring your wife, either for the cause or simply to get rid of her, you will want us to succeed."

Nazario was startled, and momentarily angry. Then he realized the truth of what Pitt was saying, and set aside his emotions.

"I did not know she brought Castillo here with her," he said, speaking rapidly. "I never met him as himself, only as an old woman who had been turned out of her home and needed a place to live, just for a while."

"And the hoax?" Pitt went on. "Did you know about that?"

Nazario looked confused. "What hoax? What are you talking about?" There was a new, stranger edge of fear in his voice. "Sofia would not trick anyone."

"The hoax to sell a huge area of relatively useless land in Canada, just empty prairie land, on the false evidence that there were diamonds or gold there." Pitt put forward his theory, curious to see how Nazario reacted.

"Diamonds? In Canada? I have no idea what you are talking about. Is that what Castillo said?" Nazario frowned, trying to make sense of it.

"That was the hoax," Pitt explained. "Hall paid a fortune for the land, on behalf of the Church of England. He has much of their money to invest."

"Ah!" Nazario smiled ruefully. "That is why Sofia was going to see him, to tell him. But he had already committed the money. So he is behind this? He is trying to silence her, but first he must find out what she has done with Castillo, because Castillo also knows?"

"Apparently when Castillo's partner in the hoax was murdered and left as a warning, instead of running away to somewhere he could never be found, he went to Sofia and confessed. She must have told him confession was no use without repentance."

"That is what she would do," Nazario agreed. "She would make him give back the money. So where is it? If Castillo still has it then we will never get it back now." He shook his head. "But if he had it, Mr. Pitt, I think he would have returned it by now. Why come at all, if he did not mean to give it back?"

Pitt saw the answer only too clearly. "He

didn't have it," he said wearily. "Maybe this other man did. Does he have a name?"

"I know only that he was called Alonso. And if he had it then why would Hall not take it from him and leave it alone? This is too much trouble simply for revenge. Too dangerous, and too bloody."

"Yes," Pitt agreed again. "There is still a piece that does not fit, someone else involved perhaps —"

He was interrupted by Brundage's return. He knocked on the door and came straight in.

"I've got six men, sir: Mr. Narraway; Stoker; yourself, sir; Hollingsworth and me. And Mr. Delacruz, if he's well enough?"

"I am," Nazario said, rising to his feet, almost succeeding in masking a degree of pain. "I am easily well enough."

"Guns?" Pitt asked.

"Yes, sir," Brundage replied. "And Mr. Teague is just back too, sir. He has eight men with him, and he didn't say so, but they're all armed. Can see it, sir. Man behaves different when he's got a gun. And it makes a coat hang a little different too."

"Thank you." He stood up also. "Where is Teague?"

"Just outside the door, sir. And I got us a wagon to go in. Looks like a furniture wagon."

"Thank you. Take Señor Delacruz and look after him, and send Teague in here."

"Yes, sir." Brundage offered Nazario his arm, but Nazario declined it, straightening himself up to walk out.

Brundage smiled and followed him, holding the door open as Teague came in, closing it behind him.

"Ready?" Teague asked. He was standing across the room from Pitt and staring at him with odd clarity. Now there was no pretense anymore, no affectation of alliance. Teague led Pitt along because he had not yet found any way to do this without him. Then an uglier thought came to Pitt's mind.

Teague knew exactly how he was going to emerge from this the hero, the man who rescued a woman whose beliefs he espoused, when Special Branch could not do it!

For an instant, staring at Teague's handsome, chiseled face, Pitt doubted himself. It was his own dismissive attitude that had likely driven Sofia to go to Inkerman Road. She didn't think Pitt and his men would protect her. If she had, then perhaps Hall would not have dared take her. She would never have been beaten, tortured or now facing death, if they did not succeed in getting to her before Hall finally killed her.

"Of course I'm ready," Pitt said with perfect calm. "I was waiting for you. We'd best go. I assume you have transport for your men? Food? I have for mine."

Teague's eyes widened slightly. "Do you have no intention of discussing some form of plan first? You have no idea where you're even going, man!"

Pitt looked back at him innocently, also with slight surprise.

"Is it so close we won't have time to speak before we get there?"

In an instant Teague understood. Anger and appreciation flickered in his face for a second, and then were gone.

"I'm not sure there is room for you in my vehicle," he said with a slow smile.

"Not if there are nine of you," Pitt agreed, matching his smile exactly. "But there is room for you in mine. Come on!"

Teague was too skilled to show irritation. He fell in step with Pitt and they walked side by side down the corridor to the outside door away from the hall itself.

Stoker was waiting for them on the pavement. It was still just daylight. The air was balmy and a little damp, the smell of the river discernible.

"Mr. Teague is coming with us," Pitt said loudly enough for all the assembled men to hear. "We'll not travel too closely, so we don't look like an invading army. Just deliverymen, starting the day a little early, or maybe catching up on yesterday."

"Someone who can't pay the rent doing a flit!" Stoker said under his breath.

Pitt did not bother to answer, but it was not so rare an occurrence.

In the wagon Pitt made room for Teague to sit opposite him and as the back was latched he settled as comfortably as possible and invited Teague to give them all the information he had. He saw an expression of cold acknowledgment pass between Narraway and Teague.

"We've tracked her down to an old factory backing on to the river," Teague began. "Not far by water, but you can't approach it that way without giving them at least fifteen minutes' warning, by the time you've landed and got up the steps, and that would have to be two at a time, at best. We have to go around the land side, which means going to the south first."

"Disused factory?" Pitt asked, trying to recall which one that must be, but there were too many to take a guess.

"Falling to bits," Teague replied. "Dangerous. Too dangerous for even the homeless to settle in. Bits of it falling off, rotting, rusting. Whole demon lots sinking into the mud."

Pitt did not take his eyes off Teague's face. He could imagine Stoker's expression upon hearing about such a place. He was a seaman. Storms at sea did not frighten him, although he respected their power, but the slow, sucking, stinking mud of the river appalled him.

"We'd better send someone round by the water anyway," he said. "Whoever's there might escape that way. We'd look damn stupid if they fled by boat and we couldn't stop them."

Teague nodded. "We can have two of my men take a boat, just to be safe."

Pitt raised his eyebrows, not that Teague could see him either.

"Can't wait for you to send your men back to do that. We'll send two of mine. They're just as capable of borrowing a boat, and just as willing."

Teague hesitated only a second. It gave Pitt control of the river escape, but it also greatly increased his numerical disadvantage inside the factory. Pitt knew that too, but he had no alternative.

"Any idea how many men we are facing?" he asked.

"Not many," Teague replied. "Unless he

knows we're coming, which he might, after tonight's fiasco."

"How did you find out all of this, sir?" Stoker asked, with an unusual amount of deference in his voice. Pitt hoped it was assumed! He wished he could see Teague's face in the shadows to read it.

There was a long moment's silence, then Teague spoke.

"Many questions, and then a stroke of good fortune," he replied, slowly, as if choosing his words with care. "I have friends, people who admired my career in cricket . . . supporters, you understand?"

"Oh, yes, sir," Stoker replied quickly.

"One of them came forward," Teague went on more easily. "He had seen a woman resembling Sofia Delacruz. He said she seemed to be in some difficulty, quarreling with the man who was with her. She wished to leave but he would not let her. My . . . supporter tried to help, and was told that she was emotionally disturbed. She needed restraint, or she would hurt herself. He believed it at the time. Afterward he was less sure."

"And you put the pieces together," Stoker concluded.

"Precisely."

"I see." Stoker said, apparently satisfied.

He made no mention of the pieces of the story that didn't fit, and Pitt was glad. Now was not the time to put Teague on edge.

They stopped at a wharf at Teague's instruction, and Hollingsworth and Brundage got out.

Teague directed them toward the wreck of the factory, less than a hundred yards away. Nothing else was said.

Teague returned to his seat in the wagon and they moved forward the last short distance and stopped again, in the deep shadow of the factory ruin.

Pitt got out, followed by Teague, Stoker, Narraway and Nazario. They nodded to one another, and Pitt led the way down the alley toward the wharf and the warehouse steps where Teague's men were waiting.

The night was clear and there was a three-quarter moon. It gave more light than Pitt would have wished, but there was a bank of cloud coming in from the east, and in quarter of an hour the moon would be shrouded.

They moved along the wharf but remained in the shadows of a huge crane and several stacks of timber.

There was no one else in sight. There was no sound except the continual murmur of the river below them, the ripples of the water swishing around the huge supporting beams, the suck and slurp now and then as a wave broke against the stones along the shore. It was an ebb tide, just before the turn.

Moonlight made silver patterns on the surface. It was oily, broken here and there with driftwood and patches of spume. There was no sign of anyone on watch at the factory, no silhouette of anything like a human form.

A ferry pulled away from the wharf where they had left Brundage and Hollingsworth, a hundred yards away. A boat was making its way out into the river, oars dipping silently in and out.

It was a moment of decision. They had no idea if Hall was ahead of them or behind. The question was really whether Hall knew that the man who had killed Nazario's attacker was Castillo. If not, he might be making one desperate last attempt to force Sofia to tell him where Castillo was.

But if he had already identified Castillo, then they might be too late.

Pitt turned to Teague. "Now," he said.

"No, wait!" Teague replied sharply. "If he comes from the far side, we need to stop him before he gets to her, or warns his men."

"He could be in there now," Pitt pointed out. "Come on!" He turned to signal his men forward, and Teague grasped him by the arm, bringing Pitt up abruptly.

"I had men watching," Teague hissed. "He's not here yet. He'll come the land way. Wait for that cloud bank. It's only a few minutes away. That's probably what he's waiting for. Come!" He started forward, picking his step through the debris on the path toward the street.

Pitt followed, Narraway behind him. No one spoke until they were in the deserted yard facing the street. Teague motioned them to blend into the shadows.

"Let him pass us," he whispered.

"If he's coming," Pitt answered.

"Oh, he's coming." Teague's voice oozed certainty, and satisfaction. They still sent another chill of ice through Pitt's blood. Teague had said the words with pleasure.

The cloud cover was already darkening the moon. Somewhere to the left of them, near the street, there was a very slight sound, wood against wood.

Teague froze, then turned slowly and peered toward the gate.

"Quiet!" he hissed.

Then Pitt heard it as well, a faint creak, the bump of metal on wood, and then silence for several seconds before the rattle of small stones as if someone had slithered a step before regaining their balance and moving on again.

Pitt saw him first. A tall man moving awkwardly, almost feeling his way across the last few yards of open space before the huge wall of the building, and what was left of it. It was Barton Hall. Pitt knew him from his gait, the angle of his head and shoulders, then, as he turned, his face was in the hazy moonlight for an instant before the clouds drew together again. He looked like a man who has seen his own death: sunken-eyed, hollow-cheeked, all his pain inside him, moving as if his arms and legs were all but numb.

He fiddled with the latch of the door, soon realizing that it was broken. He heaved his shoulder against it to force it open and went in through the space, leaving it ajar.

Teague swung his arm, directing them all to follow him. He went through the door first with Pitt on his heels.

Inside, Pitt looked up. It was the entrance to the enormous factory, now fallen into a wreck of its past self and clearly no longer used. The whole roof was shattered, much of it fallen inside in a patchwork of debris, shattered glass, broken rafters and beams, some hanging at crazy angles. The walls were stained, windows broken, some so shattered there was nothing left but the empty frames. A crane had rusted so badly parts of it were hanging off the structure, dangling against the caved-in walls of a loading bay. Old machinery loomed ghostly in the yard, like skeletons locked in battle. It had its own wharf, and the smell of rotting wood hung in the air along with the sickly odor of river mud.

"Perfect place to keep someone prisoner," Pitt said softly. "They could scream themselves sick and nobody would care. Anyone who heard would think it was another piece of machinery breaking, or even a seabird crying. They come upriver this far."

"For God's sake, man, don't just stand there!" Teague said with desperation sharp in his tone. "We've got to take Hall before he gets to her!"

Hall was somewhere ahead of them, but they could no longer see him.

Pitt took a step forward.

Behind him Stoker and Narraway went out to the left, Nazario to the right. Slowly they all moved across the littered space, feeling their steps carefully. A fall over a piece of rolled wood, rubble or parts of broken machinery would not only alert Hall ahead of them, but would cause disabling injury if it were over glass shards, or wood with protruding nails.

They reached the entrance to the main work floor and Teague tried the first door. It gave beneath his weight, the wooden frame rotten. As Pitt stepped in behind Teague he could smell the decay in the air, the wood rot, mold, even the breath of tidal mud.

Ahead of them there was a noise: a single thump of wood against wood, but it was clean, not splintered, just one sound. It was a human step, not the crumble of floor falling apart.

Teague froze, then looked up. He turned to Pitt and pointed to his left, then started to move to the right himself.

Pitt moved carefully, afraid of knocking into the remnants of machinery still in the place.

The cloud cleared again and moonlight shone through the open roof. Lengths of timber lay on the floor. One misplaced step could send you falling, landing hard.

Pitt stepped over a pile of chains and a crane hook. Teague was still ahead of him.

Hall was out of sight.

Rafters creaked and sagged above.

Somewhere to the left a rat scuttled across

the floor, its claws scratching on the wood. The whole place seemed to be alive with tiny movements, men walking slowly, a step at a time, small animals of the night looking for food, beams settling, the water rising and seeping upward to fill the thousand tiny channels until it covered the floor and the broken debris was concealed, a hidden trap.

Pitt froze. Was that someone moving above them, or more wood settling as the water rose?

A rat splashed off a step.

Ahead of them and to the right Teague's tall figure emerged from the gloom. Pitt could see several other men in the shadows. Teague's men? How many did he have? Some of them must have come from the river side of the factory. He could see four or five, and Brundage and Hollingsworth had arrived now too.

Brundage was over to the right, Narraway opposite him. Pitt could not see Nazario.

"Looks like this is the battleground," Teague whispered.

"I don't give a damn about battlegrounds," Pitt said fiercely. "Where is Sofia? Is she even in this place? What's happened to Hall? He's the only one who knows where she is."

Somewhere ahead of them a volley of

shots rang out. Then a moment later, several more.

Teague had disappeared.

Pitt cursed under his breath and stepped forward into the moonlight.

"Hall!" he shouted. "Barton Hall!"

There were several seconds without sound at all, then there was a movement above them, but not much more than a brief shadow across the moonlight.

"What is it, Pitt?"

Pitt looked up and saw the silhouette of Hall. He was standing at the edge of the crater made by the caving-in of the floor above. There were three beams left that crossed it. All the rest were jagged, sheared away by falling masonry, or simply rotted by seasons of rain and sun.

Teague was standing thirty feet away, on the same floor, facing Hall across the open space between them.

Stoker had his gun out.

Pitt looked up at Hall. "You can't leave here. We have the factory surrounded. Sofia can't tell you where Castillo is now, because none of us knows. He escaped after he killed the man who attacked Nazario."

Hall glanced down at him, then across the gaping space between himself and Teague. At the back of the building, the littered floor and the last of the rotting beams that stretched between them.

Pitt thought of Frank Laurence, the anger he felt against Teague and Hall, and all that he had said about school days, cheating, debt and hatred.

He looked up at Hall and Teague facing each other.

"Haven't we come a long way?" he said almost conversationally, though his voice could be heard throughout the yawning space, above the dripping water and the occasional skitter of rats' feet, or the settling of timbers.

"Do you remember the exam room? Do you, Hall? You always knew all the answers, while the rest of them were still trying to understand the questions." He turned a little. "Isn't that right, Teague? He thought like a genius, and on the sports field he ran like a duck!

"But you remember the cricket field, don't you, Teague? You were golden! All grace and strength, all skill. You could hit a ball out of the pitch, and run like a deer. You practiced enough. Kind of put you at the back for the exams, though! Didn't it? You needed Hall to help you cheat. What a disgrace if Teague, of all people, failed the exams! Golden Teague, who could do anything! A god on the sports field, a dunce in class?"

Teague came to the edge of the crater. "If Laurence could have proved that, he would have done it years ago! You're making up stories because you'd like them to be true."

"One of your masters knew, though, didn't he?" Pitt said clearly. "Do you remember him? Burned to death in his own house. Smoking. Let the hot ash fall. At least that's what they said."

Hall walked toward Teague, who was several feet across the huge, surviving beam. It cracked and a little plaster fell. Hall ignored it and moved another couple of steps toward Teague.

Pitt watched.

Teague was smiling, his mane of hair like a halo in the moonlight. "What did you do with the money, Hall?" he asked. "There must be something of it! And you're still borrowing more."

"To make up for what the hoax swallowed," Hall replied. He looked like a man staring into the abyss, but he did not sway on the beam, nor did he take his eyes off Teague.

Pitt saw out of the corner of his eye that Stoker had his gun leveled at Hall. Pitt kept his own on Teague.

Teague laughed. "You thought the mines

in Manitoba would make a fortune for you and you'd crown your success by becoming Governor of the Bank of England. Sir Barton Hall! Maybe in time Lord Hall! Save the country. Get us back to the top again."

Suddenly Pitt began to see a different picture. It wasn't about money, or about what money could buy, but what the having of money could gain for you. Glory! The gratitude of men with power to give office, and take it away. The hoax was about ruin . . . and rescue.

Pitt stepped forward and looked up at Teague, wanting to keep the situation under control.

"Was that what he meant to do?" he smiled at him as if he believed him still. If Teague turned his men on them, the results would be disasterous. "Rescue the bank and by saving one, stop the slide of all of them? Just in time?"

Teague was startled, and then he took another step forward to where he looked down at Pitt. "Very clever, Commander. You got there at last. A day or two after I did, but yes, that's what he meant to do. Step out and be the hero. Damn fool!"

In that moment Barton Hall lunged. He caught Teague in the center of the chest and they struggled for a long, desperate moment, then Hall closed his arms around Teague and both of them went over the edge, crashing onto the litter on the floor below.

Pitt ran over to them, tripping and blundering as the darkness closed in again and he found the way into the center where Hall lay absolutely still. One look showed that his neck was broken.

Pitt turned to Teague just as Narraway got there, Stoker a moment later.

Teague was still alive, but there was blood on his face, in his mouth. Pitt could see he was finding it difficult to breathe.

There was no time for mercy, and he was beyond help.

"Where's Sofia?" Pitt asked him. "And where's the money?"

"It's safe," Teague whispered. "Ask Hall . . ."

"It's too late for that," Pitt told him. "You were the partner of Castillo and Alonso. Was it your idea?"

"Good one," Teague said with a grimace that might have been intended as a smile. "That fool Hall swallowed it whole!"

"Where's the money?" Pitt repeated. "Let me put it back, and save the bank. Isn't that what you were going to do anyway? Be the hero once again, give your own personal fortune to save it, and be rewarded with governorship of the Bank of England? You would have deserved it."

"Why the hell should I tell you?" Teague gasped. He was fading rapidly. The bleeding was inside him where they could not reach it.

"Because if you do, I will put it back where it belongs," Pitt replied. "You will die the hero you always needed to be."

Teague smiled, just a twitch of the lips.

"And if you don't," Pitt went on, "then I will see that your memory is stained with the blood of Sofia Delacruz, and of the two women who died on Inkerman Road. And for all I know, that poor old master, long ago in your school days, when you hadn't the brains to pass your exams and you got Barton Hall to cheat for you. Even your cricket glory won't count for much then!"

"Why should I believe you?" Teague was clearly struggling against the encroaching darkness.

"Because I give you my word," Pitt replied.

Teague whispered something almost inaudible.

Pitt bent closer to hear it. It was a number. The last words Teague said were the name of the bank, and the man to speak to.

Pitt reached out and closed Teague's eyes, then he stood up. He looked at the other men. "We are going to say that Teague died in an accident during our raid of this place," he said without any change of tone.

They stared at him. It was Brundage who spoke. "We know he killed the women on Inkerman Road and probably the man in Spain. He might even have killed the poor old schoolmaster!" he protested.

"No, we don't," Pitt replied. "But if he did, he's dead himself now."

"He was a monster!" Brundage said hotly. "And we don't even know if Sofia is still alive! If she isn't, then he tortured her to death. Are you going to cover that up too?"

"If she's dead," Pitt answered quietly — the words were difficult to say — "then she died to keep the secret of the hoax so the banks would not crash. Do you want to punish Teague at the cost of having it all come out in the open? That would make her sacrifice worthless."

Brundage stood motionless, confused.

"No, he doesn't," Narraway answered for him. "But we're not standing around here arguing about it now. Let's find Sofia, if she's here." He lowered his voice. "And arrest Teague's men! We'll decide what to charge them with later. We don't want a damn gun battle!"

Brundage looked around him, hand on his gun now. "What about Hall's men?"

"I don't think he had any," Pitt answered. "He was only here because of Teague. I think he just wanted to end it." As he spoke he was moving back into the shadows. They were too vulnerable where they stood in the fitful moonlight, exposed one minute, shadowed the next. He thought Teague's men might surrender, now that their leader was gone. They might even be bitterly disillusioned, perhaps not even have really understood what they were doing. But he did not intend to rely on it for his men's safety.

And Nazario had a gun. If they did not find Sofia alive, he might be tempted to take revenge. Pitt would not blame him if he did, and he really did not want to have to arrest him for it.

He left the others to round up Teague's men and he and Nazario began a systematic search of what remained of the factory, watching carefully for broken beams, floors with rotten wood, boards that would give way beneath them. They moved silently, not calling out in case there were any of Teague's men hiding, frightened now and believing they had little to lose.

The stink of tidal mud was everywhere. Everything seemed to settle lower with each creak, as if it were drowning half an inch at a time. The tide was on the ebb. Below the high water mark, everything dripped.

It was Pitt who found her. She was lying on the floor in one of the lower rooms. He had to splash through a pool of river water to get to the door, and up the last step.

There was a man guarding the door. He raised a gun toward Pitt.

Pitt hit him as hard as he could, all his weight behind the blow. The shock of it went right up his arm and the man dropped like a stone and did not move. If Pitt had injured his arm he barely felt it. He stepped over the man and went to Sofia.

She stirred, opened her eyes and flinched as if she expected to be struck.

"It's all right," he said softly. "I won't hurt you."

She stared at him in the faint moonlight.

"Pitt," he told her. "Thomas Pitt. Can you sit up?" He put his arm out and it was only when she took it to pull herself up that he felt the pain. Not that it mattered in the slightest. He closed his hand over hers and took her weight.

"Can you stand?" he asked. "Lean against me. We'll get you out of here, and to a doctor." He lifted her as gently as he could.

She was standing, swaying a little, when he heard a noise at the door and snatched his gun out, knocking her away to leave his arm free to fire.

But it was Nazario who stood in the doorway, the moonlight showing tears of relief running down his face.

"Thank you," he said huskily. "Dear God! Thank you." He came forward and took Sofia in his arms.

She clung to him for a moment, and then straightened herself with difficulty and obvious pain. She turned to Pitt. Her clothes were torn, her hair matted, her face was filthy, dark with bruises and swollen out of shape, but she stared at Pitt with a slow smile.

"I knew you would come for me, Mr. Pitt, but I am profoundly grateful that you were not much longer. I don't think I could have lasted. What are you going to do with Mr. Teague?"

"He's dead," Pitt replied. "I gave him my word that he would be buried with honor, as long as the money is where he told me."

She took a long, slow breath and her face was beautiful with gratitude. "Thank you, Commander Pitt. You do know what it is you believe, and it is good . . . very good."

ABOUT THE AUTHOR

Anne Perry is the bestselling author of two acclaimed series set in Victorian England: the Charlotte and Thomas Pitt novels, including *The Angel Court Affair* and *Death on Blackheath,* and the William Monk novels, including *Blood on the Water* and *Blind Justice.* She is also the author of a series of five World War I novels, as well as twelve holiday novels, most recently *A New York Christmas,* and a historical novel, *The Sheen on the Silk,* set in the Ottoman Empire. Anne Perry lives in Scotland.

www.anneperry.co.uk

The employees of Thorndike Press hope you have enjoyed this Large Print book. All our Thorndike, Wheeler, and Kennebec Large Print titles are designed for easy reading, and all our books are made to last. Other Thorndike Press Large Print books are available at your library, through selected bookstores, or directly from us.

For information about titles, please call:
(800) 223-1244

or visit our Web site at:
http://gale.cengage.com/thorndike

To share your comments, please write:

Publisher
Thorndike Press
10 Water St., Suite 310
Waterville, ME 04901

The employees of Thorndike Press hope you have enjoyed this Large Print book. All our Thorndike, Wheeler, and Kennebec Large Print titles are designed for easy reading, and all our books are made to last. Other Thorndike Press Large Print books are available at your library, through selected bookstores, or directly from us.

For information about titles, please call:
(800) 223-1244

or visit our Web site at:
gale.com/thorndike

To share your comments, please write:
Publisher
Thorndike Press
10 Water St., Suite 310
Waterville, ME 04901